OPERATION DURANGO CONNECTION

To Nick,
I hope you enjoy
"The Race"
Mike Gg...
aka Mott

OPERATION DURANGO CONNECTION

▼

> In the War on Drugs,
> just who are the Good Guys,
> and who are the Bad Guys ?

MATT GAVIN

Writers Club Press
San Jose New York Lincoln Shanghai

Operation Durango Connection

Writers Club Press
an imprint of iUniverse.com, Inc.

For information address:
iUniverse.com, Inc.
5220 S 16th, Ste. 200
Lincoln, NE 68512
www.iuniverse.com

ISBN: 0-595-15805-6

Printed in the United States of America

To my cherished friend, Connie Selwood, who has proven throughout the production of this novel that God was, and is, a woman.

And to all the Good Guys and Bad Guys portrayed in the "War on Drugs." They were extraordinary characters, and the author feels privileged to have known them.

Chapter I

▼

DURANGO

There were many times in Joe Fruin's career as a drug cop he wished he'd thought before he'd reacted. He was a passenger on Mexicana Airlines flight 103 from Mexico City to Durango when he realized he'd done it again, jumped-off without considering the dangerous consequences that could result from following a target into a country where he had no more power than the average "Joe Tourista." Seated two rows behind his archenemy, across the aisle in a window seat, he suppressed the voice of caution by telling himself, what the hell, it's too late to worry now.

Fruin sat back in his seat as a smiling hostess placed a beer on the tray in front of him. "Gracias," he said, noticing everything about the señorita from her lustrous black hair down to her shapely legs.

"Enjoy," the hostess replied sweetly.

Fruin sipped on his beer until his eyes drifted across the top of the Wall Street Journal the passenger seated next to him was reading. "JUNE 6, 1980," the newspaper announced. It was an appropriate date, he thought. June 6, 1944 was D-Day, the invasion of Europe, the beginning of the end for Adolph Hitler. He felt in his bones this trip would be the start of his target's downfall. For over three years, Angel Herrera was at the top of the DEA's most wanted list, and for good reason. He was suspected of smuggling into the United States each year more than one ton of heroin, with a street value of more than one-hundred million dollars. The DEA and Chicago police had reliable information indicating Angel Herrera controlled his heroin empire from the Rio Loro, an innocuous appearing nightclub located on Chicago's Southwest Side. But years of intense effort to penetrate the Rio Loro and install electronic overhear devices proved frustrating. A disgusted Joe Fruin had told several of his task force agents one evening after a few beers, "We keep getting our noses rubbed in shit."

Fruin's eyes burned into the back of Angel's head as he silently vowed, I'm gonna take you down you frickin' drug dealer.

Apparently unaware that one of the plane's passengers harbored malicious intentions, Angel traveled in his usual style: expensively dressed, gracefully mannered, and most importantly, adoringly accompanied by an attractive young woman. His custom tailored blue shirt and slacks accentuated a good physique and striking Latino features. Olive black eyes, constantly examining everything and everyone, hinted at predatory instincts. Fruin leaned forward in his seat and watched as Angel raised a glass filled with a dark red wine, rolled the stem between his thumb and forefinger, and said, "Salud."

Jenni Bueno responded instantly by touching her wine glass to Angel's, and smiling sweetly said, Salud." She was thrilled. It was her first time in a jet airplane, her first visit to Mexico since immigrating to the States as a teenager. And she was elated about becoming the mistress of one of the richest, most talked about men in Chicago's Latin community.

Fruin squeezed-up his face and silently cussed. Angel's carefree, big-bucks life-style irritated him almost as much as his drug trafficking activities. On a DEA agent's salary, he was barely able to afford a nice house on

Chicago's Northwest Side, a Ford, and a one week fishing vacation in Wisconsin with his wife and son, while Angel flaunted luxurious houses and Lincoln cars. Still worse was that solid gold watch and necklace with the golden Madonna dangling from it. The glitzy jewelry Angel adorned himself with cost more than he had made in the last six months.

Fruin's thoughts were interrupted by a voice crackling over the intercom in rapid Spanish. The flight attendant with great legs and captivating smile told passengers to fasten seat belts and prepare for landing in Durango. She eyed Fruin as she repeated the message in English. It wasn't necessary. His wife taught Spanish in a Chicago high school and had prodded him for years to become fluent in Spanish. He was grateful now that she had been so insistent, for he never could have pulled off the trip to Durango without his knowledge of the language.

Willard Smith, agent in charge of the Drug Enforcement Administration's office in Chicago, had at first refused to approve Fruin's unique plan to follow Angel Herrera to Durango. "Too risky," Smith had snorted.

"Contrary to a popular belief in this country, Chief," Fruin had tactfully argued, "everyone in the world doesn't speak English. In Mexico, we are foreigners. The agent you send must be bilingual. And dammit, Chief—this is my case."

The familiar whine and resounding thud of the plane's landing gear lowering into place jarred Fruin out of the past and into the present. What awaited him in a town controlled by people who hated nosey drug agents from the States, he wondered. Would the traffickers try to torture and kill him as they had two agents from the DEA's Houston office? He glared at Angel, feeling an instinctive hatred for drug traffickers rippling through his body. It felt good; it smothered all fears. He startled the passenger next to him when he mumbled, "I'll get you first, you son-of-a-bitch!"

"Huh? Que, señor?" the passenger said.

"Nada," Fruin snorted.

Joe Fruin was a professional cop. No matter how hard he tried at times to disguise it, wrinkled, loose fitting suits and rough-edge mannerism betrayed him, as did a serious and sincere nature. He had grown up on Chicago's South Side, where fighting was a way of life, and where the endless confrontations had hardened the lanky, sinewy youth to physical violence. And he had gotten used to being shot at and the smell of death while serving as a sergeant in the Green Berets in Vietnam. During a search and destroy mission behind enemy lines in 1969, his platoon was entrapped by an experienced, well-armed force of Viet Cong. After darkness settled over the jungle, Cong mortar shells began falling like sleet, blowing his buddies to pieces. Just before morning light and the arrival of reinforcements, he was so certain the Cong marksmen could put a mortar shell anywhere they wanted he took off his helmet and held it upside down. "Come-on, you slant-eyed assholes," he kept saying. "Let's see you put one right here."

He was one of the ten Green Berets to survive the slaughter, and he returned home to Chicago with a chest full of ribbons and an unquenchable lust for action. He found that working as a drug agent provided the intrigue and danger he needed. He often lectured rookie agents, "Undercover drug work is like jitterbuggin' in Nam. That's a strategic tactic where Green Berets are deployed by chopper at a selected site in the jungle. If contact isn't made with the Viet Cong, the Berets are picked up and dropped off again until the enemy is located and engaged. That's what we do in Chicago. We go out on search and destroy missions."

In 1973, Congress authorized the creation of the Drug Enforcement Administration. The newly appointed director, operating with an abundant budget, devised a plan to fight the drug war with regional task forces and asked Joe Fruin to form and lead one in Chicago. "I'll take the job on two conditions," he replied. "First, I pick the agents who work in my task force. Second, I be allowed to go after drug kingpins with all that new electronic surveillance gear the CIA has developed."

"Do what you gotta do," the director had said.

Shortly after Fruin had gotten his task force ready for combat the character and dimension of the drug war changed. Appearing to be giant octopuses aggressively spreading their tentacles, Mexican drug cartels began to systematically monopolize the marijuana and heroin industries. Ironically, for the first time in more than 50 years, Mafia families in Chicago, New York and Miami were muscled out of an illicit business that was making millions. After a few years of battling drug traffickers in the States, Fruin became convinced that the constant flow of drugs across U.S. borders could never be stopped if he didn't do something innovative and aggressive. He boldly told his boss, "Chief, we've got to stop the flood of heroin into the United States right where it starts—in Mexico. We've got to infiltrate the land areas where the opium poppies grow with informers and undercover agents. And, Chief, I'm the only one who can set up an operation down there."

A man on his way up in the ranks of the DEA, Willard Smith had to be politically correct at all times, and he had to make certain Joe Fruin took the heat if anything went wrong. "Okay, Joe, you have my unofficial blessing to do what you gotta do to interdict drug smuggling. But don't act like Popeye Doyle," he cautioned, referring to the famous New York police officer who used trench warfare tactics to expose and dismember the French Connection. "This time the battle will be fought from Chicago, not New York, and against Mexicans, not Frenchmen and Italians, and more significantly, by one of my task forces."

"I gotcha, Chief," Fruin had said. The aircraft taxied to within a few yards of a small, white building which served as the Durango airport terminal, then came to a sudden stop. Fruin stood and positioned himself immediately behind Angel so that he could get a good look at the brown leather valise Angel had placed under his seat and protectively straddled after take-off that morning. Prior to boarding the flight in Chicago, Fruin was told by surveillance agents at O'Hare Airport that the case had been x-rayed by a drug agent posing as an airport employee. The scan had revealed several three-by-five inch packages.

"Clearly stacks of money," the agent had opined, "money extracted from drug buyers in Chicago and destined to bolster the coffers of the Herrera cartel in Durango."

Having been warned that the Herrera cartel controlled the police and politicians in Durango and that he'd have to operate discreetly if he wanted to stay alive, Fruin decided to show his tourist and voters cards to security officers in the terminal. His plan called for him to act the part of a mid-level government bureaucrat who was too square to be a danger to traffickers. It was going to be hard to change his persona from lion to lamb, but he was determined to try.

When the casual Mexican entry formalities were completed, Fruin stepped outside through the doors of the terminal in time to glimpse Angel and Jenni being driven away. Thinking he recognized the driver, he began to search his memory. Ah-ha, he thought, Señor Manuel Herrera himself. He was in Durango only a few minutes and the many long hours spent in his office memorizing the faces and descriptions of the ranking Herrera cartel members had paid off. He watched the car until it faded into heavy traffic, then turned his attention to the milling crowd. Seeing no one who remotely resembled an agent from the federale police, he politely moved through the crowd to the end of the terminal where the baggage area was located. He had waited for his travel bag for only a few moments when a voice startled him. "Taxi, Señor, taxi?"

Turning quickly, he glanced down at the short, mustachioed man who had suddenly appeared at his side. Before he could respond, the man whispered in broken English. "Commandante Gonzales tell me to come for you and bring you to his office."

Uncertain of the taxi driver's veracity, Fruin slowly nodded his assent and then watched as the little man picked up his travel bag and walked toward the waiting taxi. He had seen his type before: the round, wrinkled face, the droopy-eyed, almost sleepy expression, the slow shuffled walk. He wondered if this man was as harmless as his appearance suggested. Choosing to trust him for the moment, he followed after him, entered and seated himself comfortably in the back seat of the taxi, and then scanned the crowd for a hint of hostility. He saw shy, benign faces, except for one. A creepy looking character with slick, black hair and mustache and large dark sunglasses shielding his eyes was surveilling him.

They had driven a short distance from the airport through crowded streets when the taxi driver turned and said, "I am Jorge. I work for Comandante Gonzales."

Fruin replied in Spanish, "Hello, Jorge. Thanks for picking me up. But how did you know that I was the man you were to meet at the airport?"

There was a sound of relief in the thick voice that no longer had to struggle with broken English. "El Comandante told me to meet a gringo by the name of Joe Fruin who was a passenger on the flight from Mexico City. You were the only gringo."

Fruin jerked upright in his seat, as if someone had punched him in the gut. Damn, he thought, I jumped right into a pile of shit this time. I'm alone against an organized army of bad guys, all armed with automatic weapons and dreaming about blowing away a Yankee drug cop.

Jorge was the typical Mexican taxi driver, unoffensively asking question after question as he dodged in and out of traffic, blowing the horn frequently. And Fruin was just beginning to enjoy Jorge's rank efforts to glean information when he pulled the taxi to the curb and stopped. "Here's your hotel," Jorge said. "El Comandante told me to have you check into the El Paraiso before meeting with him."

Fruin glanced out at the hotel facade and was pleasantly impressed. The scene resembled something right out of a tourista's picture postcard: sun-bleached stucco walls, arched windows laced with ornate grill-work, a veranda formed by porticos, and large, carved oak entrance doors. He recalled the motels and inns where he and his family had spent their modest vacations. The charm and inviting atmosphere of this hotel made them seem pale. "I'll just be a few minutes," he told Jorge as he stepped out of the taxi and looked around.

"The days are hot in Durango," Jorge replied. "You should change out of that Chicago suit."

Fruin examined a car parked twenty yards up the street. "Why, Jorge, so the guy sitting in that car watching me in the rear-view mirror won't recognize me?"

Jorge's face flushed, and he nodded.

Fruin registered at the hotel desk and then went to his room where he quickly showered and slipped into lightweight slacks and shirt. His meeting with the legendary Comandante Gonzales was his only commitment that afternoon, and he planned to keep it brief and informal. He wanted plenty of time to find out just how the Herrera cartel functioned in Durango without police or army intervention. And he wanted to know if the Herrera cartel bosses were money-mad, narco-terrorists as reputed, or cunning businessmen in search of fame and fortune, as Angel had often bragged.

The chance for narco-terrorism caused Fruin to remove his snub-nosed .38 Special from his travel bag, strap on his ankle holster and fit the gun into it. The pea-shooter would be used only in an emergency. It would be pitifully insignificant against the Herrera cartel's arsenal of automatic pistols and assault rifles. Returning to the street, he found Jorge sitting patiently on the front fender of his red and white 1970 Chevy, seemingly content to sit there until "manana." And the tail was still there, eyes glued to the rear-view mirror. "Insultingly amateurish," Fruin said as he slid in to the taxi.

Jorge hunched up over the steering wheel and drove as fast as the congested streets would allow. "I'll lose that tail," he said. Fruin watched the comical driver for several minutes before he sat back and pretended to doze off. He wanted to collect his thoughts about his target and the top secret intelligence reports which were stuffed into the two file cabinets in his office. The cabinets were labeled in large black letters: OPERATION DURANGO CONNECTION. He had given his get-Angel

Herrera campaign the code name in honor of Morgan Murphy, a crusading Illinois Congressman, who while speaking before a crowded House of Representatives, said, "Chicago is connected to Durango by a pipeline of heroin, and that pipeline is controlled by the Herrera cartel in Mexico." Jorge's thick voice jarred Fruin out of his thoughts. "Do you carry a gun, Mr. Fruin?"

Fruin's eyes narrowed. "Do you think I'll need one?"

"It depends on how dangerous the traffickers think you are," Jorge replied.

Fruin grunted, then said in a casual manner, "I'm an unimportant bureaucrat. I just push pencils and shuffle papers."

Jorge was puzzled, but after thinking about his passenger for several moments, he said, "Yes, Mr. Fruin, carry a gun. And you must remember that the people of this town live from the profits of the opium plant. Ten years ago, things were different. The campesinos—the farmers, as you gringos say—were starving and struggling to clothe their children. There was no plumbing or electricity in their adobe houses. With the money they now make from farming and processing the opium plant, the compesinos are able to live better than they ever dreamed; and the people of Durango know they owe it all to one man. They will fight and die for that man."

"Shit!" Fruin growled. "El Padrino. The Godfather. What are we dealing with in this town, a Mexican mafia?

Jorge shrugged his shoulders. "The drug cartels here in Durango are like the Mafia families in Chicago and New York in lots of ways."

While he had experienced the total spectrum of drug trafficking in the States, from junkies to pushers to major dealers, Fruin was now fathoming for the first time the vastness of the heroin industry. Here in Durango the overwhelming power of his enemy was suddenly and staggeringly apparent, and his mind raced with the realization that the

Herrera cartel controlled the heroin industry just like the Italian
Mafioso controlled alcohol, prostitution, gambling and loan sharking
in the United States. Many similarities were now so obvious. Each
organization honored only money; and there was the insatiable appetite
for blood and violence, the vendetta, and the conspiracy of silence.
"Hoodlums are hoodlums the world over," he said.

"Don Gonzalo is not a hoodlum," Jorge argued. "He runs his cartel
like your president runs the United States."

"Yeah, sure, Jorge. Have you ever met El Don?"

"Of course!" Jorge gushed. "El Don talks to everyone, just like the Pope
does. I took my family to meet him several times at parties and celebra-
tions in Durango."

Fruin laughed. "It seems, Jorge, you and the people of Durango think
of El Don as a Robin Hood. He breaks the law but helps the campesinos.
He's a hero."

Jorge nodded and smiled. "Yes, everyone likes and respects him."

Fruin eyed Jorge for several moments before asking the big question.
"Do you think El Don knows I'm in town?"

Jorge's reply was barely audible. "Maybe. Many public officials and
police are on his payroll, and one of his close relatives got off the plane
just before you did. Do you know the man I speak about?"

"No," Fruin replied firmly. "I didn't know anyone on the plane."

"The man on the plane," Jorge said in a conspiratorial tone, "is very
important to El Don. If El Don thinks you are in Durango to hurt Angel
Herrera in any way, you'll be dead by tomorrow morning."

Fruin pivoted in his seat and peered out the taxi's rear window. The
tail he had scoffed at outside his hotel was following several car lengths
behind—still looking and acting like he was auditioning for a role as the
Bad Guy's henchman in a classic James Bond movie. Paranoia gripped
him again and he considered the tail and the surrounding vehicular and
pedestrian traffic from a different perspective. He was all alone, and he
was in danger. "Wonder who that tail works for?" he said.

"Don't know," Jorge replied in a suspicious voice.

Fruin sat back in his seat and studied the little man with the kind face and gentle nature. He didn't trust Jorge now. He glimpsed Jorge's eyes in the rear-view mirror, focusing on him then darting away, moments before the taxi slowed and turned onto a strangely deserted road. He was in a precarious situation if Jorge was leading him into an ambush. Sliding his hand down his leg, he removed a gun from an ankle holster, held it next to his knee for seconds, then pointed it at the back of Jorge's head. The words of his platoon's master sergeant at the start of each mission in Vietnam rang out in his ears: paranoia is the first line of a good defense. Resolute, he said, "Jorge, I think you should know; you're going...."

"Federale garrison," Jorge blurted as the taxi rolled to a stop in front of an adobe building.

Fruin didn't believe Jorge until he pressed his face against the taxi window and saw a barbed wire fence extending out fifty yards in each direction from the building. Immediately inside the doorway two heavily armed men were glaring out at him. They wore the same olive-green uniforms as the regular Mexican army personnel did, except they carried M-16 assault rifles over their shoulders instead of M-1's. The largest and fiercest looking federales ambled over to the taxi and, recognizing Jorge, saluted in a joking manner. "Buenas tardes, General."

Jorge smiled and puffed out his chest.

Fruin breathed deeply, lowered his gun, and slid it under his leg.

"This is Joe Fruin," Jorge told the federales. "He has an appointment with Comandante Gonzales."

In one movement, Fruin reached for the door and reholstered his gun. When he was outside the taxi, he looked down into Jorge's large brown eyes and said, "I was saying, you're a great driver. If you ever need a job, look me up in Chicago."

Jorge's face lit up with a broad grin, his eyes reflecting a childlike wish for a job in the United States.

Poor bastard, Fruin thought as he turned away from the taxi. Good thing I didn't get a chance to finish telling him I was going to shoot him first if he led me into an ambush.

Chapter 2

▼

MEXICO'S ELLIOT NESS

"Follow me, Mr. Fruin," a federales guard said politely. "My name is Sergeant Diaz."

At first glance the garrison guards appeared tough and crude, and the building which served as a secured entrance-way to Durango's Federales Judicial Police Station looked like it belonged at Poncho Villa's stronghold during the 1916 Rebellion. But things changed as Fruin walked onto the garrison compound. The sergeant took on a likeable persona, and the other federales policemen he passed and the barracks where they lived impressed him. "Your comandante runs a real sharp operation here," he said.

"This garrison is the best in all Mexico. And the reason for that sits inside this door." The sergeant halted in front of a door with a makeshift sign above it. "COMANDANTE'S OFFICE," it announced.

Immediately after Sergeant Diaz knocked on the door, Fruin heard a deep, booming voice, "Entre." He wasn't sure exactly what he had expected of Comandante Alfonso Gonzales, but he was mildly surprised when he pushed open the door and saw him seated behind an old, worn, wooden desk, deeply engrossed in stacks of papers and documents. Gonzales sprang to his feet and rushed around his desk to welcome his visitor. "Buenas tardes, Señor Fruin. Bienvenido a Durango."

"Hello, Comandante, it's a pleasure to be here. I've heard much about you and your work."

Gonzales smiled, pleased with his visitor's response in fluent Spanish. He said, "I'm delighted the U.S. government sent a gringo who speaks Spanish. Most of your leaders in Washington think everyone in the world speaks English."

Fruin sat down on a chair across from Gonzales. A wily look crossed his face as he replied, "Our political leaders in Washington aren't any different than yours in Mexico City. They didn't make it there by what they knew; it was who they knew."

Gonzales laughed. He didn't respect most Yankee bureaucrats, as he called the agents and minor officials sent to Mexico to oversee the war on drugs. Yet he sensed Fruin was different; he was a man of courage and honor like himself, a man who could understand why the federales hadn't eradicated all the opium poppy fields within weeks after the Yankee bureaucrats told him how easily it could be done. He critiqued the joint United States and Mexican effort to halt the flow of heroin into the States, then summed up his feelings, "Your president, senators and congressmen in Washington refuse to understand that we will never be able to smother the supply side of heroin in Mexico until the U.S. government eliminates the demand by users in the States. They don't understand simple economics."

Fruin disliked playing games with people he respected. Still, he couldn't divulge his beliefs without tipping his true identity and mission. "Right," he said. "The Justice Department wants only the kingpins. The users are given a pass."

"We have similar problems here in Durango. I'm ordered to arrest the major traffickers but leave the campesinos who grow the opium alone. We can't win a war that way. We have to—"

"Comandante!" Sergeant Diaz said as he burst through the door. "One of our men has been injured in a shoot-out with traffickers."

As Gonzales and the sergeant hunched over a map and engaged in animated conversation, Fruin sat back in his chair and used the opportunity to scrutinize the famous drug fighter. El Comandante was average height, squarely built with a predominant barrel chest. His dark, piercing eyes flashed with determination. His bearing left no doubt that he was as tough and as trustworthy as he was reputed to be. He suddenly felt foolish for allowing paranoia to grip him and cause him to distrust everyone in Durango. During the taxi ride from the airport, he had suspected the old woman he had seen peering from a window and the young boy playing in the street of being spies for the Herrera cartel. And there was Jorge; he was going to shoot him.

Intelligence reports in the Operation Durango Connection file had provided Fruin with a profile of the thirty-nine year old professional soldier who had risen through the ranks of the Federales Judicial Police. Alfonso Gonzales was tough but fair with his men, having earned their respect and loyalty by leading dangerous raids rather than sitting back and directing them. He had been assigned the year before to command the thirty-three man garrison in Durango, and throughout most of that time had been engaged in a running battle with the drug traffickers. One of the few men in the Durago area the CIA and DEA trusted, he sometimes found himself doing the bidding for Uncle Sam with Mexican government officials. His biggest accomplishment had been getting a poppy eradication program approved by the corrupt politicians in Mexico City who referred to the brash Comandante as Mexico's Elliot Ness.

Shortly after his arrival in Durango, the traffickers made contact with Comandante Gonzales and attempted to bribe him, as they had his predecessor. Although he felt gravely insulted that anyone would believe he could be bought so easily, he politely refused the payoff and sent a message back to the heads of all known drug cartels. "If all drug trafficking is phased out over the next six months, I will guarantee immunity from arrest and prosecution for past crimes."

Upon learning of the Comandante's refusal to play the money game, Angel had said, "There's something wrong with that guy. No Mexican in his right mind would turn down a large cash bribe."

Shortly after the peace offer was made, rumors of an assassination attempt by several disgruntled traffickers reached Angel. At a hastily called meeting, Angel tried to impress upon them that killing Comandante Gonzales would be stupid and self-defeating. He told them, "I have learned a valuable lesson in Chicago watching the Mafia operate prostitution and gambling businesses. The Mafia's success over the last fifty years can be attributed to living up to its number one rule: never kill a cop; it brings too much heat."

Thinking it was time for the Herrera cartel to move over and give up some of the control it held over the heroin industry, Pablo Lucero openly defied Angel. "No," he shrieked, "we must kill Comandante Gonzales and all those who try to drive us out of business!"

Angel's eyes flashed with anger. "You are a Mexican dummy, a fool who will destroy us all. I warn you. Stay away from Gonzales.

Lucero backed-off from a confrontation, but in the days following the meeting he convinced several of the small time traffickers to join him in a scheme to kill Gonzales. "We get him when and where he least expects it," he said. "Gonzales will taste narco-terrorism right after he prays to the Lord for forgiveness."

Señora Gonzales cherished Sundays. It was the only day her husband put away his guns and tough talk and became the gentle family man she wanted him to be. After mass, she gathered Alfonso Jr. and little Maria around her and began preparing the traditional parrillada. This Sunday the large tray would be covered with a wide variety of seafood and served in the family room. It was a time for happiness and rejoicing.

Totally absorbed with his family and the sumptuous meal, Alfonso Gonzales failed to hear the car come to a stop in front of his house or see the three hooded men running toward the large glass patio door which led to his family room. The first sign of danger was the sound made by a man trying to force open the locked patio door. "Get down!"

Gonzales screamed as the serene setting exploded with the sound of machinegun fire and glass shattering.

Without thinking, Gonzales reacted and dove for his pistol. With a crazed look in his eyes, he charged the patio door, firing at the hooded men until they fled.

The next day a grim looking Comandante Gonzales removed two chrome-plated Colt .45 automatics from his desk drawer, loaded seven bullets into each clip and inserted the weapons into holsters so that they dangled at his hips. "Two bullets for each terrorist who raided my home and tried to murder me and my family," he vowed.

Methods of law enforcement changed dramatically in Durango after the attempted assassination. It became a virtual holy war, with the battle plan designed to overcome and eradicate an evil enemy. And the first devil to be brought to justice was Pablo Lucero, the outlaw who had violated not only the laws of Mexico but those of his own pack. The traffickers made him an outcast and then sent an anonymous tip to Comandante Gonzales. The note read: "PABLO LUCERO LED THE RAID ON YOUR HOUSE. HE HIDES AT THE GARCIA RANCH NORTH OF DURANGO."

Believing there was no evidence that could implicate him in the raid, Lucero surrendered without a fight and remained defiant as the interrogation began. That pleased Gonzales, who said, "I will give you to the count of three to tell me who planned and took part in the raid on my house."

Lucero became visibly frightened, but remained uncooperative.

Primal instincts told Gonzales he had the right man. "Ahh, that's good," he said. Turning to one of his federales, he ordered, "Strip him and spread eagle him while I get my favorite instrument of persuasion."

Lucero's eyes bulged when he saw Gonzales return with an electric prod. He started screaming before the prod was rammed into his testicles. "Stop! Stop! I'll tell you everything I know." He continued to scream for endless minutes as each jab of the prod sent excruciating pain throughout his body.

Within hours after their names and whereabouts were provided, Lucero's four henchmen were rounded up and given a dose of the electric prod. Each quickly admitted his participation in the raid and provided valuable information concerning trafficking in Durango. Still, confession and jail weren't enough for Gonzales. He labeled his captives narco-terrorists and executed them by putting two .45 slugs into each man's head.

Fruin had read the background information about Alfonso Gonzales in the Operation Durango Connection files with skepticism. He had told one of his agents, "No one can get away with enforcing the law like Gonzales does." But now that he had met the man and observed him giving orders to Sergeant Diaz, he was certain the reports were true. He imagined what it would be like to have the fanatical drug fighter allied with him in Chicago in the war against the Angel Herrera organization. Maybe he could negotiate a deal with Gonzales, he schemed, the two of them against the whole freaking Herrera cartel. He waited until the sergeant hustled out of the office before trying to find out more about Gonzales' objective and loyalties. He said, "I overheard some of your conversation but not the whispered part about the fate of the drug traffickers. I'm curious. What happened to them?"

"Killed resisting arrest," Gonzales replied in a casual tone.

"You play a dangerous game in Durango, Comandante. We'd never get away with rough stuff in the States."

"If we didn't, we'd all be dead long ago. Our system of justice is not like yours. Sometimes it's necessary for us to be judge, jury and executioner. Quick and harsh justice is the only thing traffickers and banditos can understand."

Fruin nodded. "I guess that's the difference between our law enforcement system and yours. You're at war, and all the evil rules of war apply. Kill or be killed. There's something honorable about doing things like that. No pretenses or self-deceptions."

"Honorable?" Gonzales queried. "I don't understand."

"In the States, there's no honor connected with drug dealing. Most dealers are scum-bag, low-lifes who'd snitch on their own mothers to beat a one year jail rap. And the worst thing about my job is that I have to protect a dealer's constitutional rights when I'm conducting an investigation or making an arrest. Shit! If I ever killed one, I'd be prosecuted and sent to jail."

Gonzales flashed an all-knowing smile. "That's why we have a drug problem all over the world. The United States can't control drug users or dealers."

"It's all our fault, huh? Users in the States create a demand which suppliers here in Mexico feel a moral obligation to meet? You could be right, Comandante."

Gonzales methodically struck a match and lit a Havana cigar. "I have been instructed to afford you every courtesy while you are in Durango. Is there anything specific I can help you with? Anything you'd like to know about Angel Herrera?"

Fruin was surprised by the question. It appeared probable El Comandante didn't trust him either. Feigning ignorance, he said, "No. Who's Angel Herrera?"

"The Herrera cartel's big boss in the United States. He arrived in Durango on the same plane you did, Joe. Didn't you recognize him?"

Gonzales was probing to find out if there was a connection, legal or illegal, with Angel. This caused Fruin to become more protective of his plan and the trap he was setting for Angel. He said, "My assignment is to obtain intelligence about heroin traffickers here in Durango and determine if we can set up a joint operation to interdict them at the Texas border. Individuals like Angel—what's his name?—don't interest me."

"That figures," Gonzales said with a sparkle in his eyes. "You gringo drug cops think like desk jockey bureaucrats rather than street fighters. You want to fight the drug wars by pushing and shuffling papers."

It was getting harder, but Fruin felt he had to keep playing the role. "Shuffling papers. That's where we are losing the war. Every time a DEA agent arrests one of the Herrera's mules with a pile of heroin a Chicago lawyer by the name of Matt Gavin shows up in court, shuffles his papers, makes spellbinding arguments to judge and jury, and then walks his client out of court a free man."

Gonzales chuckled as he said, "I had planned on shooting Matt Gavin until I had the opportunity to meet him in Brownsville, Texas, last January. Manuel Herrera was prosecuted in the federal court there for conspiracy to import ten kilograms of heroin into the States, and I was asked by the prosecuting U.S. attorney to provide information about Manuel Herrera's role in heroin trafficking. That's when I first saw Mr. Gavin work his miracles."

Fruin knew the Chicago lawyer major drug traffickers called Abogado del Diablo—attorney for the devils—rather well. "I'm sure," he said, "any run-in you had with Matt Gavin was filled with fireworks."

"That it was," Gonzales replied. After Gavin used his persuasive abilities on the jurors, and Manuel was found not guilty, I made arrangements to—let's say, bump into him on the courthouse steps."

Fruin laughed. "Alfonso," he said, "the more I hear about you and your style of doing things, the bigger fan of yours I become. But I must tell you; you were screwing around with the wrong man."

"Yes, I discovered that. After I bumped into him hard, he took two steps back and told me that if I had a problem we could go some place private and settle it man-to-man. He looked so dignified and non-combative in the courtroom I never imagined he would offer to slug it out with me."

"Abogado del Diablo fooled you too, huh?" Fruin said. "Everyone in Chicago knows his reputation. He's a real nice guy until angered. Then all the experience he gained as a linebacker for the University of Illinois football team comes out."

"I sensed he was a fighter when he took off his suit coat and tie. So…when he offered to buy me a couple of drinks in the bar across the street and try to talk out our problems, I agreed."

"Smart. Real smart," Fruin said. "Did you resolve anything?"

"Yes," Gonzales said with a sly look on his face. " After several drinks Gavin told me his reasons for fighting so hard to protect drug traffickers from prison. I pretended to understand his viewpoint. Then I told him mine. I told him that from now on I was going to shoot every drug trafficker I caught so that lawyers like him couldn't pervert the law with slick tricks."

Fruin said between spasms of laughter, "I would have loved to see the lawyer's face."

When the laughter died, Gonzales focused his eyes on the tough, intelligent drug cop who sat before him still pretending to be a gringo bureaucrat. He enjoyed doing business with men like Joe Fruin, and wanting to be helpful said, "What can I do for you, Joe, while you're in Durango?"

"I've always wanted to see where the opium poppy is grown, how it's harvested, where the heroin business begins."

Gonzales played his new friend's game. "You're a lucky man, for the day after tomorrow we are going into the mountains with helicopters to look for fields the campesinos are harvesting."

"That fits my schedule perfectly," Fruin said as he rose to leave. He had planned on having some fun in the cantinas that night and then playing the sober bureaucrat with Mexican government officials the next day. Everything was falling into place just as he had hoped.

"I have instructed two of my best men to take you back to your hotel and to remain with you throughout your stay in Durango," Gonzales said, pointing his smoldering cigar. "You are an easy mark for any drug trafficker who hates Yankees."

"Thanks for your concern, Alphonse. But I think it would be better if I had Jorge take me to my hotel in his taxi. I don't want the drug traffickers thinking I'm an important person."

Gonzales hunched over his desk, took a long draw from his Havana cigar, and then deliberately exhaled a long stream of smoke. His eyes turned fierce as he said, "Jorge left here five minutes after you arrived, and within sixty minutes after that was at the Herrera compound informing El Don of your visit with me."

"Well, I…I…" Fruin stammered, "I thought Jorge worked for you?"

"He does. He works for me, and he works for the Herreras."

Fruin shook his head in disbelief. "Tell me, who the hell should I trust in Durango?"

Comandante Gonzales stroked his chin with his thumb. "Only your mother—if you happened to bring her along."

Chapter 3

▼

EL DON

If Angel Herrera suspected that an obsessed DEA agent was tailing him as he arrived in Durango, he didn't show it. He smiled broadly as he and Jenni deplaned into a sundrenched, invigorating atmosphere. "Durango," Angel said. "I'm home. This is where I'm the happiest man alive."

Jenni moved close to him as she said, "I feel like I'm home too. Let's stay here forever."

Angel spotted cousin Manuel standing just inside the terminal, mouth agape, leering at Jenni. "Hey," he shouted in mock protest. "Stop looking at my lady like that."

Manuel Herrera let a soft whistle escape as Jenni walked into the crowded terminal dressed in a skin-tight mini-skirt and blouse cut in a "V", so as to expose the cleavage and unrestrained rise of firm breasts. He shook Angel's hand, then hugged Jenni. "Welcome to Durango," he said.

Jenni's face erupted with a shy smile as she whispered, "Angel, I feel like everyone is staring at me."

Manuel responded with a spontaneous flair of panache, took Jenni by the arm, and led her through the crowd and out the terminal door. "We don't see ladies like you in Durango," he said.

Jenni's eyes sparkled. The money and power people she had fantasized about for years were treating her as if she belonged with them. She was going to enjoy every moment of this trip, and she smiled at Angel as she thought about how she was going to show her appreciation when they were alone at his villa. Manuel's car was parked at the curb, and a big police officer was guarding it. The officer politely opened the door for Jenni, and she slid into the rear seat. Angel was sliding in next to her when she gasped, "Oh, Angel, my travel bag. Everything I own is in it."

"Don't worry," Angel replied calmly. "One of my men will get our bags and bring them to the villa for us. Besides, we have to hurry and lose that gringo drug cop who followed us all the way from Chicago."

Jenni and Manuel turned toward the baggage claim area and spied a gringo with broad shoulders and square-set jaw. He appeared awkward in his effort to blend into the crowd.

"How do you know he's a cop?" Jenni asked.

"I have a little hair that stands up and wiggles when one is around," Angel replied smugly.

"Oh, is that the hair you showed me last night?" she teased as she moved close to him.

The car sped off, leaving the airport in a cloud of billowing dust and headed west away from the congested city. Jenni paid special attention to the landscape when it changed to lush, green rolling hills. Her parents were born and raised in the hill country outside Guadalajara, and she wanted to see and feel how life would have been had they not immigrated to Chicago. It would have been terrible, she thought. My career as a singer and dancer would have been smothered. Life would have been a bore.

At the base of a steep hill, Manuel turned the car onto a tree-lined road that bisected fenced pasture land. Five of Angel's prized horses, grazing along the fence, quickly jerked their heads up as Angel passed them. His favorite Arabian stallion, a great muscled animal, nodded and loudly snorted an uncanny welcome home. Set back from the road a half-mile, his well-appointed hacienda rested on top of a small ridge.

"Here's my home in Durango," Angel said, helping Jenni out of the car. "Go in and make yourself comfortable, I'll be back in a few hours." He paused for a moment, savored her face and body, then said, "Take a nice bath."

Jenni put her arms around Angel's waist and looked up into his eyes. With an impish tone to her voice, she said, "Oh Angel, I can't wait, come in with me now."

Laughing, Angel turned to Manuel and said, "Let's get out of here before I forget about our meeting with El Don." Gently he pushed Jenni away and got back into the car.

They had driven only a short distance when Angel turned and asked, "How has he been?"

"El Don is fine," Manuel replied. He eagerly awaits the chance to talk with you."

Angel had always shown respect to his uncle, Gonzalo Herrera, but after the Durango Connection became established, he addressed him as all the others did—El Don or Don Gonzalo. He and Manuel were now fiercely loyal to him. "We owe him much," Angel said, "I remember clearly the days when we didn't have two pesos."

Angel and Manuel had grown up together on adjoining farms on the outskirts of Durango where their parents scratched out meager livings from small plots of corn and beans. It seemed there was never enough food or clothing, and with no hot water or toilet facilities, life was demeaning. When Angel was fourteen his father, frustrated and embittered, left for Chicago to find work, any work which would provide enough income to live a dignified life. Returning to Durango six months later, he packed his family and worldly possessions into an old Chevy pickup truck and began the long trek northward. Tears welled in

Angel's eyes as the overloaded truck pulled away. He believed he would never see Manuel again. Ironically, a grim twist of fate would prove him wrong. As years passed, heroin addicts who conspired on the dimly lit back streets of Chicago created an incessant demand for a drug that would once again unite them, this time in one of the most powerful criminal organizations in history.

Shortly after Angel and his family left Durango, Manuel took over the duties of running his family's farm and quickly learned all about soil and indigenous crops. He studied agriculture at the university in Mexico City and became the first family member to graduate from college. Upon his return to Durango, he found himself besieged by local campesinos for help. His reputation as a magician, able to produce abundant plant life in the arid, unforgiving Mexican soil grew to a point that when he started a fertilization business success came rapidly. That reputation caused El Don to go to him with a request for help. He wanted to know how an opium poppy field could be planted and farmed to produce the greatest yield.

Conversely, Angel wanted no part of the land and farming. He was glib, outgoing, an instinctively good businessman. Unable to speak English when he arrived in Chicago, he had difficulty at first adjusting to big city life. But a good intellect and willingness to work hard catapulted him through high school and one year of night school at a city junior college. Angel's father, who became a bricklayer's helper after arriving in Chicago, persuaded a friendly masonry contractor to give Angel a job as an apprentice mason. Construction was booming in the Chicago area, and it wasn't long before Angel had worked himself up the ladder and became a card-carrying union bricklayer. The Angel Herrera family had discovered the "American Dream." They had come to the United States poor and uneducated, and in eight short years became middle-class Americans. Angel made things official by becoming a U.S. citizen shortly after turning twenty-five.

By the time Angel was twenty-seven, he had saved enough money to buy a tavern on West 26th Street, where the Mexican community in Chicago was burgeoning. Foreseeing the demand for bands and singers from Mexico, he borrowed money from local businessmen and remodeled the nightclub called Rio Loro. Being the first place in Chicago to feature well-known Mexican singers and bands, it was an instant success. And with success, Angel's inherent taste for the sweet life became apparent: flashy and expensive cars, tailored clothing and a succession of attractive young women.

His reputation as a good businessman preceded him to Durango in the fall of 1971. Uncle Gonzalo and Cousin Manuel contacted him and said they would like to talk to him about a new business venture. At that meeting the Durango Connection was born: Don Gonzalo the financier and boss of the cartel, Manuel in charge of growing the opium poppy and processing opium into heroin, and Angel in charge of the importation and distribution network—the Pipeline—in the United States. A capable work force made up of trusted Herrera family members lay in waiting, eager to serve in any capacity. El Don had summed up the new business venture when he said, "There is an unlimited demand for drugs that we can meet with an unlimited supply; we have all the capital needed and a skilled and dependable labor force. Gentlemen, we should be millionaires within a few years." All reservations that Angel and Manuel had harbored about drug trafficking suddenly evaporated.

Manuel drove south for approximately a half hour before he slowed and turned off the highway onto a narrow dirt road that passed within feet of a shabby adobe house. The residents, a man, his wife, and five children, hurried out to see who was in the car. Angel and Manuel were quickly recognized by the innocuous appearing sentries, and no alarm signal via CB radio had to be given to the Herrera ranch.

The road widened and then wound down along a creek bed until it ended abruptly at an iron barred gate. A high barbed wire fence extended out from the gate until it blended into, and was hidden by, trees and rock formations. Manuel opened the car door, got out, and then waved to the guards. One of the guards waved to Manuel before rushing to open the gate.

"I see Don Gonzalo still believes in tight security," Angel said as the car passed through the gate.

Manuel nodded his head. "It would take a small army to overrun this ranch. Those are .30 caliber machineguns in the sandbag bunkers and the weapons the guards have just been issued are AK-47 assault rifles."

Approximately one-half mile from the gate, nestled in a clump of trees in the center of a ravine, sat a large, modern ranch-style house that was appointed with all the amenities of a movie star's home in Southern California. A broad smile spread across Angel's face as the front door of the house swung open and Don Gonzalo Herrera strolled out. "Hello, Don," Angel said as he got out of the car and moved quickly to greet him. El Don—a title reserved for aristocracy or important persons—aptly fit the patriarch of the Durango Connection.

El Don embraced Angel affectionately as he said, "I've eagerly awaited your visit." Angel was special to El Don, many suspecting it was because he mirrored his own lust for the sweet life. Grasping Angel and Manuel by the arms, he led them through the expensively decorated house and out onto the patio where they sat down at a table under a large shade tree. Just off the patio a shimmering pool tacitly beckoned Angel to plunge in.

El Don's appearance and demeanor didn't fit the image of a heroin trafficker. A lustrous mane of gray hair, handsome Latin features, trim figure and gracious manners distinguished him from the movie and TV stereotyped drug kingpin. He chatted, as if a corporate executive or clergyman, for an hour before withdrawing from the table talk. Angel and Manuel knew the mood change signaled the start of business. Leaning forward over the table, El Don said, "We have lost two shipments and a lot of money in the last three months. What has gone wrong?"

"Two things," Angel replied. "First, informers. Second, the DEA and Chicago police have stepped up enforcement of drug laws. Cops are everywhere and seem to have a great deal of money available to buy information and drugs. As strange as it may seem, suddenly there are more informers trying to make buys than there are legitimate buyers."

"You must start dealing harshly with informers," El Don said. "You must make an example out of one or two of them so that those who consider informing to the police will be frightened to do so."

Shrugging his shoulders, Angel replied, "It's not that easy, because most drug users are potential informers. A heroin addict is easy to roll over. Whenever one is arrested and held in jail for more than a day, his body starts crying out for a fix. In that state he will do anything, even inform on his own mother. It happened just last week to our Cousin Arturo. He was arrested and his house searched as a result of information given by a snitch. I have bad news for you, Don. The police found two kilograms of heroin and $100,000 in cash that was on its way to you."

El Don's face flushed and his eyes disappeared into slits. Quickly calculating the loss in his mind, he asked, "And how about Arturo? Is he alright?"

"I talked to our lawyer just before I left Chicago," Angel said. "He told me he got Arturo out of jail on a $10,000 bond. And there's a good chance of winning the case and getting part of the money back."

"Good! If Matt Gavin told you that, then Arturo will be all right. Our lawyer has always been trustworthy."

"Yes," Angel said. "Matt Gavin has always taken care of his devils."

El Don nodded and smiled. "Tell him Arturo is very important to me, and that we will pay whatever he asks."

Angel rubbed the palms of his hands together as he said, "Money talks, and defendants walk."

"Now," El Don said, "tell me about my old friend, Mario. I heard he was very lucky last week."

Angel had a gift for storytelling, and he chuckled as he told El Don and Manuel about Mario Garella, one of his most capable and reliable mules. Mario was sent to Nuevo Laredo to pick up a load of heroin. While gone, the same two Chicago cops who had arrested Arturo got a tip Mario would be returning to Chicago with three kilos of heroin secreted inside wheels of ranchero cheese. Hopeful the tip would prove accurate, the cops started watching Mario's house day and night. One evening, Iris Herrera, who lived next door to Mario, went to the alley to dispose of her garbage. The two men who were hiding behind her garage frightened her at first, but then came the recognition. She had acted as an interpreter for several defendants in the Cook County Criminal Court building in Chicago and had seen the cops there, testifying in various criminal proceedings. The next day when Mario called his wife from Texas, she told him of Cousin Iris' discovery. Mario changed course, stopped at his brother's house and asked him to keep three wheels of cheese for him.

El Don interrupted the story. "It seems ol' Mario used good sense."

Angel grimaced. El don wasn't aware that Mario was an actor at heart, always jumping at the chance to play the jokester. "Good sense, no, "he said. "That would have caused him to stay away from his house for a week. Instead, he nonchalantly drove up to his house and walked into it carrying his suitcase in one hand and two wheels of cheese in the other. He had no sooner put the cheese on the kitchen table and kissed his wife when the back door caved in with a loud crash. In charged the two cops beaming with confidence that their many hours of surveillance had paid off with the seizure of a large amount of heroin and the arrest of a key man in the Durango Connection. 'Okay,' one of the cops told Mario. 'Do you want to break the cheese or should we?'"

A broad smile spread across El Don's face as he nodded, urging Angel to continue.

Angel said, "Mario gave an Oscar Award performance. He told the cops he had brought nothing from Mexico except his suitcase and his cheese. One of the cops scoffed at Mario as he picked up a butcher knife and began cutting into a wheel of cheese. When the first couple of cuts didn't reveal the brown, lumpy powder believed to be concealed inside, the cop began flailing wildly, sending pieces of cheese flying in all directions. 'It's in here somewhere,' the cop kept mumbling.'"

Manuel had at the edge of his seat throughout the story, beaming amusement. "I hope," he said, "Mario told the cops he was going to sue them for destroying his cheese."

"Not Mario," Angel replied. "He sat down and meekly began eating pieces of cheese that were scattered about the table. That enraged the cops, and they stormed out the door, swearing to get Mario if it was the last thing they did."

El Don and Manuel were laughing uncontrollably as Angel finished the story. They found the inherent danger that permeated every facet of the heroin business exhilarating. El Don reveled in the minor victory until once again his mood became stern. "Did you have any trouble with the other fifty kilos we sent you last month?" he asked.

"Everything's fine," Angel assured him. "Twenty keys went to New York, ten to Detroit, ten to Gary, and we kept ten for Chicago. At $21,000 a kilo, we should have a profitable month. I have collected most of the money, and have part of it in my valise. The balance will be sent to you over the next few weeks."

Angel's report alleviated El Don's anxieties concerning the loss of profits, and he reconciled himself to the fact that the time was gone when exorbitant profits could be made from exporting and selling heroin. "Is the demand for our product still strong?" he asked.

"Our problem is that we have more buyers than available drugs," Angel replied, mindful of the pressing problem he faced in Chicago. "In fact, that is the reason for my unexpected visit. I promised a Puerto Rican dealer from Miami twelve kilos by next week. The guy looks like he's going to be a real good customer, so I'd like to show him we can make quick deliveries."

El Don tried to be helpful. "Other than the eighteen kilos we are preparing to ship to you for our best customer, we have none ready at this time. Comandante Gonzales and his federales have been hurting us badly by spraying the fields with a herbicide that kills the poppy. The only thing I can do is send someone into the mountains to find out if one of the campesinos can harvest enough opium gum in the next few days to process into twelve kilos."

"I can go tomorrow," Angel volunteered. "The Puerto Rican will be a good account, and I don't want to lose him. He says he can dump ten kilos a month in Miami and San Juan." Angel looked to Manuel, silently soliciting his help.

Manuel had someone else on his mind, and he was searching for answers. "Angel," he said, I haven't been able to get that gringo drug agent who arrived in town with you out of my mind. He has the eyes of a jaguar, and he seems confident in the midst of his enemies. Do you think he followed you here from Chicago?"

"If he has, I hope he is having a good time. There is nothing that he saw or can see that would hurt me with the cops in Chicago. All that he can say is that I came to Durango with my lovely Jenni and visited relatives."

"Is that the same gringo Jorge picked up at the airport?" El Don asked.

Angel chuckled. "It must be. There was only one gringo on the plane."

"Then he could be dangerous," El Don said. "Jorge told me that after taking him to the El Paraiso Hotel he took him to a secret meeting with our enemy, Comandante Gonzales."

"What do you think should be done about this intruder?" Manuel asked.

Angel felt in his gut that the gringo was someone important and that injury to him would bring intense reprisals from both the U.S. and Mexican governments. He said, "Let's watch him closely and make our minds up later. If we went after him we could end up shooting ourselves in the foot."

El Don agreed. At the moment drug agents didn't concern him as much as informers did. He wanted some plan devised to deal with them, to make them pay for their treachery.

Angel had to sidetrack El Don. Trying to convince him that the treacherous deeds of informers couldn't be avenged in Chicago the way they were in Mexico was a hopeless task. He said, "El Don, I'd like you to meet my new paramour.

Manuel caught the hint and described how stunning Jenni looked as she walked from the plane. "That skirt and blouse she wore were so tight, she looked like three pounds of beans in a two pound bag."

"I look forward to meeting Jenni at my dinner party tomorrow night," El Don said.

If the ploy didn't work, El Don would have talked business all night, a night Angel had planned on spending wrapped in Jenni's arms. Angel raised his glass of wine and toasted the end of the business meeting. "To fine wine and even finer women."

El Don ushered Angel and Manuel to their car, where a reflective mood struck him, and he said, "It's crazy that the United States government should fight so hard against the importation of heroin and spend millions of dollars here in Mexico to eradicate the opium fields."

"Why so?" Angel asked, somewhat bewildered.

"Because the United States is responsible for all the opium fields in Mexico today and for all the heroin that is shipped into the United States. You were too young to know and history books never told you that in 1914 officials from the United States came here to Durango and paid my father and other campesinos to plant their fields with opium. It was a high priority program made necessary by the outbreak of World War I and Turkey's siding with Germany and other Axis powers."

"You see," Manuel interrupted, "our families helped win the war."

El Don nodded and continued, "The United States had purchased the majority of its opium imports from Turkey for refinement into morphine—the only pain killer at that time. With the supply of morphine cut-off and American military forces about to enter the war, government officials in Washington became desperate and looked for a new source of supply. They looked to the Mexican people for help, and we complied, sending the pain deadening morphine for wounded soldiers and sailors until the end of the war. Then suddenly, the U.S. stopped buying it because the same government officials preferred to do business with Turkey again. The opium industry was smothered in Mexico."

"Well then," Angel said, "the U.S. shouldn't complain about us giving it back to them."

El Don rolled his eyes and continued, "The Yankees didn't give a good shit about the Mexican campesinos when they smothered the morphine market. The campesinos had to replant their fields with corn and beans and return to meager living conditions. But they couldn't forget the money they had made, and in the hope that a new market would open, a few kept small plots of land planted with the poppy."

"Tomorrow, Angel, you will see how those small plots have grown into high yield acres," Manuel said proudly.

"Be careful, compadres," El Don cautioned, "that savage Comandante Gonzales and his men will not be gentle with you if they should capture you near the poppy fields."

Darkness had settled over the countryside by the time Manuel turned onto the driveway leading to Angel's hacienda. The night was quiet, and a large, full moon illuminated the house so that a figure of a woman could be seen standing on the veranda. Manuel said, "I don't believe she's waiting up for you, especially since the only thing she has to look forward to is that little hair she talked about earlier."

"Compadre, she's going to get a lot more than a little hair wiggled at her."

"Make sure you leave a little strength for tomorrow," Manuel said. "We'll leave for the poppy fields as soon as I can break free from a business conference."

Angel got out of the car and walked toward the entrance to his ranch house. Jenni had positioned herself so that her body was a silhouette framed by a candlelit window directly behind her. As Angel approached, she rushed towards him and threw her arms around his neck, pressing her body tightly against his.

"Where have you been all night? Come into this house right now!" she demanded.

Once inside Angel leaned back against the door, forcing it closed, and Jenni turned to face him, her eyes reflecting the passion raging inside. Angel opened the closet door and began to remove his shirt, when she reached down and took the hem of her dress in each hand, then standing erect, pulled it over her head. He heard the soft rustling of her dress as it fell to the floor. She seldom wore a bra or panties, and as she stood naked in a venus-like pose, he savored the full expanse of her firm young body. She moved slowly toward him, put her arms around his neck and then kissed him passionately. Her warm, moist lips moved about his neck and ears, and, continuing to kiss him, she slid her hand down his body and began gently stroking his hardening groin.

"Wait, Amorcito, let me take my shirt off," he whispered, fumbling with the buttons.

She didn't hesitate, but unzipped the front of his pants, slipped her hand inside and pulled out a now fully erect Angel. Then with her soft brown eyes drifting upward to meet his gaze, she glided to her knees, moistened her parted lips, and moved forward onto him. Passion flooded his body, and his knees weakened; he didn't speak or move for fear she would stop.

Jenni sensed the pleasure that had consumed Angel, and wanting to please him fully reached up with one hand and finished unbuttoning his shirt, all the while using her lips and tongue to roam over and around him. "Off, take it off," she said as she tugged on his shirt sleeve.

Angel limply wiggled his shoulders, allowing his shirt to slide off his shoulders, but before he could free his arms, the unrelenting Jenni unbuttoned his pants and let them drop to the floor, so that they cuffed his ankles. "Amorcito, stop a minute!" he pleaded, "I'm go—" With the initial stages of orgasm gripping his body, his shirt binding his arms and pants tethering his legs, he lost his balance and fell backwards into the darkened closet. The ungainly fall didn't interrupt Jenni's amorous appetite. She stayed with Angel and made love until the passion within him erupted.

Moments later, when the scene and his predicament registered, Angel burst into laughter. "Help me off with my pants and shirt. I can't move," he gasped.

She began to giggle as she tugged on the legs of his pants. "I can't get them over your shoes," she said, just before she lost her grip and fell backwards onto the floor.

Angel crawled over to where she lay, his eyes roving over her well shaped legs and thighs and then her enticing triangle. As he slowly lowered himself to within inches of her, to where he could inhale her spellbinding scent, he whispered, "I'm going to drive you so wild you'll scream."

Chapter 4

▼

THE POPPY FIELD

This ain't bad, Joe Fruin thought, as he sat back in his chair and glanced around his hotel's poolside restaurant. The brunch he'd just finished—Spanish style eggs, enchiladas and fresh fruit—was a pleasant change from his usual breakfast fare of coffee and donut gulped down enroute to an arrest scene or his office. Even more enjoyable was the generous expense allowance his boss had authorized. With a little practice he figured he'd be able to spend the taxpayer's money like the Fat Cat politicians in Washington did. He promised himself he'd change his conservative ways right after he put Angel Herrera in jail.

The prior evening he had taken a big chance when he slipped away from his two federale bodyguards and casually strolled around Durango's downtown business district. The streets, the restaurants, the cantinas—that's where the real Mexican people were. Rubbing shoulders was the only way he could identify with the genuinely warm and charming Mexicans, the ones who were decent and law abiding. They had been so refreshing, so unlike the sleazebags who had been the focus of all his attention in Chicago.

He made several sincere attempts to get up from the table and begin his workday, but each time he did so an obliging waitress rushed to his side and filled his coffee cup. He couldn't say no. He had never tasted coffee so smooth and fullbodied, and he discovered the pool patio was an idyllic place to dine. There was a young woman seated three tables away whose dancing eyes and sweet innocence reminded him of his wife. He watched her as she talked and laughed until a tinge of nostalgia crept through him, bringing with it a longing to be with Maria and little Jimmy, his ten year old son. He fantasized they were with him, excitedly planning a hike into the mountains where they would find a stream and fish and then just lay back and enjoy one another. The impulse to telephone Maria and ask her to catch the next plane to Durango gripped him. If she would, he'd promise her he'd never mention his work or drug trafficking. But would that be a lie, he wondered. Could he change if Maria and Jimmy were there, or would he remain obsessed by his work. Maybe Maria was right when she complained that his outlook on everything in life had become stilted. Drug law enforcement had consumed his thoughts and ambitions for at least the last five years. His only friends were DEA agents or Chicago cops who were equally obsessed with their work. At social events, dinners and parties, he was always shy and withdrawn, choosing to drift into a deserted corner of a room at first chance to chat confidentially with someone carrying a badge. It was just last week when Maria complained, "Sometimes when we're making love, I look at your face, and I know you're thinking about the Angel Herrera case and not being with me."

I'll change, he vowed to himself, when I bust Angel's ass and put him in the shithouse. For now, though—He was jarred from his thoughts when a waitress placed a telephone on his table and said, "There is a call for you, Mr. Fruin."

It was El Comandante. His voice vibrated with excitement as he said, "The foray to the poppy fields will begin at sun-up tomorrow. Tell no one. Not even my men know the purpose of our mission."

"Thanks for the invite," Fruin replied. "The trip will give me a rare insight into drug trafficking." As he pushed the phone away from him and stood up, a grin spread across his face and he murmured, "I'm going to fuck-up that Durango Connection."

        *   *   *   *

Meanwhile, Angel had been wrestling since sun-up with a ghost, one that had been nagging him far too often in recent months. At first he was going to wake Jenni and ask her to replay the prior night's closet scene. But seeing her sleeping soundly, he decided the next best therapy for the unsettling desire to get out of the drug business was a horseback ride to Angel Point. He saddled his Arabian stallion and rode hard into the hills, not stopping until he came to the top of a ridge that overlooked his hacienda. There he proudly surveyed his property, his real home, and thought how fortunate he was to have accumulated great wealth and power in a few short years and to have lived a lifestyle men fantasized about. Someday, he thought, he'd give up the drug business and become a respectable businessman or banker or movie producer. But for the immediate future, he couldn't. He had a pressing commitment to deliver 12 kilos of heroin to his new customer.

"Come on, big boy! Let it all hang out," he said as he urged the great horse into a full gallop. Skillfully avoiding trees and boulders, he raced to meet his appointment with Cousin Manuel at the airstrip at the Herrera ranch.

A business meeting in Durango had delayed Manuel. It was near noon when he arrived at the airstrip, testy and anxious to get airborne. "Get in," he told Angel as he kicked over the engine of the Cessna Skyhawk. Seconds later, he pushed the throttle forward and started the plane rolling down the crude runway.

The quick take-off caught Angel with one leg dangling out the door and hands engaged in a frantic search for his seatbelt. "Flying with you," he groaned, "is never a pleasure. It's more like a combat mission."

"What do you mean?" Manuel said as he pulled back on the yoke and guided the Skyhawk into the air. "You know I always evade combat."

"Bullshit." Angel said. "How about the time you lost those two army planes in the mountains by flying ten feet off the canyon walls."

Though he reveled in daredevil flying, Manuel took his ability to pilot an aircraft seriously. He told Angel in a scolding tone, "I'm not a Sunday afternoon pleasure flyer who takes off and lands on well-groomed runways with controllers to provide weather, air traffic and other good things. Most of the runways I negotiate are secreted mountain fields the campesinos clear, then disguise with boulders and shrubbery."

Angel chuckled. "Quit bitching, compadre. You're just like most pilots involved in trafficking. You wouldn't trade the highs gotten from the risks for anything."

Manuel smiled proudly as he leaned forward in his seat. "There's O'Hare Airport off the right wing."

"Don't I wish," Angel said wryly, anticipating another harrowing experience. "That landing strip looks like a postage stamp."

"That's one of the better ones. I'll make a pass over it and show you what I mean."

Angel spotted numerous boulders and other obstacles littering the field. "Yeah, it's real good if you can play leapfrog."

Manuel banked the plane and half-circled to make a final approach to the landing field. "There they are," he said. "Look, just a little north of the field, at the mouth of that cave."

Angel saw a man waving, then came the recognition. "It's the Francisco Alvarado family. They're some of my favorite campesinos."

"I'll bet he'll have the poppy gum you need. He left his ranch two weeks ago and brought his wife and three children here to harvest the poppy fields."

Angel had known Francisco for many years. Before he had started farming opium poppy fields life had been harsh. Now, he had a new ranch house, with modern conveniences, and his children ate well. There was even extra money to buy a few luxury items. The last time

Angel had met him, Francisco had said, "I will be forever indebted to you for allowing me to work for the Herrera's. The Alvarados will pray for your safety every night."

Don Gonzalo and Manuel had established a system for producing more revenue for poppy growers in one year than in several years combined. In late November, they planted poppy seeds so that opium gum would be ready for harvest when the dry season began in June. Then in the summer, they planted marijuana seeds so that the plants would be ready for harvest in late October. The campesinos were fully subsidized: seeds, fertilizer, loans, and advice were provided. And, cash was paid upon delivery for the harvested opium gum.

Manuel taxied the plane to within forty yards of the Alvarado camp and cut the engine. He smiled when he saw a teenage boy and two young girls running to see his new plane. Not expecting to find Angel on board, they became excited when they saw him push open the plane's door and yelled to their parents, "It is Angel! It is Angel!"

The youngest of the Herrera cartel's poppy growers were dressed in the traditional clean, off-white cotton blouses and loose fitting pants and wore infatuating smiles. "This is the best welcoming party I've ever had," Angel said.

When Francisco Alvarado saw Angel walking toward him, he quickly adjusted his wide brimmed sombrero and the serape which was draped over his shoulder. Beaming proudly, he said, "Welcome to our camp." Then he told his family, "Angel and Manuel have descended from the sky like great condors. We should ask them to stay and share our meal."

The children gathered around Angel, their awestruck eyes pleading with him to stay. He was a legend to the campesinos around Durango, a hero who had fought many battles against corrupt government officials and soldiers. Stories portrayed him as a man of super size and strength, ferocious in a fight. But the man who stood in the middle of the Alvarado family was under six feet tall, with a trim athlete's build. There was a twinkle in his sensitive eyes, and his voice was gentle when he said, "We will be honored to visit with you and share your meal."

Manuel smiled, aware Angel had found the serenity of the Alvarado campsite and the aroma of beans and tortillas cooking in an open cauldron over a slow burning fire irresistible. "Angel," he said, "there are times when I think you are a campesino at heart."

"This is what life is all about, compadre," Angel replied. "It's simple, but beautiful."

Angel must be getting old and soft, Manuel thought as he walked off toward his plane. He had to get the Skyhawk ready for a quick takeoff in case the federales came nosing around.

Angel had an ability to enjoy life to the fullest in spite of the dangers that constantly surrounded him. He relished the unpretentious meal and the sweet simplicity in which Señora Alvarado served it. After taking a drink of wine from a bota bag, he said, "That's the best food I've had in twenty years."

Señora Alvarado smiled shyly. The compliment was a priceless gift.

Angel stretched his legs out in front of him, sat back against a rock, and studied the faces of his hosts. He didn't want to bring up business, yet when he saw Francisco's eyes become large and questioning, he felt it was time. "It's important," he said. "I need twenty to thirty kilos of poppy gum. We thought a couple of your fields may be ready for harvest."

Francisco's eyes fixed on the ground, and he droned, "We collected gum from one of our fields today. But just ten kilos."

"I must have more," Angel pressed.

Francisco rubbed his forehead with the palm of his hand, then pointed to a high mountain ridge to the west. "Maybe you're in luck, Angel. Two fields over that ridge may be ready for harvest."

Angel smiled approvingly. "I knew I could count on the Alvarado family."

Francisco wasn't capable of understanding the urgent need for his opium gum. The Puerto Rican, the users in Miami who were awaiting the fruit from his poppy plants, and the entire drug culture were beyond his wildest imagination. He firmly believed he was placed on earth to be a farmer, and when he did it well, the Blessed Virgin smiled on him. He said, "We will work hard for you tomorrow and try to collect the gum needed. You are welcome to stay the night and go with us to the fields tomorrow."

Angel quickly considered the risks and the alternatives. He'd have to chance ambush by federales and give up a night of sexual escapades with Jenni if he stayed. The decision was made when he looked into the large brown eyes of Antonio. Lying cradled across his legs, silently waiting to be noticed was the M-1 rifle his father had recently given him for his sixteenth birthday. He said, "Are you as good a shot as your father?"

"I'm the best shot in these mountains," Antonio replied proudly.

Angel expected a challenge from Francisco. Instead, the proud father grinned and shrugged his shoulders as he said, "Antonio has an instinctive feel for a gun and an eye as sharp as an eagle's. While in these mountains, he'll be your bodyguard."

"In that case, we'll stay," Angel said. And I feel sorry for any federales who try to harm me."

"Oh, no," Manuel groaned as he glanced at the ground and mountainous terrain. "Are you sure, Angel, you don't want to spend the night with Jenni at your beautiful villa?"

"Positive," Angel said.

*   *   *   *

The sun, glistening bright orange and bringing the first rays of warmth, barely breached the mountain ridges when Angel was awakened by the sounds of burros baying and stamping, protesting the fittings of bridles and harnesses. He attempted to sit up, but stiffened muscles from a sleepless night on an unmerciful, hard, cold ground hindered him. He looked at the form lying next to him shrouded by a blanket and chuckled. "Come on, compadre!" he said, shaking Manuel's shoulder. "We have to go to the fields."

"I'm frozen stiff," came a pained voice from deep under the blanket. "Let's wait until the sun comes up and warms the air."

Francisco and his family had work to do, and they had no time to wait for the two visitors who had grown soft from a life replete with luxuries. He had loaded empty plastic jugs on the backs of the burros and, with the children guiding the burro train, started up the mountain-side. Angel and Manuel, realizing they would be left behind, dragged themselves up and mounted two horses that were left for them. They soon caught up with the swiftly moving procession, much to the delight of Antonio and his sisters who looked over their shoulders and flashed broad smiles.

Reaching the top of a high ridge, Angel raised up in his saddle to search the lush valley below for the vivid hues that distinguished the opium poppy plant from other vegetation indigenous to the area. "I know the fields are down there somewhere," he said, "but I can't spot them."

"There! There! Under the rocky ledge is one field," Francisco said. "Over across the valley to the right of those trees is another."

Angel looked at the poppy field below him. It was 250 feet long and 100 feet wide and terraced to stop soil erosion and retain moisture. "You did a fine job selecting your sites," he said. "It would be almost impossible for the federales to spot those fields from the air."

"I hope so," Francisco said. "I saw a federale helicopter fly over here last week."

A concerned look crossed Manuel's face as he said, "Angel, I think we should get the fuck out of here."

Angel was so driven by his desire to meet his Puerto Rican customer's order for twelve kilos of heroin that he disregarded the danger zone they were in. "Let's see what Francisco can harvest for me," he said. "Then we'll get out of here."

Francisco led Angel and Manuel to the poppy field and then between the rows of poppy plants, where he examined several of the hanging pods. "You're in luck," he said. "The pods are ripe and bursting with gum."

Examining one of the dark brown, egg-shaped pods, Manuel said, "Mother Nature gave you some help, Angel. The poppies have ripened earlier than usual due to a warm, dry spring."

Angel felt confident for the first time that he'd meet the delivery schedule he had set for his new customer. "Ah, it's good to know Mother Nature is on my side too. But tell me, how long will it take to harvest and process the gum?"

Manuel pointed to the Alvarado family who had spread throughout the field and were working the pods. "Today, parallel cuts will be made across the pods so that the milky white sap inside can ooze out. By tomorrow, the sap will have dried and turned into a brownish gum which can be easily scraped from the pod with a dull knife."

Angel and Manuel decided to watch the harvest from under a rock ledge, out of the sun and in the company of a bota bag gorged with wine. Angel lay back on the ground for several minutes before he brought up a subject which somewhat startled Manuel. "Tell me truthfully, do you ever think of getting out of drug trafficking?"

"Never," Manuel replied. "It's too profitable."

The almighty dollar, Angel thought. That's what the whole fucking world is about. Every person in his organization looked at heroin like it was just another commodity—corn, wheat, beans, or something easily changeable into money. "In Mexico," he said, "there's no evil connected with heroin, just money."

Manuel had noticed the change of attitude gripping Angel and decided it was time for another philosophy lesson. "When heroin leaves our hands, it can be used for either good or evil. It's the user's choice. We're like a car or gun salesman."

"It's easy for you," Angel said, "because you've never seen the effects heroin has on a person."

"That's not our problem. Our product can be used for a painkiller like morphine was for centuries, or it can be used stupidly by losers to space out, to get away from the problems of everyday living. It's the Americans who pervert a useful drug."

Angel watched the Alvarados move throughout the poppy field laughing and chattering. They were as happy as people could be on this earth. "Strange," he mused aloud, "but the happiness and self-esteem we see down there all stems from the fact we will pay Francisco $70 for every pound of opium gum harvested. That gives him a feeling of success. If he were still farming corn, he'd be getting $1.50 a bushel and feeling like a piece of shit, like most of the campesinos in Mexico."

"So would we," Manuel retorted. "If it weren't for the opium poppy, we'd be middle-income businessmen living from paycheck to paycheck. Can you see yourself doing that?"

Angel grunted. "Definitely not, but it may be better than jail. Every form of opium and heroin is against the law here in Mexico and the States."

"Fuck man's law," Manuel said. "It doesn't concern me. Only God's law, the law of morality counts. When we sell multi-kilos of heroin, we don't' hurt anyone. A user desires our product so much he is willing to pay a lot of money for it. We don't push it down his throat or inject it into him. The user has the free choice to buy it or not, use it or abuse it. A man who buys heroin is just like a man who buys a bottle of whiskey."

Where is he wrong, Angel wondered. Surely a man should be free to put whatever he wants into his body. And laws have always been made by crooked politicians for self-serving reasons. "Yeah, right!" he said. "Fuck man's law!"

Manuel burst into laughter. "Let's drink to that." He pointed the nozzle of the bota bag at Angel's mouth and squeezed. Wine streamed through the air and, missing its mark, splashed over Angel's face.

As the wine dripped from his nose and cheeks, Angel said, "Come to think of it, Manuel, we'd better stay in the drug business. You couldn't make it as a bartender."

Chapter 5

---▼---

WAR

The same sun that had awakened Angel and Manuel and guided them to the poppy field cast an eerie reddish haze into the hotel room where Joe Fruin was sleeping soundly. He might have missed the first violent meet-up fate had ordained for him and his designated target if his wristwatch alarm didn't start beeping. Just as his finger found the shut-off button, the face of Comandante Gonzales appeared on his mind-screen. "Damn, I'm late!" he groaned as he jerked upright and swung his legs over the side of the bed.

Sergeant Diaz was standing in the middle of the hallway, an anxious look on his face, when Fruin bolted through the door. "I was getting worried, Mr. Fruin. I thought you had a young girl with you and didn't want to leave her."

Fruin realized that he might be at fault for the good-natured sergeant receiving an ass-chewing. "I'll take the blame if we're late," he said.

"No problem," Diaz droned. "If we're late, Comandante Gonzales will go without us."

Fruin felt like he had been punched in the gut. Some force was compelling him to go to the poppy fields to see where the illicit drug that caused so much misery and suffering was born and nurtured. It was where the kickoff in the big heroin game was taking place. "Let's move fast," he told Diaz.

Diaz raced through the streets of Durango while Fruin held tight to the jeep seat to keep from being ejected. He whistled softly when the jeep passed through the garrison gate and jerked to a stop.

"Stay in that jeep!" Comandante Gonzales shouted. "We're leaving immediately."

Fruin looked to his right and saw a grim-faced Comandante standing in front of his office door, legs spread and arms folded. He wore green combat gear and boots, with large sunglasses shielding his eyes and two chrome-plated .45's protruding from holsters. Fruin smiled and waved.

Gonzales spun on his heels and walked into his office. He returned a minute later carrying an M-16 rifle. "Here," he said, "I believe you used one like this in Vietnam."

Fruin examined the gun. "Am I at war with someone?"

"No, but you should be armed. The campesinos do not give up their poppy crops easily."

Two jeeps roared out of the garrison and sped along the road leading north out of Durango. Sergeant Diaz drove the lead jeep with Gonzales and Fruin seated in back. Four federales sat in the second jeep which had an M-60 machinegun mounted in the rear. Gonzales was constantly alert for danger. His eyes darted from face to face and from open window to balcony, before riveting on a suspicious looking trailing car. Surprised, Fruin asked, "Why the worry, the townspeople seem peaceful?"

"Joe, we worry about a man we may have never seen before—a father, brother, or a son of a drug trafficker we killed in a drug raid. The people from Durango are different. Vendetta is a natural way of life. If a family member is killed, a man's honor is at stake if he does not avenge the injury. Not being from my country, it is hard for you to understand that the people here in Durango have never liked or trusted the police or government officials. They do not ask them for help, and most trust the Herreras more than the politicians."

Fruin's inate disgust for drug dealers was apparent in his voice as he said, "We don't have to worry about honor with drug dealers in the States. They do nothing for honor. They wouldn't put their necks on the line for any cause. Shit! I must have been involved in a thousand arrests and saw only one dealer try to shoot it out with us."

"Do you know how many men Al Capone killed in 1929?" Gonzales asked.

Fruin was amazed that even here Big Al's reputation was known. "A lot, I'm sure," he replied.

"It has never been reported in newspapers, but even though there are only 160,000 residents in Durango, there were more murders recorded here last year than there were in Chicago in 1929. Virtually all the killings were directly related to drug trafficking." Fruin sat back. The corners of his mouth began to twist up as the adrenalin began flowing through his body. Let the war begin, he thought. Townspeople and campesinos alike are fair game. "Where do we meet the choppers?" he asked.

"For security reasons," Gonzales replied, "it is necessary to drive approximately five miles outside the village to a pickup point. The last time a chopper picked up some of my men in town, it was ambushed and shot down."

"Who shot it down?"

"We don't know," Gonzales replied with a shrug of his shoulders. "It could have been drug traffickers, bandidos or just some of the townspeople who hate federales."

Fruin was amazed at how different the drug traffickers in Mexico were from those in Chicago. "It's hard to believe," he said that you and your men can't control all the banditos and drug traffickers in the area."

"Joe, I think this visit will help you understand what we are fighting here in the area you gringos so aptly named Mexico's Golden Triangle. The thirty-three men under my command must police more than 26,000 square miles of remote mountains and valleys without cooperation or help from anyone."

"How about the army and local police? No help?"

"There is an army garrison just outside of Durango. However, Generalissimo Garcia is in charge of the garrison there." Gonzales paused for a moment, then said, "Need I say more?"

"I've heard of Garcia's reputation, and I think I know what you mean," Fruin replied.

Gonzales was silent for moments, then said, "The Generalissimo is just like Jorge, the taxi-driver. He works for both the Mexican government and for the Herrera cartel. The local police are no better. The Herreras are so powerful that they have picked the public officials and the police chiefs they want!"

"So then, it is you alone against the drug traffickers."

"Yes, we are alone against the traffickers, the army, the local police, the politicians, the townspeople and the campesinos. You will understand more the longer you are in Mexico's Golden Triangle."

Fruin gritted his teeth. He was now fully aware that his plan to eradicate heroin smuggling at its source in Mexico depended on one man—Comandante Gonzales.

The jeeps turned off the road and started up the side of a dry, barren hill, the engines groaning and straining in low gear until, in a cloud of dirt, they reached a small plateau on a hilltop. Fruin leaned forward in his seat as he examined the scene before him. "Those two helicopters," he said, "look like the Hueys we had in Vietnam."

"They are," Gonzales replied. "They're war toys your government can't use anymore, so they were given to us.

Fruin knew the story behind the choppers, having been one of the first to recommend their use in the war against the growth of the opium plants in Mexico. He said, "The HU-1B helicopters were affectionately dubbed 'Hueys' by our guys in Vietnam. They're manufactured and supplied by the Bell Corporation of Dallas, Texas."

Gonzales said smugly, "I'm happy to report that your Congress has finally put its money where its mouth is. Six months ago we got those two choppers and several highly skilled mechanics to service mechanical problems, all at a nice cost to the American taxpayer."

"I know, more than eight million a year," Fruin replied over his shoulder as he climbed out of the jeep and walked over to examine one of the choppers. Nearing the cockpit, he heard a voice from inside, "Hello, gringo."

Shielding his eyes from the glare of the sun reflecting off the glass cockpit, Fruin saw a lanky, sandy-haired man with sunglasses seated behind the controls. Momentarily surprised by the sudden appearance of an American, he said, "You don't look like you were born in Durango."

"Madison, Wisconsin. Mark Jones the name."

"Joe Fruin's mine. What the hell are you doing in this business, Mark."

"After serving in Nam," Jones said, "I couldn't find a job which provided excitement and big bucks. When I heard the federales were looking for pilots, I volunteered my services."

Fruin grinned. "A mercenary, huh?"

Jones laughed. "Call it what you want, but the federales couldn't fight the drug traffickers without guys like me, and I couldn't make it without the pay."

"Are you winning or losing the war against the opium poppy?" Fruin asked.

Jones replied tactfully. "We're gaining ground. When Comandante Gonzales took over in Durango, things began to change. He's trustworthy and tough."

"From what I've seen of his federales, I would have to conclude they're a rough and ready force," Fruin said, soliciting information.

Jones said, "Comandante Gonzales and his men are the best. I would have liked having them with us in Nam."

Fruin turned and watched Gonzales directing his men, all of whom moved sharply in accordance with commands. Two federales removed the M-60 machinegun from the jeep and were anchoring it in the doorway of a chopper. After weapons and gear were loaded into the choppers, a sergeant and two federales got into a jeep and drove over a hilltop and out of sight. They had been ordered to proceed to a point near the target valley that was to be searched and to stand by in the event of a shootout with the campesinos.

"Get in!" Gonzales directed as he approached Fruin. Moving with agility, Gonzales slid into the seat next to the pilot, Mark Jones. "The other chopper has been equipped with a tank filled with a potent herbicide and two sprayers. That chopper will spray the fields we find, and we will direct the operation from this one. Let's get airborne!" he ordered.

The whirling rotor blades and lift-off reminded Fruin of Vietnam. The federales were men of war with grim looks on their faces, sitting hunchbacked in the bowels of a whirlybird with M16's, instruments of death,nestled between their knees. The same tension that prevailed during pre-dawn raids on Viet Cong positions prevailed here. It's incredible, he thought, all this sophisticated military equipment and firepower was needed to attack peasant farmers and destroy a poppy field. "Who the hell are we fighting today, General Rommel and his Africa Corps?" he blurted out.

Gonzales chomped on his unlit cigar before he responded. "Rommel would be easy. These Mexicans are tough. If you look back in history many years to old Mexico, you'd find that the area around Durango has always produced the toughest breed of Mexicans. They inherently love weapons and are crack shots with pistols and rifles. Not far from here is where Pancho Villa and his men had their stronghold and fought off in many famous battles the Mexican army. For two hundred years the Mexican government has been unable to control the men from this area."

Fruin frowned and shook his head. "And I thought my job was complicated. I can see now that it's much easier to arrest and jail a dealer in the States than it is one who fights to protect a historical way of life."

"You are correct. The campesinos are basically good people, as are the people who work in Durango for the Herrera family. But they violate the law I'm sworn to uphold, so...."

Fruin had always been closed-minded about drug dealers and users, lumping them all into what he called a bag of slime. But he was now beginning to realize that motives, involvement and rewards varied with each link in the heroin trafficking chain. "I guess one can't blame the campesinos," he said, "since all those uneducated farmers do is grow a beautiful and innocent-looking flower. The gum they collect from the poppy and transport to the lab is harmless in that form. They never see the illicit end-product of their work. And because no one in these mountains uses heroin, they never see how it affects a person."

"That's right, Joe. That's what makes this war against the opium poppy so tough. The campesinos use their wives and children to help work in the fields, and when the opium gum has been collected and started down the mountain trails to the labs, the children are used to guide the burros. Except for the money earned, they place no more significance on an opium crop than one of your gringo farmers would place on a potato crop. For that reason, we try not to arrest the campesinos. Our job is to destroy the poppy fields, either by spraying with herbicide or by cutting off the poppies before they are ripe."

But what if the campesinos should resist while you are destroying their livelihood?" Fruin asked.

"Then it may be necessary to shoot a few of them," Gonzales replied tersely, as he studied an aerial reconnaissance map. "I sent a chopper out last week to take photographs of this sector here," he said tapping his finger on the map. "I think we will find two or three poppy fields in this narrow valley."

Fruin examined the terrain below. "What do we look for?"

"Joe, you must think like a campesino and ask yourself, where would I plant the opium poppy if I didn't want the federales to find it." Gonzales stroked his chin with his thumb, then continued, "I generally look for a fertile valley about twenty to thirty miles from the closest village, a valley that is difficult to reach over land except by burro or horseback. Then I look for a terraced section of land on the side of a mountain about one-half the size of one of your football fields."

"Nothin's easy in this frickin' business," Fruin said.

Gonzales correlated the terrain below with his map until the chopper crossed over a distinctively high mountain ridge. Suddenly he stiffened and grabbed Mark Jones' knee. "Radio the other chopper! Tell them our target is just ahead!" he barked.

As the federale choppers approached the target area, an aura of innocence and peacefulness hung over the Alvarado family. They chatted and giggled as they worked their way through the rows of opium plants. Violence was inconceivable until Antonio suddenly became rigid. His sharp eyes searched the horizon as he raised his hand, signaling to the rest of his family for quiet. "I thought I heard a helicopter," he said.

Seconds later, the whining roar of engines broke the silence, followed closely by the appearance of two choppers emerging over the crest of a ridge to the south of the field. Seeing the federale markings on the Huey choppers as they swooped down from the ridge, Angel yelled, "Quick, run over here!"

"There! There!" Gonzales said when he saw figures scurrying for cover under a rocky ledge.

Jones veered the chopper toward the ledge, made a whooshing pass over the poppy field at 100 feet, and then flew a short distance up the valley.

"Get in close!" Gonzales ordered. "I think I saw poppies."

The chopper tilted to the left, on a forty-five degree angle, made a half-circle and glided to a hover above the poppy field. "Bingo!" Jones said. "We hit Durango gold."

"Okay," Gonzales said in a confident tone, "tell the other chopper to get to work."

Jones moved the chopper to a vantage point above the ledge Angel and the others were hiding under and then directed Lieutenant Flores, who was piloting the other chopper, to make passes over the field from north to south and then back south to north.

Flores spread the sprayer arms out from under his chopper, and with them fully deployed, moved forward approximately 50 feet off the ground. Reaching the edge of the poppy field, he released the defoliant, and it fell to the ground as if it were being sprayed from a large fire hose.

Knowing the importance of the gum to Angel and crazed by his fierce loyalty to and Manuel, Antonio raced to his burro and pulled his rifle from a saddle holster. As the chopper flew past him, he fired.

"Is that crazy bastard firing at us?" Lieutenant Flores said as he maneuvered his chopper into a position where his door gunner could return fire. The first bursts from the M-60 machinegun ripped into Antonio's midsection, nearly tearing him in half. He slumped to the ground without a sound and lay there with blood spurting from gaping holes.

"You bastards!" Angel hissed as he dashed toward the fallen body, recklessly ignoring the chopper and its firepower. He dove to the ground next to Antonio, then looked up into the threatening eyes of the chopper's door gunner, who responded with a burst of machinegun fire. Shells tore into the ground around him, and he heard and felt several hitting Antonio's lifeless body. Ripping the rifle from Antonio's frozen hands, Angel raised the gun and squeezed out several shots. One of the shots hit the door gunner, knocking him backwards out of the door. Another ripped through the fuselage of the chopper and severed a fuel line, causing a black puff of smoke to erupt. The chopper lurched forward and up; it's engine sputtered loudly; it's tail section swayed from side to side out of control. "Gotcha, you cold blooded savages!" Angel screamed.

Realizing his chopper was struck in a critical spot, Lieutenant Flores tried to fly out of gunshot range. "We've got to land and scramble," he told his crew.

Angel had the chopper in his gun sights and was about to squeeze the trigger when the chopper lurched upward and onto its side, then exploded into a bright orange ball and plunged to the ground engulfed in flames. "Burn in hell, killers," he snarled.

Gonzales didn't know the other chopper had been hit by ground fire until moments before it exploded. The gunfire had occurred so suddenly, so unexpectedly, that no alert could be given by the downed pilot. But when he saw the burst of orange flame surround the stricken chopper, he swirled in his seat and began firing an M-16 at the man he saw retreating to the safety of a rock ledge. He kept his finger on the trigger until the man dove out of sight behind a large boulder.

Mark Jones had been in similar situations in Nam and knew a chopper was a sitting duck for ground fire. Without waiting for an order from Gonzales, he quickly jockeyed his chopper away from the poppy field, slowing to a hover when he passed over the burning wreckage of the downed chopper.

Thinking he saw movement in the inferno, Gonzales yelled, "Land! Land! Someone's alive."

A twisted smile crossed Angel's face when he saw the federales chopper gliding down for a landing. He jammed a new clip into the M-1 and fired. The shots ripped through the chopper's cockpit and fuselage, one missing Fruin's head by inches.

"Let's get the hell out of here," Gonzales ordered. "My men have all been cremated."

Jones applied full throttle, and the rotor blades whirled faster. As the chopper rolled on its side and climbed from the burning wreckage, Jones stared down, hoping to see his good friend, Lieutenant Flores, free of the wreckage and alive. "Not one survivor," he muttered.

"Raise the support jeep on the radio and determine their position," Gonzales ordered.

Jones put the radio mike to his mouth. "Jones to Sergeant Diaz. We're under fire; need your support now."

The radio crackled with an excited voice, "Terrain impassible! We are approximately five miles from target area and will have to proceed on foot."

Vividly recalling similar circumstances in Vietnam, Fruin said, "It'll take Sergeant Diaz two hours to reach us. Comandante, we can't chance attack without support."

Gonzales looked at his watch, then turned to Mark Jones and said dejectedly, "Tell the jeep to return to base. We'll have to get those killers later. One of their shots might have done damage to our chopper, and I can't afford to lose another one. Besides, they have burros and horses. We'd never catch them on foot in these mountains."

The chopper gained altitude and roared down the canyon past the still burning wreckage. Fruin and Jones scanned the area, still hoping for survivors. Gonzales, however, was more concerned with attempting to see who was under the ledge. "I hope I can see at least one of those killers," he growled. "I want to come back and turn him into fertilizer for the next poppy crop."

When the federale chopper was out of sight, Angel scrambled from behind the boulders and went to where Antonio's body lay. The awesome hush born of shock pervaded the air as Angel picked up the limp, lifeless body and carried it to a spot alongside the poppy field the young boy had given his life defending. He and Manuel dug a grave while the Alvarado family knelt and prayed to the Blessed Virgin. Then they lowered the body into the ground.

Racked with grief and remorse, Angel was unable to speak or move away from the gravesite. It seemed as if some mysterious force anchored him to the ground that covered Antonio until Francisco broke the trance. "Will the federales be back today?"

"No," Angel replied. "Not today, maybe tomorrow."

Francisco turned to his wife and children. "We have work to do."

Slowly, solemn faced, the Alvarado family picked up their tools and returned to their work in the poppy field.

Chapter 6

▼

THE LABORATORY

The Cessna Skyhawk slowly circled the poppy field, dipping its wingtips in final salute to Antonio, the young warrior. Angel stared out the plane's window at the Alvarado family working the poppy field and tried to fantasize that Antonio was still alive, still tending the poppy crop with his family. It didn't work. Escape from reality was shattered when his eyes focused on the smoldering wreckage of the federales chopper, and he vividly recalled the carnage which had occurred hours earlier.

"The federales are savages," Manuel said as he turned the plane and headed for home field.

Angel had seen men killed before and had always accepted death as inevitable, coming one way or another, sooner or later. Antonio's death was different though. His bullet-riddled body and the grief suffered by his parents left him feeling ashamed and guilty. Barely audible, he said, "Antonio was killed because he thought it was important to prove his bravery and courage to me."

"Don't blame yourself," Manuel replied hoping to jar Angel from his somber mood. "You should feel proud that he respected you enough to give his life to protect the gum you needed."

"Proud? I feel stupid. Why didn't we let the federales destroy the crop? It's just brown shit."

"You're wrong, Angel. It's a way of life. Antonio instinctively understood that, as you once did. And he would feel he gave his life for nothing if he knew you were acting like this. Our organization must go on unimpeded by emotion."

Angel had wanted to stay at the poppy field and provide protection for the Alvarado family, but Manuel had become forceful, arguing, "If the federales return, it will be with overwhelming firepower and men. Everyone will be lost."

"You were right", Angel said, "If you hadn't dragged me away, I might have screwed things up for you and El Don. My only hope now is that the Alvarados can finish harvesting the balance of the gum and bring it down to the lab before the federales return."

"Francisco knows what he's doing," Manuel said. "That's why he insisted we take the poppy gum he had at his camp. Now, if he sees federales choppers coming soon enough he and his family can jump on burros and escape."

It was late in the day and the sun had just dipped behind mountain peaks when the landing strip at the Herrera ranch appeared over the right wing. "There's home field," Manuel said.

"Will Cousin Luis be at the lab this late?" Angel asked, more determined than ever to make delivery as agreed to the Puerto Rican.

"Our problem is we can't keep him out of the lab. Since he became our chief chemist, he thinks he's the world's greatest scientist. Now, we must all address him as Dr. Luis."

Angel said, "Dr. Luis has done an excellent job improving the quality of our heroin. We haven't had one shipment returned in over a year."

"Dr. Luis is the best," Manuel said. "He's been working nights in the lab trying to find a filtration process which will make our heroin as white as the Turkish and Asian."

Angel grunted. "He doesn't like the term Mexican Mud, huh?"

"Not our Cousin Luis," Manuel said. "He wants to produce the best heroin in the world.

Angel adjusted his seatbelt for what was going to be a fast landing, then said, "Our cousin is a real company man. Maybe I should be too. Maybe I should take the time to find out how the hell heroin is made."

Manuel twisted quickly in his seat and took hold of the top of one of the ten-gallon jugs resting on the plane's rear seat. He shook it vigorously a few times, checked the fluidity of the liquid and then did the same to another jug. "It's a simple process," he said. "The first step is to separate the good shit from the bad shit by mixing the freshly harvested gum with a slake lime and water solution. It appears from the looks of the fluid in these jugs that Francisco has concocted a proper mixture. Once the opium juice is separated, it is up to Dr. Luis to refine it into morphine, then heroin."

"Clear as mud," Angel said. "But what's the difference between morphine and heroin to a user?"

"Hell, Angel, I don't know. I just grow it. I wouldn't degrade myself by sticking a needle in my arm if my life depended on it. We'll be on the ground in a minute. Why don't you stop by the lab and ask our mad scientist about it?"

Manuel brought the Skyhawk to a stop under a clump of trees. As he shut down the engines, two men began to camouflage the plane by enveloping it with a large earthen colored cover. "A few precautions," he said, "makes it difficult for the federales to determine what type of aircraft we are using."

"It's strange," Angel said as he slid out the plane's door. "I never cared to spend any time at our labs. Do you think if I stopped by for a visit, Dr. Luis might be persuaded to cook up the twelve kilos I need?"

Manuel smiled obligingly. "I guess I'm not going to deter you from your trip to Cousin Luis' lab, so I'll join you." He led Angel to a pick-up truck, then said, "Climb in."

Angel and Manuel waited as the jugs of opium juice were removed from the plane and loaded onto in the back of the truck. The lab, converted from an old sheepherder's cabin, was located fifteen miles from the ranch, deep in the hill country. The road into it was passable, but only by a well handled four-wheel vehicle. Wanting the Herrera ranch free from all traces of opium gum, or its derivatives, El Don placed the labs in locations that couldn't be easily connected to him. And, ironically, El Don and Angel were alike, reluctant to go near heroin until it was sealed in heavy gauge plastic and ready for shipment. They preferred to look at heroin solely as a cash commodity, not as the lumpy, brown, illegal powder it was.

As the truck came to an abrupt stop in front of an old wooden cabin, the putrid odor given off during the refinement of opium engulfed Angel. He put his hand to his face, covered his nose and mouth, and gasped, "No wonder El Don won't visit the labs."

Manuel laughed. "I predict this will be your last visit. Look at the grass and shrubs surrounding the cabin; everything is withering and dying."

Angel was about to agree when Luis burst out the cabin door, a white surgical mask covering his face. A long, white smock covered his body. His slightly round shape and white attire made him look like a ball of wool. "Cousin Angel, I'm honored to have you visit my research project," he said.

"Hello, Dr. Luis," Angel said, bowing, suppressing a smile. "I am honored to be in the presence of such an great scientist."

Luis jerked to a stop and feigned insult. "Angel, if you don't stop joking with me, I'm going to concoct a potion that will make you impotent."

The men roared with laughter as they walked into the crude, one room cabin that served as Dr. Luis' workshop. In one corner on a long table were large vats and other apparatus used to process the opium gum.

"Yes, yes, over there on the table," Luis directed the worker who had unloaded the plastic jugs from the truck and was looking for a place to put them. "Now, go tell El Don that Angel and Manuel are with me and that I will have them at the ranch house in time for his dinner party tonight."

The roar of the truck engine faded in the distance before Manuel turned to Luis and said, "Angel and I would like to see your new process for turning opium juice into heroin."

"All right, gentlemen, it will be a pleasure. Stand back and let me have the papaver somniferum," Luis said with a sly smile across his face.

"Huh? The what?" Angel stuttered.

"That, compadres, is Latin for flower of sleep." Luis lifted one of the plastic jugs and began pouring the dark brown liquid into a large vat on the table. "Now watch as I start the refining process by separating the morphine base from the opium juice."

Angel moved closer to the table. "I'm watching" he said. Luis continued, "Francisco put the raw opium gum into these plastic jugs containing water and slaked lime solution.I generally drain off as much water as possible while the juice is in the vat, heat the juice that is left, and then strain out the visible impurities."

Angel was still perplexed by the most often heard criticism of his product. "Why is our 'Mexican Mud' dark brown and the Turkish and Asian heroin white?"

Cousin Luis, thoroughly enjoying his lecture and the opportunity to demonstrate his importance to his family, replied, "That is because labs in Marseilles and Bangkok are professionally equipped, and the chemists refine the morphine base several times through expensive charcoal filters. In Mexico we refine the morphine base once through cheesecloth filters and omit many cleanup procedures."

Manuel grinned. "Our product is like pussy; it looks bad but feels real good."

Luis nodded. "And it has just as much umph as Asian white. Our customers seldom complain about the quality. It's a small percentage of users who get a product which has been stepped on who complain. Unscrupled street pushers sometimes cut the strength so much that the high gotten from shooting up is more psychological than physiological."

A new marketing plan for the their business raced through Angel's mind. "Dr. Luis," tell me more," he said slyly.

Luis was happy to do so. "The next step in the process is the mixing of the morphine base with acetic-anhydride. The chemical reaction created by mixing acid and morphine makes heroin ten times more potent than morphine. We add procaine as an adulterant to build up the bulk, and we are ready for shipment." Luis paused for several moments, then continued, "You may ask next, why do we have to build up the bulk? Because it takes about ten pounds of raw opium gum to produce one pound of morphine, and morphine is concentrated into heroin at a one to four ratio."

"When you build up the bulk," Angel said, "can you control the percentage of heroin in the mixture?"

"Certainly, within a few percentage points. Our product leaves here anywhere from forty-five to fifty percent in strength."

This was the first time Angel looked at the infamous drug as something other than a commodity to be packaged and sold for a profit. Turning to Manuel, he said, "Dr. Luis is in a conspiracy with Mother Nature to produce a drug that brings relief from mental and physical suffering. Why are we the Bad Guys for selling it?"

"Did you ever use it?" Luis asked in a suggestive tone.

Angel shook his head, thinking he'd handle and sell the commodity, but he'd never stick a needle into his arm and pump heroin into his veins. "Hell, no! I can sell that shit without ever knowing what it feels like."

Manuel said proudly, "There's no place in the Herrera organization for a heroin user."

*   *   *   *

It was dark when Angel and Manuel returned to El Don's ranch house, and as they washed and dressed for dinner, they deliberately delayed each movement, hoping to stall off as long as possible reporting Antonio's death. Sensing something was awry, El Don saved them the initial step when he walked into their room and with a puzzled look on his face asked, "Did everything go well today?"

"Don," Angel said, "El Comandante has killed Antonio, the son of Francisco Alvarado." He related the details, emphasizing the heroic efforts of their young soldier.

Suddenly, El Don became noticeably proud. "Imagine the courage it took to look down the barrel of that M-60 machinegun and to stand ground and shoot it out with only an M-1 rifle."

"Yes, El Don, Antonio died a hero, a death every campesino dreams of but can seldom achieve."

"In that case," El Don said, "we can never let his name or courageous action be forgotten. We'll see to it that newspapers and books memorialize him for many years to come."

"What about his family?" Angel asked.

El Don took hold of Angel's hand and squeezed it tightly. "See to it that they are well taken care of—all their needs."

Satisfied Antonio's memory would live on in the hearts and minds of the people of Durango, Angel said, "It is now time to celebrate life. Tomorrow it could be us, compadres."

They entered the courtyard where flickering candlelight illuminated a large oak table that was laden with assorted fruits, cheese, and wine. A bottle of brandy with the label Vino Del Lago was conspicuously placed at the end of the table. It caught Angel's eye instantly, and he picked up the bottle and cradled it for inspection, then adroitly half filled three brandy quaffers. "Salud," Angel toasted as he lifted his glass, sniffed, and then savored the brandy. "Ah, a wonderful bouquet, and it tastes as good as my favorite French import."

El Don beamed. "Coming from a connoisseur of wines and liqueurs, I'll take that as a great compliment."

Angel eyed the man who deserved recognition for pioneering the wine industry in Mexico, and he silently thanked him for increasing the value of his financial portfolio. In under three years El Don had proven the self-annointed wine making experts and investment bankers wrong. They had warned him that a winery was a foolish investment, that no vineyards were located within several hundred miles of Durango, and that Mexican grapes were notoriously poor in quality. El Don took the experts admonitions and used them to his profit. If the local banks wouldn't lend construction and working capital funds, then he would tap the Durango Connection's cash proceeds. And if Mexican grapes were bad, then he'd import grape juice produced in California wineries, and from those select juices he'd ferment a choice burgundy, rose' and chablis. Those wines were marketed throughout Mexico under the label Vino Del Lago.

Angel took a sip of brandy. "How are our wines selling?"

El Don's eyes sparkled. "Sales are booming. We now sell more wines than any other Mexican producer." He held up a bottle."This new brandy should be very successful. We distill it exactly like the Christian Brothers Winery in California."

The shrewd fox, Angel thought. He used the profits from heroin to buy cattle, lumber mills, and start a winery, and in a few short years has turned them into highly profitable businesses. "I think you will be wealthier than Aristotle Onassis one day soon, Don Gonzalo."

"And so will you and Manuel. Your interest in our businesses must be worth over several million dollars. In fact, our financial holdings have become so diversified that I am presently negotiating to buy a bank that will provide us with funding for major investments."

Angel had to determine El Don's intentions and plans for their heroin business, and he asked, "Do you think we'll be able to quit drug trafficking soon and devote our energies to legitimate businesses?"

El Don chose to evade the question, but in doing so, tacitly gave Angel the answer he was seeking. "But enough talk of business," he said. Let's leave that for our business meeting tomorrow. Tonight we—" He turned to see Jenni and Manuel's wife walk into the courtyard. Jenni's long radiant, reddish-gold hair and sparkling green eyes instantly captured his attention.

Overwhelmed by the scene, Jenni looked lost and forlorn. A nervous giggle escaped as El Don walked to her, took her by the hand and escorted her to the table. "You sit right here next to me," he said graciously.

Angel smiled, for he knew El Don delighted in the company of a beautiful woman, and that he was going to be a charming host that evening. Raising his brandy glass in a toast, he said, "I salute you, El Don, for this magnificent dinner party."

As the evening progressed, Angel discreetly observed the scene he was part of, and for the first time in years felt proud of his business activities. Honeysuckles and jasmine plants were arranged around the courtyard so that the air was bathed in a fragrant scent. And a mariachi group played a soft ballad as servants instantly responded to the slightest, most gracious of movements by El Don. He watched the party chat and dine in a splendor that only extreme wealth could provide before allowing his eyes to focus on a vase that sat inconspicuously in the center of the banquet table. It was filled with stunningly colorful flowers— flowers that offered the only clue to the source of the opulence.

Chapter 7

▼

REGGIE BEGOODE

During the return flight from the poppy field, Comandante Gonzales seethed with subdued rage. His blood red face and eyes, so large they appeared ready to burst from their sockets, caused Fruin to caution him, "Settle down or you'll have a stroke."

Gonzales hissed between clinched teeth, "We should've stomped out those campesinos like bugs."

While engaged in fierce combat in Vietnam, Fruin had seen men act like barbarians. That had been stereotypical behavior in war for thousands of years. With his buddies in Vietnam, it happened because the young soldiers were following orders and tradition, were scared, and acting so out of character. But Comandante Gonzales was a different type of soldier. With him, the most undesirable expressions of human nature—hate, revenge, and the proclivity to kill—seemed to be the good and right way to enforce his country's drug laws. And that's what now worried him. If he helped Gonzales do his job, then Operation Durango Connection would have to be shit-canned. "Comandante," he said, determined to protect his own case, "you performed your job as well as possible under the circumstances. The shot that brought down the chopper was pure luck, a one in a million."

Gonzales squeezed up his face. "Yes, lucky for the campesinos, unlucky for me. The exploding chopper and fiery death of my men are clear in my mind. I'll never be able to think of anything else until I get even with those bastards."

"But who are they?" Fruin probed. "Until you know, you have to forget about how the four federales died. You have to think of doing your duty, not a personal vendetta."

Gonzales grunted, then turned in his seat and peered out as the chopper settled down in front of his office at the federales garrison. "I wish I were returning a victor rather than a disgrace," he groaned.

Fruin empathized with his comrade in the War on Drugs. "The only thing that will get you out of the bad mood you're in is a bottle of Tequila. I just happened to have one in my hotel room, next to a bucket of ice and a fresh lime."

Gonzales nodded. "Yes, I've got to get away from my men and talk with someone who can understand me."

Several hours later, Gonzales found Fruin's hotel room and ten shots of tequila were just what he needed. The look of homicidal passion left his eyes, enabling Fruin to see another side of his comrade. The defeat of his well-equipped federales by a group of poorly armed peasant farmers was a blow to his sense of self-esteem and courage, and that humiliation was more intolerable than the loss of his men. Certain Gonzales would do all he could to save face with his superiors in Mexico City and with his men, Fruin asked, "What are your plans for the campesinos who were at the poppy field?"

In a casual tone, Gonzales replied, "I'll kill them all."

"When are you going after them?" Fruin pressed.

"Tomorrow morning."

Fruin wanted no part in the slaughter of campesinos, but he had to stay involved in the search and destroy mission. He had to find out if the man who shot down the chopper had been identified by anyone. Shortly after sun-up the following day, he was seated in front of Gonzales' desk with two federale staff officers when Comandante Gonzales marched in, grim and determined, and told his officers, "I have contacted my superiors in Mexico City and received authority to step up the poppy eradication program, using whatever force necessary." He jabbed his finger at a large map on the wall, assigning and coordinating positions, becoming livid with anger as he did so. Pointing to the valley where the chopper was shot down the prior day, he proclaimed, "This area is mine!" Although the stated purpose of the full scale attack with four choppers and twenty-five men was to eradicate poppy fields, Gonzales kept emphasizing that all resistance should be met with force. "Shoot to kill," was his order.

Fruin waited until the staff officers rushed from the office to assemble the attack force before he tactfully continued his quest for information. He hadn't been candid at the poppy field when Gonzales asked if he had seen the man who had shot down the chopper. Later, he said he wasn't certain, that due to the pitching of the helicopter, he had gotten only a brief glimpse of a man sighting down the barrel of a rifle. He lied. He thought the man was Angel Herrera, and now he felt in his gut it was him. This created a dilemma, for if it had been Angel and Gonzales found out about it, months of investigation and a major bust would have to be flushed down the drain. Gonzales would see to it that Angel never made it back to the States alive. A self-righteous interest in protecting his case prevailed when he said, "You don't think one of the Herrera bosses was at the poppy field, do you? Say, someone like Angel Herrera?"

Gonzales laughed sarcastically. "You'd never find Angel any where near poppy fields. You can go back home, Joe, knowing I will find and kill those men responsible for the death of my men."

"How will you find them, Alphonse? And how will you know who did it?"

Gonzales pulled his knife from its sheath. "No man can resist talking with his cock laid across a rock and a sharp knife held to it. The campesinos we round up will tell us who tends that poppy field and where he lives, or there will be nothing but cockless men running around those poppy fields."

Feeling that unpleasant ache again, Fruin said, "Ya know, my balls have shriveled, and if I don't want them to stay that way I'd better get back to a more civilized way of enforcing the law."

Gonzales grinned as he offered his hand. "Goodbye, good friend and partner. May the good Lord always protect you during your war on drug traffickers."

Fruin left the office and was walking across the compound when he heard Gonzales shout, "Attention!" Turning, he saw three ranks of federales snap to attention. As he watched Mexico's law enforcement officers, he wondered if this was what he really wanted when he persuaded his bosses in Washington to spend millions of taxpayers' dollars to wage war on drug trafficking in Mexico. The federales were trained by U. S. personnel, and modern weapons—automatic rifles, grenades and machine guns—were supplied. No one in Mexico was fooled. The U.S. was providing technology and weaponry and supporting military operations against disorganized and poorly armed peasant farmers, innocents who were on the periphery of the drug cartels. The farmers were at war with the law only because they proudly, but ignorantly, defended a way of life. He wished, as he had done so often in Vietnam, that the big bosses in Washington, the Fat Cats who sat behind desks and pushed buttons, could see just once the misery, suffering and death their decisions caused. If they could be transposed to a combat zone to be shot at and bombed, to have the shit scared out of them, they wouldn't be so eager to wage war. "No way," he murmured as he strode toward his car. He was resolved to put Angel Herrera in jail by playing by the rules.

Fruin returned to his hotel room and placed a call to his office in Chicago. While he was awaiting the connection, Angel Herrera's face peering over a M-1 gunsight appeared on his mindscreen. He questioned himself. If it were Angel, how and when did he get to the poppy field? He didn't see a plane at or near the field, only burros and horses. It was crazy, yet the more he thought about it, the more convinced he became it was Angel.

The raspy voice of Bob Cass drifted through the phone, "Hello, agent Cass speaking."

"Como esta, amigo," Fruin said in a jovial tone.

Joe Fruin was a friend first, a boss second, to Cass and the other task force agents in Chicago. Concern had turned to fear when he neglected to call the office and report on his progress. "Did you forget the office telephone number?" Cass asked in a peeved tone.

"No, I've been busy. Besides I've been gone only three days," Fruin replied, thinking how soothing Cass' voice was. It caused him to conjure up good thoughts of the office and home.

"I really wasn't worried about you," Cass said facetiously. "I just wanted to tell you that our snitch Martinez has really opened up. He told me he received word a few hours ago the Angel Herrera deal is to go down in a motel near Joliet within a week."

"Great!" Fruin said, now confident Angel didn't recognize him at the poppy field as he stared down from the chopper. If he had, he would have cancelled all drug deals for a while. "Any chance Martinez is playing games with us so that he can stay on the street and sell drugs?"

Cass grunted. "Chief, I got news for you. Martinez is going to be the greatest snitch in the history of the drug war. You know how we've been busting our asses for years to put Reggie Begoode out of business. Guess what? Martinez says he's Reggie's supplier—says he can put him in the bag for us, wrapped real nice."

"Gawd! Angel Herrera and Reggie Begoode in the same week. I think I might say a prayer of thanks."

"Don't waste your time, Chief. You know God doesn't come close to the drug business."

Fruin restrained a laugh as he said, "Well, then, let's make a deal with the devil. Whatever it takes to get that piece of shit Reggie Begoode off the streets."

"I thought you'd feel that way, so I took it upon myself to meet with an old pal who is the chief exec at the telephone company. I told him about the problem we're having with Reggie—four Cadillacs with mobile phones, five apartments, and an army of teenage runners pushing his shit."

Fruin knew the score, but he had to ask, "Did you try for an eavesdrop warrant?"

"No. I was afraid Martinez didn't give us enough to satisfy a magistrate that probable cause existed. Plus, you know we don't have the equipment or skill to put a wire on a mobile phone yet."

"Sad, but true, Bob. By the time our technology catches up with the drug dealer's hi-tech, someone puts something new on the market. Those mobile phones and beepers have been a boon to the dope business."

"It's just going to take a little ingenuity, Chief."

"Can your pal handle it?" Fruin asked.

Cass sounded confident "My friend says to trust him. Says he checked things out and found that Reggie uses the New Deal Answering Service on the South Side. It seems New Deal utilizes a computer system to record Reggie's incoming messages and then sends them out on an assigned frequency to a beeper."

"I always knew you had ingenuity, Bob. But give me the bottom line."

Cass cleared his throat. "A computer in the bowels of the telephone company will instantly analyze and record all calls from Reggie's mobile phones. The same will be done for incoming calls. We're going to get everything that slime-bag says."

"I'll be back in a few days," Fruin said. "If we can take Reggie down we may save a lot of school kids a lifetime of shame and agony."

*   *   *   *

Meanwhile, the man who was looked upon as a god to many elementary and high school students in the heart of Chicago's South Side exited the Dan Ryan Expressway in his shiny, silver Cadillac El Dorado, oblivious to the fact he had become a target of the United States Drug Enforcement Administration. Reggie "R Bag" Begoode picked up his car phone and punched in the number and code of one of his runners. Hearing the double beep, he spoke into the receiver, "Buzz me right away, mother fucker!" He then dialed two more numbers and left the same message, except the inflection and accent on each "mother fucker" varied.

On the South Side, Reggie could get away with calling anyone anything he wanted. He was a highly visible success story, a role model of choice for inner city black kids. At 26, he was a millionaire drug dealer, owning a fleet of luxurious Cadillacs, five apartment buildings, and hoards of jewelry. What made him a hero to the wanna-be drug dealers, though, was the harem of women he constantly adorned himself with and the wads of $100 bills he carried in his pants' pockets. Ironically, very few legitimate businessmen on the South Side had been able to accumulate a fraction of Reggie's wealth after long years of work and respectability. Worse, the businessmen were looked down upon with disdain while Reggie Begoode enjoyed celebrity status.

Reggie was also the beneficiary of an elaborate protection system. For $3,000 a month he bought a police captain who was politically powerful. In turn, the captain passed the payoff-off money around to the beat cops who patrolled the streets where Reggie's runners were pushing drugs on corners, in school yards and phony churches. To keep the cops from confusing his runners with competitors, Reggie bought them yellow, silk jackets with the name "R Bags" emblazoned in large black letters on the back.

Then there was the El Rukin street gang, an organization of extremely violent young men. El Rukin hit men kept everybody in line for Reggie by using any degree of force necessary. Over the years, Reggie had pointed his finger at dozens of men and women who he said had crossed him or who had posed a threat to his burgeoning drug empire. The victims of Reggie's wrath generally met a violent end.

When his beeper sounded off, Yosef was standing in an elementary school yard negotiating with a group of 8th graders for some pot. The students burst into a raucous laughter when Reggie's message was broadcast.

"Listen up," Yosef said. "I's got to jingle The Man. Does anybody want dis R Bag of pot or some good H befos I's leaves?"

Stefanie looked at him with large brown eyes as she whined, "I's wants that bag of pot, but I's got only seven dollars."

Yosef grinned with expectation. "Little lady, does you know what's make Reggie Begoode the prince in a ghetto dream? He's ridden the dope business from poverty to riches with these little R Bags of good shit. The pot. The H. The coke. It all sells for ten dollars—never a penny less."

"Shoot," Stefanie said, aware of the rules of the game.

Flashing a gold-tooth grin, Yosef leered at the shapely and pretty fourteen year old. "Listen, little lady, if you want to give up some pussy, I'll drop several of these zip-lock bags on ya."

Stefanie thought for a few moments. "Whose does I's have to gives it up to?"

"First, Reggie Begoode!"

Stefanie held out both hands. "Gimme three bags of H and three pot."

"Reggie will await you at his pad on 34th street," Yosef said over his shoulder as he headed for a pay phone.

Reggie was only a mile away from his turf—a depressing wasteland of graffiti, cracked and stained buildings with boarded-up windows and garbage strewn everywhere—when Yosef's call came in on his car phone. "Where's you at, mother fucker?" he said.

Yosef laughed. "I's across da street from Ring Elementary School. I's been engaged in commerce."

"Stay there," Reggie ordered. "I'll get you in a few minutes."

The El Dorado slid to a stop in the center of the street, and Yosef sauntered over and got in. None of the drivers in the cars which were backed up behind blew a horn or protested the road block in any way.

Recognizing the car and driver, they decided a display of impatience could prove costly.

"You've got some explaining to do," Reggie told Yosef. "You were low man this month."

Yosef slumped back in the seat. "Man, how could I's be? I's got twelve kids hustling R Bags for you. What the fucks, man. I's got to be doing thirty bags of shit a day."

Reggie glared at Yosef, keeping the pressure on. Even though he had worked for him since they were freshmen in high school, he was there to shake him up, like he was going to do to all his street pushers. "Looka here," he said. "I'm expecting a new load of heroin, some of that Herrera shit right from Durango. My man, Martinez, says the Mexican Mud will be here in about a week. I want you to bust ass and push R Bags in every school yard that's in my turf."

Yosef flashed his gold teeth. "Now I's understand. You're one bad motherfucker, Reggie. The baddest drug dealer ever to live."

Slapping palms with Yosef, Reggie said, "That's right, now get the fuck out, mother fucker!"

Yosef said, "Just so you know I's always thinking of you, I'm sending a little present to your pad on 34th street. I's gives six bags to a little lady a short time ago. Stefanie's goin' to pay you with some puss."

Reggie grinned. "Does she look like we can hook her?"

"Ain't no doubt," Yosef replied. "Get her on H for a week, and you can turn her out on the street to work her pussy. She'll be a big money maker."

"Get out," Reggie said. "I's got business to take care of at my pad."

Chapter 8

▼

VENDETTA

After his phone conversation with Joe Cass, Fruin felt for the first time that his innovative methods of law enforcement were beginning to pay off. Both Angel and Reggie were superstars in the drug culture, and if they were put behind bars for a long time every dealer would recognize his own vulnerability. He pounded his fist into the palm of his hand as he mumbled, "Snitches and electronic bugs. That's how we're going to win the war on drugs. Fuck the silly laws and the judges who protect the sleezebags."

Reports of Comandante Gonzales' raid on the poppy growers started coming in the day Fruin returned to his office in Chicago.

Recognizing the official versions of what happened at the Alvarado poppy field for what they were—government propaganda—Fruin chanced a telephone call to Gonzales. "This is confidential," Gonzales told him. "We went back to the same poppy field and saw the Francisco Alvarado family harvesting opium gum. When he saw our choppers moving in on him, he put his family on horses and burros and sent them scurrying down the mountain, away from danger. That fool remained behind, hidden by rocks in a mountain pass, waiting to ambush us. In the shoot-out that followed, Francisco killed four of our men before running out of ammunition."

Fruin concealed his only concern. "Did you capture him or anyone else in the Herrera organization?" he asked.

"No, the fool charged us with an empty M-1 rifle, swinging it like a club. A barrage of bullets knocked him to the ground in a bloody heap. Before he died, he choked out something like, 'Antonio has been avenged.'"

"Did you get anyone else?"

"Yeah, we rounded up about twenty campesinos who tried to stop us from spraying three poppy fields. But no one has told us who his boss is yet."

"You're one tough drug cop," Fruin said. I think we'll make a great team, and I look forward to working with you again."

*   *   *   *

Meanwhile at the Herrera ranch, the mood was distinctively different. A somber Angel and Manuel sat at the sides of the banquet table which only two nights before had been the centerpiece for a festive occasion. Now, it was a war room, and the presiding general was tapping his fingers on it as he made plans for an attack. "All the members of our organization are outraged by the atrocities committed by the Comandante Gonzales and his federales. They look to us to avenge the death of Francisco and Antonio. I feel revenge is our duty."

Angel said, "Gonzales has become a fanatic. He also forgot a simple truth: Before one starts down the path to revenge, he should first dig two graves."

"So true", El Don said passionately. "Honor dictates a direct attack, face-to-face combat with that killer."

Angel focused his eyes on the man he admired and respected. "Don," he said tactfully, "whatever you decide, I'll be with you. But think of the consequences of all out war. Everything we worked so hard for would be lost. We should try to make Comandante Gonzales' death look like an accident so that we can stay free of any direct blame."

Manuel believed El Don's way of waging war belonged to history. He said, "If we kill Gonzales and all his federales, the government will send in 500 well equipped soldiers to attack us and destroy our homes and businesses. If we kill that 500, then soon 1000 more will follow."

"What do you suggest, Manuel?" El Don asked. It was totally out of character for El Don to even consider compromising his pride, but he appeared willing to listen.

Manuel cleared his throat. "We have to poison him."

El Don grunted out a short laugh, a look of disbelief spread across his face. Angel sat motionless, eyes riveted on Manuel.

"Cousin Luis," Manuel continued, "can get a poison that causes death by paralyzing muscles and nerves of the heart. The drug takes twenty-four hours to work, and death will appear to be caused by heart failure."

"That leaves one slight problem," El Don said, still skeptical. "How do we give El Comandante the poison?"

"Vasquez will put it in his coffee." Manuel replied, exuding the confidence that accompanies a well thought out plan.

El Don sat up quickly, the impact of the Machiavellian plot startling him. He had thought of having Private Vasquez assassinate Comandante Gonzales, but by a show of force and not by stealth. After all, it was he who had hand-picked Arias Vasquez when he was a teenager to perform sensitive and dangerous missions. And, it was he who had Arias relocated from Durango to Mexico City, given a false identity and background, and infiltrated into the Federales Judicial Police. "We were very fortunate," he said, "when Arias was assigned to the garrison in Durango. If the poison plan doesn't work, we will lose our most valuable source of intelligence."

"If it is successful," Manuel said, "no one will suspect him and he can remain in the strategic position."

El Don's mindset softened. "But no one will know he died by our avenging hands. His death will mean nothing."

"It will," Angel urged, "because we will be rid of a powerful enemy, and word will spread that we caused Gonzales' death. And for an added bonus, the new comandante may be willing to shut his eyes to our business activities."

"What about the doctor who examines the body?" What about the autopsy?" El Don pressed.

"That can be arranged," Manuel replied smugly. "The pathologist who will perform the autopsy is loyal to us."

"Case closed," El Don said. "We'll leave this matter in Manuel's capable hands. Is there any other business to discuss?"

"Don Gonzolo," Angel said, "I have business in Mexico City the day after tomorrow. After that I should return to Chicago."

El Don understood. Angel's heart was in Durango, but he had to get out town fast. "Yes, leave," he said. "If the federales attacked us or something messes up our plan for El Comandante, you'd be right in the middle of things."

Angel nodded and cleared his throat. "That leaves us one last thing to talk over before I go. I'd like to change the way we distribute our product in Chicago."

"Why?" El Don asked in a defensive tone. "Haven't our ways of smuggling heroin and selling it been successful? And haven't I taken the profits from heroin sales and invested wisely in wine, cattle, and other businesses critical to the Mexican people? We're making millions."

The attitude of drug agents and the vast majority of people in the States toward drug traffickers had changed dramatically. Angel feared that if the distribution end of their business didn't change too many of his mules and distributors in the States would soon be arrested and jailed. In a sincere tone, he said, "Yes, Don, we've made lots of money, thanks to you. Your great talent for money management reminds me of the Chicago Mafia. The mob guys make big cash profits from prostitution, gambling, and loan-sharking and then invest those profits in legitimate enterprises. But it's time for us to change, and it's time for the Mafia to change. I suggest a marriage of convenience."

"Marriage to hoodlums?" El Don said, waving his hand to dismiss the thought.

Angel pressed his point. "A couple of mob guys I know met with me and offered a deal. We sell only to their group in Chicago. We cut our risk of arrest because the mob guys will handle all the distribution in the United States."

"Never," El Don said. "This is our family business from the beginning to end. We control the growth and production. We don't need the Mafia to sell it."

El Don's attitude didn't surprise Angel. Everything El Don knew about the Mafia came via movies and TV programs. He believed the mob's tough guys were treacherous and untrustworthy. And, when it came to profits from heroin sales, that money was to be shared only by the compesinos, lab men, mules, and the distributors. Angel said, "Everything you say is right, El Don, but why should we risk going to jail when we can let the Mafia take all the chances?"

El Don squeezed-up his face as he said, "We should stay loyal to our family and organization. I don't want Mafia bosses getting richer."

"It is not the bosses who want to muscle into our business," Angel retorted. "The boss in Chicago, Tony Accardo, hates drugs, especially heroin. He gave orders to his lieutenants and soldiers to stay away from drugs. It's the younger hoods—the Wise Guys—who feel they don't have a big enough piece of the action. They want their fair share of the big money that always went to the bosses. Drug trafficking not only provides the chance for instant millions, but also the long awaited opportunity to divest power from a few aging men who control organized crime in the United States."

"We don't do business with hoodlums. We're entrepreneurs," El Don protested.

Angel continued, "In New York and New Jersey it's different. Several of the Mafia families there have bankrolled drug deals since the early

'60s and are used to making enormous profits. But since their connections in Sicily and France have been cut off, they're looking for new sources of supply."

"If they're greedy, they'll make mistakes that will eventually destroy us," El Don argued. "Why do business with such people?"

"In my opinion," Angel said, "the Mafia offer should be accepted for two reasons. Heroin users and sellers are so hated in the States that it won't be long before U. S. drug agents use every gun they have to halt drug trafficking. The U.S. government is already spending millions to smother the growth of the opium poppy in Mexico and the Middle East. An increasing number of our mules have been arrested and given long jail sentences, and large amounts of our drug money has been seized by the DEA. In short, Don, we can't beat the U. S. Government. The heroin business is on its way out, and we must make changes."

El Don stiffened and looked directly into Angel's eyes. "Rather than doing business with the Mafia, why not limit our risks in another way?"

Angel shook his head in frustration. "Once again, Don, our major problem is informers. Snitches, as they're called in the States, are responsible for all arrests of our men and seizures of our product. Drug agents would never make an arrest if it weren't for snitches."

"Eliminate the treacherous bastards!" El Don snarled.

Angel felt like giving up. El Don had never experienced the drug culture and its unsavory characters so void of honor and dignity, and he could never understand the constant danger informers posed. But he decided to try once more. "Over the last two years," he said, "fifteen percent of our shipments of heroin have been seized somewhere between the Texas border and one of our safe houses in Chicago. Because every drug user and pusher is a potential informer and we are helpless to do anything about it, business projections must be based upon losing over twenty percent of our shipments."

"Shoot the bastards," El Don said.

"Contrary to your views, El Don, I'm against killing informers for example's sake. The public furor would cause the drug cops to put greater pressure on us."

Manuel said, "I agree, the drug cops would sensationalize the killings in the news media and make hideous monsters out of us. Then no one would care if the drug cops broke the law when they arrested and jailed us. Soon no one would care if the cops shot us instead of arresting us."

Angel said, "Don, why not think about my plan for a month? I'll stall my contacts."

"Agreed," El Don said.

Angel stood and shook El Don's hand as he said, "I'd better get my mules lined up for their trip to Chicago. Cousin Luis told me that he switched orders, and the 12 kilos I need for the Puerto Rican will be ready to leave the lab in a few days."

El Don gripped Angel's hand firmly and said, "You've been such a good businessman that I'm giving a dinner in your honor tonight."

"Who will we break bread with?" Angel asked, aware only the most important politicians and businessmen were invited to the Herrera ranch.

El Don replied, "We will be entertaining the Honorable Mayor of Durango, Alberto Cetone, and Federal Judge Pedro Salinon. And in light of our conversation concerning Comandante Gonzales, I think we should definitely invite Manuel's good friend, Dr. Bolivar."

Manuel grinned and quickly agreed. "Since Dr. Bolivar performs all autopsies for the State of Durango, I think his attendance would be appropriate. As a wise man once said, 'If you prick us, will we not bleed; and if you poison us, will we not die; and if you injure us, will we not seek revenge.'"

Angel's eyes drifted from El Don to Manuel as he said, "Revenge is an iron rule of nature, and we must do what comes naturally."

Chapter 9

▼

THE MULES

On Chicago's West Side, where the loop ended and the ghetto began, two cops cruised past a run-down, dingy apartment building in a Blue and White. The driver, Sergeant Crowley said, "Our snitch told me Amador Rios is expecting a new supply, coming any day from Durango."

Officer Mullin gazed out the squad car window at the second floor apartment. "He's in there. Do you want to crack the little jerk now and see if he'll roll on his supplier?"

"Naw. Let's come back tonight. By my calculations he'll be strung out by then."

Amador knelt at his apartment window and watched the police car creep past. "Com-on, mother-fuckers," he said in a whiny voice. "Hurry up."

Two of Amador's friends were seated at a table behind him mixing a dark brown powder with a white one in a small metal container. None of the young men had worked in the years since arriving from Puerto Rico, the price for their drugs coming from thefts from cars, houses, stores.

Amador returned to the table and examined the mixture of heroin and cocaine. "Go!" he urged. "I'm shaking apart inside."

"Easy," Pepsico said as he poured a liquid into the powder and lit a match, heating the powders until they liquefied.

Even though the container was red hot, Amador grabbed it and began to stir it with the tip of a syringe. "Man this is good shit," he said, not caring that the syringe had been used by others many times before, or that the powders could have been cut with anything from sugar to arsenic. His god beckoned him. The needle hovered over his vein, just below the crook in his arm for a few seconds, then disappeared below the skin. A drop of blood oozed out from the needle puncture as he slumped back in his chair, arms crossed and held tightly against his chest, eyes closed. Grunting out a laugh, he said, "Man that speedball is good shit."

Persico shot up next and then passed the syringe to the third man.

Amador felt like superman. Never wanting to get way down again, he said, "I ain't got a fucking dollar to make a buy."

Persico's grin was sardonic. "I know this ritzy house in the Western suburbs. We should be able to score big with jewels, TVs, nice things.

Amador droned, "Let's hit the mother-fucker. Then I'll tool down to 26th Street to visit Jose Herrera. He's supposed to have some good shit comin' in from Mexico."

*   *   *   *

It was late morning when Sal Veta's phone rang. Recognizing the caller's voice, he listened carefully to the message: "I understand you'll be flying from Laredo to Durango tomorrow."

As the message registered, a hint of a smile crossed Sal's normally dead-pan face. "Okay," he said, then quickly hung up and put the phone back in place. Swelled with a feeling of self-importance, he turned to his wife, Rosa, and said, "Duty calls."

A childlike look of pleasant expectations crossed Rosa's face as she began helping her husband make preparations for his trip to the Herrera ranch and then his long drive to Chicago. Mindful that the money they would receive for this trip was needed for braces for their daughter's teeth, she said, "Do you need me for anything?"

"No," Sal replied. "Claudio is going to be my back-up driver this time. Besides, you have to take Yolanda to the dentist."

Sal Veta and Claudio Cillas were two of the Durango Connection's most trustworthy and experienced mules, and they were paid well by Angel to transport loads of heroin from Durango to Laredo, Texas, and then onto Chicago. Sal Veta was a shrewd businessman whose primary duty it was to provide load cars from a used car business he owned and operated in Laredo, Texas. When a load car from the Herrera ranch arrived at his car lot, Sal switched the load into one of his many used cars and then either drove it to Chicago himself or arranged for another mule to handle the driving duties. If bad luck struck, as it had on two occasions, and the load car was intercepted and seized by the police, Sal quickly arranged a backdated transfer of title to a fictitious person. When cars returned safely, they were put back on the lot and marked for sale, potential buyers never suspecting the use they had been put to.

Claudio Cillas was traditionally Mexican, with a "manana" attitude. An hour or a day made no difference to him, except when it came to his job with the Durango Connection. That was sacred to him, and he met Sal at the Laredo airport exactly 15 minutes before their plane was scheduled to leave for Durango. "How come we're flying to Durango to pick up a load?" he asked.

Sal was thoughtful for several moments before he said, "Don't know. This load must be very, very important to Angel."

Though Angel was bright and imaginative, his manner of shipping multi-million dollar loads of heroin was primitive and risky. From the moment a mule left Durango, he had to worry about an army roadblock

and car search or a band of cutthroat banditos. After successfully negotiating the hazardous trip from Durango to Nuevo Laredo, the real worries began. A mule had to drive a load car right under the noses of the
United States Customs agents stationed at the bridges on the Rio
Grande River. Then came the Texas State Police and the DEA. But Angel
wasn't about to change a good thing. In spite of the potential dangers at
every turn in the long road north, the transportation system had been
successful, with over 85 percent of heroin shipments safely reaching
Chicago. That success was predicated on several factors. In the United
States, law enforcement agencies were at a disadvantage because of the
dense vehicular traffic on the highways and the veil of secrecy that covered the load cars. In Mexico, success was due in large part to "la mordida"—the bite—as a bribe was referred to. It kept the Pipeline well
oiled and functioning smoothly, and provided the insurance that the
blockade searches were conducted on the cars of the other Mexican
travelers, the ones who couldn't afford to pay "la mordida."

Sal and Claudio arrived at the Herrera ranch and went directly to a
garage where skilled mechanics were working on a 1974 Chevy. The car
looked like thousands of other cars, faded and dented. But characteristic
of the Herrera cartel, looks were deceiving. The engine had been rebuilt
by one of the cartel's mechanics, and the car was rumored to be the
fastest in the State of Durango. Sal got into the car, turned the ignition
switch, and listened to the finely-tuned engine respond with a roar.
Then he looked over the back seat. There was a lot of heroin stashed
somewhere, but there wasn't a clue as to where.

"Don't worry," Manuel Herrera said as he walked up to the car. "The
load is concealed well."

Sal slid out of the car. "Manuel, I'm not worried about the load being
seen. I'm worried about a dog sniffing it."

Manuel pointed to the back seat arm rests and said, "Secret com-
partments have been built in behind those arm rests. Twenty-four,
one kilogram packages of heroin are in there wrapped in heavy gauge

plastic bags and tightly wrapped with gray duct tape. Those drug-sniffing dogs won't be able to detect our product."

Sal smiled. Nothing was going to stop his load from getting to Chicago. "Get in," he told Claudio. "I'll drive the first two-hundred miles."

Seventy miles northeast of Durango, where the mountains stopped and the vast Mexican plateau started, Sal and Manuel saw the cars in front of them come to a stop, a makeshift gate barricade blocking their way. It was the first of the army roadblocks they would have to negotiate. Soldiers manned sandbag bunkers on each side of the road and trained M-1 rifles on the approaching cars. A few of the soldiers took great pleasure in aiming their rifles at the occupants of a car and then smiling menacingly over the gunsights, much to the consternation of the travelers. A feisty young lieutenant approached Sal's window, glared at him, and then began searching the interior and trunk areas of the car. Although the army general in charge of the area was paid well by El Don not to impede his mules, many times an uninformed lieutenant would mistake a Herrera cartel shipment for that of a competitor and carefully search the car.

Watching the lieutenant perform his duties, Sal worried for a few anxious minutes about what the man knew, what his orders were, and what side he was on. His questions were answered when only a calculated cursory inspection was conducted, and he was waved through the gate. "Ah, la mordida," he whispered to Manuel, grateful El Don and Angel had foreseen the problem of roadblocks and had taken the necessary precautions.

Nuevo Laredo, Mexico, was a critical point in the Pipeline. It was there the heroin was switched from the load car which brought it from Durango to one of Sal Veta's cars bearing Texas license plates. In the early days of the Pipeline, the switch from one load car to another was made in a parking lot that adjoined a busy nightclub. Procedures changed after a few years of prosperity. Angel persuaded his cousin, Pepe Herrera, to relocate from Durango and buy a service station. With financial aid from El Don, Pepe became the proud proprietor of his own business, one that thrived by day selling gas and repairing cars, and by night switching a load of heroin from one car to another.

Nuevo Laredo was an important point in the Pipeline for yet another reason. El Don and Angel felt confident transporting heroin from Durango to Chicago for distribution throughout the central United States. However, Angel didn't trust most of the large dealers in New York and Los Angeles, preferring to be insulated from personal contact with them once the terms of sale were agreed upon. Thinking the drug laws in the U. S. were similar to those in Mexico, Angel believed he could not be convicted and sent to jail as long as he wasn't caught in possession of heroin. For that reason, whenever he did business with a viable heroin purchaser he didn't trust sufficiently to deal with on a hand-to-hand basis, he would make arrangements for the sale to be consummated in Nuevo Laredo. And, there were many drug dealers in Chicago, New York and Los Angeles who began as one of Angel's mules or soldiers only to find that ambition caused them to break away and become independent operators. They, of course, desired to buy heroin at the lowest possible price and sell it at the going street price to those they hoped to keep as exclusive customers.

Angel's cash-and-carry plan was simple. When the agreed upon purchase price had been delivered to Angel or one of his men in a back booth of the Rio Sangre Cantina, the buyer's car would be driven to Cousin Pepe's garage and loaded with packages of heroin. In the event the buyer was suspicious about the quantity and quality of the heroin when his car was returned, he was given a chance to examine the tendered product before starting the perilous drive north.

When Sal and Manuel arrived at Pepe's service station, they were exhausted from the long drive from Durango in an old car with no air-conditioning. Vanity and a desire for a comfortable drive to Chicago caused Sal to arrange for a brown over white 1978 Buick to be driven from his car lot to Pepe's garage. Upon seeing the car, Pepe complained, "There's no time to solder in a false compartment. I'll have to deflate the spare tire and put the 12 kilos Angel wants inside, then put the tire back on the wheel. The other 12 kilos I'll keep here until the next car goes north."

Sal shrugged his shoulders and tried to sound unconcerned. "Transporting the shit in the spare tire should be no problem."

"Yeah," Pepe replied. "The border cops at the bridge have been searching only a few cars out of thousands. And a car driven by a Texas resident and bearing Texas plates shouldn't cause suspicion."

Sal smiled weakly. The unusual way his cargo was hidden did unnerve him, but he was bound to say nothing because Angel had told him during a phone conversation an hour before, "Get the load to Joliet as fast as you can."

It was 8:00 a.m. when Sal and Claudio got into the Buick and started toward the bridge that served as the port of entry from Nuevo Laredo to Laredo, Texas. They were counting on the hundreds of Mexican day workers who were streaming across the bridge on their way to work in and around Laredo to provide cover.

"Here we go again," Claudio said.

"Yeah. It's going to be a piece of cake," Sal said as he drove the car over the bridge arch. He sat upright in his seat and came to a stop behind a line of cars queued up in front of the United States Customs and Immigration booth. Nervousness turned to fear as he drew closer to the booth and saw an unusually large number of Customs officers on duty. This could only mean there was an alert, and agents would be stopping and inspecting all cars that aroused suspicion. Fear turned to outright panic as he looked to the right of the entry booth and saw a Customs agent with two large German Sheperds on leashes standing alongside of him. "Damn!" he said. "Those fucking dogs have been sniffing out lots of shit lately. Every week they pull out a bag of drugs."

"I hope—" Claudio stiffened when a hostile looking Customs agent approached Sal's window and looked in at the two men.

"Where were you born?" the agent asked Sal.

Displaying his green card, Sal said, "I was born in Nuevo Laredo, Mexico, and I have been a legal resident of the United States for twenty years."

Speaking English fluently, Sal had a little difficulty convincing the Customs agent that he resided legally in the United States and had the right to enter without further investigation. However, Claudio was a different matter. He spoke very little English and had difficulty understanding the Customs agent. Sal attempted to interpret, but to no avail. The Customs agent gazed at Claudio for a moment and then told Sal, "Pull over to the side and park right in front of that building." Training and instinct had aroused his suspicion.

"Get out of the car and open the trunk," another agent ordered Sal.

Sal considered jamming the gas pedal down, making a break for it, but he decided against it when he saw Border Patrol cars ahead of him. "Shit!" he mumbled as he started toward the trunk, watching the German Shepherds whining and pawing at the ground, straining to perform their task. Though the animals acted no differently than usual, a guilty conscience caused him to believe the dogs had sniffed the heroin from over thirty feet away.

Sal stepped back as the dogs were led to the trunk. "Go!" their handler ordered. The dogs attacked the car, one leaping into the trunk and poking his nose at every square inch of it. The second dog jumped into the interior of the car and excitedly romped throughout. Not having been able to understand the Customs agent when he had told him to get out of the car, Claudio sat motionless as the playful dog sniffed under, over and around him.

Sal waited until the Customs agent motioned with his finger, signaling he was free to go, before he drove off the bridge and onto United States soil. "Damn!" he said. "If those dogs had sniffed the shit we'd be on our way to prison for at least fifteen years. La mordida doesn't grease our movements as it does in Mexico."

Claudio was noticeably shaken from his encounter with the dog. Deeply engrossed in brushing dog hairs from his pants legs, he said, "It's just a matter of time before Angel makes contact and takes care of things with the Yankee judges."

"For sure, Claudio, for sure. Men are the same the world over. Money speaks a language everyone understands. For the right price, U. S. judges can be had."

"I hope Angel gets to Judge John Seely in El Paso," Claudio said. "Mexicans got nothing coming from him."

Sal grunted. "That's why we don't cross the border at El Paso. Maximum John warns everyone he doesn't apply constitutional rights in his courtroom for Mexican traffickers. Everyone gets found guilty and gets the max."

Claudio droned, "Judge Roy Bean and Maximum John. Fuck El Paso."

Sal examined Claudio's chubby, expressionless face. The heavy black mustache and large eyebrows seemed glued to a mask of bronzed stone. "What do you think?" he asked. "Should we push on or stay in Laredo tonight?"

"Stay," Claudio groaned.

Sal decided to decoy the car, to use it as bait to detect police surveillance. Instead of proceeding north to pick up the interstate highway, Sal turned west toward Laredo's business district, eyes darting from rearview mirror to intersecting street, suspicious of any car that looked like it might contain a DEA agent. Taking a circuitous route, he approached "Sal's Used Car Sales" from a side street, pulled onto the lot, and then maneuvered the car to one of the more prominent spots up front near the road. It was left there that night with a "for sale" sign on the window—immune from the slightest suspicion that heroin with a street value of over $1 million was secreted in the trunk.

Chapter 10

▼

FATAL MISTAKE

During the flight from Mexico City to Chicago, Jenni filled Angel's thoughts. He had cut short all important business meetings so that he could meet her that night as he had promised. This bothered him because he had never before allowed a romantic interest to interfere with the affairs of the Durango Connection. Was she different from all the others, he wondered. Had she cast a spell over him? Was he sensing and responding to a siren's call, a call that would lead him into serious trouble.

Ernie Kummer was standing at the end of the Customs inspection counter at O'Hare Airport when Angel deplaned. He greeted Angel with a broad grin on his face, "Hi-ya. How'd things go in Mexico?"

"Great," Angel replied, avoiding any talk about drug trafficking.

"Your wife know you're home?" Ernie asked, wanting to know how he should play the game.

Angel waved his hand. "Tomorrow, amigo, tomorrow."

Ernie took Angel's travel bag. "Follow me," he said. "I gave the cop in front ten bucks so he'd let me park my car at the front door."

Jenni had been waiting in front of the El Sombrero Lounge for several minutes when Ernie's car came to a stop at the curb. Seeing Angel, she turned her head haughtily, feigning indifference.

Ernie whistled softly. "Look at the boobs on her."

Angel had already noticed the wine colored dress that revealed Jenni's curvaceous body. "Ah, the things I do for love," he said.

"Better be careful," Ernie cautioned. " She can't be a day over nineteen."

"Amigo, there are some things worth taking risks for."

The raucous laughter of the two men caused Jenni to walk over to Ernie's car. She smiled, then slowly moistened her lips with the tip of her tongue and leaned forward to show her breasts. "C'mon, Angel. I've been waiting ten minutes. Some guys just tried to pick me up."

"Where are they? I'll blow their cojones off!" Angel bellowed in mock rage as he bolted out of the car.

Jenni threw her arms around him and kissed him. She was in love with Angel and wanted to show him at all times just how much. Still embracing her, Angel turned his head to Ernie and said, "We'll be at the All American Motel in Cicero tonight if anything comes up."

"Yeah," Ernie responded, still unable to take his eyes off Jenni.

She caught his stare and leaned forward again, swaying her shoulders so that the exposed portion of her breast rolled.

"That's all. I'm going." Ernie said.

Walking from the car to the door of the El Sombrero, Angel put his arm around Jenni's waist, then slid his hand down to the curve of her buttocks. Through the thin cotton dress he felt soft, warm flesh. "My God!" he gasped, "where's your panties?"

Her eyes sparkled as she whispered, "I don't have any on. I didn't feel like wearing any."

Suddenly, Angel felt a surge of warm blood to his lower abdomen, and he turned to her and said, "One quick drink and then let's go where we can be alone."

She smiled contentedly, instinctively aware her lover was under her spell and couldn't resist her charms. She had sensed it for the first time the night she had left Durango, when Angel had insisted she return to Chicago alone, ahead of him. "An emergency has arisen in Mexico City," he had explained. "I have to go there without you."

Jenni had pouted and balked at traveling alone, and when that hadn't worked, she had sobbed. Angel's resistance melted, as tears rolled down her cheeks. "Okay, amorcito," he said. "If you stop crying, I promise I'll finish my business in two days and when I return to Chicago, I'll rush to your arms."

The large roll of $100 bills Angel carried and spent freely made him a preferred customer in the restaurants and nightclubs around Chicago. "El Señor Herrera," as he was known to the employees of the El Sombrero, was a regular customer, and one of the best booths had been reserved for him. He and Jenni were seated for a few minutes when Jenni saw Angel's eyes focus on a man seated at the bar. He nodded, excused himself saying, "I'll be right back," and then sauntered toward the bar.

Although young, she recognized the fact that Angel lived every minute of his life as if he were playing the lead in a movie about international espionage. When he would turn to her and excuse himself, she was not surprised. Angel would often recognize a man at a bar, drift off and have a private conversation, then return after a few minutes. She knew better than to acknowledge the meeting, or ask any questions, or even whisper a word about it. Tonight was no different, except when Angel returned to the booth, he appeared aggravated.

"Can we be alone now?" she asked as he sat down next to her.

The man at the bar told Angel that the mule who was to pick up the 12 kilos of heroin from Sal Veta in Joliet had been arrested the night before and was still in jail. This foul-up in plans left Angel with a distressing decision to make. He'd have to find someone else to send to

Joliet or go himself. For a fleeting second his cold, logical business mind prevailed, and he turned toward Jenni to tell her she must go, that he must tend to his duties. But a deep look into her pleading eyes destroyed his resolve and the job of contacting another mule was put off. He said, "I'm your slave for the rest of the night, amorcito."

"Good, then dance with me." she said.

As a bewitching melody drifted across the dance floor, Angel pulled Jenni close to his body so that they moved as one. "Let's go," he whispered in her ear.

Angel used the All American Motel on 28th and Cicero often. It had a reputation for being a place cheaters used since an identification or credit card wasn't required to register, and trouble was quickly and discreetly smothered. He and Jenni took a cab to the motel, registered, and went hurriedly to their room. Once inside, the fast sex, lack of commitment atmosphere a motel room portrayed caused an unsettling sadness to creep through Jenni's body, and she turned away from Angel.

Thinking it strange she hadn't pranced into the room, friskily peeling off her clothes and flipping them in all directions, Angel slid his hands around her waist and then crushed her body to his. When his hand cupped her breast, she stiffened and attempted to move away. Convincingly sincere, she said, "Angel, will we always be together? Do you really love me?"

"Of course, amorcito," he mumbled weakly. Until professing his feelings, Angel had never considered love. Jenni and his other girlfriends and mistresses were for fun and games. His wife, Celia, was for love. An unfamiliar emotion overcame him. Damn, he thought, maybe I do love her.

Angel's rough edges melted as he changed into a sensitive lover. With one smooth movement, he raised Jenni's dress up her body and over her head. Then sweeping her off her feet, he carried her to the bed, carefully laid her down, and began to softly trace her nipples with his finger. "What happened to my wildcat?" he asked. "I've never seen you like this."

"I got the feeling I'll never see you again," she said.

Angel stood up and finished undressing, conscious of her lying still, wide-eyed, watching his every movement. "I'll always be here for you," he said, as he lay back down and snuggled close to her, moving his hand down to the dampness between her thighs, caressing her. Resistance waned and then vanished as her hips began to pulsate rhythmically, then uncontrollably. Releasing a subdued moan, she pressed her mouth against his with a startling ferocity.

*   *   *   *

The drive from Laredo had been uneventful. Excepting gas stops where the driving duties were alternated, the mules had driven straight through. Claudio was growing restless, and when shifting his body from one side to another couldn't provide comfort, he asked, "How much longer?"

Before Sal could answer, the lights of the Safe Harbor Motel came into view. Claudio sat up, squinted through sleep-filled eyes, grunted, and then wearily sat back in his seat. The men knew the motel well, for they had used it many times before. Just why Angel insisted they stay in the Joliet area, a good 25 miles south of Chicago's Mexican community, was confusing. But Angel was the boss, and they did exactly what he told them to do.

It was four o'clock when Sal turned off Interstate 55 and decelerated. He brought the Buick to a stop in front of the motel office, and then glanced over at Claudio who had lapsed back into a sound sleep. Not wanting to wake him, he slid quietly out the door. His compadre's job was now over, and he wanted to let him rest up for the drive back to Laredo.

Sal startled Mrs. Batson when he entered the motel's office door. She was generally apprehensive at that time of night, being alone and many minutes away from help. But tonight was different; she was frightened. The hot, humid weather that had turned Northeastern Illinois into a giant steam bath made the night air eerie. And then she had caught glimpses of men whom she thought acted strangely as they hung around the pool area and parking lot. She eyed Sal as he strode slowly toward the counter, observing his olive skin, his tall, slender built, and thinning black hair, neatly cut. A Latino, and nice looking, she thought. The man's light blue, open-collared sport shirt was damp with perspiration and stuck to his body at his armpits and in the hollow of his chest. That wasn't unusual for an evening like this. It was a good sign actually. To Mrs. Batson, it meant that he probably had driven a long way, and that he was just another traveler on the Interstate looking for a place to sleep.

"Do you have a room for two, ma'am?" Sal asked in a soft voice with a slight Texas drawl. His manner was pleasant, and a gentle nature revealed itself when he spoke.

Feeling a slight tinge of shame that her anxieties may have been noticeable, she said, "Sure" and handed him a registration card. She examined it when he had completed it and slid it back. "Oh, you're from Texas, Mr. Perez?"

"Yes, ma'am, Laredo."

"How long will you be staying, Mr. Perez?"

"Jus' tonight, ma'am," he replied.

"Then that will be $26.00 for the night," she said, smiling. "Your room is 208. That's on the second level, but you have to go through the door on the other side of the building, then up the stairs. You can park right over there, though." She turned slightly to her own right and pointed to indicate the building separated from the office structure by a breezeway.

Sal counted out the $26.00 in cash, and with a casual smile on his face said, "Gracias." He turned, went back through the glass door and walked out to the car. Stopping at the passenger's side, he leaned through the window and shook his traveling companion, who was still dozing, head tilted back against the headrest. "Ey," he said. "Wake up. We made it one more time."

Claudio opened his eyes and sat up, smiling for the first time since leaving Nuevo Laredo. "Tomorrow," he said, "I'll be back with my bride of one month."

Sal laughed as he jokingly said, "Mrs. Cillas doesn't care how long you stay gone as long as you bring home lots of money. After you give her the money you make for this trip, she's going to give you a great screw."

"The Yankee dollar," Claudio replied, "buys a wife's respect and pussy."

After Sal had moved the car to a parking place next to the north wing of the U-shaped motel, both men got out, opened the trunk and removed a few items needed for the overnight stay. As they walked from the car across the asphalt parking area, Sal carried only a brown toilet kit and Claudio a clean shirt. They didn't plan on remaining in the Chicago area any longer than the time required to deliver the cargo they transported.

As they walked toward the stairway, Sal looked back over his shoulder to see if anyone was watching them. The big glass windows that formed the outside wall of the motel rooms reflected the orange of the parking lot's helium-arc lamps and illuminated the automobiles that stood in the lot. They appeared empty, no one, nothing to arouse suspicion.

Pausing when they reached the landing at the top of the stairs, both men surveyed the courtyard and passageways. The pool below was like a mirror, reflecting the soft yellow lights that illuminated it. Seeing the courtyard was deserted and silent, they walked the forty feet to room 208. "Chingo," Sal said as he fumbled with the key and then stabbed at the lock.

"Hey, Sal, pretend the hole has hair around it."

Sal grunted as he slid the key into the lock, turned it and reached for the light. "I'm going down to the office to call Angel," he said as he dropped his toilet kit on the bed.

Claudio only grunted as he pulled back the covers on the bed. His job was finished, and he thought only of sleep, and of the $700 he was going to receive for the trip, and how good he and his wife were going to live.

The moment Sal left the room and set foot on the walkway, his instincts told him something was wrong. Then he saw a man, a large man wearing a white cowboy hat sitting on the edge of one of the pool-side lounge chairs. He wasn't there a minute before. I wonder who he is, Sal thought. Couldn't be police. That hat is too obvious. Still, things just don't feel right. He quickly and nervously headed down to the office where he proceeded to use the pay phone on the office wall. He wasn't about to make the same mistake he'd made the last trip when he'd used his room phone. Angel had screamed at him, "Always use a pay phone and always use code words!"

"Why the worry?" Sal had protested.

Angel had gotten angrier. "I'm warning you. The telephone is the most dangerous thing a trafficker can use. It has been sudden death for many who talked too freely."

Sal wasn't able to understand electronic eavesdropping. Bugs and overhear devices were far too sophisticated for him. But if he wanted to keep his job he'd have to do what Angel wanted. He entered the motel office, and after soliciting a smile from Mrs. Batson, reached into this right pants pocket. "Cabron!" he said.

Mrs. Batson looked blankly at him, not reacting to the Spanish expletive.

Sal fumbled in his other pocket as he loudly said, "Hijo de la chingada!" Again he checked the woman's reaction. Certain she would have called the police had she understood Spanish, he took out his wallet, withdrew a dollar and said, "D'ya have change for a dollar, ma'am?" smiling like an old friend.

"Sure thing." She pushed the button on the cash register, opened the drawer and exchanged coins for the bills.

Sal quickly dialed Angel's number and waited as the phone rang twice. Angel's wife answered, "Hello."

"Is Angel there?" Sal asked.

"No, not now. Is this Sal?"

"Yes, how are ya, Celia?"

"Okay, I guess."

"Do you know where Angel is?" Sal asked.

"Last I heard he was in Mexico City."

"Listen, Celia, try to contact him and tell him I'm at the same motel. He knows the one."

Celia hung up the phone. She couldn't react for a moment, a flash of hurt pride consuming her as she agonized over the thought of Angel being with a girlfriend. Sighing deeply, she picked up the phone again and dialed. "Hi, Ernie. It's Celia. Where's Angel?"

Ernie Kummer was on the spot. Celia wouldn't have called if something important wasn't going down. Deciding on a half-truth, he said, "I picked him up at O'Hare and dropped him off at El Sombrero. He said he had to meet and talk business with some—"

"Listen," Celia interrupted, "a friend of Angel's from Laredo called and said to let Angel know he was at the same motel."

"I'll see if I can find him," Ernie said, eager to be of assistance even though he did not know the exact nature of the cause he was furthering.

"Tell him to come right home," Celia said.

Visualizing what Angel and Jenni were doing at that very moment, Ernie telephoned the All American Motel, and when the motel operator answered, he asked for Mr. Duran, the alias Angel was to use when he registered at the motel earlier that night. After a couple of rings, a man's voice answered. "Angel?" Ernie said.

"Hello," Angel replied in a deep chuckling voice. "Anything wrong?" It was difficult for him to talk with Jenni lying across his chest.

"An amigo from Laredo called your house, said he was at the same motel. I thought it might be important."

Angel nudged Jenni and sat up quickly. "Buddy," he said, "do me a favor, will you? Pick me up and drive me to a motel near Joliet."

"Jesus, Angel, I picked you up at O'Hare Airport just a few hours ago."

"I know, but Celia has my car, and I can't call her."

"All right," Ernie said, "but on one condition. We don't touch no shit. You know I don't want to go near that stuff."

"Yeah, good buddy, don't worry. None will be close to us," Angel lied.

"Okay," Ernie replied, "I'll be there in half hour." He hung up the phone, then turned to see if his wife had been awakened. Sylvia raised herself upon one elbow and said, "What's up with Angel?"

"Oh, he's got to meet a guy in Joliet, and he doesn't have a car."

"Be careful," Sylvia warned. "I hear he's been taking chances lately."

"Angel promised there wouldn't be shit near us," Ernie said in an uncertain tone. "Anyway, he's your brother, and he needs a favor."

Sylvia let her head fall back onto the pillow. Nothing more had to be said.

Ernie walked to the kitchen, where he took a six-pack of beer from the refrigerator. His mind was still fuzzy from the beer guzzled earlier that night, and he needed his usual eye opener. Certain this was one time Sylvia wouldn't complain about his drinking and driving, he said, "I need a little energy for my trip to Cicero."

Chapter 11

▼

THE ARREST

Ernie was late, and Angel was becoming irritated. Wrapping a towel around his waist, he walked to the window, pulled the drapes slightly apart, and peered out. It was a hot, windless morning and heavy, humid air enshrining cars in the motel parking lot created a surreal haze. No one was in sight, nothing moved, and the only sound was Jenni's gentle breathing. Angel walked back to the bed, thinking it would do no good to worry about Ernie. He was hopeless, just not persuaded to the virtues of being on time. Last month the easy-going hillbilly had told him boastfully, "Ah ain't so good lookin', and I don't dress so fine, but the girls all likes me cuz I takes my time."

Angel quietly slipped back into bed and snuggled up closely against Jenni. He was content to let her slumber, for nagging questions kept flashing through his subconscious. Why was he violating one of the major rules for survival in the drug world by going to Joliet to pick up the heroin? Why was the deal with the Puerto Rican driving him? Could the cops have learned about the load, and Sal's arrival with it at the motel?

"Ah, bullshit!" he said as he jumped out of bed and put on his pants and shirt. He walked to the room table, sat down, and began reviewing his plan in his mind. After meeting Sal, he'd drive to the safe-house in Chicago, and while the heroin was being unloaded and stored behind false wall panels in Cousin Rodolfo's house, he'd make contact with the Puerto Rican and tell him the delivery site had been changed from the Joliet area to a place to be designated on the Southwest-Side of Chicago. The only ones who knew about the heroin were Sal and Claudio, and they were totally trustworthy. Nothing could go wrong, he told himself.

Minutes later, the sound of an idling car and squeaking brakes broke the morning silence. Bolting to the door, Angel opened it and waved to Ernie, who responded by maneuvering his Buick into a parking space in front of the room's door. A few minutes later Ernie's short, stocky figure stood framed in the doorway. His face bore an impish smirk, "Hi-ya," he said.

"Where have you been?" Angel asked in a hushed voice. "It's almost five o'clock."

Ernie glanced in the direction of the bed. "I had to get some gas. Besides, I didn't think you'd be in a hurry to leave."

The strange voice awakened Jenni. Realizing she lay uncovered from the hips up, she fussed with the sheet a moment, pulled it up snugly around her, and then smiled teasingly.

"Ah got a good idea, Angel. You take my car and I'll just stay here for a while."

Angel snorted and stifled a laugh as he started toward the door. Nearly reaching it, he was stopped short when Jenni said, "Hey, how about me?"

"I'll be back for you about nine o'clock," he said, as he leaned over and kissed her. "Get some sleep, you'll need it when I get back."

"Promises. Promises," were Jenni's parting words.

Ernie was careful not to make any unnecessary noise as he drove his car past the motel's office. Then after looking both ways twice, once for traffic and once again for police surveillance, he turned south on Cicero Avenue and headed for I-55, the major freeway which carried motorists southwest. As long as there was no heroin nearby, he enjoyed the glamour and intrigue that came with acting as Angel's wheelman.

Reaching the I-55 on-ramp, Angel snapped, "Hit it!" Ernie floored the gas pedal and as the Buick sped onto the super highway, Angel twisted around in his seat and stared out the rear window. "No one following us," he said.

Ernie was becoming increasingly worried. He knew that Angel lived every day of his life openly conscious of tails, phone taps and other forms of police surveillance. But tonight, he saw Angel was overly cautious and tense. "Ya know," he said, "dealing in contraband isn't new to me. As a boy in Tennessee I staked my share of stills, and after coming to Chicago in my teens I delivered white lightning for my uncle to all the hillbillies in town."

"Hell," Angel said. "Ain't nothing wrong with selling a little moonshine, or drinking it."

"Nope. It's part of my hillbilly heritage."

Angel had heard from Sylvia that the only thing which had kept Ernie in high school was the free breakfast and lunch program instituted by the Chicago Board of Education. When the public aid money his parents received couldn't support the family any longer, he had to drop out of school to work in a gas station. He shifted from job to job, but could never keep a permanent one, always falling into the lower class trap of getting stone drunk in the middle of the week and sleeping through a wake-up alarm, or simply deciding that he'd rather be fishing out on the lakefront than working. "How much did you have tonight?" Angel asked, glancing down at the three cans of beer cradled between Ernie's legs.

"Maybe I'll never be anything but a drunken hillbilly, like Sylvia and you say. Maybe I've sold a little white lightning, maybe so, but that never hurt nobody, and I've never really broken the law and ain't never been near heroin."

The poor hillbilly is really shook, Angel thought. Quickly deciding that a slight deception was necessary, he said, "Good buddy, I won't get you mixed up in anything. I've got to meet somebody from El Paso and give him some money."

"Jesus!" Ernie said, thumping the steering wheel with the palm of his hand. "You mean he's got some shit with him?"

"It's hidden in his car. We won't be near it," Angel said in a serious tone. "I'll see him in his room, drop some money and then we'll return to Chicago—you in this car, me in another."

Ernie had every reason to trust Angel. In the five years since he had married his sister, he had gone to him a dozen times desperately in need of money. Angel had always given him a loan and never asked for repayment. "There isn't much Sylvia and I wouldn't do for you," Ernie said. "I'd better shut up and hope you watch out for me."

"Nothing can go wrong. And even if we were busted, the cops would have to let you go. You've never had anything to do with drugs."

Ernie took a long drink from his beer can. "Yeah, I guess I'm...."

"There it is," Angel said, pointing to an illuminated area ahead. "Turn at this exit."

Ernie decelerated and turned onto the exit ramp. As he turned east, back toward the Safe Harbor Motel, he saw the red morning light breaking on the horizon.

"Pull up to the office, and I'll check what room my man is in," Angel said.

Ernie pulled into the waiting zone, and as Angel got out he flicked on WMAC, the popular country and western music station in Chicago. He wanted to catch the truckers' early morning show.

Angel went through the motel's front door. "Do you have a guest from Laredo that got in last night?" he said.

Mrs. Batson, who had been dozing, her head propped in her hands, her elbows on the desk, woke up slightly embarrassed.

"Laredo? Oh, yes, a Mr. Perez?"

"Did he come in with another man?" Angel asked, observing her reactions. His eyes darted around the motel office, looking for signs of danger.

"That's right. They're in room 208, on the east side facing the pool." Mrs. Batson watched Angel as he nodded and started to leave, then called after him, "But you have to go up the stairs on the other side of the building, sir."

Angel nodded again and walked back to the car grateful that Mrs. Batson didn't remember that she had given him similar instructions at least twice before.

"This place is dead," Angel said, as he slid into the front seat. "The old lady at the desk is the only one here and she suspects nothing."

Ernie reached over and switched off the radio just as Merle Haggard finished his rendition of "Just Foolin' Around." He began to regret his earlier comments concerning drug trafficking and even more regretted showing signs of weakness.

Angel was jovial and eager to get to Sal Veta's room. "Hurry, park next to the car with the Texas plates," he said. "I think that's Sal's." Angel opened the car door and started to get out, but hesitated and then turned toward Ernie. "Want to stay here or come up?"

Ernie's eyes stared at nothing for a moment, then he said, "Aw, I gotta piss. I'll go up with ya."

Angel scanned the parking lot as he slid out of the car. Seeing nothing suspicious, his attention focused on the motel rooms, and when the stare from his piercing dark brown eyes had been met only by the glare from the lifeless, glass windows and closed, expressionless doors, he began to walk across the parking lot toward the stairway. He saw no one. Nothing aroused his primal instincts. His move was Ernie's signal to follow. The two men crossed the parking lot, headed for the stairway door, and went up the stairs to the second floor. "Here's Room 208," Angel whispered as he rapped on the door.

"Who is it?" a soft voice challenged from inside the motel room.

"Angel. Come on, open up compadre."

The door swung open and a sleepy but grinning Sal Veta, clad only in his pale blue boxer shorts, appeared. "Entra, entra," he said, stepping back. Then he froze, his eyes fixed on Ernie.

"This is Ernie, my friend," Angel explained mostly in English, for Ernie's sake. "My car broke down, so he drove me."

"Where's the pisser?" Ernie asked. "I gotta piss, then I'll wait for Angel in the car."

Sal got the message. Ernie wasn't part of the deal. "Over there," he said.

Claudio, who had been sleeping, jerked up, and resting on his elbow said, "Hi, Angel."

Angel waved. "How was the trip?"

Claudio shook his head wearily and smiled.

"Do you have it with you?" Sal asked, his chin lowered, eyes looking directly out from under his eyebrows.

Angel moved next to the bed table, tilting his head, beckoning Sal. Reaching into his pants pocket, he withdrew a roll of $100 bills and placed the money on the table. "Twenty-five hundred," he whispered.

Sal took the money without counting it and slipped it into his toilet kit. "It's in the spare in the trunk," he said.

"Good, Ernie can drive back alone, and I'll drive your car to the safe-house, unload it, and have it back here this afternoon. I'm—" Angel paused when Ernie's broad frame appeared in the bathroom doorway.

Embarrassed for putting Angel in an awkward position, Ernie said gruffly, "I'll wait down in the car."

"Just a minute," Angel said. "Let me go out first." He began to open the door, but suddenly stiffened as if an electric shock had jolted his body. He was looking into the muzzle of a .357 Magnum held by a large man with a sardonic grin on his face. Behind him were several other men—all with guns pointed at his head.

"Surprise, Angel!" the grinning man said, as he shoved the barrel of the gun flush against Angel's nose. "I'm DEA agent Joe Fruin; you're under arrest!"

Before Angel could react, Fruin put his large hand in the center of his face and shoved him, sending him sprawling back onto the floor. Drug agents poured through the door, guns nervously pointed at the startled drug traffickers. While one agent talked into a two-way radio, another approached Ernie.

"Hey! What's goin—" Ernie was hit above the left eye with the barrel of the agent's gun, and he dropped to the floor on one knee, blood streaming from a deep cut.

"Shut up and don't move," the agent ordered, pointing his gun directly at Ernie's head.

Angel was on his back, spread-eagled on the floor, Fruin on top of him with one knee in the center of his chest and the barrel of his .357 Magnum resting on the tip of his nose. "Roll over and put your hands behind your back!" Fruin barked. When another agent had fastened handcuffs to Angel's wrists, he was forcefully picked up and slammed against the wall. "Put your forehead against the wall and don't move or I'll blow your nuts off!" Fruin said.

Angel could see out of the corner of his eye that Ernie and Sal were pushed alongside him, hands cuffed behind their backs. The blood from Ernie's wound was running down into his eye and cascading down his cheek onto his shirt.

Claudio was apparently overlooked in the initial excitement. As he sat in bed with a bewildered look on his face, Agent Cass approached menacingly. "You are under arrest. Move over to the wall with your hands up!"

Not able to understand, Claudio just sat still, a deadpan expression on his face.

Cass pulled Claudio up by the arm and flung him against the wall, "I said move, asshole!"

The agent holding the two-way radio raised it to his mouth and spoke excitedly, "The suspects are under arrest and secured. Do you read me?"

"Ten-four," the radio crackled.

Fruin walked over to Angel, who had turned his head enough to hear and see what was going on. "We finally got you, Señor Herrera," he said. "After a whole year of getting our noses rubbed in shit, it's great to see you sick and scared." He was unable to control himself and began punching Angel in the kidneys and back, causing him to flinch in pain. Releasing the frustration that had built up after months of around-the-clock surveillance felt good. "Read them the Miranda warnings," he ordered.

Cass removed a printed card from his wallet and began to read. "You have the right to remain silent. If you give up the right to remain silent, anything you say can and will be used against you in a court of law. You have a right to have an attorney present during questioning. If you cannot afford an attorney, one will be appointed for you."

"Now do it in Spanish, Cass, for our amigo there."

"But Chief, I don't speak Spanish!"

"Try. The words are printed underneath on the card."

"Oostid teeney el duretcho di no desir mayda!" Cass stopped after stumbling through the first sentence and mispronouncing everything except "el" and "no." The four other agents in the room roared with laughter.

"Okay, Cass, that was great," Fruin said. "Now go down and help search our prisoners' cars. Hill and I will search the room." He turned quickly on his heels and glared at Angel. "Where is it? Save us the trouble of looking for it, and I'll see you get only ten years."

Angel had rehearsed in his mind many times what he'd do if he were arrested—remain silent and stay cool. He turned his head towards the three men lined up against the wall next to him and whispered in Spanish, "Say nothing; this asshole has nothing on us."

"Comprendo," Fruin yelled as he leaped at Angel, jamming his head into the wall with the heel of his hand. The enraged drug cop stuck his gun high between Angel's legs so that the hammer pushed between the cheeks of his buttocks and the barrel pressed hard on his testicles. "Shut up. Don't say another word or I'll blow your balls off! Your girlfriends wouldn't like that would they, lover boy?"

"Are you crazy?" Ernie shrieked. "Angel didn't do nothin' to you. We're going to sue you for civil rights—"

For a moment it looked as though Fruin was going to shoot both Angel and Ernie.

"Chief," agent Hill said, "killing them won't be worth it."

"Yeah, yeah," Fruin said as he turned away from Angel and walked to the wall-length mirror hanging over the vanity. He stared trance-like at himself for several seconds before he told agent Hill, "Go down and see if they found anything in the cars."

Agent Cass had taken car keys off the bedstand before joining other agents in the parking lot. He was searching the trunk of Sal Veta's car when agent Hill walked up. "Did you find anything in Angel's car?" Hill asked.

"Nothing," Cass said as he began rummaging through the trunk. "It was clean." Something about the spare tire caught Cass's attention. It looked worn, half inflated. "I'll bet it's there," he said, lifting the tire from the trunk and laying it on the ground behind the car. Using a jack handle, he popped the tire from the rim. "Hot damn! We hit it big! There's 12 to 13 kilos of shit here." He pulled out two packages, each one being the size of a small loaf of bread and wrapped in gray tape. In his five years as a drug agent, Hill had never been in on a seizure of more than ten ounces of heroin. His eyes bulged as he said, "This case will make history."

"I'll take one package up to Fruin and show him what we got," Cass said. He raced up the stairs and re-entered the room where he was amazed to see Fruin in the middle of what resembled the debris from a hurricane. "We hit it big," Cass said, waving the gray taped package. "There's a lot more just like this in a spare tire."

"Which car?" Fruin asked.

"The one with the Texas plates," Cass replied.

"Aw shit!" Fruin hissed out between clenched teeth as he led Cass by the arm into the privacy of the bathroom. "The bust is no good," he groaned.

"Whadda ya mean, Chief?"

"You didn't find a fucking thing in the car Angel came in, did you Cass?"

"Naw, it was clean," Cass said. "But we musta found 12 keys in the other one!"

Fruin groaned. "Shit. None in Angel's car. He's clean. He'll walk."

Agent Cass had been with the DEA for only fifteen months and still was not familiar with the laws of arrest, search and seizure, or what constituted a prosecutable case. "I don't think so," he argued. "No judge will let Angel walk away from all this."

"Listen up, Cass. I know what I'm talking about. I've testified in court against drug dealers a hundred times, seen cases against drug dealers who were dead bang guilty dismissed because arresting officers didn't protect the slimebags' Fourth Amendment rights."

Cass' eyes narrowed, "How ya going to play the game, Chief?"

"This is no game, like some Monday night football spectacular between the Bears and the Green Bay Packers. We're in a war, where agents get blown away by drug dealers and where addicts burglarize homes and hold up grocery stores with stolen pistols in their shaky hands. No way, Cass. I vowed after I lost the last motion to suppress evidence that a guilty drug dealer would never again walk free on a legal technicality."

Cass' mouth gaped as he tried to anticipate his boss' next move. "Whatever," he said.

"Give me that." Fruin snatched the package from Cass and tore the tape off. Through the inner plastic wrapping he could see a brown powdery substance. "That son-of-a-bitch walks if we don't do something." He opened the bathroom door, the package of heroin in his hand, and walked directly toward Angel with a malicious grin on his face. "Look what I found right next to where you were standing, Señor Herrera."

The three agents guarding the prisoners stared at Fruin, uncertain at first whether he intended to plant the heroin on Angel. His grim face removed all doubts.

"What are you going to charge Angel with?" Cass asked.

"All of it," Fruin replied, holding the booty up with two fingers and thumb. "Let's take Señor Herrera and his gang downtown and show him the kind of hospitality he can expect for the next twenty years."

Angel had felt safe throughout the room search. Without heroin on or near him, he was confident a judge would order him released. But the plant of heroin changed the rules of the game. No one would believe he had been framed. "You crooked bastard!" he snarled as he reared back his head and spit into Fruin's face.

In virtually one movement, Fruin wiped the fluid from his face with the back of his right hand and shot his left fist forward, his huge hand crashing into Angel's nose, knocking him flat on his back on the floor, blood squirting from his nostrils. With cat-like movements he took several steps toward Angel and began kicking him. Angel rolled and squirmed as best he could, taking the kicks in the legs and back instead of the groin where they were aimed.

Seeing the potential for serious injury, Cass grabbed Fruin from behind. "Easy, Chief, you'll kill him! We'll be on trial, not him."

"Get this bastard down to the car!" Fruin yelled.

Cass pulled Angel to his feet, and then stood protectively in front of him. Though blood was streaming down his face and his body ached, Angel didn't utter a sound. He stood glaring defiantly at Fruin.

"How are we going to explain all this blood?" Cass asked.

"Get some towels and clean up our prisoners," Fruin ordered.

Cass did the best he could, stopping the heavy flow of blood from Angel's nose and the cuts above Ernie's eye, before Fruin lined up the four prisoners and started them toward cars in the parking lot. Each prisoner was placed in the rear seat of a separate official government vehicle, Angel going into the lead car with Cass and Fruin. It was about seven o'clock when the caravan of vehicles turned onto Interstate 55 and began winding north toward the DEA offices located in the Dirksen Federal Building in downtown Chicago.

"You suppose we were too rough in the room?" Cass asked, barely audible, conscious of Angel in the back seat.

"You mean when they resisted arrest?" Fruin shot back. "Naw! Besides if we didn't nail 'em, there would have been twenty-five pounds of heroin on the streets within the next forty-eight hours. Reggie Begoode and Amador Rios would be shooting it into their arms and selling it to school kids."

"Yeah, Chief, I guess you're right. We gotta get it off the streets to protect the kids."

Fruin settled back in his seat, calculating the time it would take to process his prisoners: fingerprinting, photographs, typing of arrest reports and incarceration forms, and finally, putting them behind bars. His role in the war was just about over. Starting the next day, the Angel Herrera case was going to be in the hands of United States Attorney Sam Stevens and his capable assistants who, he was sure, would be willing to bend a few rules to gain Angel's conviction. He looked down at the packages of heroin piled on the seat next to him and mused aloud, "Do the ends justify the means?"

Cass glanced at his boss and friend. "Only when we ain't the poor bastards who are the victims of the means and the ends."

The image of Comandante Gonzales' face, distorted by hate and frustration, flashed across Fruin's mindscreen and brought with it the awareness that he had an awful lot in common with the fanatical enforcer of Mexico's drug laws.

CHAPTER 12

▼

ABOGADO DEL DIABLO

It was a few minutes after seven when Matt Gavin awoke from a peaceful night's sleep. He lay still for a while, thinking about his hectic Monday morning schedule. Then all his thoughts focused on the warm, alluring back pressed firmly against him.

Tricia had been awake for some time, but unwilling to end the enchanting night they had spent together clung tightly to the embracing arm draped around her. She sighed deeply as Gavin parted her hair with gentle nudges of his nose and kissed the nape of her neck, igniting a gentle glow of passion. She reached back for him, to pull him closer, when the spell was shattered by a short, muffled ring from the phone on the bedside table. "Damn," she said softly.

Neither moved, each thinking it would be easy to ignore the inconsiderate caller who intruded upon their special moments of intimacy. After three rings, Gavin said, "I'd better answer. The ring does have a sound of urgency to it." He tried to turn away from her but couldn't. "Let go, please."

Tricia reluctantly released her grasp, allowing him to reach quickly for the phone. Though conscious of the fact a phone call at that time of morning usually meant a client had been arrested during the night and was desperately in need of his help, he wasn't prepared for the shocking sound of panic in the voice he heard. It was Celia Herrera and she was babbling incoherently. He held the phone away from his ear until the voice stilled, then said, "Calm down; who's in jail?"

"My God, Mr. Gavin, they got Angel! He's in jail now. You've got to help him." Celia pleaded.

Stunned, but fighting to keep a business-like tone, Gavin said slowly and calmly, "Don't worry, everything will be okay. Now tell me, what was he arrested for?"

"Don't know, something to do with drugs! Angel telephoned ten minutes ago and told me to get in touch with you—say he was arrested by drug agents and is being held in the lockup at the federal courthouse. Please help him! Please!" she gasped.

No sense pushing her, Gavin thought. Celia Herrera knew little about her husband's drug dealings, or the problems he now faced. The one legally required phone call Angel had been allowed to make most likely had been made in the presence of arresting agents, and no doubt, he had refused to say anything more than was necessary. "It'll be all right," he assured the distraught wife. "I'll do everything I can to get your husband back home where he belongs."

After putting the phone back in place, Gavin sat silently on the side of the bed for a moment, then shaking his head said, "Angel Herrera of all people."

Tricia rose on her elbows, her eyes mirroring concern. She had met Angel several times when he had come into the office for conferences and, aware of his reputation, recognized the seriousness of the early morning call. Sliding over, she put her arms around Gavin's waist and then nestled her head against his back. "How bad is it, hon?" she asked.

"Intuition tells me Angel is in serious trouble. I'd better get over to the federal courthouse and find out." Gavin strained to get up, but as he did Tricia tightened her grasp around his waist and pressed her body firmly against him. Preoccupied with Angel's incarceration, he almost failed to recognize the message she tacitly conveyed. She needed that last touch, a reassurance from him that last night's activities were expressions of love and not just sexual gymnastics. He swung around in the circle of her arms and rolling her on her back, embraced and caressed her tenderly until she let out a wistful moan and relaxed her hold. Gently, but quickly sliding out from her arms, he stood up, and with a wily smile breaking across his lips said, "Be on time for work today or I'll see to it that you're fired."

"You can't fire me, buddy. I'm too darn important to your law firm."

Gavin smiled and nodded, somewhat surprised by Tricia's display of spunk, "You're—" He stopped short of telling her she wasn't too far off the mark, that she was becoming a very capable trial lawyer, and that he'd have trouble getting along without her. His mind raced back a year, to the night he'd met a prim and proper looking Tricia Berglund at a Lawyer's Association meeting. She was so vivid in his mind's eye, wearing the necessary touch of make-up, hair swept back and tied in a bun and clothes designed to conceal a curvaceous figure. He had been thinking about bringing a woman into his firm, and Tricia fit the image he wanted perfectly: intelligent, dedicated to her profession, driven but not a super-achiever, and safe—no romantic involvement foreseeable.

The more he learned about her the more impressed he'd become. She told him that after graduating from DePaul School of Law she started her career with an old-line, prestigious law firm that specialized in corporate and tax law and worked in that stuffy atmosphere for almost two years. "I'm bored stiff," she complained, "with my job of shuffling papers and creating billable hours of work to justify large fees. I want to be where the action is."

He had casually handed her his card. "Stop in and see me. I may have a spot for you."

Her eyes had scrutinized his face as she so obviously had wondered if he was on the legit, interested in her for her legal abilities and not for an amorous escapade. In a defensive tone she had asked, "Do you think I'll be accepted in the all-male enclaves that control the criminal defense business?"

He had replied in a challenging tone, "Don't know. Do you have the balls to give it a try?"

Tricia's resolve had electrified the air around them. She was going to do what she had to do to get the job and become the best criminal defense lawyer in the city, but she was never, ever going to get romantically involved with Matt Gavin. "I'll be in your office tomorrow morning at eight, ready to start work."

"Miss Berglund," he had cautioned her, "you'll have to start as a trial assistant and researcher. I have a unique type of practice in that a client charged with murder or major drug offense or white-collar financial crime wants only me to try the case. It'll be at least a year before you can handle major litigation yourself."

"That's fine," she had called after him as he walked to the podium to address the lawyer's meeting. "Just being part of high profile litigation fits my career plans perfectly."

Sensing he'd been lost in pleasant memories involving her, Tricia watched Gavin rushing about, showering and dressing. "Darn you," she whispered, suppressing the passion he had playfully ignited and then left to smolder. "You've changed my life so much."

Gavin heard her as he rushed past the bed. "How'd I do that?"

"Well, to begin with, my vow of celibacy lasted for only a few months around you."

Gavin laughed. "I'd say that change was for the better."

Tricia had known from the start of their relationship that a strong, undeniable magnetism drew her to him, yet she used the moment to silently probe for a more explicable reason for her feelings, examining his features, physique and demeanor. She thought how his face was

sensitive and intelligent at times, and others when it was ruggedly handsome, fitting perfectly with an athlete's build.

Watching her eyes drift over his body, he said, "Why am I so irresistible
to you?"

"It's a certain mystique I can't describe." She wouldn't say it, but there
was more. He had the ability to turn off his charm during business
hours, becoming aloof, almost immune to her sensuality. She liked it
that way; it made a love relationship and a career feasible.

Gavin walked toward the apartment door in a teasing manner, thinking it would be just a matter of steps.

"Hold it right there!" Tricia demanded. "Are you going to kiss me
goodbye or dash off like I'm not even here."

"Oh, well, if I have to," Gavin said moving to her. He touched his lips
to hers and then turned and walked out of the bedroom.

It was approximately one mile from Matt Gavin's lakeside condominium to his office on LaSalle Street, a distance he preferred to walk
every day, even though there were days when he believed he was running
a Marine Corps obstacle course. "Neither rain nor snow, mud nor blood
can stop me," he had often told his secretary as he strode into his office
dripping wet or covered with snow. Irene would always glance up and
reply, "Yeah, Chicago is a great place to work and make money, but it's a
shitty place to live."

There would be no more complaints of foul weather this year, he
thought, as he crossed Lake Shore Drive and entered Grant Park. A
warm, cheering sun was breaking over Lake Michigan, and a balmy
breeze brushed over the rows of vividly colored flowers that lined the
park's walkway. The summer day Chicagoans had waited months for
had suddenly appeared. Even the Chicago Loop, looming before him,
had taken on the appearance of an inviting and invigorating place to
conduct business rather than the cold, gray place to work that it had
been throughout the seemingly endless winter months.

The summer weather reminded Gavin he had reached an important milestone in his career: he had started his sixteenth year in the private practice of law. How had the time passed so quickly, he wondered. From early high school days, through college and law school, his only goal had been to be a criminal defense attorney. He was totally content now that he had chosen the law profession and dedicated his life to it. It had been richly rewarding in many ways.

Like several of his colleagues in the criminal defense business, Gavin had started his career on the other side of the fence, as a prosecutor for the Cook County State's Attorney Office. It was an invaluable position for a young lawyer seeking trial experience and insight into the political infrastructure of the Big City. He learned all there was to know about criminal law the hard way, by prosecuting every type of crime on the books. When he wasn't in the courtroom, he spent his time learning about political power and the Richard J. Daley Democratic Machine, one of the most dazzling political organizations to ever exist. Watching "His Honor's" political maneuvering had been a rare privilege.

To survive though, he also had to learn about bribes—and the payoff as the Chicago cognoscente referred to it—and judicial and political corruption. The bribe happened to be a way of life, an institution, which had to be considered every time he walked in to a courtroom. It became second nature. He'd look for the "handshake" which would covertly exchange a wad of $100 bills, or the wink, or the unwarranted arrogance of an amateur player. It was disgusting at times because it seemed that lawyers who bragged they could buy anyone or anything hung out near the doorways leading to every courtroom in the Criminal Courts Building.

Convinced he couldn't change things had he wanted to, Gavin began studying the many skilled and honest lawyers who reached the pinnacle of success without resorting to the payoff. There were lots of them, many being the best lawyers, prosecutors and judges in the city, and they made the state and federal courts in Chicago a gratifying place to practice.

Drug cases were rare when he had started in the criminal defense business. Prosecutors at the federal courthouse busied themselves prosecuting bank robberies, counterfeiting, and fraud cases, and occasionally the political corruption case. Unless a drug case involved a large quantity of marijuana, cocaine, or heroin, it was no big deal. And the rising number of rapes, robberies and gang related crimes in the inner city kept the state prosecutors from actively pursuing drug dealers. Things changed dramatically in the space of ten years. In 1979 everyone involved with the criminal justice system suddenly realized state and federal courts were inundated with drug cases, and defense attorneys were amazed to find that accused drug dealers comprised 30 to 40 percent of their practices.

Gavin took his share of abuse from colleagues when speaking before local bar associations. He'd retort when his representation of drug dealers came under fire, "It's the only area of law where an attorney gets the opportunity to fight for the preservation of the constitutional guarantees of due process and fair trial." Law schools were much easier places to lecture because of the students' experience with the drug culture. There he was free to warn, "The constitutional rights of persons charged with drug law violations are being unreasonably infringed upon and abrogated by drug agents, prosecutors and judges." At his last lecture at Northwestern Law School he warned, "Drug dealers have become the scorned, the lepers of the criminal justice system, unable to get a break or benefit of the doubt from a judge or jury. It's a reverse form of corruption because drug dealers are singled out for prosecution and for unreasonably harsh prison sentences. Sellers get all the blame for America's most disturbing social problems, while illicit drug users blatantly use and abuse in restaurants and bars, in parks and at parties, and even in the grandstands at athletic events. Our politically responsive criminal justice system gives the users a pass, because in many instances the users are the sons and daughters of the rich and powerful, and 'Little Johnny' or 'Cute Debbie' just couldn't be at fault for his or her own problems. Americans have been brainwashed into believing the drug problem is all the seller's fault."

When one of the students suggested that the drug laws were unconscionable, Gavin tried to distinguish between the drug laws and enforcement of those laws. "I've no quarrel with the drug laws as they were enacted by Congress. If the majority of Americans want to outlaw the use of pot, coke and heroin, it's okay with me—provided constitutional rights aren't abrogated and grotesque, draconian, immoral twenty to fifty year prison sentences aren't dished out like handshakes at a political convention."

An audience of three hundred fifty students and faculty stood and applauded when he had finished.

Matt Gavin's introduction to Angel Herrera and his Durango Connection came when a cousin of Angel's was caught by Chicago police officers with a kilogram of heroin in his car. Señor Pepe Herrera had been stopped for a minor traffic violation, but the suspicious and aggressive arresting officers searched the trunk of his car without probable cause.

"Nothing more than a fishing trip," the Criminal Court judge said, as he ruled that the state prosecutor couldn't use the heroin in evidence. "Police are not, at least in this country, given the unbridled right to search private places in the hope of getting lucky and finding contraband." With the use of heroin suppressed, the state prosecutor dismissed the charges against Señor Herrera, and he walked from court a free man. Word of Matt Gavin's expertise spread quickly throughout the Latino community, and after several similar dispositions, Angel Herrera walked into his office and introduced himself. Aware of Angel's reputation, Gavin was reserved, almost defensive at first. However, it wasn't long before it became apparent that Angel was like any other businessman in control of a large corporation. He wanted the best legal representation available in the event of an emergency.

Deciding to set the record straight right from the start, Gavin had looked sternly at Angel. "I'll give every person who walks through my doors and requests my help the best legal defense I can. But I don't want to know anything about your day-to-day business. I work nine to five, and only in the courtrooms."

Angel understood the message clearly and respected Gavin for defining the boundaries of his representation. He was confident his new lawyer would do all he could within the limits of the law to protect him and the men of his organization against unreasonable or outrageous government action. But there would be no help outside the courtrooms, no facilitating the operations of the Durango Connection. "El Abogado Del Diablo," Angel said.

Gavin put his thumb to his chin and studied his new client. "El what?", he said.

"You are the attorney for the devils, counselor."

Chapter 13

▼

THE DRUG WAR

The Dirksen Federal Building, a modern high-rise with steel and glass walls, presided majestically over the south end of the Chicago Loop. The Courthouse, as the building was usually referred to, was where some of the most powerful people in the United States gathered to play their part in the law enforcement system. It was where senators and congressmen hung out and were influenced to pass laws which were aimed at eliminating drug trafficking. It was where FBI and DEA agents set up investigations, stings, and busts. It was where assistant U.S. attorneys, the prosecutors, reigned with awesome power. And it was where men and women with average mentalities and skills donned black robes and stepped up on benches to become supremely powerful district and appeals court judges. It was a mind-boggling building, an arena where a person charged with a crime could lose his life, liberty, or property if his lawyer didn't strap on his six-guns and shoot it out with the System's designated hit men.

Matt Gavin pushed through the Courthouse's revolving doors and walked up to a security guard's desk. Metal detectors and searches weren't needed prior to the trial of the "Chicago Seven" in 1969, but the gaudy spectacle Judge Julius Hoffman turned into a Hollywood terrorist show prompted the Marshals Service to take bomb threats seriously. Defendant Abbie Hoffman and his yippies had a profound and everlasting effect on the federal court system. Now it was routine for guards to search the coats and handbags of all but the well-known. Most people respectfully complied, even though they were made to feel like common criminals.

"Good morning, Mr. Gavin," a guard said.

"Mornin'," he replied, as he strode past the security desk and headed for the elevator, conscious of the fact the guards were doing their job, giving him the once over, looking for something unusual in his dress or demeanor.

Angel Herrera's face flashed across Gavin's mindscreen as the elevator whisked him to the twenty-fourth floor lockup where the prisoners awaiting court appearances were detained. Jail had to be a tough deal to handle for someone like Angel who had so much macho pride and so much of the sweet life going for him. He had told Angel on several occasions, "If you can't do the time, don't do the crime." In retrospect, it was probably the best advice he had ever given to the boss of the Durango Connection, because the judges, prosecutors, and the drug cops—those who made the criminal justice system what it was—were changing dramatically. They were going to get down and as dirty as they had to win the war on drugs and put traffickers like Angel in prison.

The trigger symbol happened as Gavin stepped off the elevator. The infuriating sound of the large, black iron lock-up door slaming shut sent the message it was time to go to war again against the top guns—intelligent and skilled prosecutors who were charged with prosecuting, convicting, and jailing his client. It was the Big Leagues. Adrenalin poured through his body, eroding memories of the idyllic night he had enjoyed with Tricia. Behind that iron door, which locked in despair and frustration and shut out everything of value, sat a client who trusted him with his life. Clang! Bang! The iron door sounded again, and Gavin was ready for combat.

The marshal seated at a desk inside the lockup looked up when he heard the loud knock on the small square of bullet-proof glass to the right of the iron door. A smirk spread across his face as he pushed the button, triggering the electronic latch. Gavin pulled the heavy door open and walked in.

"We were expecting you, Mr. Gavin," said Ed Kerski, the marshal in charge of the lockup. "They got a big one with 25 pounds, I hear. You ain't gonna win this one, counselor."

Gavin feigned indignation. "What would you do for excitement if you didn't have me knocking on your door?"

"Probably get some rest, counselor."

"Yeah, sure, Ed. The only thing you enjoy more than playing the court-house jester with me is watching the White Sox play the Yankees with your favorite seven course dinner—a six-pack of beer and a bag of pretzels."

Kerski grunted and shook his head. "You lawyers always have an answer for everything."

"I'd like to see my client," Gavin said.

"I'll put him in room one for you," the gentle giant replied as he shuffled toward the cells with a large ring of heavy brass keys dangling from his huge hand. "But he'd better get used to a jail cell," he said over his shoulder. "He's going to be in one for a long time."

Gavin walked back to the attorney interview room, confident Kerski would fetch his client without delay. He sat down in front of the large glass pane that partitioned the small room and scooted his chair forward so that he was inches away from the voice box through which he could talk to his client. More from instinct than reason his eyes darted from point to point throughout the room, searching for an overhear device. He knew if a bug had been secreted somewhere in the room it would have been professionally done and not easily detected. Still, the futile search was consoling.

The door swung open, and Angel Herrera shuffled in and sat down. He waited until the door was shut and marshal Kerski gone before he looked up sheepishly. "Hello, Matt," he said.

Gavin was appalled. Angel looked like a whipped puppy. Gone was the proud, macho, almost arrogant bearing. The left side of his jaw was red and puffy, and dried blood was caked on his lower lip. Gavin's insides rolled at the sight of his client, and he quickly decided to skip formalities and get on with the business at hand. "Como esta?" he said.

Angel nodded. "Okay, I guess."

Gavin cleared his throat and said in a loud, firm manner, more for the sake of those who may have planted an electronic listening device than for Angel's comfort, "Tell me about it, Angel, and tell it to me straight. You know that anything you tell me is confidential and can't be used against you."

Angel leaned forward so he could speak directly into the voice box in the glass pane. His face was flushed, and he couldn't mask the turmoil that showed in his eyes and contour of his face. "We got busted in Joliet at the Safe Harbor Motel. It's a bad deal. There was nothing in the room when the agents came in. It was all in the car."

"Okay, Angel, start at the beginning."

"See, Claudio and Sal brought in a load. I was supposed to meet them when they got here, pay them for the trip, and then have someone drive the load car to Chicago. The next day the car was to be returned to them empty. I went to their room, and I no sooner shut the door when I heard footsteps. When I opened the door, a DEA agent was standing right there with a gun in my face. He pushed the door open and knocked me on my ass!"

"What happened then?" Gavin said.

"The fucking agents searched the room. But I swear, Matt, they didn't find a thing. One of the agents, I think his name is Fruin, got violent when he couldn't find any heroin. He knocked me all around trying to make me tell him where the shit was hidden."

Gavin attempted to respond in a supportive manner. "Well, if that's the truth, I'll have you out of here in an hour."

"But wait," Angel said, "here's where I think the problem is. That fuckin' cop said he found a kilo of heroin in the room."

"Come on, Angel," Gavin cautioned. "If you don't tell me the truth you'll hurt only yourself." He knew from years of experience that Mexicans from Durango who trafficked in illegal drugs rarely, if ever, admitted to being caught with a load of drugs in their possession. He suspected Angel, like others, would let machoism stand in the way of telling him the embarrassing facts. "If you or your mules didn't bring the stuff into the motel room, then how did it get there?" he asked, probing for the truth.

"I swear, Matt, agent Fruin or one of his men got the keys to Sal's car off the dresser and went down to the parking lot, brought a kilo up, and then put it on the chair right beside me."

"Did you see who did it?" Gavin said.

"No!" Angel replied. "Other agents had me with my face against the wall and hands in cuffs. When I tried to turn around, they whacked me, and treated me like a dog. We were up against the wall for at least fifteen minutes while the agents searched the room and cars. Then I heard that prick Fruin say, 'We got you now, Big Shot!'"

Gavin studied his client's face, searching for signs of credibility. Joe Fruin and his agents had reputations for being straight guys, not corrupt, not known for planting heroin. Yet Angel did look like he was telling the truth. "Okay," he said, "I'll check with the prosecutor and case agents to determine what offense you are going to be charged with."

"Thanks, counselor. I knew you'd take good care of your big devil. But you've got to help Ernie too, get him out of the mess I got him into."

Gavin was amazed. "Ernie Kummer? How the hell is he involved?"

Angel spoke rapidly, pleading Ernie's case. "He drove me to the motel in his car, but he had nothing to do with the deal. He had to take a leak, so he came up to the room. He was leaving when the agents came through the door."

"Come on, Angel. He knew you were going out on a drug deal, didn't he?"

"He knew I was going to do something, but none of the details. You know how he hates drugs!"

"Who is going to put up the bonds and pay attorney's fees for the others?" Gavin said.

Angel replied as expected. "Me. I cover all my soldier's legal expenses. And if their families should need any money while they're locked up, I'll handle it."

Gavin nodded.

"But tell me," Angel said in an urgent tone, "what's going to happen now? Can you get us all out of this shithouse?"

Gavin rose and knocked loudly on the iron door. "You and your amigos will be brought before Magistrate Hamilton for a bond hearing in a few minutes. If I can get the marshal to let me out of here, I'll meet you in the magistrate's courtroom."

Marshal Kerski wore a mischievous grin as he let Gavin out and ushered him to the lockup door. "Wanna bet ten skins?"

"On what?" Gavin said, as he brushed past the marshal and walked toward the magistrate's courtroom.

"That Señor Herrera won't get out of the slammer on bond."

"You got a bet, marshal."

Magistrate Alex Hamilton's courtroom was small and unpretentious in comparison to those of the district court judges. The bench was elevated only one foot off the floor and was modest in size and construction. A counsel's table for the prosecutor and one for the defense team was placed in front of the bench, and behind them were eight rows of bench seats. Stepping into the courtroom, Gavin was surprised to see it was filled to capacity with drug agents, news reporters and spectators. One agent stunned him when he said derisively, "Here comes Matt Gavin. That means that son-of-a-bitch Herrera is going to walk on a low bond."

"He's a fucking shyster!" another agent said.

Turning in the direction of the voices, Gavin nodded at two agents who were leaning up against the courtroom wall, glaring at him. He showed little emotion, for he had reached a point in his career where he understood the agent's animosity. "Just here to do my job," he said, hoping they too would understand when he took them on in head-to-head combat and tried to tear their testimony to shreds.

Assistant United States Attorney Terry Mack sat at a counsel's table, head bent forward, concentrating on case reports which were spread before him. "Good morning, Mr. Mack," Gavin said. "I see the best prosecutor in the courthouse has been assigned the job of trying the Angel Herrera case."

"Morning, Mr. Gavin," the prosecutor replied without raising his eyes.

The reason for Mack's stiffness stood behind him, casting solicitous smiles. Gavin nodded greetings to two news reporters who were aggressively seeking a scoop about his client.

"Hey, Matt," one reporter shouted, "is Angel Herrera really the boss of the Durango Connection, the biggest heroin ring operating in this country?"

"That's sheer fantasy," Gavin scolded as he turned and walked to the court clerk's desk.

The reporters pressed harder, "A case agent told us Angel Herrera smuggles over twenty million dollars of heroin a year."

Gavin had to try to stop a media frenzy. It would kill any chance he had to have his clients released on reasonable bonds. Magistrate Hamilton was politically conscious and extremely sensitive to pressure created by the media. Gavin warned, "If any news reporter in this courtroom publishes any facts about my client other than the ones that come out in the upcoming hearing, I'll slap him with a million dollar lawsuit."

The tension was broken when the door leading to chambers opened quickly, revealing a big, broad-faced man dressed in a flowing black robe. Alex Hamilton lowered his head and charged toward the bench. His mindset concerning the case he was about to hear was strikingly obvious. Silence prevailed in the courtroom as he took his seat. Gavin gazed at the imposing figure with affectionate eyes, recalling the first time his associate, Tricia Berglund had appeared before him to argue for a bond reduction.

"Chrissakes!" she had complained after leaving the courtroom. "Hamilton tried to intimidate me with his rough looks and then verbally tackle me."

Gavin had replied in a facetious tone, "Law's a contact business with him. He likes to tell young lawyers he got his mangled nose in courtroom battles."

Tricia had laughed as she had said. "I heard he got those twists and bumps on his nose playing football before face masks were worn."

Gavin didn't tell Tricia at the time that the nose and gruff mannerisms were part of a persona the magistrate had no intention of changing. He was once overheard in chambers boasting, "I enjoy scaring the shit out of defendants who stand before me charged with crimes against society." He practiced what he preached when it came to drug dealers, whom he accused of being "those demons who provide the chemical guts for killers, rapists and stick-up men." It was rumored around the courthouse that when a prosecutor wanted a high bond set, he'd simply step into the magistrate's chambers before the case was called and tell the receptive magistrate that the drugs the defendant was charged with possessing were destined for teenagers in city high schools. There was nothing which could be said on behalf of a defendant after that. He was going to stay in jail.

Magistrate Hamilton glanced down at the complaint before him and then around the courtroom. "Where are the defendants?"

"They are being escorted—" Marshal Kerski was interrupted when the courtroom door swung open and three burly marshals ushered Angel Herrera and his three alleged co-conspirators to the defendants' table.

Gavin had known Ernie Kummer for several years, but this was his first glimpse of Sal Veta and Claudio Cillas. Neat appearing and overly polite, nothing in their appearances indicated they were involved in the business of illegal drugs. Huddling the four men together, he said in a hushed voice, "I'm going to have the judge set bonds for all of you. I expect them to be high, but don't be alarmed. I will get your bonds down to where you can make them within the next few days."

Angel and Ernie nodded, their eyes showing fear and confusion about the proceedings which were about to start. Sal Veta said "Our only hope for freedom rests with you, Abogado Del Diablo."

"United States versus Angel Herrera, Ernie Kummer, Sal Veta and Claudio Cillas," the court clerk announced.

As Gavin walked to the podium, everyone in the courtroom focused undivided attention on him. The media reporters were especially discerning, scribbling their appraisal of everything about him, from his black, wavy hair to his penetrating eyes to his dark blue, three-piece suit. They wanted to tell their readers or viewers just what sort of man represented the most notorious drug dealer ever arrested in Chicago.

"Good morning, Your Honor," Gavin said respectfully.

"Good morning," the magistrate replied gruffly. A few in the courtroom recognized the magistrate's standoffishness whenever Gavin appeared before him for what it was, a facade. It was widely rumored in the legal community his friendship with Gavin dated back to their college days, when the University of Illinois played Michigan at Ann Arbor. Hamilton was a raw-boned tackle who had gained all-conference honors for the Wolverines the prior season, and Gavin an Illinois linebacker assigned a defensive position directly across from him. Their introduction that Saturday afternoon came in the form of several violent head-on crashes, as Gavin tried to play off Hamilton's blocks and move to the ball carrier. Gavin still vividly recalled one vicious block that knocked him to the ground. Getting up, he told a teammate, "Hamilton charges off the line like a rampaging bull." In recent years the game provided him with the means to lure Hamilton into a quiet bar, where he would then argue long into the night that Illinois had really been the better team and should have won the game. Hamilton cherished the brew talk and the camaraderie, but he never let it interfere with the administration of justice when attorney Matt Gavin litigated a matter before him.

Alex Hamilton was appointed a magistrate shortly after Congress had created the post in 1966. Congress had responded quickly to complaints by federal judges that too many criminal cases were bogging down the federal court system and hindering the administration of justice. Hamilton was just the sort of lawyer the district court judges at the federal courthouse in Chicago had in mind for the job, and the judges selected him over twenty-five qualified applicants for the position. He instantly assumed the sense of power and prestige that came with the Black Robe and title. And the new respect paid to him by the legal community was enjoyed immensely. Ironically, his only complaints were leveled at his bosses, the district court judges, who when exercising their power to direct and control him had a tendency to be petty and demeaning. The fact that many knowledgeable lawyers considered his job insignificant didn't bother him. After all, he reasoned, the low pay and limited authority to hear only motions for bond, preliminary hearings and misdemeanor cases would change in time. And, providing he didn't offend the powerful cabal of judges who controlled the federal court in Chicago, he'd be a district court judge soon.

Hamilton read through the complaint lying on the bench before him, then looked up at Gavin. "Each of the defendants has been charged in a complaint signed by agent Ben Cass with conspiracy to possess and distribute heroin in violation of 21 U. S. Code, Section 846. Have you received a copy of the complaint?"

"Yes, we have, Your Honor," Gavin replied respectfully.

Hamilton's eyes drifted along the row of defendants as he continued, "Each of you is entitled to an evidentiary hearing to determine the legality of your arrests. This means the government must show that the arresting agents had probable cause to believe each of you committed the crimes charged in the complaint. Do you all understand?"

"The defendants stood with heads bowed, eyes riveted on the floor. Gavin interceded, "The defendants understand the charges made against them."

"All right. Then that brings us to the matter of preliminary hearing. Are you ready to proceed?"

"We are ready for preliminary hearing," Gavin responded, radiating confidence. It was a bluff, but there was little risk involved in the deception, for he knew the prosecutor would request a continuance. It was the policy of the prosecutor's office to bury suspected drug dealers in jail for as long as possible after arrest by stalling bond hearings and other preliminary matters as long as the law would permit. An incarcerated drug law offender feeling helpless and forsaken by friends and business associates was much more likely to panic and cooperate than one who has bonded out shortly after arrest. It was obvious Joe Fruin and the prosecutor were intent on using the high bond tactic on Sal Veta and Claudio Cillas. If the mules cooperated they figured they could put Angel Herrera away for fifty years.

"Terry Mack for the government, Your Honor," the prosecuting attorney greeted the court in his amiable, outgoing manner. He had established a reputation as an outstanding trial attorney during the seven years he had served the U. S. attorney's office, and Gavin respected him greatly for his competence and professionalism. "The government is not ready for hearing, Judge," Mack continued. "We will need two weeks to get the case agents into court."

"Very well," the magistrate announced, "next Wednesday at one o'clock." While Mack would have preferred a longer continuance, Magistrate Hamilton, swayed more by the presence of the media reporters than the constitutional rights of the defendants, demonstrated his intent to provide the defendants with their right to a speedy hearing.

It was now time to raise the issue everyone in the courtroom eagerly anticipated. Magistrate Hamilton was growing edgy, tapping his pencil against the top of the bench, obviously agitated because he was going to have to do something contrary to his sense of fair play. Mack returned to counsel's table, acting as if the hearing had ended. The four defendants stood alongside Gavin, faces flushed, eyes burning with anxiety, hoping their lawyer would speak up for them then, before it was too late. Gavin felt his clients' desperation as he said, "At this time I request this court to set reasonable bonds for all the defendants."

The magistrate cleared his throat. "Mr. Gavin, give me the background on the defendants."

"One moment, Your Honor." Gavin huddled with his clients for a short whispered conversation, and then returned to the podium and began to search his mind for the best argument to use. He flashed a grim smile at Hamilton when he concluded no argument would work; his clients were going to get screwed. "Magistrate Hamilton," he began, "Angel Herrera is a naturalized citizen and resides legally in Chicago. He is married, the father of three children, and presently employed as manager of the Rio Loro Restaurant. He has never been convicted of a criminal offense." Gavin then pointed toward Ernie Kummer, Sal Veta and Claudio Cillas. "All three of these men have good records of employment and are good family men. Most important to this court, "he said passionately, "is the fact that none of the defendants has been previously arrested for a criminal offense." He sat down, certain that a long impassioned plea for reasonable bonds would be futile.

Prosecutor Mack sprang to his feet. "Your Honor, the government is asking the court to set a one million dollar cash bond for Angel Herrera, and five-hundred thousand dollar cash bonds for each of the other three defendants. Angel Herrera is the head of the infamous Herrera cartel in Chicago, and if he were allowed free on a low bond, he would flee to Mexico tomorrow. The other three pose such significant risks that high bonds should be set to insure their presence for trial."

Magistrate Hamilton's face flushed; his eyes narrowed. Anxious to do what he had to do, he said, "One million cash for Angel Herrera. Five-hundred thousand each for Sal Veta, Claudio Cillas and Ernie Kummer!"

Gavin stiffened but said nothing. As he turned away from the bench, his attention was drawn to the drug agents in the rear of the courtroom. They sprang to their feet, smiling broadly, exuding great satisfaction. Their arch-enemy, heroin king, Angel Herrera, was in jail to stay.

Angel took the high bond order well. Confident his lawyer would take care of his devils and have the bonds reduced before long, he held his head high and showed little emotion as the marshals led him mana-cled from the courtroom and steered him, with his three co-defendants trailing closely behind, toward the lockup. The procession of men had to pass between the grinning drug agents who, after leaving the court-room, lined the corridor walls to bask in their victory.

"Bastards," Gavin said, barely audible. "Like a bunch of vultures queued up waiting for a struggling animal to die."

"Hey, Matt, how soon will Angel have the one million cash raised?" Joe Fruin asked.

"I've got it right here in my valise, Mr. Fruin," Gavin replied smugly. "Angel will be out within the hour."

Fruin's face blanked. With any other defendant, he would have scoffed at the jest, but not this time, not with Angel Herrera's alleged financial prowess. "We'll see 'bout that bullshit," he said as Gavin brushed past him.

Marshal Kerski knew from years of experience that Matt Gavin never took an adverse ruling well and that he'd be pounding on his lockup door at any moment. He put the prisoners in the largest of the attorney interview rooms, then skipped to the lockup door, opened it quickly, and stood there projecting a self-satisfied look. His timing was perfect. Gavin didn't have to break stride to pass through the doorway. "Smile," he said as he pushed past the amused marshal. "I'll bet you a Polish sausage with beer Angel will be out on bond within three days."

"You're on, Counselor; I'll pick the restaurant."

Gavin entered the interview room to find his four clients silent and gloomy. They had been prepared for high bonds, but no one had expected, or could now comprehend, the bonds that were set.

"What the hell happened, Matt?" Angel asked.

"I think the bonds are the most unreasonably high bonds that I've ever seen set in this jurisdiction. The arresting agents must have pumped up the prosecutor and Magistrate Hamilton before the hearing."

Angel pressed his mouth against the voice box and rolled his eyes as he whispered, "Can you reach the magistrate? Whatever he needs to...."

Gavin pretended he didn't hear his client, who by instinct believed every judge wore a price tag on the palm of his hand. "I'll get the bonds reduced, but it will take some time. Your arrest is going to get major TV and newspaper coverage. No judge will go near a motion to reduce bond until the incendiary publicity settles down."

"But, Matt," Ernie Kummer drawled in his rural Tennessee accent, "I didn't do nothin' wrong. Ain't I being punished before I've been found guilty of somethin' I ain't done? Ain't that unconstitutional?"

Beginning to believe Ernie's claims of no criminal intent, Gavin said, "If you weren't part of the conspiracy to distribute heroin, and Angel was framed as he so emphatically claims, then your arrest, jailing and high bond is a tragic perversion of justice."

Angel still didn't get the message. "Do what you gotta do," he said, winking.

Gavin rose and walked out the door. Trying to convince Angel that la mordida didn't buy everyone and everything in the federal courthouse the way it did in Mexico would be a waste of his valuable time.

Chapter 14

▼

THE DEFENSE

The opening skirmish had gone decisively for the prosecution team of Terry Mack, Joe Fruin and DEA case agents. Matt Gavin didn't like the feeling of defeat, and he muttered, "Shit," as he entered his office and brushed past Tricia Berglund. "I feel like I got kicked in the gut."

Tricia noticed that certain look in Gavin's eyes as he sat down at his desk. A basic instinct had been aroused. "We're at war again, huh?"

Gavin hunched up over his desk as he said, "Call me a zealot or obsessive compulsive, but I've got to beat Terry Mack and his prosecution team. I'm going to do whatever I've got to do to win, so insulate yourself from the case if you want."

Tricia's face flushed. Her eyes sparkled as she said, "Matt, both my personal and business life with you have been bombastic, orgiastic. But I wouldn't want it any other way. Count me in."

"Miss Berglund, the Angel Herrera case is going to be different. I sense trouble ahead."

Tricia sat back in her chair, crossed her legs, and in a professional tone said, "Let's get down to business. What was Angel's bond set at?"

She let out a soft whistle when she heard Angel's bond was one million cash, then returned to the pointed questioning. "Well, what do we do now? Will we get his bond reduced?"

"Until a few months ago I'd say, yes. Now, it's maybe. In the not too distant future I'm afraid my answer would be, no."

Tricia's eyes blinked. "Well, I guess if he's guilty, he's going to—"

"Counselor!" he interrupted in a scolding tone. "Angel Herrera and Ernie Kummer are our clients. We presume them innocent and protect all their constitutional rights until they are found guilty by a jury of their peers."

"Whoops. Sorry," she said in an appeasing tone. "But sometimes it's hard to close your eyes to reality. After all, our clients were caught with a lot of heroin."

"Lesson number one for today, Tricia. In the criminal justice system, what appears to be isn't, and what is claimed not to exist, often does."

"Are you saying Angel and Ernie are not guilty?" Tricia asked.

Gavin smiled. "We deal only in the facts, not personal conjecture. For example, prosecutor Mack and agent Fruin swear that our clients were found in possession of twelve kilos of heroin. Our clients swear there was no dope in their motel room. They say the agents planted it."

"If what Angel says is correct, U. S. drug agents are bigger crooks than he—" Mildly embarrassed by the slip, Tricia covered her mouth with her hand.

Aware she didn't want to believe a flagrant flaw might exist in her country's criminal justice system, Gavin said, "Tricia, it will take a few more years of practice before you become cynical of politicians, judges, and cops and suspect every official act is self-serving. The combination of maturity and experience will bring the awareness that once a man achieves a position of power his every action is motivated by his desire to keep power. People and fundamental human rights become secondary."

Tricia sighed. "God. That's depressing. How can you stay so upbeat?"

"I understand man's nature and look at our criminal justice system as a game," Gavin replied.

"Game!" Tricia shot back. "Agents and prosecutors shouldn't play games with people's lives."

Gavin liked her reaction and decided to fan her smoldering indignation. "But what can we do about it? The planting of heroin boils down to Angel's word against agent Fruin's. Which one do you think will be believed? And both the prosecutor and the magistrate knew the law. A person charged with a crime is entitled to be free on bond until guilt is proved beyond a reasonable doubt at a trial. To incarcerate a person and cause him to suffer the humiliating aspects of jail life prior to guilt being established violates our constitution."

Tricia grew angry. "Are those tactics unique to Angel's case, or does that sort of thing go on all the time?"

"Most of the time our system works justly and fairly for those who get caught up in it," Gavin replied. " But unfortunately for many, dirty tricks have become common practice. The drug world phenomenon has been responsible for creating exigent circumstances wherein drug agents and prosecutors rationalize dirty tricks are necessary. There was always a small amount of corrupt conduct by agents, but it has exploded in recent years."

"Well," Tricia said, "I'm not going to let any drug agent get away with breaking the law under the guise of enforcing the law."

Gavin grinned proudly. "Defense attorneys like us are given a significant responsibility. Insidious or corrupt conduct by agents, prosecutors, or judges has to be exposed in a courtroom during a public hearing. And, if we should fail to do our job, you can bet constitutional rights will systematically fade into history."

Tricia tried to be helpful. "Maybe we should ask the press and TV and congressmen for help?"

"Wrong, Tricia, we're all alone. No one will help when an infamous drug dealer is getting stuck in the ass by the System. No one dare buck strong public opinion."

Tricia's face blanked. She had always been a staunch supporter of the System, always had faith in its integrity. She, like most Americans, was disposed to believe judges were good and honest, and prosecutors were sincere in their representation of all the people, a duty which included defendants. Until recently, she had the tendency to believe the one charged with a crime was the one who was wrong and guilty until proven innocent. "How do you know who to trust in this business?" she said.

"You'll discover that secret over time, Tricia. For now, you'll have to come to grips with the fact all men are corruptible, there being a thin line between those who enforce the law and those who break it."

She cleared her throat and in a determined voice said, "Matt, I plan on doing all I can to find out just who's telling the truth, who are the Good Guys and who are the Bad Guys."

"Whoa, wait a minute, Miss. Did I say you were assigned to this case?"

"No," Tricia said. " I did. And if you try to keep me out of it, there'll be no more fooling around like last night."

Gavin rocked slowly back in his chair and said slyly, "That sounds like a clear-cut case of extortion to me. I think I'll call the cops."

The following morning Gavin began the walk to his office at seven o'clock. Rounding the corner at Washington and LaSalle streets, beginning the final two block walk to his office building, he saw the morning editions of the "Tribune" and "Sun Times." The newspapers were prominently displayed on the front of his favorite newsstand. "Major Drug Bust," the headlines screamed to passersby.

"Your picture's on da front page, Mr. Gavin," the stand vendor said as he handed off the newspapers to Gavin who passed by in full stride. "And I saw ya on TV last night," he called out after him in a raspy voice.

Angel's arrest and bond hearing had been the major news story on TV. It bothered Gavin now that he had been so prominently pictured on the screen and misquoted from brief interviews with reporters. Normally, criminal defense attorneys would do or pay anything for that type of exposure. It was good for business and insatiable egos. However, times were changing. Drug dealers were considered sleaze, in a class with child molesters, by a quickly increasing number of people. And rumors emanating from the Justice Department in Washington portended troubled times ahead. Orders were reportedly going out to regional United States attorneys to open grand jury investigations of high profile lawyers who represented major drug dealers. Next case, he promised himself, I'll hide from all the reporters.

His thoughts were suddenly interrupted when he got off his office building elevator on the tenth floor and saw light streaming from under the large, oak doors of his suite. To his surprise, the doors were unlocked. "Darn," he mumbled, suspecting he'd been beaten at his own game.

"It's about time, boss," Tricia greeted him. "I've been waiting an hour for you." She was seated behind Gavin's desk, a broad smile spread across her face, and steaming cup of coffee in her hand.

"Unbelievable," Gavin said. "I bet you stayed up all night so you could be the first here this morning."

"When there's important work to be done, I'm always the first here," Tricia said.

Gavin agreed silently. She had become a competent and dedicated professional. And because she was so important to him, he was going to have to give her some bad news. He walked over to her and nudged her with his hip. "Up," he said.

"Okay, boss," she said as she vacated the desk chair. "The helm is all yours."

Gavin sat down, and quickly setting the business tone which would prevail for many months, said, "This is the first conference in the matter of the United States versus Angel Herrera, et al. I will, of course, represent Angel and be lead counsel. Tricia, you'll be in charge of research and preparation of witnesses."

Tricia nodded and smiled weakly. She had hoped to represent either Sal or Claudio, even though she knew she didn't have the required experience.

Seeing her disappointment, Gavin tried to explain. "We'll have to get three other attorneys from law firms not connected with us to represent Ernie, Sal and Claudio. There is too big a risk a conflict of interest would develop during the trial. If that happened we'd catch a lot of flak from the trial judge. I think we'd be wise to avoid the problem." He paused for a moment; his emotions were prevailing over a logical business mind. "Besides," he continued, "your expertise is needed in the Stanson embezzlement case."

Tricia's eyes brightened. It was her type of case. Russ Stanson, well-known multimillionaire and president of Standard Bank, had been charged with embezzling ten million in bank funds for construction of a hotel-casino in Las Vegas. "What will the defense be?" she asked.

"Extortion and duress," Gavin replied. Some Mafia wise guys got to him and squeezed him as only they can."

"Well," Tricia said, "maybe we can work out a good deal with the U. S. attorney's office in return for Stanson's cooperation."

Gavin cleared his throat and shifted in his seat. Tricia didn't understand that she'd be signing Stanson's death warrant if she even mentioned cooperation. "Counselor," he said, "this firm will represent Russ Stanson provided he stands trial and presents a viable and vigorous defense. Any signs of cooperation, we withdraw."

Tricia's face blanked. Her introduction to the criminal defense business in Chicago was coming in shock waves. "Okay, Matt," she replied weakly.

Gavin pushed the Angel Herrera case file to Tricia and then watched her as she sifted through the legal documents within. After several minutes he said, "As you know, this case is fraught with problems. For beginners, which version of the arrest should we believe? Every large drug dealer I've ever represented swore he was innocent, swore that the arresting agents fabricated the story. I generally don't put one ounce of credence in the denials, yet for some strange reason, I believe Angel and Ernie. Experience with the Durango Connection's way of doing business tells me Sal and Claudio wouldn't take the heroin from where it was secreted in the trunk and bring it into the motel room. They were mules. Their only job was to deliver the heroin."

"That's right," Tricia said, anticipating Gavin's conclusion. "Angel didn't have to see one package of the heroin. He knew exactly what the load consisted of, and he was going to take all the heroin from the spare tire that night."

Gavin said incisively, "Assume there was no heroin in the motel room when the agents entered, and assume further that the agents had no probable cause to search the car. The necessary conclusion is that Angel and the others would have to be let go. No arrests. I'm afraid the scene was ripe for a plant."

"But Joe Fruin!" Tricia protested, "It's hard to believe he'd plant heroin on anyone. His record with the DEA is unblemished."

Forcing a stern look, Gavin said, "I want you to get out of here and get all the facts relevant to this case. I'll interview Terry Mack and Joe Fruin; you take the rest of the agents and witnesses."

Tricia's large, emotion-filled eyes burned into Gavin as he busied himself reading legal documents. A good case of female possessiveness set in, causing her to wonder if she'd be able to keep their personal life from interfering with business, if Gavin's feelings would change, if she'd lose him. His tendency to be a workaholic who became totally absorbed in a trial had bothered her so much two weeks before that she had blurted out, "Mr. Gavin, you can be downright obsessed at times." Things had been so different, so easy, her first months on the job. She had been single-purposed, career-minded, intent on not letting a close personal relationship develop. A soft moan escaped as she resigned herself to the fact that a relationship with Gavin was ordained and inescapable and that she'd have to learn to live with the little hurts.

Sensing inner struggle, Gavin looked up and met Tricia's intense gaze. "Everything okay, hon?"

She rose gracefully from the sofa, smiling confidently. "Yes, once again your eyes have answered my questions. And with that problem solved, there's something I'd like to say. I know that most people want to trust and believe in public officials as much as I do. Maybe I'm naïve. But you know, Matt, just maybe the government is right, and Angel and his crew are bullshitting us."

"The only way to find out is to go to work," he taunted.

*   *   *   *

Three days after Matt Gavin's mandate to get all facts relevant to the Angel Herrera case, Tricia appeared in the office doorway holding a bulging legal file under each arm. She placed the files containing the fruits of her hard work on top of Gavin's desk, backed up to the sofa and flopped down, kicking off her high-heeled shoes in the process. "I need a drink."

Gavin reached into the large drawer of his desk and retrieved a bottle of Jamison's Irish Whiskey and two glasses. "Pour a little touch for us," he said.

Tricia reached for the bottle. "My pleasure."

A scowl formed on Gavin's face as he skimmed through the statements Tricia had taken from four of Joe Fruin's task force agents. When he finished, he removed his glasses, let them drop to the desk, and imitating an Irish brogue said, "Bejayus! It looks like an informer did Angel in. What did you find out 'bout da dirty informer', as me dear auld mudder youse to say."

Tricia was eager to show her work product. She referred to her notes and then summarized, "Juan Martinez was arrested by Joe Fruin's task force on May 13 for possession of one pound of heroin. The agents were armed with a search warrant when they cracked Martinez' house, and the search and arrest appear to be legal. After he was in jail for a week, the agents made him a deal he couldn't refuse—go to jail for ten years or cooperate and get a probated sentence. After a few more days of confinement, the snitch threw out his trump card. He gave valuable information concerning Angel Herrera. Upon hearing Angel's name, Joe Fruin swore to do Martinez' time for him if a judge wouldn't go along with the deal, and promised five-thousand dollars cash, allegedly for expenses, and government protection for one year. With the unsavory deal sealed, Martinez told Fruin that Angel agreed to sell 12 kilos of heroin to a Puerto Rican from Miami and make delivery within two weeks. Angel reportedly was to travel to Mexico, and when he returned, the deal was to go down in a motel near Joliet."

"Nice piece of investigative work," Gavin told Tricia. "Did you find any witnesses that will controvert Joe Fruin's story?"

Tricia shook her head, then offered an opinion. "There can be no doubt that a large amount of heroin was illegally seized from our clients. We have to file a motion to suppress and attack the search of the room and seizure of the heroin. If we are going to win this case, we'll have to do it with pre-trial motions."

Gavin nodded in apparent agreement, but he seemed to be hiding something. "I've got a strange feeling," Tricia said. "Do you know something I don't, and maybe should?"

Feeling honor-bound not to reveal a conversation he'd had the prior evening with a good friend, one who was a DEA agent and took part in Angel's arrest at the motel, Gavin replied, "Yeah, but not now."

Tricia flashed a wily smile as she said, "Why do I feel you know what really went down at the Safe Harbor Motel?"

Gavin breathed deeply. "Because I do. But I won't use what I know until the appropriate occasion."

Chapter 15

▼

MEXICANA HILTON

The sleek, triangular shaped building with concrete walls and distinctively slit windows was dubbed the Mexicana Hilton by the destitute Latino immigrants who were being detained for deportation to Mexico and other Latin American countries. Politicians and high-ranking bureaucrats called it the Metropolitan Correction Center. However, most people involved in the criminal justice system referred to it as the MCC. The twenty-six story building was located in downtown Chicago, a short distance from the federal courthouse and from the internationally famous Board of Trade and State Street's bustling department stores. It was a strange place for a high security federal jail.

Angel and Ernie were housed on the thirteenth floor of the MCC along with forty other pre-trial detainees who had not been able to make bail. Angel chose to do his time like a hermit, hiding away in his cell, talking to no one except Ernie. He would have liked to have had his compadres, Sal Veta and Claudio Cillas, near him, but they were kept on the fifteenth floor, purposely separated from their boss. Ernie liked to play cards with the other inmates, and when he wasn't "making some money playing spades or gin," as he bragged, he pulled a chair up close to one of the TVs which blared fourteen hours a day, and vegetated. Angel was thankful Ernie had some diversions. It eased the feeling of guilt he felt for his friend's incarceration.

Angel was surprised to discover after a few days as a guest of the government that for a large number of prisoners life in jail was considerably better than what it had been on the outside. All essentials were provided free of charge. Ernie had said it best after an especially good Sunday meal, "This joint ain't bad. Ya get three hots, a cot and a TV, just like ya gets in a resort."

Angel stared incredulously at Ernie, "Ain't bad?" "This is the most disgusting place I've ever been in," he said.

"Angel, if you think this joint is bad, you ought to see one of our county jails in Tennessee. Now, that's disgusting."

Angel conceded silently that life at the MCC wasn't hard to endure from a physical sense. What made things bad was the psychological torture. Being kept in a cage and told when to eat, sleep and crap was demeaning. And the sleazy prisoners he was forced to live with, mostly heavy drug users, made his skin crawl. He considered them society's subhuman rejects. Still worse was the separation from his wife, family and friends. And then there was Jenni. That caused a mental and emotional anguish he had never experienced before.

As the days and nights passed, Angel spent more and more time gazing out through the narrow slit that served as a cell window. Although he tried to concentrate on the throngs of passersby thirteen floors below, his thoughts would invariably drift to the motel and to his arrest. In the few moments it had taken Joe Fruin and his agents to rush inside the motel room and place him under arrest, he had fallen from the sweet life to the pits. He wanted to kick himself for making the mistake of going to the Safe Harbor Motel himself rather than sending a mule.

The spark had been there for several days, but Ernie threw high octane gas onto it one evening when he walked into Angel's cell and flopped down on the bed. "How," he drawled, " did that fuckin' cop Fruin know you were going to be at the Safe Harbor Motel? Who told him about Sal and Claudio and the shit in the car? Who's the snitch?"

An inferno of hate roared through Angel's body as he became consumed with the idea that an informer was responsible for destroying his life. He couldn't figure out exactly who it was, but he began making plans for that man's future. "I'll find out no matter what I gotta do," he hissed.

*   *   *   *

It was 9:30 Wednesday morning when Angel's floor officer notified him his attorney was on his way up from the lobby. After the required, and particularly repugnant, strip search by a security officer who seemed to enjoy looking at naked men, Angel was escorted to an attorney interview room on his tier. There he saw his only hope for freedom sitting at a table. A wide grin spread across his face, and his eyes reflected gratitude as he said, "I thought you forgot all about me."

"Naw, couldn't do that," Gavin assured him. "Besides, the ten days in jail has done your wife a lot of good. She told me yesterday that this was the first time she knew what you were doing when you weren't home."

"Not funny," Angel said as he sat down at the table across from Gavin. His eyes darted around the stark, unfurnished room, then focused on the third chair at the table.

Gavin guessed what was on his client's mind and said, "I tried to have Ernie brought in for this conference but was told by a gung-ho young lieutenant that it was impossible because he's in the hole. I figured I'd wait and find out from you what happened to him."

Angel shook his head as he said, "The dumb shit got in a fight yesterday with another inmate over the TV. He was watching his favorite country-western videos when a guy walked up and switched the channel to some soap opera. After a few heated words, Ernie punched the guy out."

Gavin laughed as he said, "Can't mess with a hillbilly when a good ol' tear-jerking tune is playing." He pictured Ernie in the hole, disciplinary segregation, as it was formally called.

"Can you visit Ernie today?" Angel asked.

"No." Gavin replied without explanation. He didn't want to tell Angel that the only time he visited a client in the hole was when an absolute emergency required it. He detested the entire concept of the hole: squalid eight by ten foot cells, the cold iron slabs and dingy mattresses prisoners were forced to sleep on, the way prisoners were treated by the archetypal jailers who controlled sado-masochistic jails. Whenever he did interview a client there, he always felt like he was visiting a monkey in a zoo rather than a fellow human being.

Angel sat back in his chair, expecting the worst. "Well, Matt, I know you're here for some reason. Give it to me straight. Will you be able to get me out on bond?"

"I've got some good news and some bad news. Your case has been assigned to Judge Sam Matyan, about the best man you could draw for this type of case. Tricia is in his courtroom now trying to have your motion to reduce bond set for this afternoon."

In spite of the circumstances, Angel was alert. "Why did you say Judge Matyan's courtroom?" he asked, thinking he would be brought back in front of Magistrate Hamilton.

"That's the bad news. Terry Mack telephoned early this morning and told me that an indictment was returned yesterday."

"How can that be? What was I indicted for?" Angel pressed plaintively.

Gavin explained, "It may sound like a lot of legal mumble-jumble, but after your arrest the U. S. Attorney's office had two choices. One, let the case go to a preliminary hearing before Magistrate Hamilton for a probable cause determination, or two, seek an immediate indictment from the grand jury. At a preliminary hearing the prosecutor would be required to show a reasonable cause for your arrest by putting Fruin or another agent on the stand to testify to the facts of the arrest. The witness, who'd be subject to cross-exam by me, would have to testify that heroin was found in the motel room. If no heroin was found in the room, the magistrate would have to let you go free."

Angel said, "I assume the second choice was indictment. But how can the prosecutor get an indictment without someone saying I had the shit in my possession?"

Gavin grunted. "One of the most potentially dangerous tools in the hands of a corrupt or overly ambitious prosecutor's office is the power to control a grand jury. The preconditioned, politically and legally naive jurors feel it is their duty to return an indictment against anyone a prosecutor charges with a crime. As a matter of fact, most indictments returned are based on hearsay evidence, with no minimum standard of proof required."

"What do you mean, hearsay?" Angel shot back.

"It means the prosecutor's office could get around a perjury issue by having one of the case agents, one other than Fruin, testify before the grand jury that he was told heroin was found in the motel room."

"Matt, who the hell is framing me—Fruin and his DEA agents, the prosecutor's office, or both?"

Gavin replied in a wry tone, "The first thing you must realize is America is not an Alice in Wonderland society. You'll never find a judge courageous enough to rule that a plant of drugs by agents or a meritless indictment by a prosecutor is anything more than excusable over-zealousness. In a drug case like yours, we'll have to deal with what the prosecutor says the facts are and not with what actually happened."

Angel's shoulders and head slumped. "I never would have dreamed," he groaned, "I'd have to worry about getting fucked by the Good Guys."

"Angel, you once questioned, who are the Good Guys? I have a lot of confidence in prosecutor Mack's integrity. He wouldn't go along with the frame up of a man he thought was innocent. But he's no one's fool. He knows the heroin was yours and that Sal and Claudio worked for you."

"So what!" Angel replied belligerently. "No one can testify I ever touched that heroin or ever went near Sal's car. So what in the hell can they charge me with then?"

"Conspiracy," Gavin said.

Angel's face became ashen. While his arrest and incarceration had been shocking, they were situations he could take in stride and remain hopeful. But when he heard that he could be charged, contrary to his belief, with a crime even though he never physically possessed the heroin, he became visibly unnerved. "Why, even in Mexico," he said indignantly, "I couldn't be charged unless I was caught with the shit."

"That's right. Mexico doesn't have conspiracy laws. There, a person can be charged only with a wrongful overt act. But in the United States a person can be charged under the conspiracy laws for a purely subjective plan, a scheme to commit a crime. The forbidden act need never be committed, nor need the offender come close to committing the crime."

"You mean all I have to do is talk about selling drugs with a compadre and it's a crime?"

"Basically, that's right," Gavin said. " People are now being punished for the lust they feel in their hearts, so to speak."

Angel understood the message conveyed in the parody and nodded. "It looks like President Carter started something, huh? And, Abogado Del Diablo, if I'm to be punished for lust in my heart, then I'm guilty and deserve one hundred years in jail!"

Gavin caught the smirk on Angel's face and stifled a laugh. In reality it wasn't humorous, he thought, not when the new breed of prosecutors appeared to be generic, the men non-masculine and the women non-feminine. He visualized some of the neo-prosecutors indicting Angel for lustful conduct, for a conspiracy to carry out sexual escapades with Jenni. "If you're lucky enough to get out of this mess," he said. "I advise you to live the life of a trappist monk for a long while."

Angel was about to respond when the sound of keys rattling against the door-lock caused him to stiffen. An instant later Tricia burst through the door. Radiating pride, she said, "I have good news, gentlemen. I have skillfully talked Judge Matyan into hearing the motions to reduce bond at one o'clock today. He agreed with me, of course, that the motions were emergency matters and should be heard without the required forty-eight hour notice to the U. S. Attorney. And," she emphasized, "this was in spite of Terry Mack's vociferous protestations."

Angel's mouth dropped and his eyes widened. He understood that Tricia had accomplished something, and that something had been done on his behalf. But Tricia's energy and sincerity shocked him, and he groped for the right thing to say. "Ahhh...will I have to testify?" he asked.

Tricia didn't give Gavin a chance to reply. "You may be required to testify to your personal background under oath, and what you say and how you say it will be very important. If the hearing goes off well, your bond will be reduced."

"How much do you think I'll need?" Angel said, obviously encouraged. "And what about Ernie?"

"I would guess fifty to sixty thousand dollars for you and five to ten thousand for Ernie. Start making your calls right now so that the money will be available shortly after the bond is set. I want to get you out as quickly as I can." Gavin reached across the table and put his hand on Angel's arm. "With a little luck, we'll have you out of here this afternoon."

"What about Sal and Claudio?" Angel asked, with a look of urgency.

"Tomorrow. I don't want to frighten or confuse the judge. If we isolate on you, we stand a good chance. Sal and Claudio both live in Texas and have other problems that will cause the judge alarm. If he's faced with lowering the bonds of three risky defendants, he'll probably take the easy way out and let the bonds remain where they are. Let's worry about you today, and Sal and Claudio tomorrow."

Angel agreed with the strategy. It was an iron rule of the Herrera cartel: every soldier was subject to sacrifice for Angel's protection. But once free on bond it would be Angel's turn to show loyalty. He'd have to raise the cash necessary for Sal and Claudio's bond, no matter what the amount. He leaned up over the table and whispered, "When I'm out on bond I want to help you prepare my defense. But first I have to know who informed on me; who set me up."

Gavin understood what Angel really meant, and he was about to tactfully postpone giving the information he'd eventually have to give when Tricia said, "Our investigation revealed a guy by the name of Juan Martinez gave the DEA information concerning a sale of heroin you were to make to a dealer from Miami. He told the agents the deal would go down in a motel near Joliet."

Gavin saw the pupils in Angel's eyes turn the color of an erupting volcano and then Tricia's face pale as she realized what she had so innocently done. As he rose to leave, Gavin found himself hoping the prosecutor's office had a fool-proof witness protection program.

Chapter 16

▼

SENTENCED TO MEXICO

It was shortly after one o'clock when two marshals escorted Angel and Ernie into the holding cell adjoining Judge Matyan's courtroom. Marshal Kerski took charge of the prisoners, removed their handcuffs, then secured them in the iron-barred cell. Opening the door into the courtroom, he spied Matt Gavin seated at defendant's table. He nodded, in typical fashion, tacitly offering Gavin a chance to conference with his clients.

"Thanks, Mr. Marshal," Gavin said, "I don't think this courthouse could run without you."

Kerski squeezed up his face. "Yeah, yeah, more lawyer bullshit."

Gavin was still laughing when he reached the iron bars. Angel took it as a good omen and said, "It looks like maybe you've got a couple aces up your sleeve."

"Just the Constitution, Angel. That's all we're going to need."

"Thought maybe you put Fruin in a trick bag, made the prick confess to what he did," Angel said, showing signs of pent up frustration.

"Don't even think about it," Gavin said. "Fruin's proud and tough. He'll never crack."

That fierce look, the one predicated on blood revenge, spread over Angel's face. "Okay, Matt. For now we'll do things the proper way, so tell us what we should do."

"Think about this bond hearing, Gavin counseled. " When you're before the judge, I want you guys to sit up straight, look smart and respectful. And Angel, if he asks you about your past, remember the things Tricia and I told you about your citizenship, work history, and no criminal record. Ernie, I think the fact you're a good ol' hillbilly with no criminal background will be enough. The judge should reduce your bond to a reasonable amount. I'll…."

The door to the lockup swung open and Marshal Kerski's large body appeared. "The judge is ready, Matt."

Judge Matyan had already mounted the bench and was seated by the time the procession of Gavin, Angel and Ernie reached the podium. The judge appeared to be in a hurry, yet in a good mood. He said, "All right, Mr. Gavin, what's your motion?"

Mr. Herrera and Mr. Kummer are asking this court to review and reduce bonds which have been set by Magistrate Hamilton."

"All right, let's take Mr. Herrera first," the judge said. What do you have to say, Mr. Prosecutor?"

Mack had a great deal to say, and when he finished he was confident he had said enough to paint Angel Herrera as one of the most dangerous criminals in American society, a man that should not be allowed free on the streets. He began by going into the facts of the case, stressing the amount of heroin that Angel allegedly possessed when arrested, and finished with a long tirade on Angel Herrera's alleged control over the heroin industry in the United States. "Judge Matyan," he said dramatically, "if Angel Herrera is allowed free on bond, you will never see or hear from him again. He'll flee to Mexico."

"What do you have to say, Mr. Gavin?" the judge broke in, satisfied he fully understood the prosecutor's position.

"Your Honor," Gavin argued, "integrity and decency have been traditionally the hallmark of the U. S. Attorney's Office here in Chicago. Recently, however, prosecutors have discarded those noble standards when a prosecution involves a drug dealer. Then anything goes."

"Objection!" Mack screamed. "I resent that spurious accusation."

"Proceed, counsel," the judge ruled.

Gavin nodded to Mack, then continued, "As this court well knows, federal law unequivocally provides that a person arrested for a non-capital offense shall be admitted to bail. The Eighth Amendment to the United States Constitution has provided a right to a defendant to be free until convicted. This provides the defendant with the ability to be unhampered during preparation of a defense. Moreover, it serves to prevent infliction of punishment prior to a conviction. Judge, unless this right to bail before trial is preserved, the presumption of innocence, secured only after centuries of struggle, would lose its meaning. In the case of Angel Herrera, I cannot ask this Court to set a low bond. I would ask that a reasonable one be set. The bond should be such that it will give adequate assurance the defendant will stand trial and submit to sentence if found guilty. If bail is not set in an amount that can be reasonably calculated to fulfill this principle, then it is excessive under the Eighth Amendment."

"I agree, Mr. Gavin," the judge interrupted, "a person that is merely charged with a criminal offense is presumed innocent and, therefore, should not suffer the punishment of incarceration, unless," he emphasized, "that person poses a risk of flight or a danger to society."

"Gavin said, "That's correct, Judge, and there is absolutely no reason why Angel Herrera should flee the jurisdiction of this court. The facts brought out so far indicate that he has a meritorious defense and will be found not guilty. Additionally, Mr. Herrera resides here legally in the United States and has an excellent work record. He is married and has three children. More importantly, he has never been arrested or convicted of any criminal offense other than a minor traffic violation."

"What is Mr. Herrera's bond at present, Mr. Gavin?" the judge inquired.

"One million dollars, cash. Bond was set by Magistrate Hamilton immediately after the arrest."

"All right. In the matter of Angel Herrera," the judge ruled, "the bond will be reduced to five hundred thousand dollars, secured."

Gavin was elated. His client would have to post only ten percent of the five hundred thousand to walk free, a sum that could easily be gotten together within a few hours. He glanced at the prosecutor and saw his face redden and heard a nervous effort to swallow.

"Judge," Mack wailed, "Angel Herrera will have that bond posted within an hour and be out on the streets. He will be in Mexico by tomorrow."

"Well then, Mr. Mack, I guess the sentence order will read, sentenced to Mexico." Becoming stern, the judge said, "Are you trying to tell me this country would not be better off without the likes of Mr. Herrera? We would have fifty thousand dollars in the U. S. Treasury and a good chance of collecting four hundred and fifty thousand from various assets Mr. Herrera has amassed. Taxpayers would then not be forced to support him while in prison."

Prosecutor Mack's mouth gaped. "But judge—"

Not wanting to discuss the matter any further, the judge queried, "Now what about Mr. Kummer? His motion alleges he is a citizen of the United States, has resided in the Chicago area all of his life, and is gainfully employed. He has no criminal record. Is there any reason, Mr. Mack, why he should not be allowed out on a ten thousand dollar bond?"

For the record, Mack was required to object to a bond reduction. Personally, he didn't care, and it showed in his voice when he replied, "The government requests that the bond be substantial."

"Then it will be ten thousand dollars, secured, for Mr. Kummer."

Gavin huddled with Angel and Ernie at the side of the podium, and in a whispered voice said, "Okay, Angel, get the money together, and I'll have you two released this afternoon."

"Wait a minute, Matt," Angel said. "What does all that stuff mean? How much money do I need?"

"Have your wife bring fifty-one thousand dollars to my office, and we'll have you out of the slammer today."

"How can I call her, get hold of her?" Angel asked.

Gavin's eyes focused on Marshal Kerski as he said, "I'll ask the marshal to let you make a call from his office, and I'll phone Celia as soon as I leave here."

The news of Angel's bond reduction spread quickly. As Gavin walked out through the courtroom door, Joe Fruin and several other agents rushed down the hall, nearly knocking into him. Thinking Judge Matyan would order the bonds to stand, they hadn't bothered to appear for the hearing. Hostile now, Fruin was looking for Terry Mack to demand an explanation. His face was shrouded in disbelief, and his frustration was obvious as he said, "That pinko liberal judge lowered it, huh? I'll bet Angel will swim the river before the next court date. But if he does," he growled, "I'll swim right after that son-of-a-bitch!"

Considering the mood Fruin was in, Gavin decided to smile, lower his eyes and pass through the half-circle of agents without a word. Nothing could be said anyway. It was a good bet Angel would fugitate if conviction seemed imminent. Everyone thought it, even Judge Matyan, when he made the stultifying comment—sentenced to Mexico.

Before stepping onto the elevator, Gavin glanced over his shoulder and saw Fruin pressing Mack against the wall, face flushed, demanding that Angel Herrera be dragged back before the judge for another bond hearing. He had seen that same attack posture during the last argument he had gotten into with the hot tempered drug cop. He'd never forget that night at Capo's, a happy-hour bar, located across the street from the courthouse.

"What's a high-priced lawyer like you doing in a joint like this?" Fruin had said as Gavin slid onto a bar stool next to him.

Gavin nodded greetings. "I thought I'd find you here fueling up for your commute home. I'd like to buy you a drink."

Many beers later, after Gavin's business had been disposed of, the same old argument began. "Ya know," Fruin said, "I'm getting tired of making cases on drug dealers, then have them skip to Mexico as soon as you get them released on bond."

"Who you talking about now?" Gavin asked.

"Jesse Salgado. He fugitated about three months ago, just before his trial."

"Shit," Gavin said, "Jesse was just a dumb kid, a mule who had a very minor role in a minor drug conspiracy. I think it worked out best for everybody."

"No, it didn't," Fruin snapped. "If I had a chance to squeeze him, he would have spit up on his bosses. Then it would have been a major drug case."

"I think justice was served," Gavin argued. "Just think of all the tax-payer's money that was saved. No trial. No housing and feeding Jesse's wife and kids while he sits in jail for ten years. And he'll never come back into the States. He's too frightened."

Fruin's eyes blazed as he said, "I don't care if Jesse was a fucking seven-teen year old nun. He drove a kilo of shit from Mexico. He belongs in jail."

"Joe, you're a cold-blooded son-of-a-bitch. Cops like you have jails across the country jammed with decent young men like Jesse, men who never hurt anyone in their lives. What good does it do? None. And the sentences are more evil than the crime."

Fruin struggled to hold his voice down as he replied, "For a guy who used to be a man, you sure as hell turned into a pinko liberal too. I remember when you were with the State's Attorney's Office. You and I prosecuted the bad guys together. That was before you became a pinko."

Gavin bit his lower lip. He felt like smashing Fruin in the mouth. "Don't call me a pinko again," he said, "or we're going outside."

Fruin was suddenly ornery drunk. "Put your arm up on the bar," he said. "Let's have a little arm wrestle."

Gavin thought of leaving, quickly. Several bar patrons were staring at them, straining to hear what the argument was about. And the bar owner looked like he wanted to check out his dram shop insurance coverage. Gavin breathed deeply as he said, "I'll try one more time with you, Joe. The drug war has made all you cops myopic sadists. Don't you ever think of the spillover injury a prison sentence causes? Just think of your wife and little Joey and the agony they'd suffer if you were sent to the slammer for ten years. They'd be thrown out of the home you worked fifteen years for. All your savings would be exhausted, and they'd have to go on public aid or welfare to survive. Their lives would be destroyed."

Fruin sat hunched over the bar, staring at his glass of beer. "I don't wanna hear that shit," he growled. "If the opportunity came along for me to do drugs, I wouldn't because I wouldn't want to hurt Maria and Joey. Fucking drug-heads don't care who they hurt until they get caught. Then they start sniveling. If they really cared a good shit about anyone but themselves, they wouldn't do drugs."

"Look, Joe, I'm not arguing it's right to do drugs or that the laws against drug use and dealing are wrong. It's the excessive sentences I think are wrong. They're way out of line most of the time."

Fruin laughed derisively. "Fuck em," he growled. If they can't do the time, they shouldn't do the crime."

Gavin stripped off his suit coat as he moved toward a table. "Okay, Joe, let's get it on."

Fruin rolled up his shirt sleeve and sat down across the table from Gavin. As the men locked grips, the bartender reached for the phone. It was time to call the cops.

A year had passed since the brawl at Capo's Bar, and Fruin was still a fanatic nut case. Gavin let a soft whistle escape as the elevator door closed and shielded him from the frustrated drug cop who just couldn't understand how Judge Matyan could let Angel out of jail on a fifty-thousand dollar bond. He didn't need any more personal combat with Fruin. That night at Capo's had been enough. The arm wrestling match had left him with muscles so sore he couldn't hold a pen to write for three days. And he had been thoroughly embarrassed when the two young cops who broke up the wrestling match that ensued by pulling him and Fruin off the floor learned he was a well-respected lawyer and the other brawler a high-ranking DEA agent. Fortunately, the Chicago way of doing things had prevailed. After discreet handshakes the cops had left Capo's with smiles on their faces, and the bartender had gotten amnesia shortly after getting a $50 tip for his troubles.

Gavin half-ran, half-walked the two blocks to his office, where he planned on hiding out until Angel was bailed out of the MCC. He figured it highly unlikely that Mack and Fruin could persuade Judge Matyan to change his mind about Angel's bond order, but he was certain they were in the judge's chambers trying to do just that. Sam Matyan had never allowed a prosecutor's political or personal reasoning to influence him, yet he had cause to worry. The number of federal judges who protected the constitutional rights of drug dealers was growing small. If Angel had been charged with a bank robbery or mail fraud or a tax case, the majority of judges would have staunchly defended his constitutional right to a reasonable bond, but when a drug dealer stood before those same judges, the rules of the game changed. Pressure generated by the general public, the news media and hypocritical politicians who sought to curry favor with voters was too much to buck. It was much less controversial for judges to side with prosecutors and harshly enforce the law than provide a drug dealer with due process and equal protection under the law. Gavin wondered if he were sitting as a federal judge would his sense of fairness and justice change with the political winds? Would he manipulate the law just so he could remain within his political and cultural power base? The view is always different depending on where you stand on the mountain, he reminded himself, as he walked into his private office and closed the door behind him.

Celia Herrera posted fifty thousand dollars bail money for Angel and the one thousand for Ernie within an hour after the bond reduction orders were entered. She then posted herself in the lobby of the MCC, resigned to wait as long as necessary for her husband. While it seemed like an eternity, it took less than an hour for the office that processed inmate arrivals and departures to order Angel's and Ernie's release. Celia was voraciously attacking her fourth fingernail when she saw her husband, with Ernie trailing behind, emerge from the elevator and walk unchallenged past the security desk. Not wanting to take the chance that an agent or prosecutor would change the judge's mind about Angel, she took him by the hand and hurried him out the lobby door to her car which was parked at the curb. It was only when she was settled in the back seat and the car moving toward her home that she allowed the tears she had forced back for a week to cascade down her cheeks.

Angel drove until the slimy feeling that had permeated his body every minute he had been in custody at the MCC dissipated. Then he pulled alongside a public telephone booth and performed an obligation. He dialed, and when he heard the deep, modulated voice, he said, "Hey, Abogado, you did it again, huh?"

Gavin had been expecting the call. The rakish voice sending the clear-cut message caused him to smile. "Angel, you got a real break today."

Angel chuckled, "Yeah, sure." He was convinced his release had been gained by a payoff or by some other unsavory deal, as it would have been done had he been arrested in Mexico. He instinctively believed "la mordida" was the only way good things ever came from a politician or judge.

While his client's typically Mexican attitude annoyed him, Gavin was not about to try to change a belief which would have been realistic in many courthouses the world over. Avoiding the issue, he said, "I have a copy of your indictment here. You've been charged with conspiracy and possession of all twelve kilos of heroin."

"Well, Abogado, I guess Fruin went and did it."

"It appears that way. It's up to a jury of your peers now. Maybe they'll cut through the bullshit, give you the benefit of the doubt and set you free."

"I'm not too hopeful of that happening," Angel said.

*   *   *   *

The System's wheels continued to grind and on the following Wednesday, Angel and his three co-defendants were ordered to appear for arraignment. Gavin found his clients anxiously awaiting him outside Judge Matyan's courtroom. He was surprised to see Ernie Kummer's mood had changed from beaten and submissive to one of pitiable anger. "What the fuck they goin' to do to us now?" he said.

Gavin summoned up a professional tone and replied, "The next step in what must seem to you to be Joe Fruin and Terry Mack's insidious scheme to convict you and put you away is your arraignment. You'll be brought before the trial judge and formally notified of the indictment and the charges contained therein, and then given the opportunity to plead guilty or not guilty."

"Why all this formal legal stuff?" Ernie asked. "Fruin and Mack know I'm innocent. Why do I have to go to court just to say it?"

"Because the Constitution says you have to," Gavin replied in an understanding tone, aware that very few criminal defendants were capable of appreciating the significance of the judicial procedures they tread their way through. "All of you had a right to a preliminary hearing within a short time after your arrest. A bond hearing was held to set reasonable bail pending trial. You were indicted by a grand jury of your peers, and now you have an upcoming arraignment where you will be formally charged in open court. All those judicial proceedings are constitutionally mandated safeguards protecting individuals who have been arrested for an alleged criminal offense. Those rights didn't come easily. Lives, legs, and precious pieces of flesh were the price."

"Just like Mexico, huh?" Angel said.

"Exactly, except in Mexico, it was the Spaniards. We had the bloody British. Back in 1787, the American colonists, who had been tyrannically deprived of virtually all human rights by mother England, insured that the succeeding generations of Americans would not suffer the anguish of outrageous government oppression when they provided for a Bill of Rights in the first Ten Amendments of our Constitution. The Fourth, Fifth, Sixth and Eighth Amendments are the ones we hope to have enforced in your case."

"The Constitution is just a piece of paper," Angel said. "Powerful men like Fruin and Mack can make that paper work for them."

"True, but for over two hundred years, the Bill of Rights has endured though legislators, judges, prosecuting attorneys, and cops have periodically attempted to erode or abrogate its various provisions. Fortunately, for the American people, somewhere along the line in the criminal justice system, a judge with a sense of common decency and fundamental fairness has come to the forefront and stopped the assault on constitutional rights."

"It all sounds good, Matt, but will it work for me, a major drug dealer?" Angel asked.

"You never know in this business. Sometimes you're lucky; sometimes you're not. But I think you've got about as good a judge as you could get."

Disgusting and frightening memories of the MCC were fresh in Sal Veta's and Claudio Cillas' minds. Thinking the judge might revoke his bond and put him back into the slammer, Sal Veta said in a shaky voice, "What should I say or do?"

"Nothing. Stand next to me and look respectful to the court. I do all the fighting," Gavin said as he opened the courtroom door and led his clients to the podium.

The four defendants were certain their case was the only one Judge Matyan had on his docket that morning and that they were the only persecuted defendants in the courthouse. In reality the overworked and, as he often complained, underpaid jurist considered United States versus Angel Herrera, et al, just another case which was going to be handled in a routine manner. Picking up the indictment lying before him, he read through it quickly, then looked down at the four defendants and said, "You are all charged in indictment number 78 CR 0137 with violating the drug laws of the United States. Count one charges: On or about June 21, 1980, each of you conspired to possess and distribute a controlled substance, to wit, heroin, in violation of 21 United States Code, Section 846; and in counts two and three each of you is charged with possessing with intent to distribute heroin, in violation of 21 United States Code, Section 841."

"Your Honor," Gavin acknowledged, "each of the defendants received a copy of the indictment, has read and understands the charges. Each enters a plea of not guilty to all charges contained in the indictment."

"All right, gentlemen," the judge continued, "the recently enacted Speedy Trial Act requires that criminal trials be disposed of in an efficient manner, and with that in mind, you gentlemen will be expected to abide by the following dates: September 15th for hearing and disposition of all contested motions, and I'll set a tentative trial date of February 14, 1981."

"Will we go to trial on February 14, or can the case be continued to a later date?" Angel asked, as he followed Gavin out through the courtroom doors and into the hall. Ernie, Sal and Claudio huddled in close to them, eager to hear the answer.

"It's just a tentative date. The judge has a long backlog of criminal and civil cases that he'll probably not dispose of by February."

With the fear of being sent back to jail gone, Sal Veta's thoughts quickly turned to his family and used car business. He said, "What about Claudio and me? Do we have to stay in Chicago?"

Gavin shook his head, "The conditions of your bonds have been enlarged to allow you to travel to your homes in Laredo, Texas. But be sure to be in court on each court date, unless you are excused. One unexcused absence and your bonds will be revoked. And, we have to make arrangements for another attorney to represent you at trial."

Sal's face flushed. "You mean you won't represent us?"

"I can't, Sal. The court would never allow it." Gavin had not wanted to rattle Angel's three co-defendants prior to their arraignments so he didn't tell them that they would have to be represented at trial by three other lawyers. "Don't worry, Sal and Claudio," he said. "I've got two good lawyers for you."

Ernie's shoulders sagged. He trusted only Matt Gavin and wanted him to fight for him in court. "What about me?" he said.

Gavin put his arm around Ernie's neck. "Trust me," he said. "I'm always going to be with you. But I had to get another laywer for you. His name is Jim Reilley, and he's one of the best criminal defense lawyers in the country. He's very savvy, knows all about fanatic agents like Joe Fruin."

"With you and Jim Reilley representing me, I gotta win," Ernie said.

Turning to Angel, Gavin said, "Keep your nose clean, cut out dealing in that shit. If Fruin gets you again, you'll go to the slammer for keeps."

"You have my word, Matt. I don't want to do one more day in jail."

Gavin didn't believe Angel. There was no way he could walk away from the Durango Connection and turn his back on his family and the cartel. But he wanted his client to know he was involved in a game as lethal as Russian Roulette. Fruin and his agents would be watching every move Angel made, and one more mistake would be his last.

Chapter 17

▼

VILLA DEL MAR

Tricia Berglund walked into Gavin's office with a stuffed case file under her arm and a scowl spread across her face. Stopping abruptly, she tossed the file onto the desk so that it spun to a rest with the caption facing Gavin. Amused by Tricia's pretense of displeasure, Gavin glanced down at the file and read the caption and case note next to it: "USA versus Judge Dave Cowan. Prepare motion to suppress evidence obtained from illegal wiretap."

Tricia flopped into a chair across the desk from Gavin, a forced martyr's look flooding her eyes. "I was just thinking," she said, "we don't have any trials scheduled for the next two weeks. I've caught you daydreaming several times in the last couple of days. And suddenly all the legal work is ending up on my desk. The way I figure it you're going to take off for the Caribbean and leave me with all the work."

Tricia had read the signals perfectly. For days Gavin hadn't been able to think of anything but an uninhabited island in the Caribbean. Feeling a tinge of guilt, he tried to take the sting out of the work load.

"You've become very knowledgeable in wiretap law. That last memo of law you prepared was the best argument against the unfettered use of phone taps by FBI agents I have ever read. And if you don't do as good a job on the Cowan case, the good judge is going to go to jail for a long time."

It didn't work. "Matt," she protested, "you've tried more electronic eavesdropping cases than all the rest of the defense lawyers in the city added together. How did I get to be the expert? Damn! I need your insight."

Gavin smiled. "Okay. The motion and supporting memo of law shouldn't be difficult. The FBI had no reliable information that anything illegal was going on in the judge's chambers before they planted a bug in the headrest of his desk chair. The eavesdropping was a fishing trip to gather information. There are several cases right on the point. If the FBI had no probable cause to bug the chambers, all the recorded conversations concerning bribes and payoffs can't be used as evidence against our client."

"It's that simple, huh?" Tricia retorted, now resigned to the fact the job had been delegated to her. She had to put up a little fuss, but the bottom line was there were very few things she wouldn't do for the man who meant so much to her. "How long do I have to get the Cowan wiretap memo done?"

Gavin cleared his throat. "Two weeks."

Then what was really bothering Tricia came out. "Well, I hope you think of me while you're off sunnin' and funnin' in the Bahamas on your yacht."

Gavin laughed. During the past six years, it had become routine for him to juggle trial dates and rearrange business appointments so that he could slip away to the Platis, his floating home. A seagoing yachtsman by nature, he had cruised extensively throughout the Bahamian Island chain, the Turks and Caicos, and the Virgin Islands. Cruising was his passion, his avocation, and he was unable to resist the siren's seductive call from an island which loomed on the horizon. His eyes twinkled as he said, "You're half right. I'm going boating, but this time I'm going to explore the reefs and islands off Mexico's Yucatan Peninsula."

Tricia pouted. "Sounds great. I've heard the barrier reef there is second only to the one off Australia. But where are you going to stay?"

"Angel offered to let me use his villa near Tulum."

"Are you sure you...." Tricia's voice trailed off when her secretary interrupted and told her she had an urgent phone message.

Gavin eyes followed Tricia as she left the office. He had played a game with her, wanting her to feel a little miffed that he didn't invite her to go with him to Angel's villa. He spun in his swivel chair so that he could gaze out the window. He wanted to think about the Yucatan, with its sun-drenched sandy beaches and warm turquoise waters and coral reefs. There he'd slip into dive mask and fins and float for hours among God's most splendid creations. There he'd dive down and shoot lobster and grouper with sling and spear and afterwards, with subtle pretentiousness, cook and serve them for dinner. But he needed someone to do it all with, someone who would make it all super-sensational, someone who would be a mate and companion. "Tricia," he whispered. "She'll go with me."

When Tricia began working for his firm, he never imagined their relationship would turn out to be what it was. He hired her because during job interviews she seemed to have a subdued sensuality and seemed more concerned with succeeding in her profession than looking for a lover or husband. For several months, it was a platonic, professionally handled work hours association, with Tricia guarding herself at all times by wearing loose fitting skirts and blouses and only the necessary dash of makeup. Then things began to change. They began to spend more time together, during and after work hours, chatting about everything and anything. Then it became pleasurable to touch one another, at first by accident, then by design. When Tricia's eyes began to focus on him with a certain radiance about them, each realized it was useless to pretend any longer.

Gavin believed a man never seduced a woman. When a woman was ready to make love, some primal instinct caused her to pick the time and place, and then let nature take its course. The night that changed their lives forever started, when at the close of a business day, they found it difficult to separate and go their separate ways. They invented excuses to linger until Tricia said something about going to her apartment and working on a client's case, and that she wished she had some help on the difficult legal issues. He took her by the hand and led her out of the office. Months of charades ended five minutes after they entered Tricia's apartment. Powerless to impede or halt the magic of sex which had taken control of their senses, they were drawn into one another's arms, their bodies exploding with passion, and they made love for endless hours with an almost unbearable intensity.

As it turned out, Gavin had not fooled Tricia. She reentered his office, sat down with a precocious look in her eyes, and said, "Yes, I'm going with you to the Yucatan. I've wanted to learn to snorkel and scuba dive for years. I love boats and will be a good mate. And besides, I don't want you running off to the Caribbean without me anymore."

Their first trip together was sheer ecstasy. Flying in the first class section from Chicago to Cancun, a trendy resort island on the northern tip of the Yucatan, they enjoyed all the amenities of the privileged class: champagne with appetizers and a fine moselle with breast of chicken for the entree. When they had finished dining, Tricia put her seat back and snuggled in tightly against Gavin. He felt her large blue eyes searching his face. There was something bothering her and she wanted him to chase it away. But what was it, he wondered? Like a weary kitten, she'd daintily pawed around several sensitive issues. He began to think about the clues she had given. During dinner she jokingly said she thought it ironic that they, of all people, were going to vacation at a drug kingpin's villa, and then she innocently questioned if any drug trafficking would go on while they were out on the boat. Knowing she'd beat around the bush for days without saying what bothered her, Gavin ventured a guess. "I think you're worried what effect a social relationship with Angel will have on our professional reputations."

"Well, I did think about it," she said.

"The truthful answer is, I really don't know. Looking at things objectively, we aren't breaking any laws. And if we refused to stay at a place or eat at a restaurant because the owner was an alleged criminal, hells bells, we couldn't stay in or eat at half the places in Las Vegas or Atlantic City. Organized crime figures own several of the hotels and restaurants in those towns."

"I know, Matt, but Angel's a drug dealer, and in most people's minds that is different than an organized crime figure."

Gavin nodded his head. "No question the vast majority of Americans have been brainwashed by movies and TV programs which depict the heroin dealer as evil to the core, devoid of a decent, humanistic side. But it's not all that simple. A man has many facets to his nature."

"Are you saying that every human being is a complex mixture of good and evil?"

Gavin imitated an Irish brogue. "Well, as my dear auld mudder useta say, 'if de best man in de world had his wrongful acts written on his forehead, he'd haveta wear his hat awful low.'"

"What would your dear auld mudder say about Angel?" Tricia said.

"In all the years I have known Angel, I have never seen him use an illicit drug or heard him talk about the use or distribution of heroin. Socially, Angel has been charming and considerate. But 9 a.m. to 5 p.m., symbolically speaking, he is like several of my friends who are chief executive officers at large corporations or commodity traders or stock brokers or car salesmen. The almighty dollar is their only God, and no law is going to stand in the way of making a profit. After work hours, these people lead exemplary lives."

"Money," Tricia said, "is really at the root of all problems."

"Money is both good and evil. We work—break our asses sometimes—for it. And don't ever forget the posh, luxurious vacation we're about to enjoy is in essence a payment of money, lots of it."

It was another shocking education for Tricia. "Oh," she said, "is everything being paid for by Angel?"

Gavin pressed his lips against Tricia's ear. "Yes. It's a bonus for our services rendered. And it's tax free."

"Darn," she said as she put her finger on Gavin's knee and moved it slowly along the inside of his thigh. "End of business. Let's enjoy ourselves."

*   *   *   *

Knowing Gavin's favorite recreational vehicle was the Volkswagen Safari Jeep which was kept at the Villa Del Mar, Angel had an employee drive the jeep to the airport at Cancun and hand deliver the keys to him in the airport parking lot. It was a three-hour drive along the Yucatan coast to the villa, four if they stopped to sightsee the Mayan ruins at Tulum. Gavin busied himself stowing the luggage and putting the jeep's canvas top down into the boot while waiting for Tricia, who had decided to change from the slacks and blouse she had traveled in to something more appropriate for the jeep ride. He knew women liked to take an inordinate amount of time in ladies rooms, but when there was no sign of her for over fifteen minutes, he walked back into the terminal. He was relieved when he saw her standing at the counter of a cosmetics shop, doing some last minute shopping. But relief turned to amazement as she turned her head and smiled teasingly over her shoulder. "Chrissake!" he mumbled.

She was stunning. In a scene where beauty was commonplace—gorgeous airline stewardesses, counter agents, and tourists—her splendor stood out and caught the attention of all those nearby. She was so professional 9 to 5, Gavin thought. But now she was all woman. As she walked toward him, he noticed the soft blonde hair flowing down over a head held proudly erect, and the soft golden skin of her face radiating health, and the white silk blouse opened to the cleavage of her breasts, firm mounds that burgeoned up from the confines of her bra. His eyes were gliding over her well-shaped hips and legs when she noticed the expression on his face. Drawing near to him she asked, "Do you approve?"

Gavin cleared his throat and then took her by the hand. "Definitely."

"Good," she said softly, "because everything you see is all yours."

They drove south along the coast until they came to Tulum, the site of an ancient Mayan civilization. Playing archaeologist, Gavin took Tricia by the hand and led her onto and over astonishing stone pyramids which had existed since 900 A.D. Conscious that the Indians who had built them had mysteriously disappeared without a clue, he said, "How could a whole nation of people just disappear?"

She remembered the research she had done on the Mexican people. "Don't know. It's a baffler, especially in light of the fact the Mayan's were a sophisticated society, writing and recording history in hieroglyphics."

"I wish we could spend a month right here exploring the mystery."

The charm of the Yucatan had totally captivated Tricia. "Let's!" she said excitedly. "Next month."

A few miles south of Tulum, Gavin saw what he had been watching for—an old adobe house with a corrugated tin roof. He turned onto a dirt road which ran past the side of the house and stopped just as a pleasant faced woman came out the door and waved. "My husband is at the villa," she hollered in broken English. If the woman had not recognized Gavin from his last visit to the villa, the reception would have been different. The innocuous looking little woman and her family had proved in the past to be fiercely protective of the villa and its guests.

Fifty yards past the house and beyond sight of the highway, the road suddenly changed from dirt to well-paved asphalt. Thick, lush green jungle foliage grew to the edge of the pavement, making it seem like a smooth, canyon floor leading to the sea. As they came across the crest of a hill, a magnificent panorama appeared before them. A stunningly tranquil Caribbean Sea, more vividly colorful than any other sea in the world, stretched out before them. And a palm-fringed, white sand beach, without the trace of a footprint, lined the sea. An inlet, approximately 30 yards wide had been cut through the beach to connect the sea with a small bay. Baja de Herrera not only protected Angel's yacht, El Lobo, from hostile winds and waves but was the focal point for all villa activity.

Even more breathtaking was Villa Del Mar. Looking like an ancient Mayan temple, it reigned majestically from atop a hill which overlooked the surrounding area. Tricia stared incredulously. "It's marvelous. I've never seen anything like it." Her eyes glowed as she examined the off-white stucco walls and red tile roof, the Bougainvillea which curled down from the patio roof, and the palm trees which graced the grounds.

Baltazar, the villa's amiable caretaker, burst out the front door of the villa just as the jeep rolled to a stop. "Welcome to Villa Del Mar," he said, the diligent effort spent learning English showed signs of paying off. He removed the travel bags from the rear seat and led Gavin and Tricia into the luxuriously decorated living room. "Shall I hang up your clothes, Mrs. Gavin?" he asked, innocently mistaking Tricia's status.

She gazed at the short man with jet black croppy hair covering a head which was too large for his body. "Thanks twice," she replied, eyes beaming. "But I can manage."

Gavin was conscious of the fact Baltazar, like the majority of Mayan Indians, had an unassuming, child-like nature. Things treated with indifference by others could embarrass or hurt him. "Baltazar," he said softly, "please tell the cooks and maids to stay home for the rest of the week. We'd like to manage by ourselves." He had stayed at the villa several times before as a special guest of Angel, and there had been an over abundance of patronizing maids and cooks. This time he wanted solitude. He wanted to relax in the enchanted paradise, far from the incessant ringing of a phone, far from the society where he was forced to compromise his pride and values and engage in pretensions. Here, he could be the man he wanted to be.

Baltazar's large olive-black eyes focused on Tricia. He was confused, for the Latino women of wealth and class who visited the villa were disdainful of the menial chores which they believed should be left to the less privileged set. Mexicans were predisposed to be class conscious, but the usual villa guests, with their Spanish arrogance, made Baltazar all the more aware of class difference.

Understanding Baltazar's hesitancy, Gavin said, "Don't worry, I'll do the cooking and cleaning."

Baltazar's mouth gaped. That's not machismo, he thought, but if that's what Señor Gavin wants, he'd oblige. "Anything you need, just call," he said politely.

Baltazar had dedicated his life to his caretaker's job, fretting over and pampering the house and grounds and personal possessions. His greatest concern when Gavin was at the villa was the El Lobo, Angel's floating recreational palace. There were only a few boats like it on the entire Yucatan coast. He had complained Gavin took too many chances with the boat, nosing it against the reefs, and sometimes even anchoring with only four or five feet of water under the hull and fantail coral projecting inches above the surface of the surrounding water. And the big marlin and sailfish he caught always made a bloody mess of the cockpit and decks. But it wasn't his choice to make. Angel had made a special phone call and told him, "Be sure to give the keys to El Lobo to Señor Gavin, and don't interfere with his use of the boat."

Reluctantly, Baltazar reached into his pocket and retrieved the keys to El Lobo. "I know you are the very best boat captain, Señor Gavin, but please be careful."

Tricia felt obliged to pacify the troubled caretaker and said in an assuring tone, "Mr. Gavin has a boat. He'll treat the El Lobo just like he does his own."

Baltazar's eyes widened. "That's what worries me. Angel told me about Mr. Gavin's adventures in the Bahama Islands."

When Baltazar had gone Tricia took Gavin by the hand. "Let's see our home for a week," she said with pleasure and excitement in her voice. She led him through the living room and den which were spacious with high domed ceilings and then to the kitchen where they examined all the modern appliances. "I want you to know, I do all the cooking."

Gavin smiled. After a day spent diving on a reef and exploring islands, he'd welcome the thought of turning the culinary duties over to her. "If you insist," he said.

They stood there smiling at each other for moments, then she rushed into his arms, "I believe the master bedroom is upstairs," she said.

The following day Gavin understood what Tricia had meant when she had said, "I plan on being a companion in all ways, all the time." Shortly after sun-up he slipped quietly out of bed and made his way down to the El Lobo. The engines, water, and electrical systems had to be checked out, as did scuba tanks and diving gear. Like most women, he had thought, Tricia would only be in the way. He had entered the cabin and was lifting the engine hatch when he heard a reproving voice. "Wrong! Don't think for a minute you're going to do one thing to this boat without me!"

Gavin peeked out the cabin door and saw a determined looking Tricia standing on the pier. Laughing, he said "Well then, come aboard and check the fuel and water tanks and the refrigerator for supplies."

Eager to get the boat underway, Gavin hurried through the check-outs, and then climbed the ladder to the fly bridge, where he kicked over the engines. The roar of the turbo-charged diesel engines was symphonic and the feel of the throttles in his hands exhilarating. Even though the forty-two foot Hatteras had the same design and engines his own boat did, he wished the Platis were under them. She was the queen of all yachts.

It was time to give his first command. "Okay, matie, slip those lines."

Tricia untied the aft line and threw it on the pier, then dashed forward and did the same to the bow line. She smiled up at Gavin as he edged the El Lobo away from the pier and headed it through the inlet to the open sea. The sleek yacht knifed through the calm, azure-blue waters, heading for the coral reefs and small islands that formed the barrier reef.

Tricia became instantly attuned to the sea and the islands. Like Mother Nature herself, she befriended the gulls and pelicans and the playful heart-warming porpoises that constantly played in the bow's wake. A naturally strong swimmer, she learned to snorkel well the first day and insisted upon donning scuba gear and diving to sixty feet the next. On the third day she shot her first lobster, much to the relief of the numerous immobile coral fish she had used for target practice. She had spent hours placing her spear in the rubber sling, straining to pull it back, and then releasing the projectile. The spear had invariably banged into, and then careened off, a piece of coral.

When they were not diving on a reef, they would comb the beaches of the uninhabited islands. Their favorite island, which they named Moonraker, had a bay on the northwest end that carried six feet of water to within ten yards of shore. Gavin was able to virtually tuck the bow of the El Lobo in under the palm trees that rimmed the beach. It was paradise. Each tide washed the windward beaches of the island and left it littered with exquisite shells and other booty given up by the sea. He watched as Tricia stripped off her bathing suit and ran, golden tanned, into the surf and along the beach to retrieve shells. And when she tired they would lie in the shade of a palm tree, enraptured with the beauty of the sea and island, and with each other. Totally committed to showing her love for him, she fulfilled his every sexual fantasy.

Their six days of ecstasy flew by, and before they could prepare themselves, the dreaded last day was upon them. After lifting anchor at Moonraker Island, where they had spent the day snorkeling in search of prize conch shells, Tricia had gone to the bow of the boat and straddled the pulpit, allowing her legs to dangle down towards the water that rushed past her. It wasn't safe, but the pulpit had become her favorite place to sit while cruising. It delighted Gavin to see her perched so majestically, turning often to him, flashing a smile.

When the inlet leading to Baja De Herrera and the villa came into view, Gavin pulled the throttles back to one-quarter speed so that the El Lobo could glide over the gentle sea swells and capture the balmy tradewinds under the bimini top. He heard ice knocking against the side of a glass, then glimpsed Tricia's blonde hair bouncing up the bridge ladder. "It's cocktail time," she said as she handed him a glass brimmed with rum and cola.

He pulled her in close to him, and as he gazed down at the El Lobo slicing through the Caribbean Sea, he said, "This is about as close as a person can come to having it all. At this moment, I want nothing more."

"Did I please you on this trip, master?" Tricia teased.

She had been a gorgeous genie, the perfect mate, learning how to handle the El Lobo, the docking lines, and even the heavy anchor. At the end of a day on the sea, she had cooked the lobster and fish they had speared to perfection and served the feasts in a setting which caused him to marvel. "Sweetheart," he replied," with a little more practice, you could be a pretty good cruising mate."

She knew she had become indispensable to him. "Mr. Gavin," she said wistfully, "you can't get along without me. I'm the only woman for you, and you're the only man for me."

Chapter 18

▼

FRUIT OF THE POISONOUS TREE

A pretrial conference between prosecutor Terry Mack and Gavin had been set for 11 o'clock. Already 15 minutes late, Gavin quickened his pace when he saw the large, ornate clock attached to the facade of the high-rise office building on the corner of LaSalle and Jackson. He was in the habit of cussing out the clock, for it had been a constant source of agony over the years, reminding him of his tardiness as he raced to meet appointments. The building the clock protruded from was one of many which fronted LaSalle Street and formed the sides of a stunning canyon. The buildings housed the country's largest banks, security and commodity firms, insurance companies and the majority of the city's law firms.

Gavin was proud to be part of the LaSalle Street scene. He often told his suburban friends that all one had to do to be totally captivated by the Street's charisma was to walk its pavements between 9:00 a.m. and 6:00 p.m. any weekday. Hurried traders and runners from the Board of

Trade and Commodity Exchange could be seen at one end of the canyon with trading badges proudly displayed on their blue, green and yellow jackets, while at the other end, outside city hall, lawyers, judges and politicians huddled in whispered conversations. In between the bankers, insurance company personnel and other wheeler-dealers in the business world contributed their vitality to the aura of the street.

It was election day, and most of the assistant U.S. attorneys who helped create a hectic, bustling atmosphere on the fifteenth floor of the Dirksen Federal Building were assigned the job of poll watcher at one of the voting stations scattered throughout Cook County. Using the conference with Gavin as an excuse, Terry Mack managed to avoid a job he called dreadful. In his opinion, watching over the Democratic and Republican precinct workers to make sure they didn't steal or rig votes wasn't the way a dignified prosecutor should spend his day. He felt his valuable time should be devoted to preparing a defense to the Herrera-Kummer motion to suppress evidence, which Judge Matyan had scheduled for hearing the following week. He was painfully aware that he couldn't lose that motion, for if he did and Judge Matyan ordered that the heroin Joe Fruin seized in the motel room couldn't be used during the trial, he'd have to dismiss all counts of the indictment for lack of evidence. And, since it hadn't been the practice of the U.S. Attorney's office to appeal unfavorable suppression of evidence rulings, Angel and Ernie would stroll out of the courthouse free men, cleared of all charges. The intense anxiety connected with the thought of that happening caused him to throw a scare into Joe Fruin within hours after receiving a copy of Gavin's motion. He said, "Joe, unless you can pressure Sal Veta or Claudio Cillas into cooperating and testifying against Angel, we're going to lose the case."

Fruin became defensive. "What the fuck ya talkin about?"

He had replied, "No probable cause to enter the motel room; no probable cause to search the room; no probable cause to search Sal Veta's car. That's what the fuck I'm talkin' about."

The tough drug cop frowned before saying wryly, "Okay, I'll give Sal and Claudio a try. I'll bust their asses for something, and when I got them in cuffs and leg irons, I'll do all I can to crack them."

Mack's mouth had gaped. "I hope you're kidding, Joe?"

Fruin had snorted, then said, "Yeah, sure."

Mack enjoyed shedding his three-piece Ivy League cut suits whenever business conditions allowed, and this day opted for well-worn denim jeans and flannel shirt. Gavin wasn't surprised when he walked into the prosecutor's office and found him with his feet propped up on the desk, sports page spread out in front of him, deeply engrossed in a telephone conversation about Papa Halas' Chicago Bears. An avid Bear fan himself, Gavin knew the Bears had lost Sunday's game, but he was unsure of the reason—coaching, game plan or weak individual performance. He gleaned from the unilateral telephone conversation that it was weak play of the Bear quarterback, and the game could have been won if Mack was the coach.

"Bloody blokes!" Mack exclaimed, hanging up the phone. "We could take the division title this year if we had a quarterback and a couple of defensive linemen. Shoot. I can still play better than those two defensive tackles the Bears have."

Gavin had no doubts. The prosecutor was a well-built man, standing six feet four inches, and weighing, after one of his many diets, two-hundred forty pounds. Fortunately for defense attorneys, he had a gentle nature and conducted himself as a gentleman on all but rare occasions. Gavin counted on that gentle nature as he said, "It looks like the Angel Herrera case is going to be a bitter battle. I'd like to talk about some things, and try to avoid serious problems."

"That's what we're here for, counsel."

Gavin sat up straight. "I've always known you to be a fair guy. I can't believe you would let an innocent man be framed, even if that man was Angel Herrera."

Mack lifted up a stack of typewritten pages that lay before him on the desk, shuffled through them for a moment, then let them drop to the desk top. "Explain yourself, sir," he said, face flushed.

"My information is confidential, will never be used in court, and will never be brought up by me again. This is a bullshit case, so help me, God. There was no heroin in the motel room when Fruin and the other agents entered. Fruin took a package that was recovered from the trunk of Sal Veta's car and planted it on Angel." Gavin sat back and carefully scrutinized Mack's face for a sign, for the slightest indication he was aware of what had happened that evening at the Safe Harbor Motel.

"Matt, you're a great attorney, and I've always respected your opinions, but you are way off base on this one. Unless you have some damn good proof, I don't want to hear the word frame-up again. Joe Fruin and the other case agents are the best DEA agents I've ever known, and they have great reputations. Do you really expect me to believe Angel Herrera?"

Gavin didn't want to say it, didn't want to give up a good friend, but he felt the attorney-client relationship with Angel required him to push things to the edge. "The plant," he said, "has been confirmed by one of Joe Fruin's agents, one who's very reliable. That agent told me there was no heroin in the motel room when Fruin and his agents crashed through the door."

"Then put the agent on the stand at the trial," Mack challenged, obviously thinking the claim was a bluff.

"Terry, you're a fine lawyer and law professor, but you don't know diddly shit about what's going down in the real world of drug trafficking and drug law enforcement. Every drug agent is a good guy ninety percent of the time, but ten percent of the time an agent can be a bad guy."

"Save the bullshit, Matt."

Gavin realized it was time to drop his argument. No one told, and no one ever would tell, Mack what really happened at the Safe Harbor Motel. He said, "Okay, Terry, then let's try to do the next best thing."

What do you suggest?" Mack queried in a skeptical tone.

"I'll plead Angel and Ernie guilty if you recommend probation to the judge."

"Probation!" Mack said. "Do you realize Angel Herrera is the biggest drug dealer ever caught in the United States? And he was caught with a shithouse full of heroin? I'd be fired tomorrow if I recommended probation in this case."

"So that you understand my position, I'm not arguing Angel is an innocent boy, framed by a heinous drug agent. I would be naive to argue that heroin wasn't Angel's, and that he wasn't the man who arranged for it to be brought from Mexico to the motel at Joliet. If your agents had waited fifteen minutes, they might have been lucky enough to get Angel in the load car and truly in possession of all that heroin. But as lawyers, you and I are duty bound to see that justice is done. I think that if Angel took a conviction for conspiracy to possess and distribute heroin and received five years probation for it, justice would be served. We wouldn't be forced to have five agents take the stand to commit perjury and pervert justice. We could plead Ernie Kummer out for one year probation. Maybe you could reduce the charge to—being a dumb shit."

"No deal, Matt, I'm going to believe my agents. I have no choice."

Pressing his argument, Gavin continued. "Do you really think that Sal Veta would transport the twelve kilos of heroin from Laredo to Joliet and then take one kilo out of the car and bring it into the motel just to show Angel? It doesn't make any sense. Sal was a mule. His job was to transport the shit. There was never any need for him to touch it or to prove anything about it to Angel, especially one package of it. If anything was wrong with the heroin, it went wrong prior to the time it was loaded into Sal Veta's car."

"Okay, Matt, cut it. I don't want to hear anymore about it. Argue your case to a jury. If your claim of a plant is true, justice will prevail and Angel will be found not guilty."

Gavin zipped up his brief case and stood in front of Mack's desk. "The gloves are off," he said. "I'm going to tear into Joe Fruin and his cast of actor-agents so hard that when I get done cross-examining them they're going to stink up the courtroom. And I'd like you to remember after a jury finds Angel not guilty that I tried to work things out."

The straight-laced prosecutor rocked back in his chair. His eyes narrowed as he said, "Matt, save the bullshit for the courtroom."

*   *   *   *

Gavin let all work on the Angel Herrera suppression motion slide until the day before the scheduled hearing date. Then he secluded himself in his office and reviewed the argument he would give to Judge Matyan, the argument he firmly believed would cause the judge to suppress from use as evidence the heroin allegedly found in the room at the Safe Harbor Motel. He had just about finished when he heard a soft knock on the door. His secretary opened the door several inches and then slid her face into the opening. He held up his hand and said, "I know, Irene. You're going to say, sorry to bother."

"Oh, Swami," Irene replied in a jovial tone, "How come you always know what I'm going to say?"

"After ten years of watching the best legal secretary on LaSalle Street, I should be able to guess a thing or two."

"Golly, it's nice to know I'm appreciated," Irene gushed.

He thought about how inadequate words would be to describe that appreciation. Irene had been so loyal to him and so capable. And his clients adored her. He said, "What can I do for you?"

"Mr. Herrera is in the reception room. He wants to see you."

Gavin studied Angel as he walked into the office and slumped into a chair in front of the desk. The thought of going back to jail for a long period of time weighed heavily on his mind, causing him to look like a terminally ill man. He had seen many defendants with similar decisions to make seated in the same chair. "Angel," he said, "you look like a man who lost both his wife and mistress."

Angel didn't appreciate the humor. "Celia didn't leave me, and I broke things off with Jenni right after I was released on bond. I didn't want to take the chance Joe Fruin would arrest her and charge her with conspiracy just so he could squeeze info out of her."

Realizing he had misspoken, Gavin nodded, then said, "Celia is a great woman and you should be thankful for her. And Jenni is a nice gal,but her sexy butt and legs got you into the pile of crap you're in."

"I know. I know, Matt. Pussy is every man's downfall. I swear. I've given it up."

Gavin laughed. "I know you, Angel, and don't believe you. Where is Jenni now?"

Angel lowered his eyes as he said, "I gave her ten grand and sent her to a friend's place in Los Angeles until my case is over."

"There's a good chance your case will end tomorrow," Gavin said. The facts and case law support my argument that the agents acted illegally when they entered the motel room and searched Sal's car."

"That sounds great, Matt, but I don't think that judge will give us the decision, even if the law says he should. I've got the feeling that he'll deny all our motions, and the case will go to the jury to decide if I'm guilty or innocent. If that happens, the jury will find me guilty sure as hell."

"Okay, Angel, let's be straight with one another. You're getting frightened and thinking about joining Sal and Claudio on the other side of the Rio Grande, huh?"

Angel sat up, startled. "How did you know Sal and Claudio skipped? Shit! They left yesterday."

A vexatious look crossed Gavin's face. "You just confirmed my suspicions that they would be sacrificed so that you'd stand a better chance of being found not guilty."

"Cut the bullshit, Matt! You heard from someone that Joe Fruin was out to nail Sal and Claudio. And you know that left them only one thing to do."

"They didn't have to split to Mexico," Gavin said. "They could've hid out until trial."

"Bullshit! We both know what that prick drug cop wanted. Fruin wanted Sal and Claudio to snitch on me, and he would have tortured the shit out of them until he got what he wanted."

Gavin saw dilemma in Angel's eyes. The pressure generated by the arrest, court proceedings and the unrelenting potential for jail caused him to distrust everyone. He apparently began to doubt whether his lawyer would warn him of imminent dangers. The lack of confidence bothered Gavin deeply, for he took great pride in his honesty and candor with clients. "Angel," he said, "I'll do all in my power to keep you out of jail. If I thought for a minute Fruin was going to set you up and frame you again, or Mack was going to ask Judge Matyan to revoke your bond, I'd tell you to get out of town fast. But I think you're safe for a while."

"So I got to guts it out day to day?" Angel said.

"Right, a hearing on your motion to suppress evidence is set for tomorrow, and if that motion is denied, you will have to stand trial. I wouldn't like to see you skip out before the motion to suppress evidence has been ruled on. If we win, there will be no trial and the charges will be dropped. If we lose the motion and you are convicted after a trial, Judge Matyan will most likely set an appeal bond that you could afford. You would then be free on bond until the Seventh Circuit Court of Appeals rules."

Angel slumped back in his chair, somewhat relieved. "What's the motion to suppress all about?"

"Well, did you ever hear the story about the fruit of the poisonous tree?" Gavin asked.

"Yeah, isn't that the tree that Eve plucked the apple from?"

Gavin smiled, happy Angel's sense of humor had returned and relieved he'd apparently decided to stay for trial. He explained the exclusionary rule of law. "Angel, the fruit of the poisonous tree doctrine is a theory of law promulgated by some of our finest Supreme Court jurists many years ago. Simply stated, if a tree is poisonous, so then must be the fruit that it gives forth. In your case, the tree is the unlawful invasion of the motel room in Joliet by the drug agents, and the fruit is the heroin Fruin allegedly seized next to you. The Fourth Amendment to the United States Constitution protects persons from unlawful and unreasonable intrusions and searches of places where there is an expectation of privacy."

Angel blinked several times and politely uttered, "I see. I see."

Gavin continued, "The Supreme Court held nearly half a century ago that evidence seized during an unlawful search could not constitute proof against the victim of that search. Lawyers call this the exclusionary rule, since the by-product of an unreasonable invasion and search is excluded from the trial of a case. Analyzed in relation to your case, Angel, the exclusionary rule would prohibit the government from using the heroin seized in the motel room at a trial since it was the direct result of an unlawful invasion. Think of the Fruit of the Poisonous Tree Doctrine in relation to Eve plucking the apple from the tree in the Garden of Eden and then enticing Adam to eat it. Since Eve broke God's law by seizing the protected apple, she and Adam were forbidden to eat from that tree again and were driven from the garden. Similarly, the drug agents disobeyed the supreme law of this country when they entered the motel room without a search warrant or reasonable cause and seized the heroin. The judge should drive the agents out of the courtroom."

Angel was beginning to understand. "I knew there was something I liked about old Eve and the Bible. But tell me, do you really think the judge has the guts to cut Joe Fruin's balls off tomorrow?"

"Yes, I do. Judge Matyan has granted several motions which were similar to yours."

"Is the suppression motion Ernie's motion too?" Angel asked, always conscious he had gotten his friend into a mess.

"It certainly is," Gavin replied. "This is both yours and Ernie's motion. Attorney Jim Reilley has filed his appearance and will represent Ernie from now on."

"How about the heroin in the car?" Angel asked. "Did we file a fruit of the poisonous tree motion for that, too?"

"Unfortunately not. It was Sal's car; you were not in it; and you cannot claim a possessory right in and to the car. Simply stated, you don't have the requisite expectation of privacy to support a motion to suppress."

"Ah, shit," Angel groaned, "then I'll lose anyway, won't I?"

"You shouldn't. Without the heroin in the room, there is nothing to tie you to the heroin found in the trunk of Sal's car. I think Mack would dismiss all counts. And if he didn't, I think the judge would throw the case out."

Angel's stared at his lawyer. "Throw it out? What do you mean?"

"Mack will have to find or invent someone to testify that you knew there was heroin in the trunk of Sal's car and that you had actual or constructive possession of it. Otherwise, Judge Matyan will have to grant a judgment of acquittal, and the case will never go to the jury for a verdict."

"You mean, Matt, that a judge can say I'm not guilty even in a jury trial?"

"Absolutely. Trial judges have that right, though most won't exercise their duty in a drug case, saying the jury can infer anything they want from minuscule pieces of evidence. Matyan is different. He's from the old school—pre-Reagan Administration."

"You seem to have a lot of confidence in Judge Matyan," Angel said. "Has he been talked to?"

Gavin frowned. "No, and you'd better get it through your head that he's unreachable. The only thing that will sway him is the law."

"Bullshit. I'll bet the judge is a real good guy until the right amount of cash is dangled in front of him. Then he's as crooked as the rest of the judges in the world."

Gavin studied his client. He was a savvy businessman, having taken care of his mules and distributors in courtrooms around the country for years. And la mordida had always been Angel's key to success. "Angel," he said, "you'll have to face reality. It can't be done. If you want me to drop out of this case so you can get some other attorney, I'll withdraw."

"I trust only you, Matt."

"Okay," Gavin said, "then here's how we're going to get the judge to do what we want. Tricia has spent the last two days in the law library, researching the law and authorities the judge will have to rely on when he decides whether the search for and seizure of heroin in the motel room was legal."

"You mean the judge doesn't know what the law is, that you have to tell him about some case, and that case tells him what the law is?"

"That's what we in the legal profession call stare decisis, or as more commonly referred to, authorities. A trial court must rely on precedent to make a legal decision; he must follow what an appeals court or the Supreme Court has determined the law to be." Gavin pushed an open law book in front of Angel. "For example, the United States Supreme Court held in Aguilar versus Texas that an informant must be deemed reliable before a law enforcement officer can act on his tip." Gavin rose and as if conducting cross-examination, asked, "Did informant Martinez tell any of the agents that heroin would be in Sal Veta's motel room the night you were arrested? Did he tell Fruin he saw it in the room or otherwise knew it to be there?"

Gavin's question caught Angel off guard and he was slow to answer. "Ah, no, it was never in the room, and he never knew what room or what motel Sal was staying in."

Gavin continued, "Did informant Martinez know or tell any agent that heroin would be in the trunk of Sal's car?"

"No, he couldn't have known."

"Did Martinez know you were going to go to the Safe Harbor Motel that night?"

"No," Angel replied. "I didn't know myself until Ernie telephoned."

"Why did Martinez tell the agents the transfer was going to take place somewhere in Joliet?" Gavin grilled.

"Martinez had gotten friendly with Fonze, the man who was supposed to pick up the heroin that night. Fonze must have told him the heroin would be delivered in the Joliet area, and he just figured the deal would go down there. I never told him a thing."

Gavin smiled as he said, "Then the agents just made a good guess and got lucky?"

Angel shrugged. "Lucky for them, but unlucky for me."

"I'm smiling for a reason, Angel. The only thing the snitch Martinez could have told Joe Fruin's agents was that you agreed to sell twelve kilos of heroin to a Puerto Rican, and the heroin was due to arrive in the Joliet area the second week of June. And, that's not sufficiently reliable under Aguilar versus Texas and other supporting cases. Which means—you win."

Angel became noticeably optimistic. "Let's give them hell tomorrow, Abogado del Diablo."

"Count on it, Angel. Count on it."

Chapter 19

▼

MOTION TO
SUPPRESS EVIDENCE

Judge Matyan was nearing the end of his morning motion call when Matt Gavin entered the courtroom and took his position at the head of the defendant's table. To his left sat attorney Jim Reilley, and next to him, the defendants Angel Herrera and Ernie Kummer. Terry Mack sat a few yards to his right at the prosecutor's table, and perching hawk-like on the first row of bench seats behind him were Joe Fruin, Ben Cass, Larry Hill and other case agents. All combatants for the day's big battle had assembled in their respective corners, each feeling a unique anxiety, each realizing Operation Durango Connection, and possibly a lot more, depended on the outcome of the suppression hearing.

Jim Reilley arose and walked to the podium. A flamboyant dresser, with white bristle moustache that gave him a Caesar Romero look, he was known for charming judges and juries into ruling for his clients. "Good morning, Your Honor," he said. "I'd like the record to show that I have filed my appearance on behalf of Ernie Kummer."

A familiar sparkle appeared in Judge Matyan's eyes as he nodded greetings. He always enjoyed the dialogue that resulted when Reilley appeared before him. "Are you prepared to proceed to hearing today?" Matyan asked.

"I'd like a 30 day continuance, but I know even the good Lord couldn't help me get that."

Judge Matyan rolled his eyes, and he said, "You're right, counselor. I'd like to remind you that Jesus has no standing in my courtroom, and he won't until he's admitted to practice law in the United States district courts." Everyone in the courtroom, excepting Fruin and his drug agents, burst into laughter.

Federal rules provided that Ernie Kummer be represented by independent counsel, and Jim Reilley was Gavin's first choice. He had prosecuted drug cases in a Cook County narcotics court before becoming a very talented defense attorney. And his experience with excessive and illegal police conduct made it easy for Gavin to explain the plant of heroin on Angel and his new client. "Everything and anything can happen in the drug traffickers world," he had said when he accepted Ernie's case. Experience had taught him to believe no one, and everyone.

"All right, Mr. Clerk," Judge Matyan said, "I see that finishes my morning call, and the decks are clear to proceed with the business at hand this morning. Kindly call the Angel Herrera case."

The court clerk, seated in front of and below the bench, turned and fell into a short whispered huddle with the judge. The message caused Judge Matyan to sit upright in his chair and look sternly at Gavin.

"I've just been informed," Matyan said, "Sal Veta and Claudio Cillas have decided to fugitate and not join us for this motion to suppress."

"I can't comment," Gavin replied briskly. "I don't represent Mr. Veta or Mr. Cillas, and I've had no conversations with them." He glanced over at Joe Fruin, knowing that the drug cop held him responsible for Veta and Cillas fugitating.

Fruin was still glaring at Gavin when Judge Matyan said impassionately, "Let the record show bond forfeitures and warrants to issue for the arrests of the defendants Veta and Cillas." Matyan paused for a moment, then continued, "I understand this is a motion to suppress evidence filed by defendants, Angel Herrera and Ernie Kummer, and it charges that the contraband the government intends to use against the two defendants in evidence during the trial of this case was unlawfully seized from a room they occupied at the Safe Harbor Motel. The defendants claim the case agents did not procure a search warrant before entering the motel room, which, they argue, the agents should have done. The government agrees the agents did not enter the motel room under the authority of a warrant so the issue I am confronted with is whether or not exigent circumstances existed which would justify the intrusion without a warrant. Since a search was conducted without a warrant the government has the burden of showing that it came within the constitutional guidelines guaranteed by the Fourth Amendment. Proceed, if you will, Mr. Mack."

Assistant U.S. attorney Terry Mack stood erect and announced, "The government will call Joe Fruin."

Fruin pushed his chair back, confidently walked to the stand, and began to sit down. Remembering the oath, he stood quickly and raised his right hand. Judge Matyan faced him and administered the oath that if violated by perjury would subject him to jail. "Do you solemnly swear that the testimony you are about to give in this case will be the truth, the whole truth, and nothing but the truth, so help you God?"

Fruin let a nervous cough escape and his shoulder twitched as he answered, "I do." He began his testimony by describing his position with the Drug Enforcement Administration and his experience in investigating drug related offenses. Mack artfully led him through an examination designed to show probable cause for the agents' invasion of the motel room, with emphasis on informant Martinez' reliability. Fruin testified that he arrested Juan Martinez in his home after finding one pound of heroin secreted in his bedroom closet. Martinez was well known to him as a minor drug pusher, an outlet for the incessant flow of heroin, coke, pot, or whatever else was available. He advised Martinez that with three arrests and two convictions for drug trafficking on his rap sheet he was facing prison for the rest of his life. After some gentle persuasion, Martinez decided to cooperate with the DEA and tell all he knew about Angel Herrera, his major source for heroin and marijuana for over six years. Martinez' offer to cooperate became irresistible to the DEA when he said that he had promised a Puerto Rican from Miami he would set up a deal with Angel Herrera which would provide a constant, low-priced supply of heroin. "My DEA task force went ballistic," Fruin testified, "when Martinez said that he had been present at a meeting between Angel Herrera and the Puerto Rican, Jose Cruz. Angel agreed to sell twelve kilos of heroin for $36,000 a kilo."

"Did Martinez tell you Angel Herrera told him the delivery would be made in a motel in Joliet?" Mack questioned.

"No," Fruin replied, glancing up at Judge Matyan. "Martinez didn't know for certain where the delivery would be made. He said he had heard from another Herrera organization member that the heroin delivery would go down in the Joliet area."

"What did you do then, Mr. Fruin?"

"I ordered a twenty-four-hour a day surveillance of Angel Herrera. During that surveillance, one of my agents learned Angel was going to fly to Durango, Mexico."

"Objection!" Gavin interjected sharply, as he rose and walked to the podium.

"And what are the grounds for your objection?" the judge asked, obviously aware of the forthcoming argument.

"The defense requests the court to strike from the record all of Mr. Fruin's testimony concerning the informant Martinez. It is all hearsay. Mr. Fruin is repeating what he heard from another person. That person, Juan Martinez, is not here in court and capable of being cross-examined."

"Mr. Gavin," the judge said in an amused tone, "your objection is noted for the record so that you may preserve it for appeal, but you know as well as I that hearsay evidence is admissible during a pre-trial suppression of evidence hearing. Your objection is overruled."

Gavin knew that the judge was correct and that his objection was without merit. However, he had always argued vigorously in trial courts and appellate courts that hearsay testimony should be prohibited in a suppression hearing, just as it was in a trial. And he had another reason behind the objection. "I understand the court's ruling," he said, "but under the circumstances the government should produce Martinez to testify, and if the prosecutor refuses, then all statements allegedly made by him should be stricken. He's an integral part of this case. He provided the only basis for the invasion and search of the motel room. And, he is available to testify."

"Your Honor," Mack said indignantly, "the law is clear. I'm not required to call the informant."

The judge's bright blue eyes sparkled, and his face registered pleasure with the challenge presented. "Mr. Gavin knows that, but he has subtly weaved a web. Do you think it is reasonable to allow the defendants to suffer the consequences they have been subjected to without ever producing what might be a fantasized informant. Martinez' existence and statements could be easily fabricated, and the defense would never know otherwise. That's exactly why the Constitution provides for a face-to-face confrontation and an opportunity for cross-examination. Now that the real motive behind your objection has been laid bare, what do you suggest, Mr. Gavin?"

"The only fair thing that can be done," Gavin urged, "is to enter an order requiring the government to produce the informant for an interview by me and an order requiring him to appear at trial, should one be required."

"But, but—" " Mack began.

The judge cut him short. "I agree with your logic, Mr. Gavin, and an

order will be entered requiring the government to produce the informant Juan Martinez for interview and for trial, should one be ordered."

"Good lordy," Reilley whispered as Gavin returned to counsel's table
and sat down next to him. "That order has changed the complexion of this
case completely. Do you think Martinez will have the guts to appear for
trial if he thinks he will have to take the stand and testify against Angel?"

"The government is in a fix," Gavin replied. "Martinez will act like
ninety percent of informants and do all he can not to appear at trial. If
he does, I'll wager he'll hedge on his testimony. Let's wait until the
motion is over and then determine if we won a battle or the war."

Fruin, continuing his testimony, stated that Angel was observed carrying a briefcase onto an American Airlines plane, and that the briefcase
had been x-rayed as he passed through the carry-on luggage checkpoint
at the airport. A surveillance agent reported the briefcase was filled with
stacks of money.

"What happened after that?" Mack asked.

"I boarded the same plane Angel did and I followed him to Durango,
Mexico, but lost track of him shortly after he deplaned."

"When did you next see Angel Herrera?"

"I saw him seven days later at O'Hare Airport as he deplaned from a
flight which came from Mexico City. After that he was followed to a
nightclub on 26th Street in the city and later to the All American Motel
in Cicero, where he checked in with a young woman. At about 5:00 a.m.,
he was picked up from the motel by Ernie Kummer and driven to the
Safe Harbor Motel in Joliet."

"Were any agents conducting surveillance at the Safe Harbor Motel
that night?"

"Yes," Fruin replied, "I had placed two agents at each of five motels on
Interstate 55, at the Joliet exits, in hopes of spotting the load car. At
about 2:00 a.m., the agents stationed at the Safe Harbor Motel radioed
that they had seen a suspicious looking car bearing Texas license plates
arrive at the motel and that two Latino men, who fit drug dealers' profiles,
had registered and entered a room."

"What happened then?" Mack inquired.

"I had a conversation with agent Cass, who was at the scene, and he advised me he saw one of the men in the suspect car go to the trunk and take out a package. Cass said he saw Sal Veta carry a gray tape-wrapped package into the motel room." Fruin stared at the floor, his face flushed.

A shudder rippled through those seated at defense counsel's table. "Bullshit!" Reilley said, unable to suppress his contempt. "The case reports don't show anything about carrying a gray package into the motel room."

Gavin didn't respond, just shook his head. Sal Veta had told him that he had carried a brown toilet kit to the room. Could Cass have made an honest mistake, he wondered.

"I picked up surveillance of Angel Herrera," Fruin further testified, "when he left the All American Motel in the car of Mr. Kummer and started toward Joliet. We used a Chicago Police Department helicopter to follow the car so our surveillance would not be detected. Agent Cass radioed and reported that Herrera and Kummer arrived at the Safe Harbor Motel, went to Room 208, and entered."

"What did you do then?" Mack asked, knowing all he had to do was prompt his well-rehearsed witness and all the right answers would come flowing out.

"We quickly landed the chopper at the far end of the motel parking lot. After talking to my agents, I made the decision to enter room 208. I approached the room with four other agents, and I was about to knock on the door when it opened. Angel Herrera attempted to close the door quickly, but we pushed it open and announced our office. I saw on the chair, situated next to where Angel Herrera was standing, a gray tape-wrapped package, slightly smaller than a football. It was broken open at one end, and I could see a lumpy, brownish powder through a cellophane wrapping."

Gavin looked down the table to see Angel's reaction, and their eyes met. Sullen, he showed little emotion, for he realized that no matter how loudly he screamed out it would do him no good. And he knew that a heavy burden lay on Gavin's shoulders. Somehow, his lawyer would have to show Fruin was lying.

Fruin finished his direct examination by relating how he and the other agents arrested and secured the defendants and then transported them down to DEA headquarters for processing.

"No further questions," assistant U.S. attorney Mack announced smugly.

"You may cross, Mr. Gavin," the judge said invitingly.

Gavin walked slowly to the podium, tension mounting, searching every crevice of his memory for a way to impeach Fruin's testimony. He began by attacking the reliability of the informant.

"No, I had never met or spoken to Juan Martinez prior to his arrest in his house," Fruin answered. "No, he had never shown himself to be a reliable informant prior to his arrest. No, Martinez didn't know what car the heroin was to be transported in, who the mules were, or the motel they were to stay in."

"And, Mr. Fruin," Gavin said emphatically, "informant Martinez never told you or anyone else that heroin was present in Room 208 at the Safe Harbor Motel, did he?"

Fruin couldn't vary from the truth now. Judge Matyan's ruling requiring the informant to appear at trial greatly curtailed the hearsay testimony. He'd blow his whole case if he credited a statement to Martinez he'd have to recant at trial. "No," he said.

Gavin stepped up the tempo of cross-examination. "And Martinez never told you that he had ever seen Angel Herrera in possession of heroin, did he?"

"No."

"Mr. Fruin, you didn't see Angel Herrera, Ernie Kummer, Sal Veta or Claudio Cillas violate any state or federal law that evening prior to the time you entered Room 208, did you?"

"No, I didn't."

"Now, Mr. Fruin, do you really expect this court to believe that Sal Veta went into the trunk of the car, popped the spare tire from the rim, removed a package of heroin, and then carried that package like a football in plain view across the motel parking lot?"

Fruin became surly, "I don't know what the judge will believe."

The witness was on the ropes, defensive, and Gavin kept the pressure on. "Are you trying to tell this court Sal Veta went to the trunk and removed the package of heroin from the spare tire in less than a minute?"

Realizing case reports and his testimony concerning the chronology of events left no time for Sal and Claudio to do anything more than open the trunk and quickly remove a few items, Fruin felt trapped and he blurted out, "I'm telling you what agent Cass told me he saw."

Gavin pressed, "You will agree, won't you, there was no time to remove a package from the spare tire?"

Fruin lost all appearance of credibility. "I can't be the judge of time," he replied.

"Does it sound reasonable to a man with your vast experience in drug law enforcement that a mule would take a package of heroin from a secreted place and carry it out in the open for all the world to see?"

"Yes, it sounds reasonable," he lied.

"That package was in fact a toilet kit, wasn't it?" Gavin said sternly.

"I didn't see it. Agent Cass said it was a gray tape-wrapped package."

Gavin looked into Judge Matyan's eyes and saw his reaction to Fruin's testimony. He was confident the judge recognized the bulk of Fruin's testimony for what it was—bullshit.

"Did you have a search warrant for Room 208?"

"No, we didn't have time to get one," Fruin replied.

Gavin was now poised, ready to strike for the jugular vein, and the correct response of the witness was critical. "Now tell us, Mr. Fruin, if you didn't have a search warrant, and you didn't know heroin was in Room 208, and none of the parties in the room had violated any law, why then, sir…" Gavin broke off for a moment and then rammed home his major thrust. "Why then did you crash in the door of room 208 and arrest Angel Herrera and Ernie Kummer?"

As well prepared as Fruin was, he was caught off guard, and he groped for an answer that wouldn't destroy the government's case. He glanced at Mack, pathetically soliciting a suggestion, and then to an attentive Judge Matyan.

"Well, we're waiting, Mr. Fruin," Gavin said sarcastically.

"We just suspected heroin was in there."

"You mean you violated the Constitution of the United States by invading the privacy of four people on a guess?"

"No," Fruin replied. "Based on what I heard and saw, I thought heroin was in the room."

Gavin turned from the podium, walked over to his beaming co-counsel and asked in a hushed tone, "What do you think, Jim?"

"That was great work," Reilley said. "The judge will have to find the informant unreliable under the case law and find no probable cause for entering the motel room. Hell, if those agents are allowed to break in a bedroom door every time they suspect contraband is present, we might as well strike the unreasonable search and seizure clause from the Constitution."

Gavin walked back to a position directly in front of the witness. Using every bit of skill he had gathered during fifteen years in the criminal defense business, Gavin attempted to impeach and discredit Fruin by showing he was mistaken about the presence of heroin in the motel room.

"There was no mistake," Fruin said indignantly. "That package of heroin over there on the table was on a chair in room 208 when I entered."

Gavin's eyes darted to the heroin which was displayed for maximum effect on the prosecutor's table, then back to Fruin. "Are you," he said, "aware of the penalties for perjury?"

"Objection!" Mack screamed.

"Any more questions, Mr. Gavin?" Judge Matyan said. The tone of his voice indicated he felt Gavin's point had been exhausted and that he would not allow the witness to be badgered.

"None, Your Honor."

Fruin stepped down from the stand and quickly walked past Gavin. The drug cop's fiercely competitive demeanor sent out warning signals.

Chapter 20

▼

REVISIONIST
JURISPRUDENCE

Gavin possessed the basic instincts of a criminal defense attorney. He knew when to trust or distrust, to go for the throat or back off and be gentle, to react with outrage to a prosecutor or judge's conduct or to diplomatically concede and surrender to authority. As Joe Fruin headed for the courtroom door, he turned to Reilley and said, "Where do you think Fruin's going in such a hurry?"

Reilley's eyes widened. "Do you think he's—"

Gavin replied, "Right, and one of us better hustle our butt out to the hall and make sure the prosecutor's next witness isn't given the script."

Reilley bolted from his chair and followed Fruin into the hall, where he stood guard as Ben Cass walked out of the witness room. Fruin tried to whisper a message, but when he saw Reilley glaring at him, he suddenly switched to head and hand signals.

Reilley grunted a laugh, then said, "Give it up. You know it's against court rules to coach Cass on his testimony."

Fruin replied in a sarcastic tone, "I don't need a lecture on the rules from a lawyer. The only things you guys do with rules is piss all over them."

"Maybe," Reilley shot back, "but we don't frame people by planting dope on them and then lying about it from the witness stand."

Sensing a serious confrontation was about to erupt, Cass said, "The judge is waiting for me, Joe. I'd better get...."

"Yeah, Yeah." Fruin said as he spun around and walked away. Reilley grinned as Cass brushed past him and entered the courtroom with a bewildered look on his face.

During direct-exam, Cass performed well, echoing or corroborating Joe Fruin's testimony. He looked and sounded credible when he described the discovery of heroin in the motel room, and when Mack tendered him for cross-exam, he settled back in the witness chair, wondering what was in store for him.

"Good morning, Mr. Cass," Gavin said pleasantly.

Cass narrowed his eyes and nodded.

"Kindly tell Judge Matyan what you saw on the morning in question in the parking lot of the Safe Harbor Motel when Sal Veta and Claudio Cillas arrived."

"I saw Sal Veta pull into a parking space, get out, walk to the trunk, open it and take out a package. Claudio Cillas got out, walked back to the opened trunk and took out what looked like a shirt. The package was a gray tape-wrapped package which appeared a little smaller than a football, and was the type the Herrera organization usually used to conceal heroin. Then the two men walked across the parking lot, up the stairs, and entered Room 208."

"How long did it take for Veta and Cillas to open the trunk and remove the property you described?"

"About a minute or two," Cass replied.

"And where were you located when you saw the actions you just described?"

Cass cleared his throat. "I was in the car at the far end of the parking lot. Agent Hill was in the passenger seat...." His voice trailed off as Reilley walked to a portable blackboard and affixed a photograph to it. From where he was seated, he could see the photograph was an aerial view of the parking lot. At Gavin's direction, he stepped down from the stand and pointed to the location where Sal Veta and he had parked their respective cars. He agreed, with hesitation, the parking lot was eighty percent filled with cars that night, and there were approximately fifteen cars between his car and Sal Veta's. When he pointed to where the cars were parked in the photo, he began to see the errors in his testimony. His vantage point was seventy-five yards away from Sal Veta's car, and the alignment of other parked cars made it virtually impossible to see the trunk. Furthermore, when Claudio Cillas and Sal Veta walked to the stairway, they walked away from him, so that all he could have seen was their backs. With the sudden realization his well-rehearsed testimony wasn't plausible, his face became ashen and a stammer began to punctuate his speech. Gavin increased the intensity of cross-examination until Cass recanted. "I couldn't exactly see Veta take a package from the trunk, but I assumed he did because he didn't have one in his hand when he got out of the car."

"And how would you know that?" Gavin said in a mocking tone. "You were seventy-five yards away, and it was dark and there were at least fifteen cars blocking your view."

"I saw him through the car windows," Cass shot back, credibility gone.

Gavin stood erect at the podium and tapped his pen on the oak wood top until Judge Matyan raised his eyes. He looked directly at the judge as he said to Cass, "Do you really expect us to believe Sal Veta carried the package of heroin across the parking lot just like Walter Payton carries the football for the Chicago Bears?"

"Yes."

"Now, Agent Cass, you knew if there was no heroin in room 208 when you entered, you wouldn't have had grounds to arrest Angel Herrera, isn't that correct?"

Cass remained loyal to his boss and friend. "I suppose that's right. But there was heroin in the room."

Gavin feigned contempt as he addressed the court. "I have no further questions for this witness."

Mack jumped to his feet, face flushed with anger. He was the overly protective captain of the prosecution team, and when Gavin hurt one of his players, he reacted as if he had been slapped in the face. "Judge," he growled, "we have no other witnesses." Turning, he glared at Gavin. "And unless our esteemed counsel has changed his mind, we have stipulated to the admission into evidence of one package of heroin and a chemist's report. Said report renders the opinion that the substance recovered in Room 208 was in fact heroin, with a purity of twenty-two percent."

Gavin recognized his adversary's dilemma. While common practice and trial strategy dictated Mack call the other agents who were at the arrest scene for purposes of corroborating Fruin's and Cass's testimony, he couldn't take the chance that one of them might cave-in during cross-exam and blow the prosecution's case. And it was obvious the prosecutor felt he had met his burden of proof by showing the agents had probable cause to believe a crime was being committed in the motel room. Fruin had stuck to his story that the heroin was on the chair in the motel room when he entered, and Cass stuck to his. The prosecutor figured his case was weak but sufficient for a ruling in his favor.

Judge Matyan granted Gavin's motion for a ten minute recess, a recess Gavin needed badly. Wasting no time, he and Reilley pushed through the courtroom door and walked out into the hall. When they were alone Gavin said, "What do you think? Should we put Angel and Ernie on the stand?"

"Can't do it," Reilley said, shaking his head. "We would make a drastic mistake if we did."

Gavin had already made the decision but wanted his co-counsel's advice. "Why not?" he asked.

"If Angel and Ernie testify, they might mistakenly provide a link which the judge could hang a probable cause finding on. And they really couldn't do us any good since neither one was there when Sal and Claudio arrived at the motel."

"Counselor," Gavin said, "it sounds like you are giving a bit of sage advice. Behold the fish, he never gets in any trouble until he opens his mouth."

"That's it in a mouthful," Reilley said. "Informant Martinez was not shown to be reliable, and Fruin and Cass' testimony about heroin being found in the motel room was incredible. Our motion should be granted."

The image of Judge Matyan stepping down from the bench and leaving the courtroom for recess was fresh in Gavin's memory. Sheer dilemma had reflected in the judge's demeanor. "I'll bet you ten to one," he said, "Matyan is pacing the carpet in chambers, agonizing over the call he's going to have to make."

"Why?" Reilley protested. "If he follows the law, he'll have only one thing to do."

"I wish it were that simple, Jim, but you know as well as I do that Judge Matyan is an expert in Fourth Amendment search and seizure law. But he is also a pragmatist, one who refuses to act for ideological reasons when common sense dictates the ultimate outcome of a controversy."

"Wait a minute, Matt, I don't want to hear it or believe it. Matyan is too fine a constitutional lawyer to...."

Gavin held up his hand. "To find there's no such thing as an illegal search or constitutional violation when a large amount of heroin has been recovered?"

"Sam Matyan won't hurt us," Reilley said. "You know he's an old friend and good drinking buddy."

A wily look crossed Gavins's face. "Of course, Jim. That's why I asked you to come on board."

Moments later Judge Matyan returned to the bench. Looking solemnly at Gavin, he said, "I'd like to hear from you first."

Gavin sensed that the judge was disposed to deny the motion, that he looked to him to provide some novel reasoning or bring to light some fact which was overlooked. "The law," he began, "promulgated in the Aguilar, Roper and Spinelli cases, all of which have been recently decided by the United States Supreme Court, mandate that the defendants' motion to suppress evidence be granted for the following reasons. First, the informant had never cooperated with the government prior to this case and had never given any information that could provide a track record for credibility. Second, the information, or informant's tip if you prefer, concerned itself with the expectant sale of heroin by Angel Herrera to a man from Miami. Informant Martinez didn't tell the agents that heroin was located in a particular place, at a particular time, and in the possession of a particular person. When the agents stood in front of Room 208, about to cave in the door, they had no basis upon which they could reasonably believe heroin was in the room. At best, they suspected it."

The judge bent forward, a concerned look flashed across his face, and he appeared to nod in agreement with Gavin's argument.

"The record is clear," Gavin continued, "the agents went in on a wing and a prayer, on a hunch, that heroin would be in that room. That's exactly the type of unreasonable police conduct the search and seizure clause contained in the Fourth Amendment to the United States constitution is designed to stop."

Mack, realizing he needed a knock-out punch to overcome Gavin's argument, rose dramatically, and gave one of his better theatrical performances. Stern faced, he slowly raised a finger to point at the gray tape-wrapped package of heroin. "That dope! That sinister and vile looking substance, destined for the addicts of Chicago, was found in room 208 in the Safe Harbor Motel in Joliet. When the agents entered that room, Angel Herrera and Ernie Kummer were inside with the heroin. The arresting agents acted reasonably throughout the investigation. They substantiated the informant's tip and reasonably believed a crime was being committed. And that," he emphasized, "adds up to probable cause."

"Thank you, gentlemen, for your excellent representation of the evidence and the law," Judge Matyan said. "I am convinced that the information given by an otherwise unreliable informant was made reliable by virtue of the agent's surveillance and Mr. Herrera's arrival at the motel. When Mr. Herrera arrived at the motel, all the pieces of the puzzle fit together, and at that point, the agents had probable cause to enter the motel room." He paused for a moment, looking out over the rims of his glasses to see Gavin's and Reilley's reaction, and then continued. "While your analysis of the facts and law is meritorious, Mr. Gavin, I do not agree that U.S. versus Spinelli and U.S. versus Aguilar are controlling."

"Judge," Gavin interrupted, "the Supreme Court in Aguilar set forth a two prong test for demonstrating the reliability of an informant, and thus probable cause for a search without a warrant. One, the prosecutor must show the informant has a track record for reliable information. And, two, the tip must be independently corroborated by agents."

The judge's tone changed, and he became defensive as he said, "I don't believe Aguilar is the law any longer. Even if the informer's tip is deficient under Aguilar, it may meet constitutional requirements if it is sufficiently corroborated by independent investigation by agents."

Gavin was dismayed with the judge's mindset. He had presented several motions in past years which had raised similar issues, and he had never seen Matyan search crevices or under rocks for facts or rationale to support a ruling. Matyan had always been a staunch supporter of personal liberties. "Judge," he asked, "is that your novel interpretation of the law or do you have authority for it?"

"I think, counselor," he replied curtly, "you will find U.S. versus Graham, 548 Fed 2nd 1302, is analogous." He then looked at the court clerk. "Let the record show that the motion to suppress is denied."

Needing to rethink his position and not believing in post mortems, Gavin left Jim Reilley the task of winding up business with Terry Mack and of explaining the outcome of their motion to Angel and Ernie.

Returning to his office, he was pleasantly surprised to find Tricia seated behind his desk, a warm look of understanding and sympathy in her eyes. Just the elixir I needed, he thought. "You know, honey," he said, "until I saw you an old adage kept racing through my mind—a doctor buries his mistakes, but a mistake buries a lawyer."

"Matt," she protested, "you didn't make one mistake. No one could have presented the motion to suppress as well as you did."

"I know, but lawyers bear a heavy cross. We feel we're to blame for the loss of a case regardless of the evidence, the law, or proclivities of a judge."

"It seems to me that Judge Matyan had his mind made up long before the hearing started," Tricia said, wanting Gavin to talk, to vent his frustrations.

"I'm sorry to say the ruling was the result of a conspiracy," he lamented. "The Reagan Administration, or more precisely, Reagan's Justice Department, has influenced several of our more politically powerful appeals court and district court judges to systematically erode the exclusionary rule. It's the beginning of an insidious assault on the Constitution."

Tricia said, "If they can influence Sam Matyan, they can influence any judge in the country."

"Sad but true," Gavin replied. "It appears Matyan has been brainwashed into thinking that if a person is caught with twenty-five pounds of heroin in his possession, he should not escape prosecution and conviction on a legal technicality, even though that technicality is a constitutionally guaranteed freedom."

"Do you think," Tricia said, "that Reagan's first appointment to the Seventh Circuit Court of Appeals, the ultra-conservative's, ultra-conservative Judge Bosner, is behind this scheme?"

"No doubt in my mind, sweetheart. Bosner is getting his sailing orders from Washington, but he is the judicial activist who authors policy in this circuit. Matyan couldn't hit head-on into the new wave of judicial activism, and he knew it. If he had ruled for Angel and Ernie, Mack would have appealed the ruling and Judge Bosner sure as hell would have reversed it. In the final analysis, Sam Matyan wouldn't have been able to preserve the Constitution."

Tricia was mindful that until recently she had been a staunch conservative on most political issues. "Do you think," she asked, "that the ultra-conservatives will change our legal system?" Gavin shrugged his shoulders and grimaced. "While the Fourth Amendment assures the right of the people to be secure from unreasonable searches, it is silent as to what remedy, if any, is to be provided to a victim of an illegal intrusion. Prior to 1924, no barrier existed to stop the introduction in criminal trials of evidence obtained in violation of the Fourth Amendment. The federal courts created the barrier by establishing the exclusionary rule."

Tricia thought for a moment. "I guess then Judge Bosner and other Reagan judges feel that since the federal courts have giveth, they can taketh away."

"Something like that, counselor. And the bottom line is our street ignorant federal judges will be responsible for inducing and authorizing perjury and burglary by law enforcement officers."

Tricia's eyes widened. "That's a pretty heavy accusation," she said, "especially if it includes Judge Matyan."

"I know; I know. But the primary purpose for the exclusionary rule is to deter unlawful police conduct. Cops and drug agents have been abusing our search and seizure laws in spite of judicial controls but on a limited basis. I worry that if the rule is done away with an unbridled police state will result, one similar to what can be found in Russia."

"Doesn't Judge Matyan understand these things?" Tricia said.

"He foresees the problem, but he believes law enforcement agents will exercise self-restraint and not violate anyone's rights. That's like putting the proverbial wolf in charge of the chicken coup. When judges were looking critically at searches without warrants, feeling they were unreasonable per se, there was a rein on cops. If cops wanted to get inside someone's house to conduct a fishing trip, they would have to go before a judge and swear falsely before him that they had probable cause to believe contraband was located on the premises they wanted searched. That formality, plus a trial judge's review of the facts alleged in support of the warrant during a motion to suppress hearing, kept the cops in line."

Jim Reilley came into the office during the conversation and sat down on the sofa, a wry look on his face. "Most cops it did," he interjected, "but there have always been cops like Fruin who would perjure themselves before a judge to obtain a warrant. Hell's bells! It's easy when you don't have to divulge who the informant is or anything about him. The Fruins in law enforcement simply invent an informant and a set of facts that show the informant is reliable and credible. That's all that's required for a search warrant."

"True," Gavin replied, "but the legal requirements for a search with a warrant have deterred the vast majority of law enforcement agents from illegal intrusions. As soon as word gets around that federal judges will support invasions into places of privacy without reasonable grounds or a search warrant as long as contraband is discovered, the expectation to privacy in one's home will be a thing of the past.

Tricia asked, "How long do you think the state court judges can resist the pressure?"

Gavin looked at Reilley as he said, "The judges in the criminal division of the Circuit Court of Cook County are for the most part lawyers who had extensive criminal law practices before taking positions on the bench. They are much more savvy, more aware of the proclivities of law enforcement agents for perjury. They'll resist as long as they can."

"Right," Reilley said, "the judges in state court are street smart and won't put up with Washington pressure like Sam Matyan did. Why even Terry Mack was surprised at Matyan's ruling."

Gavin looked from Reilley to Tricia. "I told you both this case was going to be a ballbuster. So let's repair our bruised egos and prepare a winning defense for trial. We're going to beat Terry Mack and Joe Fruin."

"Matt, you're the quintessential optimist," Tricia said. "You know as well as I that after today's hearing Angel and Ernie have serious problems."

You're right," Gavin said in a somber tone. "But that's because there's a new sinister twist in their case. After the testimony today revealed Juan Martinez was the snitch who brought Angel down, I would guess Martinez has a very short life expectancy. And if he's killed, Angel will probably have to skip town."

Tricia's face blanked. "Gawd," she said softly, "This case is incredible."

Chapter 21

▼

CHANGING TIMES

There were times when business could be discussed and critical issues decided better at some place other than his office. So when Angel offered to buy dinner at La Hacienda Del Sol, his favorite Mexican-style restaurant, Gavin quickly responded, "Tricia and I will be there at six o'clock with big appetites."

Angel was seated at his preferred table in the popular near-west side eatery when Gavin and Tricia walked through the door. And Julio, the personable owner, was standing next to him with a broad, welcoming smile on his face. "Hello, Abogado," Angel and Julio said in unison.

After Gavin and Tricia were seated, Julio served a pitcher of his famous margaritas. "The best in the city," he bragged.

"What special treat do you have for us this evening?" Gavin asked.

"I go to la cocina to prepare enchiladas a la preferida," Julio replied in fractured English.

Julio's persona was primarily responsible for the success of the restaurant. The short, barely five feet, six-inch, gentle natured man lways greeted his customers with a captivating gap-toothed smile. It was rumored that he dabbled in drug trafficking until he had saved nough money to buy the restaurant, but Julio always proudly pro-laimed he had worked as a dishwasher and cook until he had saved nough for the down payment. Then he knocked on Matt Gavin's door nd asked for his professional help. It had been five years since the estaurant purchase, but Julio still never referred to Gavin by his name. t was always, "my lawyer." And the elfish man had another endearing uality. He thoroughly enjoyed telling jokes and humorous stories bout the legal profession.

"Get ready, Tricia," Gavin said as he spied Julio shuffling back toward heir table. "It's joke time."

"My lawyer," Julio said excitedly as he sat down. "Me going to get a lew lawyer."

Gavin grimaced, then, playing along with him, said in a concerned one, "Why, Julio? Where have I gone wrong?"

"Me want lawyer like the woman lawyer I watched in a TV movie last light. She won a murder trial for her client and then afterwards had a wild sex affair with him."

Gavin had seen the movie. He raised his eyebrows and braced him-self for Julio's punch line.

"Si," he said. "Me want woman lawyer who will win my case and give ne pussy, too." Julio put his head back and laughed loudly.

In light of the delicious meal and Julio's joke, it took sheer dedication o turn his attention to business, but when Angel asked the unexpected question, dining etiquette was abandoned. Gavin stared at Angel with iis mouth agape for a few moments, then said in a voice rising in aston-shment. "You want me to do what?"

Tricia attempted to suppress a cough-like laugh but couldn't.

Angel sipped wine from his glass before repeating the question in a iushed tone. "Matt, I'd like you to ask the judge for permission to travel o Durango for two weeks."

"Do you realize, Angel, if I asked the judge for permission for you to travel to Mexico, he'd put me in an insane asylum and you in jail immediately?"

Tricia agreed. "It would be a dumb move because there are too many of your amigos who have gotten out on bail and then skipped. You were lucky your bond hearing came before all the hysteria about bond jumping started."

"Don't delude yourself," Gavin cautioned. "Times are changing. The courts aren't setting reasonable bonds for defendants charged with drug trafficking anymore, and that is especially true if the defendant is a Latino. President Reagan's boys at the Justice Department have a bail-reform act before Congress right now which will revolutionize the present bond system. When it becomes law, the prosecutors will be able to keep anyone they want in jail."

Angel leaned over the table and whispered, "I have a celebration I must attend in Durango."

Gavin shook his head. "Is it worth the risk of going to jail?"

Angel continued to whisper. "To my family it is. Comandante Gonzales, the head of the federales in Durango, died of a heart attack three months ago. The new Comandante is investigating the death as if it were an assassination. I've done business with the new Comandante in the past, so...."

Gavin sensed the untimely death of Alfonso Gonzales was shrouded in mystery. From what he knew about the legendary warrior, it was doubtful anyone would believe his death was from natural causes. "If you go," he told Angel, "you'll be taking a big chance. Fruin and Gonzales were friends. He probably attended the funeral and probably put an agent in Durango, just to see if you'd show. Your bond would be revoked the day after an agent spotted you there."

Angel took several swallows of wine before he said, "What's the use of sticking around for trial? I'm going to be found guilty."

"Maybe not," Gavin said. "I've got an ace up my sleeve. We got a chance of winning your case.

Angel's eyes widened. "I don't think so. I'm going to get fucked. First, it was the plant of shit by Fruin, then the judge's ruling on my motion to suppress. Now I'm in the middle of a changing law system. What's just and fair won't count at trial."

The symptoms were all present and Gavin was deeply concerned. "Angel," he said, "I don't want you to skip. I want you here so that we can fight this bullshit case together."

"What kind of time do you think I'll get if convicted?"

"I think you'd do seven to eight years on a fifteen year sentence," Gavin replied as he studied his client. Angel had obviously weighed the pros and cons of skipping town. If he did go, he could forget about the unpleasant rigors of a trial and a potential jail term and live a life of freedom and luxury in Mexico. But failure to appear for trial would mean giving up his house, his real estate and business investments, and paramount to all immigrants, his citizenship.

"I trust your advice," he said, "but why would Judge Matyan give me fifteen years when I know most judges would give me thirty?"

"Because the new Reagan judges suffer from the Judge Roy Bean syndrome. They have decided the only way to stop drug use is to put drug traffickers in jail until they are too old to sell drugs. And if Congress had authorized the death penalty, many judges would not only impose the death penalty but would walk the condemned man to the gallows and pull the lever."

"That sucks," Tricia said. "That's exactly the perverted rationale Hitler used to solve his problems. In reality the sadistic sentences are worse crimes than those committed by the drug traffickers."

"True," Gavin agreed somberly, "especially when you consider that drug dealing is a victimless crime, and most guys arrested with drugs are mules who played a very small role in the offense."

Angel attempted to pay the dinner check but Julio would not accept his money, disdainfully pushing it back at him. He had fixed one of his sumptuous dinners for, as he said, "my lawyer," and insisted that the meal was on the house. As charming and pleasant as the little man was, he could be quite firm. Angel surrendered gracefully once he realized he was not about to win the money-pushing contest. He shrugged his shoulders, tacitly saying, I tried.

Gavin watched Angel as he slipped through the crowd of people standing at the bar and walked out through the door. "Angel looks like a dead man walking," he said.

Tricia slid her hand across the table and gently rubbed Gavin's arm. "Don't, she said, "worry so much about Angel. If he

decides to jump bond, you can't stop him."

"It's not only the fear that when I wake up tomorrow morning or the next, I won't have a client, but it's the whole drug business. It reminds me of politics and religion where fanatics line up on each side of issues and never give in, each side thinking the other is in league with Satan. I'm beginning to envy the tunnel-visioned fanatics who seem to be the only ones able to clearly distinguish right from wrong."

Tricia found that she too was caught up in moral uncertainty. She was quiet and pensive as they left the restaurant, entered Gavin's car and began the drive to his condo. Having never discussed drug use from a personal viewpoint with him, she found it difficult to broach a subject which might prove harmful to their relationship. Drugs and drug use had always been discussed from a detached legal viewpoint, with the user never considered as an individual, only as a client-defendant. She broke the thoughtful silence, "What do you think? Should drugs be legalized?"

"I don't know," Gavin said. "After sixteen years in the law business, I still don't have an answer. Bottom line is use and sale of heroin, pot and coke is against the law, and the trouble one gets into for standing up for the individual's right to do drugs just isn't worth it."

Tricia was aware drugs had never been part of Gavin's life. They were just absent, never thought of and never missed. With her and her contemporaries, drugs had been as commonplace and pervasive as baseball, beer and premarital sex. She had tried pot, and on a rare occasion coke. But she had never discussed the use of drugs with Gavin. He was too close-minded about drug use. Deciding it was time to put her feelings on the table, she said, "I think drugs should be legalized. If someone wants to use pot or coke or heroin, why should a government be able to stop him?

Gavin was surprised by Tricia's viewpoint. "You're right, sweetheart. Something has to be done soon."

"But what can be done, and what can we do?" she said.

Gavin sat up in his seat. "Well, for starters, we have to identify the problem. It appears our elected state and federal legislators have followed the will of the majority of the people when they enacted laws making it illegal to use or sell hard drugs. But, was that really the will of the majority or the fanatical desire of a few powerful people who could influence congressional action?"

Tricia thought for a few moments. "I know that Prohibition was brought about by a powerful few, and it turned out to be a drastic mistake. In 1920, mass hysteria made it appear the majority of people voted for the constitutional amendment which banned the sale of alcoholic beverages. A few years later it turned out not to be the will of the majority. Prohibition was a gross mistake which created more social ills and suffering than it cured. Users bought all the booze they wanted on the black market and in speakeasies, an era of organized crime was spawned, and a mockery was made of the legal system."

Gavin agreed, "That's right. But at least the right to imbibe in an alcoholic beverage was put to a referendum. Drug laws were passed by Congress more than forty years ago, long before the American public knew what coke, pot, or heroin was."

"I betcha," Tricia said, "if drug use was put to a vote by an educated public today, most drug laws would be repealed."

"There's a good possibility, but a lid would have to be kept on the vainglorious politicians who are responsible for the hyperbole and propaganda against drugs. For their own good, they create public opinion. The best critique I've seen concerning the cocaine problem was written by a friend of mine, and it was published in many legal publications. I just happen to have a copy with me." He reached into his jacket pocket, pulled out the printed article, and said, "Read it, hon."

Tricia read aloud:

"Coke use is pervasive in our society, with frequency of use more dependent upon ability to pay for it than on legal controls and restrictions. It's the glamour drug, the one used by the sexually sophisticated and active, the over-achievers, by all those who truly believe—while in the throes of a coke habit—that it increases physical and mental well-being, performances and enjoyments.

While many argue it is not a physiologically addictive drug, it is unquestionably psychologically habituating. And, it's difficult to understand how anyone who has witnessed the downside of a coke dependency can believe it is not physiologically addicting, with withdrawal effects ranging from depression to paranoia and schizophrenia, from anxiety to suicidal tendencies, from nervous twitches to rotting blood vessels and tissues in a user's nose.

And cocaine is the swiftest and most deceiving joyride to financial self-destruction. Any sort of romance with the White Lady will cost a bundle of cash, and if the user has a serious affair, he is likely to lose a family, a job or profession, and wind up bankrupt.

Then there is the very real danger of jail for a sadistically cruel period of time. Judges, acting like they themselves are rushing with cocaine, are committing atrocities when they sentence coke traffickers to ten, twenty, thirty and fifty years in jail. Such a sentence, imposed in self-righteous and arrogant ignorance, is a much greater violation of fundamental human rights and morality than the offense committed by the sentenced drug trafficker. But it does no good to argue with the sadomasochists who arrogantly perch up on benches, drenched in black robes of justice, nor to ask for support from politicians, the news media, the general public. To them, the coke trafficker is a leper, an ugly cripple who should be locked in a cage and separated from the decent folks in the world.

In spite of all the horrendous consequences, coke use flourishes and the demand increases. Droves of people wait in the wings to step into the role of an annihilated coke dealer. The competition is fierce at all levels of trafficking-from cocoa leaf growers in Peru and Bolivia, to major dealers in Miami, to small street pushers.

And the nagging questions persist. What good has all the efforts of the President's Commission, the DEA and other state law enforcement agencies, and the religious institutions done? Has the sadistic jailing of drug traffickers and annihilation of their families been worth it? Objective viewpoint: Absolutely not. The entire war on drugs has been a sham, a charade.

Current law enforcement procedures will never stamp out the cocaine epidemic. It is bound to get worse.

Objective viewpoint: The only feasible solution to the problem is to legalize cocaine use. That's the only way to denude the fickle and treacherous bitch of all her glamour and mystique and show her for what she is. Once legalized, the affluent socialite would have to stand in the line behind the petty thief, and in front of the truck driver, at a state owned and operated store to buy coke at one-twentieth the price the illegal drug sells for. Glamorous and fashionable? Not for long. And the violent criminal element who control its importation—the Mafia families in the northeast and the Colombians and Cubans in Florida—would soon be out of business. No one would be willing to pay their price and conspire in the drug underworld as long as cocaine was legal.

More importantly, once legal the problems of drug use and abuse will be out in the open, where it should be. A drug user can't beat his habit if he has to hide it. He has to be given a chance to freely air his problem and seek help without risking cries of outrage or jail.

But will coke use ever be legalized? Objective viewpoint: Hell, no. The primary reason is paradoxical. Those in law enforcement and those in peripheral roles who so vaingloriously oppose drug trafficking would cut their own throats if they were instrumental in legalizing cocaine use or totally eliminating illegal drug trafficking. Fifty percent of federal judges, prosecutors and law enforcement agents would be out of prestigious, well paying jobs. If drug offenders suddenly stopped clogging up and overcrowding the judicial system, one hundred thousand jobs would be lost in the support ranks, such as marshal's service, court personnel, probation service and the Bureau of Prisons. State and federal prisons hold over five hundred thousand prisoners, sixty-five percent of which are incarcerated because of drug law offenses. Additionally, there are over one million men and woman being supervised by the probation departments and parole commissions.

Pity the naive, misled taxpayer. He supports through his hard earned tax dollars not only a budget breaking payroll of federal and state employees, but the object of his hatred. When a judge snuffs out a drug trafficker's life by incarcerating him for a ghastly period, the taxpayer must pay a staggering sum for his room, board, books and recreation. When will Americans wake up? Politicians—and judges are first and foremost politicians—aren't going to sacrifice any part of their sweet life for the good of society. They ascribe to the Yuppies' motto: after me comes thee."

"Nice read," Gavin said as he took the article from Tricia and slipped it back into his pocket.

"This whole drug business gets more mysterious every day, Matt."

"It sure does," Gavin said. And the American public will have to wake up before it's too late. Court systems and law enforcement systems haven't done anything but exacerbate drug use problems. It's mind boggling when you consider the amount of drug use that's going on around us at this moment." He jabbed a finger toward the sprawling four square block medical center they drove past. A prestigious hospital, medical school and clinic offered help and hope for the sick and injured. He said, "At this moment in the apartments and living quarters surrounding the hospital, several nurses, medical technicians, and medical students are doing pot, having looked forward to a toke all week. They are chatting about matters important only to them, having a good time, bothering no one. While in other living quarters and in nearby bars and cafes, the more affluent interns and young doctors are laying lines of coke out for anxious young ladies."

Tricia had been there, had seen it. "No doubt about it."

Gavin gestured over his shoulder with his thumb. "Now on my side, there are many people in that ghetto who'd like to escape for a little while, to feel the rush of euphoria that heroin brings on." He took his foot off the gas pedal, and as the car slowed he crouched up over the steering wheel so he could examine the dingy store fronts, the numerous liquor stores with cheap wines their major attraction, the litter scattered about the pavement, the look of hopelessness and despair in the faces of people who stood in front of the run down old brick and wooden houses. "I guess I can't blame them," he said. "Within four blocks of us, right now, there must be a dozen persons shooting heroin into their bloodstreams. Heroin is the ultimate escape for them."

Tricia said, "I wish there was some way of controlling its use without penalizing the user and dealer so severely."

"Not likely to happen, not as long as heroin users and dealers are considered by the vast majority of people to be the vilest creatures on earth. A lot of people can accept pot and coke use, but very, very few will ever be able to tolerate heroin use."

"Yeah, people see only the evil connected with it."

"Another paradox," Gavin said. Morphine and heroin have a legitimate medical purpose. Millions of needy people, particularly those wounded during wars, were given morphine for intense pain. And until 1900, it was legal to sell and use opium and its derivatives. In the 1890's, newspapers and magazines advertised opium as the ultimate cure-all for aches and pains. And, one could walk down and buy it at a drugstore or liquor store just as easily as a bottle of rum."

Surprised, Tricia asked, "How did they use opium in those days?"

"The Chinese get the dubious distinction for introducing opium and its derivatives into this country, so Chinatown was where the first opium dens were located."

Tricia motioned with her hand. "Isn't Chinatown located a couple of blocks to our right?"

"Yes. If this were 1890, we could stop by a 'hop joint' and smoke opium through a two-foot long bamboo pipe. In those days, the average law-abiding citizen would step into an opium den to soothe a wide variety of emotional and physical aches and pains. It was considered less injurious to the body than alcohol. About the time morphine use became widespread, the laws changed."

"Slam bamm," Tricia said. "All of a sudden the casual user was an outlaw and immoral person. That raises a profound question for legal philosophers. How can a society pass criminal laws that prohibit an act which is not immoral? Throughout history, criminal laws have followed the moral code. Virtually all crimes—murder, rape, robbery and so on—are immoral acts. No reasonable person can find one socially redeemable quality in those heinous offenses. But drug use, per se, is a victimless crime. Theoretically, it injures no one except the user."

Gavin was thoughtful for several minutes, then said, "No matter how philosophical you may want to get, the answer to your question is quite simple. The powerful majority in our country do not want the minority doing drugs. Morality or freedom of choice do not count. Those that do drugs will have to stop or find a place in this world where they can use and deal in a drug of choice without governmental interference."

"Or else, Matt, they can look forward to going to the shithouse for a long time. It's that simple."

As he turned the car north onto Lake Shore Drive, Gavin gazed out the window and saw an angry, windswept Lake Michigan breaking over the seawall, then the Chicago Yacht Club majestically perched on the shore of Monroe Harbor. The yachts and sailboats weren't lying at anchor in front of the Yacht Club yet, but it wouldn't be long. They were being taken out of winter storage and would be arriving at the harbor throughout the next month. So would the cocaine. The wealthy jet-setters from North Michigan Avenue and Skokie and Oak Brook—the sons and daughters of well-known politicians, judges and businessmen—would be bringing it with them. It was the "in thing" to do.

Gavin turned the car onto the circular drive that fronted Harbor Point, his condo-apartment building, and came to a stop at the entrance door. Taking Tricia in his arms, he said, "Why don't you go up to my pad and freshen up while I park the car."

"Hurry up," she replied softly.

After Gavin had parked his car in the underground garage and taken the elevator to the 53rd floor, he walked quickly down the hall to his condo door. He was groping for a key in his suit coat pocket when the door across the hall swung open, allowing the unmistakable odor of pot to drift out into the hallway. "Hey, Matt, how are you?" Barry Gold asked over the sound of men's and women's laughter.

The young bachelor lawyer was noticeably high, and the sounds emanating from his apartment indicated his guests were in a party mood. "Hi, Barry," Gavin said. "What's the gang over for this time?"

"A bunch who live in the building wanted to have a little get together. Come on in and have a drink or a hit of ganga if you want."

Gavin almost laughed at the irony of the situation. He studied Barry's guests for moments, then said, "Some other time. Please be careful."

"Don't worry, neighbor," Barry said as he shut his door.

Resuming the search for his door key, Gavin wondered how many residents in a building where three judges, a police captain, and many prestigious businessmen lived did drugs. He barely touched the key to the door lock when he got a pleasant surprise. The door swung open, revealing a wide-eyed Tricia clad in lace panties and a souvenir T-shirt they had brought back from Mexico. NO FRIGGIN IN THE RIGGIN was inscribed across the front.

"I might just as well join the party across the hall," Gavin teased. "You don't look like you'd be too much fun tonight."

She grabbed hold of his hand and in one motion pulled him inside and shut the door. "Why don't you try me?" she said as she touched her lips to his, allowing him to sense the warmth and scent of her body.

It always amazed Gavin how Tricia could excite him into making love with such passion. One moment he would be withdrawn, mind attuned to business or personal problems. Moments later, after she began to apply her lips and tongue to his body, he'd lose all vestiges of restraint. It took her under two minutes to lure him into the bedroom, where she demanded uninhibited lovemaking. She was everything he wanted in a woman, mentally, emotionally and physically.

When the rapture was over, Gavin lay exhausted, his head buried under a pillow. His mind, which had been temporarily separated from his body, gradually began to spin. It focused on natural law and man's instinctive right to seek revenge. "I was just thinking," he said, "about the Bad Guys doing drugs and the Good Guys retaliating against them by putting them in jail. But what if a Bad Guy got screwed, would he have a natural right to retaliate?"

Tricia took the pillow off the back of his head, propped it up behind her and sat up. Leaning back, she said, "I'm not sure I know what a Bad Guy is, but I do know a naughty one when I see one." She touched her finger to his buttocks and gently scratched.

He rolled over on his back and looked up at her. "I'm serious. Do Angel and Ernie have a right under the natural law to seek revenge against Joe Fruin or against the snitch, Juan Martinez?"

She rolled her eyes. "I don't know, and I don't care. Angel broke the law, and it's up to the drug agents and prosecutors to enforce the law as best they can. And, I know you're one of the sweet Good Guys."

"Flattery will get you another thumping."

"I'm ready," she replied coyly as she slid down next to him. "No more business talk tonight, okay."

"I just thought you'd like to talk about the philosophy of—"

"Shut up," Tricia said as she pressed her body against him.

Chapter 22

▼

ROBE ARROGANCE

The Union Athletic Club, a private all-male social and athletic club, was the after-work playground for some of Chicago's more affluent business and professional men. It was where they shed frustrations generated in executive offices or on stock exchanges or in courtrooms. Some chose to beat the stress factor by swimming in an Olympic-size pool, others by jogging or exercising in the gym. Gavin preferred to beat a small blue ball against the walls of a handball or racquetball court three times a week with some of the stiffest competition in the Chicagoland area. The match he had just finished playing had been great fun, but for his good friend, Ray Bern, it had been infuriating. Gavin fought back the urge to laugh as he walked out through the handball court door, taunting, "Just remember, brains and trickery will always win out over sheer strength."

"Ah, bullshit!" the usual stately and polite judge replied.

Gavin noticed Ray Bern was dripping with sweat and breathing hard. "You got a good workout, huh?"

"You played one of your patented handball matches," Bern moaned. "You let me win the first game by hitting into my power. Then in the second and third game you dinked me to death by hitting slow curve balls and lob shots that slid down the side walls. I ran my ass off."

After showering, Gavin suggested that before leaving the club they stop at the Rendezvous Bar for some liquid refreshment and commentary on the match. He knew it was going to take the customary whiskey and water with some tactful humor to jar his friend from his irascible mood. After the waiter had served their drinks, he lifted his glass in toast and said, "Nice game. You moved like a cat, and your kill shots were hitting the wall one inch above the floor."

"Thanks, Matt, but that was the best customer's game I've ever seen you play." A sly look crossed his face as he said, "As a matter of fact, you deserve an Oscar for the acting job you did in the first game."

Gavin sat back and studied the man who was considered one of the most brilliant and incorruptible judges in the Cook County court system. "I must be losing my touch," he joked.

They sipped on their whiskey and water and chatted about fun things for over an hour when Gavin saw Terry Mack walk into the bar. He waved to the grim looking prosecutor.

Mack nodded greetings as he slid into a chair next to Gavin. He took a deep breath and explained his unexpected visit. "Judge Matyan is in bad shape. He was taken by ambulance from his home to the hospital just a few hours ago."

"Cancer?" Gavin inquired.

"Yes, it has spread from his liver to other organs. He's not expected to make it for more than a couple of days."

Gavin looked at Ray Bern and saw his body slump and his head lower. He and Sam Matyan were close friends. Gavin's mind drifted. He remembered Sam Matyan sitting right where Ray Bern was seated, only one month before. He vividly recalled the smile on his face, the twinkle in his eyes. The judge had walked up to his table and said, "Let me get you another one of those elixirs you use for sore muscles. You look like you can use it."

"Sit down, Sam," he had replied. "My favorite uncle once told me that a man should never imbibe alone." As the judge settled into a chair, he observed him closely. Federal judges rarely allowed themselves to be seen in public with attorneys who practiced before them, especially one who vociferously and tenaciously defended those who were accused of being on the other side of the law. But that night had been different. The judge had wanted company, someone to chat with. "Someone he liked and respected," he had said, "for the way he analyzed the law and argued his positions, foregoing the cock and bull stories most lawyers came to court with."

The barroom in the private club had offered the solitude needed to drink their cocktails and talk unpretentiously, which they did until nearly midnight. He had noticed the change in the judge's physical appearance—the deep lines in his face, the pallor of his skin, the saggy look of his body. But because his eyes had retained the bright glow of an indomitable spirit, he had assumed a minor ailment had been the cause. He felt foolish now, for he should have suspected something was wrong when the judge's topic of conversation had kept drifting toward the philosophy of law and morality, subjects he had never discussed socially in the twenty years he had served as a federal judge.

"You know," the sensitive jurist had said, "this whole drug business had me totally perplexed for a long time. When President Kennedy appointed me in 1961, drug problems were limited to hippies, musicians and motorcycle gangs. I must admit it was my personal conviction that an adult should have the right to put anything he chooses into his body and that a government doesn't have a lawful right to interfere."

Gavin had felt the urge to question some of the judge's recent opinions. "Well then—"

"Lately, however, my beliefs have changed for two major reasons. One, the irrefutable fact that an illegal drug causes so much waste and injury to the self-destructing user, and two, the crimes that are a direct consequence of drug use and drug dealing. Drug users commit thefts and robberies to pay for their drug of choice, and drug dealers use every type of violence to collect a debt or silence a snitch. And, user-dealers will never change."

Gavin's attention was brought back to the table conversation when Mack said, "Judge Matyan is a great judge and quality person. I hope we don't lose him as our trial judge."

The full realization of Sam Matyan's health problems hit Gavin. "Just who," he said, "do you think we'll draw for a trial judge if Sam Matyan steps out of the case?"

Mack glanced from Gavin to Ray Bern. "I'm sure it'll be one of President Reagan's new appointments. Maybe Dalton Dart."

"Shit," Gavin groaned. "The Angel Herrera case has been a pain in the balls since day one. If Dart gets the case, he'll cut my balls off."

*   *   *   *

It was one month later when Gavin's worst fears became reality. He and Jim Reilley were ordered to appear with their clients to Judge Dalton Dart's courtroom for a status hearing. As he sat at defendant's table waiting for the judge to take the bench, he vividly recalled the last time he and Dalton Dart had met in a courtroom. It was after a bitterly fought breach of contract trial. He had persuaded a jury to award his client three million dollars, and Dart, who had represented a large insurance company, couldn't accept responsibility for the loss. Dart had made a fool of himself, bitterly accusing him of tricking the judge and jury, then storming out of the courtroom, face distorted with anger, vowing, "I'll get even with you, Matt Gavin, if it's the last thing I do."

"Hear Ye! Hear Ye! Hear Ye!" Marshall Kerski sang out in a rich baritone voice, raising and lowering the gavel that beckoned those seated in the courtroom to their feet. "This Honorable Court is now in session, Judge Dalton Dart presiding."

Gavin stood erect, more in respect for the judicial system than for the judge, and watched the short, barely five-feet-eight inches, thin man with slouched posture slowly mount the three steps to the bench. He swallowed hard, the bitter taste of frustration permeating his mouth. How, he wondered, with all the competent and worthy lawyers in this district could the Reagan power brokers pick Dalton Dart to sit as a federal judge. It was an insult to the memory of the brilliant pragmatist Sam Matyan to have Dart sit in the same chair and peer out over the same bench.

Gavin and most of the people in the courtroom were resuming their seats when the judge said, "I have a procedure that I follow every Monday morning, and that is I ask all in my courtroom to stand and recite the 'Pledge of Allegiance.'" The judge turned to face the American flag draped on the wall, placed the palm of his right hand over his heart and solemnly began, "I pledge allegiance to the flag of the United States of America and to the Republic, for which it stands, one nation, under God, indivisible, with liberty and justice for all."

Most lawyers and litigants in the courtroom remained silent, a few followed the judge's lead with weak voices. Gavin emphasized loudly, "With liberty and justice for all."

Reilley leaned close to Gavin and remarked, "I wish he'd forget the hypocritical rhetoric and just tell us if he's going to be fair and impartial."

Gavin doubted that the judge could overcome biases and prejudices and rule with impartiality when the interests of the United Stated Attorney's office were at stake. What the prosecutors who appeared before him wanted, they were going to get. He pressed his thumb against the table top as he uttered in a low tone, "He'll be a rubber stamp."

Gavin recalled the grumbling among defense attorneys which started shortly after Dart became a district court judge. Where did the Reagan administration get this guy? they asked. Did he ever get near a courtroom before becoming a judge? Trying hard to put aside his personal dislike for the man, Gavin began an investigation of the appointment process that resulted in an unqualified lawyer becoming a judge. He wasn't surprised when he discovered Dart's appointment to the federal bench had been politically motivated, with his legal abilities and personal integrity having very little to do with it. He was a prototype Reagan administration judge: age 50, young enough to exert influence on the law for a long time, and from a silk-stocking law firm that represented big oil, insurance, and transportation companies. He had no criminal trial practice, and while professing to be an intellectual, in fact had only mediocre intellect.

In June, 1981, when Judge John Crowlin announced his plans to retire, Governor Jim Tysen began searching for a man to take his place on the district court. While Big Jim ostensibly considered all qualified lawyers whose names were submitted to him, no one who was not a faithful member of the Republican Party had a chance. Dart, who had coveted the power and prestige which went with a black robe for years, realized he met the first criterion and seized his golden opportunity by sending his father to see Big Jim. David Dart, a wealthy industrialist from the Chicago suburbs, just happened to be one of the governor's financial supporters since the beginning of his political career. During the luncheon meeting with his "old buddy," Big Jim agreed it was pay-back time, and he promised the beaming father that his son's name would be submitted, with his strong recommendation, to President Reagan's staff in Washington for consideration. A grateful David Dart shook Big Jim's hand and said, "You can count on me to raise at least $500,000 for your next gubernatorial campaign."

Big Jim smiled. "David, I think your son is going to make a great judge."

Assistant Attorney General Donald Grott was a very powerful man. He not only controlled all the prosecutors around the country, but he was also in charge of selecting judges for the Reagan administration. He interviewed Dalton Dart twice, investigated his background, and then came to a conclusion that made him rejoice. Dart was a hard-core right-wing conservative, an idealogue who could be relied upon to fall in line and rule in accordance with what the policy makers in the Attorney

Generals Office wanted. Grott assured Governor Tysen that Dart's nomination file would be rammed through an FBI check-out and a Senate confirmation hearing and that the President would announce his appointment to the federal bench within two months.

With all the wheels greased, Dart became a federal judge before the lawyers who practiced in the Northern District of Illinois knew he was being considered, before anyone had a chance to object to his appointment to the federal bench for the rest of his life. It had been Chicago-style politics—the fix—at its very best.

"United States versus Angel Herrera and Ernie Kummer," the clerk announced.

Gavin and Reilley rose from defendant's table and spryly walked to the podium. "Good morning, Judge," each said respectfully.

Judge Dart acknowledged the attorneys, then got right to business. "When will you be able to start trial in this case?"

"We need thirty days," Gavin replied. "I'm scheduled to start a jury trial next week in state court. Because our witnesses must be subpoenaed in from California, Judge Bailey has given us a firm trial date."

The judge stared down at Terry Mack. "When can the government be ready?"

Mack shrugged his shoulders and replied in a casual tone, "We can start tomorrow."

"Fine then," the judge ruled, "trial is set for one week from today, at ten o'clock in the morning."

Gavin protested, "Judge, the state case is a murder-jury case. I don't think Judge Bailey will agree to continue it."

"Mr. Gavin," the judge replied drolly, "we don't set our schedule here in federal court around state court trials. You'll have to make arrangements to continue the trial in state court or have another attorney try this one."

Gavin felt the pressure build as he visualized himself standing before Judge Bailey limply requesting a one month delay in a case the judge had pushed to get to trial for six months. Deciding it would do no good to argue with Dart, he said politely, "Very well, Your Honor."

"Did that prick surprise you?" Reilley asked as he and Gavin walked out the courtroom door.

"No. I figured he'd show his disdain for me every opportunity he got. What did surprise me was his overwhelming arrogance. It permeated the air."

"It's called robe arrogance," Reilley said. "Most federal judges seem to be afflicted with it."

"Unfortunately, the little demonstration we just witnessed is going to inconvenience a lot of people. Judge Bailey is one of the most even-tempered men I've ever seen, but he's going to get good and pissed at me. He has arranged his entire schedule around our murder-jury trial. And what am I going to tell my client? If I can't persuade his alibi witnesses to come to court next month, he faces a sentence of death in the chair."

"Dart is going to be a pain in the ass for most lawyers who try to do their job," Reilley said.

Gavin took his co-counsel and friend by the arm. "The law business would be pure pleasure if our politicians would select qualified men for the bench, not political cronies. The incompetent ones cover up for their lack of ability by being rude and domineering. With the bright ones, everything goes smoothly. They can gently persuade attorneys to do what they want. They don't have to use the power of the bench to force it. Judge Matyan would have looked at me with his large, brown eyes sparkling with awareness and asked if there was any reason why I couldn't be ready for trial within the next three weeks."

"Shoot!" Reilley exclaimed. "We would have broken our butts for old Sam Matyan."

"That's a fact. The good judges like Matyan are flexible and try to work around a defense attorney's busy schedule. The bad ones, those with ego or personal agenda problems, force all who appear before them to conform to their self interests."

A troubled look crossed Reilley's face. "Do ethics and professional responsibility require us to withdraw from this case?" he asked.

"Why, Jim, because a serious conflict of personalities exists between Dart and me? Because he will harbor a bias and prejudice against our clients and deny them a fair trial because of me?"

"Right on point, Counselor. And, another right on point thing would be to tell Angel about the animosity that exists between you and Judge Dart."

"I did," Gavin replied. "I gave him the whole story. And as he walked away from me, he muttered something about starting to fight things his way."

*   *   *   *

Later that evening an ominous dark mist moved in off Lake Michigan and drifted by the federal courthouse. It took less than an hour for the cold front which was flowing in from the northeast and covering the city with a dark fog and chilling rain to reach 26th and Kostner, where Juan Martinez had just completed his twenty-first drug sale of the evening. In the six months Martinez, El Viejo as his customers called him, had been running the candy store operation from the small house on Kostner Street, business had been brisk. His customers would drive up to the front of his house, park and then dash into the house where they would choose one of El Viejo's products: coke, pot, heroin, speed. They liked doing business with the short, mouse-faced man with unkempt gray hair because they didn't worry about getting arrested. It was rumored the neighborhood cops were bribed to close their eyes to Juan Martinez' drug deals.

Martinez noticed the change of weather as he let a frail, teenage boy out the front door of the old, red brick bungalow. "Be careful," he called after his customer, "it's so foggy I can hardly see ten yards."

"Don't worry, Viejo," the boy said as he dashed for his car, two grams of cocaine in one shirt pocket and an ounce of marijuana in the other. "This weather can't stop superman."

The boy had opened the car door and sat down behind the steering wheel before he noticed his girlfriend had slid down off the seat and sat huddled under the dashboard. "Whatcha doing down there?"

"I, I was so frightened," the girl replied as she crawled up on the seat. "This neighborhood gives me the creeps."

The boy had no time to pamper his girlfriend, who was a sophomore at Hinsdale High School and had never seen anything but the affluent western suburbs, nor did he have time to think about the area they were in, even though robberies and rapes were nightly occurrences. His mind was riveted on the plastic package he pulled from his shirt pocket. "Whitney," he said, "get the tools out."

Although Whitney was still trembling, she removed a small mirror and Pyrex straw from her purse. "Let me," she said, taking the package. Carefully, she poured two lines of a fine-grained, white powder from the bag onto the mirror she cradled in her hand. She began to giggle as the boy inserted the three-inch straw into his nose and snorted loudly.

"Ha," he gushed, "I'm superman again."

Taking the straw, Whitney daintily sniffed-up the second line of coke, and as she settled back in her seat, all the realistic fears of a crime-ridden neighborhood floating away. It was now a romantic place to be, and a time to teach her shy, inexperienced boyfriend about kissing and petting.

"Wow, coke and making love!" he said as he slid down on the seat next to her.

Five minutes later, Whitney decided Larry was trying to learn too quickly, and she said softly, "If you'll take your hand out from under my bra, I'll pour a couple more lines."

They were hunched over, concentrating on partying when they heard a man's voice. Startled, they looked up over the dashboard and saw a large man standing in the middle of the street, a short distance from the front of the car. They watched him as he raised a two-way radio to his mouth and spoke, "The cars are empty and all's quiet." They slid down and laid on the car seat as the man walked past the front of the car and headed towards El Viejo's house.

"Gawd," Larry whispered, "if we'd been sitting straight up, that guy woulda seen us."

"What should we do?"

"We'll just watch," Larry said. "Don't move. That guy may be a cop."

"Oh, no," she whined, "my mom and dad will kill me if I get arrested."

As the man reached the front steps, he was joined by another man who had been waiting at the side of the house. The man raised his radio again and said, "We're going in." Slipping the radio into his jacket pocket, the man walked up to the door and knocked twice, paused, then knocked once more.

"Who is it?" Martinez asked.

"Friends," the man replied.

Martinez quickly opened the door and greeted his visitors with a broad smile. "What's up?"

"Come on outside," the man said, motioning with his head. "We've got to talk."

Martinez stepped out and closed the door behind him. As he reached the sidewalk, he sensed something was wrong. The men were acting strangely. "This is far enough," he said. "What do you need this time?"

"You fink!" the man said as he pulled a .22 Beretta semi-automatic pistol from his pocket.

The instant Martinez saw a silencer had been attached to the barrel, he fell to his knees. "Don't shoot me," he pleaded, "I didn't snitch. I ain't working for the feds. I swear."

The man aimed the gun at Martinez' mouth. There was a small flash of fire and a faint popping sound as the bullet crashed into its target. "Bullshit! Fink!" the killer said as his victim crumpled to the sidewalk, blood gushing from his mouth.

Casually, as if they were handling a drunken friend rather than a murdered corpse, the men picked the body up and carried it to the street where they dropped it in front of Larry's car. The killer held the radio close to his mouth. "Come on, hurry up," he said. Moments later, a car glided to a stop next to the two men, and the limp body was dumped into the trunk. "Now, let's give the fink a proper burial," the killer said.

Whitney's eyes were so large and white with fright they seemed to illuminate the front seat of the car. Trembling, she said, "Will they kill us too?"

Larry watched the car disappear into the fog before he said, "No, they're gone and we're getting the hell out of here."

Chapter 23

▼

VOIR DIRE

T-DAY for United States of America versus Angel Herrera and Ernie Kummer finally arrived. From a procedural and evidentiary aspect, the trial wasn't going to be much different from most of the major drug cases Gavin had defended in the federal and state courts. But when the constitutional safeguards of fundamental fairness and due process of law were considered, the trial was going to be a once in a professional lifetime ballbuster. Angel and Ernie were innocent of the charges, and he and his co-counsel had the awesome responsibility of convincing a jury of it.

Gavin had planned on being in court early so as to bolster the confidence of his client, but an emergency bond hearing at the Criminal Courts Building took priority. He was more than one hour late when he pushed through the courthouse doors and trotted past understanding security guards. Anticipating a perturbed judge awaited him, he entered the courtroom and sat down at the defendant's table before he noticed how crowded the courtroom was. There was standing room only.

"We were beginning to think you weren't going to make it," Reilley said.

Gavin smiled and nodded to Angel and Ernie before he asked, "Where's our judge?"

Reilley raised his eyebrows as he said, "He finished his motion call ten minutes ago and retired to chambers to await your arrival. He told his clerk to notify him as soon as you grace the court with your presence."

A panel of 42 prospective jurors sat randomly spaced over the rows of bench seats on the right side of the courtroom, while Celia Herrera and Sylvia Kummer sat in the first row on the left side in front of the spectators. Gavin noticed that most of the prospective jurors had their eyes fixed on him, wondering if he were one of the actors in the drama that was about to unfold before them. Wanting to create some good will with a captive audience and at the same time find out who the new man was sitting at prosecutor's table with Terry Mack and Joe Fruin, he walked over to Mack and said in a confident manner, "Good morning, gentlemen. Do we have anything else to discuss before trial starts?"

Mack stood erect, and acting the part of the fair, unruffled prosecutor replied, "Mr. Gavin, if you care to discuss this case, I suggest we step out into the hall."

Mack was used to Gavin's courtroom antics, but Fruin wasn't. His face flushed and his eyes darted, unable to keep contact. He looked deflated, guilt-ridden, Gavin thought. Or was it the presence of the jury that bothered him. He was aware that 12 fair and impartial jurors selected at random from the community held the formidable power in their hands to determine his credibility and decide the ultimate issue of Angel's guilt or innocence.

"Oh, by the way," Mack said in a hushed tone, back turned to the jurors, "This is Jay Doff. He's with the President's Commission on Organized Crime in Washington. He'll be helping with this prosecution."

"Hello, Jay," Gavin said. "Ganging up on me, huh?"

Doff nodded his head and returned to reading case documents that lay before him.

CRACK! The gavel sharply sounded, as Judge Dart, long black robe flowing behind him, took the bench.

Gavin was taking his seat when Reilley leaned toward him, smiled, and then raising his eyes to the ceiling quipped, "God has arrived."

As if he had overheard, the judge glared condescendingly at Gavin for a few moments. "So glad you could join us this morning, Mr. Gavin. Are you ready to proceed?"

Gavin weighed for a moment whether to apologize for his tardiness or ignore it. Considering the mood the judge was in, anything said would probably be turned around and used to place him in an uncomfortable position. He decided no excuse be given and replied curtly, "The defense is ready for trial."

Judge Dart directed his stare to the rows of prospective jurors who were sitting silently, eagerly waiting to be informed of the nature of the case that was to be tried. In a newly acquired judicial tone, he said pleasantly, "Good morning ladies and gentlemen. First let me tell you a little about the case twelve of you will be selected to hear." He picked up the indictment, read through it quickly, and then paraphrased it for the jurors. This is a criminal case, and the government in count one of the indictment charges that in June, 1980, in the Northern district of Illinois, Angel Herrera and Ernie Kummer and others did conspire to possess with intent to distribute 12 kilograms of a controlled substance, namely, heroin. It is charged in count two of the indictment that on the same date and in the same place the defendants possessed with intent to deliver 12 kilograms of heroin. It's my duty now to examine you, collectively, to determine who is qualified to sit as a juror."

Gavin's eyes focused on each juror's face, searching for signs of predisposition, bias or prejudice. It was at this point in every jury trial that Gavin wished he were a mind reader. The 12 individuals seated before him were strangers at this stage of the proceedings, but they would soon have to band together in a close working relationship and arrive at a common goal. Until then, they would be center stage, the object of the judge's and lawyers' fawning attention. When all the cards were played, they alone would decide Angel's and Ernie's guilt or innocence.

"A criminal trial is different than a civil trial," the judge told the prospective jurors. "In a criminal case, the defendant is presumed innocent until all the evidence has been presented and you go to the jury room to deliberate. And the burden of proof is greater in a criminal case in that the government must prove the defendant guilty beyond a reasonable doubt."

Seeing the judge lower his eyes and check his notes, Gavin leaned close to Reilley and said, "Here comes the loaded question, the one that will signal the mood and feeling of the jurors toward a drug case."

"At this point," the judge continued, "I must ask if any of you believe you cannot be a fair and impartial juror?"

Several hands shot up instantly and another few hesitantly. Judge Dart stared incredulously for a moment, as if disbelieving what he saw, and then asked a man who had quickly raised his hand, "Why do you feel you cannot be an impartial juror?"

"I just couldn't be fair in a heroin case," he replied. "I've read a lot about the family with the same last name as that one man. I know that family controls—"

"Sir," the judge interrupted, "you do not want to be a juror in this case?"

"No, sir."

"All right then, you will be excused for cause. Give your juror card to the marshal on the way out." Eight other prospective jurors who stated they couldn't give a defendant in a drug case a fair trial were also summarily excused by the judge.

"Chriss-sake," Angel hissed, "I wouldn't believe this if I didn't see it with my own eyes. One-fourth of the jury panel said they couldn't give me a fair trial."

"I was afraid of that," Gavin replied. "The average person around Chicago hates heroin so much it's almost impossible to find a jury that will give a person charged with heroin trafficking a fair deal. What concerns me more is that the most unbiased and impartial jurors may have just been excused. Who knows what prejudices lurk in the hearts of the remaining jurors, or worse, if they answered the judge's questions mendaciously. Maybe one saw a relative or loved one turn out to be a heroin addict or was the victim of a burglary or robbery committed for drug money, and he's just waiting to punish someone for it."

The last of the excused jurors sheepishly left the courtroom as the judge was turning to the courtroom marshal and saying, "Will you have twelve jurors take seats in the jury box, please?"

Marshal Ed Kerski picked up the stack of white cards with the names and personal information of the prospective jurors printed thereon and read off twelve names, mispronouncing all but the most common Anglo-Saxon ones. A pleasant-faced woman unsuccessfully attempted to correct the marshal several times. Taking her seat in the first row of the jury box, she looked at the judge and with an impish smile across her face shrugged her shoulders.

Judge Dart responded immediately to the cue, and turning to the already embarrassed marshal said, "Marshal Kerski, if you don't cease murdering our jurors names, you may find yourself on trial here."

The prospective jurors laughed, becoming noticeably comfortable for the first time and pleased that the judge had made them part of the proceedings.

Gavin didn't crack a smile. Turning to Reilley, he said, "Dart will try to have every juror eating out of his hand before the trial begins. Then he'll try to subtly motivate them to do exactly as he wants."

"It's one of my biggest gripes about the federal system," Reilley said. "In state courts, lawyers pick the juries."

Engrossed in obtaining personal and background information from the jurors, Dart didn't notice Reilley walk over to the clerk and hand him a sheet of paper. He looked up in surprise as the clerk turned in his chair and laid the sheet of paper in front of him. He glanced at it, watched Reilley walk from the podium, then turned toward the jury box.

"Mr. Reilley requested that I ask you the following question. Have any of you read anything in the newspapers or seen anything on television about this case, or in the past seen anything in the media about either one of the defendants?"

Three prospective jurors quickly raised their hands. Several others began to, but changing their minds, settled back in their seats.

"Would anything you have read or seen start you out with a feeling of prejudice against the defendants?" the judge asked.

Each juror responded with a weak no or shake of the head.

"Well, here goes the opening round," Gavin said to Angel as he rose to address the Court. "Judge, I have a motion, and I think it should be heard outside the presence of the jury."

Anticipating Gavin's motion, the judge replied, "All right, Mr. Gavin, I suppose we might as well dispose of the pretrial publicity issue right now. I will see the court reporter and lawyers in chambers."

Mindful that Angel and Ernie had never seen a criminal jury trial before, Gavin attempted to explain what had happened and the purpose for his motion. "Angel, this trial has received so much television and newspaper coverage that I think virtually anyone able to see or hear has learned something about this case. In addition, one of our local newspapers has been running an exclusive series on the Herrera Family and its control of the heroin industry. There is no question the newspaper and television stories have influenced everyone in the community. The question is—will the media coverage prejudice the jurors to a point where they will find you guilty even though the evidence does not warrant it? There is no need telling you again, Angel, we need every break we can get in this case."

"That jury looks like it would find me guilty right now," Angel said dejectedly.

"Yes, unfortunately it is a typical federal district court jury. They're middle-class Americans who have absolutely no tolerance for crime or criminals. In their minds you are guilty until you prove yourself innocent."

"What do you think the judge will do about your motion?" Angel asked.

Gavin put his hand on Angel's shoulder. "He'll deny it, but it will be one more ground that I can take to the appeals court in case of a conviction. The appeals court has thrown back several cases because the proper safeguards weren't provided to criminal defendants when the issue of prejudicial pretrial publicity was raised."

When Gavin entered the judge's chambers, Judge Dart was already seated at the head of a large oak table with the court reporter alongside him. Prosecutors Mack and Jay Doff sat on one side and Reilley on the other. Anxious to get the trial underway, the judge dispensed with formalities and said, "What's your motion, Mr. Gavin?"

"Motion to excuse and discharge for cause all the jurors in this panel on the basis pretrial publicity has rendered them incapable of giving the defendants a fair trial."

"Mr. Gavin, is it your position that just because a prospective juror has read something in the newspaper or seen something on television concerning a criminal case that he is immediately prejudiced and incapable of giving the defendant a fair trial?"

"Not in all cases, Judge. However, a drug case is different from other criminal cases. I would wager this is the first time this court has ever seen eight prospective jurors ask to be excused because they could not fairly decide guilt or innocence. Newspapers, magazines and television have been blasting the Herrera name for several years. A significant number of jurors on this panel have acknowledged learning about this case through the media. Any criminal defendant by the name of Herrera who is charged with dealing drugs would be found guilty by association."

"I must disagree with you, Mr. Gavin," the judge replied. "If I were to buy your argument, I would have to conclude that only the illiterate and ignorant members of our community are qualified to decide the outcome of a criminal case. The criteria is whether or not the pretrial publicity has so prejudiced a juror that he is not capable of giving the defendant a fair trial. I don't feel just because a person has read something about a case or recognizes the defendant Herrera's name that he or she is tainted with prejudice."

"That's textbook theory," Gavin shot back. "We are faced with a very practical problem. Eight jurors out of forty-two have already stated that the news media has so tainted them that they couldn't give the defendants a fair trial. Now we have at least three more in the jury box who indicated they have seen media coverage concerning Mr. Herrera."

Dart sat back, focusing unsympathetic eyes on Gavin. "So what? The purpose of selecting a jury is to find twelve impartial, unprejudiced people who will give a defendant a fair trial. I find what most defense attorneys want is a partial jury, one that is predisposed to give the defendant a break or to swallow some emotional argument. That's why I don't let lawyers interrogate jurors during the voir dire. We'd spend the next six months selecting a jury in this case if I were to strike someone for cause who had read something about this case or the Herrera Family's alleged involvement in drug trafficking."

"Wait a minute," Reilley argued. "The Sixth Amendment imposes a duty on this court to insure the defendant a fair trial. You should ask each juror, individually here in chambers, what he or she saw or heard in the news media and how it affected them."

Judge Dart shook his head. "I don't do that in this court. I don't put jurors on the spot."

Reilley played an ace card. Opening the morning's Chicago Sun Times and Chicago Tribune to marked pages, he laid them before the judge. "Did you see these articles? They're the biggest pack of lies and half truths I've ever read."

The judge scanned the papers. "No, I didn't get a chance to read this morning's papers," he said.

Gavin glanced over the judge's shoulder and saw the same editions lying on a credenza. It gave him an idea. "Judge, why don't we ask Marshal Kerski to go to the jury room and see if there are any morning papers lying about."

"Hold it! Hold it!" the judge lashed back, becoming angry. "I'm not about to send someone to sneak around and check up on jurors."

"But read the articles," Gavin said. "They're all propaganda, false information deliberately given to the press for only one purpose—to prejudice the right of the defendants to a fair trial." Gavin looked at Mack. His face became flushed and his eyes darted to the floor. Doff reacted differently. His eyes widened, and he glanced from the judge to Gavin to Reilley with a smirk on his face.

"The First Amendment," Dart said, groping for a rationale, "prohibits me from restraining a free press. What do you suggest I do, violate the Free Press Doctrine?"

"I suggest you do two things," Gavin replied. "One, inquire of Mack and Doff if they were responsible for the press releases. Two, bring each juror into chambers and determine if anyone was tainted."

The judge was agitated. "Without a showing that pretrial publicity has biased or prejudiced a juror, I will not grant your motion." Satisfied his ruling was politically correct, he ruled, "Motions are denied. Let's get back to work."

"Thank you, Judge," the prosecutors said in unison.

Judge Dart breezed through the voir dire, eliciting names, addresses, work affiliation, and other background information. "You're first, Mr. Mack," he said, giving the prosecutor the opportunity to challenge any juror he felt would not give the government a fair verdict.

Mack was satisfied with nine of the prospective jurors. They were all middle-class Americans who had worked at their respective jobs for long periods of time, were married, and had raised families. They were just the sort of jurors a prosecutor wanted in a drug case. He did excuse three of the panel that didn't meet his criteria for fairness. One was a well-dressed and groomed man who said he helped run a rehabilitation center for young men and women with drug problems.

"How many preemptory challenges do we have?" Reilley asked, not wanting to use up his right to challenge a juror without having to state his reason or motive.

"The Federal Rules prescribe that each side is allowed five," Gavin replied. "Normally judges will grant additional challenges if there are two or more defendants. Our Honorable Judge Dart has decreed that we have six preemptories between us."

Aware that Ernie Kummer was going to need twelve of the finest jurors ever selected in a court of law, Gavin sat back and prayed as Jim Reilley analyzed the eyes and faces of the prospective jurors. They had agreed on a strategy, and Reilley followed it when he politely excused six of the jurors, four of whom were from the inner-city, where drug abuse would have had to touch their lives. Normally blacks made good jurors, but when it came to drug cases the middle class and hard working blacks were devoid of compassion. Reilley opted for twelve jurors from suburban areas, hoping their lifestyles insulated them from the drug culture.

Gavin always felt slightly embarrassed for the dismissed jurors as they stepped down from the box and left the courtroom in the throes of personal rejection. Even if they were indifferent toward jury duty, it hurt to be one of a handful singled out and rejected. The twelve jurors who were ultimately chosen appeared to breathe a collective sigh of relief, not only because they wanted to be part of a newsworthy case, but because it gave them a feeling of self-importance. The power to decide guilt or innocence had been placed in their hands. And they realized now that they, not the judge or attorneys, were the most important people in the courtroom. The seven men and five women smiled and nodded their heads as the judge thanked and dismissed them until 9:30 the following morning. Then the jurors anxiously filed out of the courtroom, eager to get home and tell family and friends about the exciting day spent at the Dirksen Federal Building.

Summoning the attorneys before him, the judge commended them for the professional and efficient way they had selected the jury. Gavin bit his lip when the judge intoned, "Justice is best served when efficiency is done."

Chapter 24

▼

TRIAL

The following day Judge Dart hurried through his morning motion call, testily allowing attorneys to make only brief statements in support of their motions. Gavin and Reilley sat at counsel's table watching several attorneys approach the podium, present their motions, then swallow their pride and dignity for the sake of their clients as the judge flaunted his black robe power. Reilley pushed his chair back on its rear legs and rocked slowly as he said, "I'd like you to kick me right in the ass if I ever cow-tow when appearing before a judge."

The expected barrage from the bench came suddenly as Judge Dart demanded, "Explain the charge you made in your motion. What does orchestrating the news mean, Mr. Gavin?"

Gavin winked confidently at Reilley as he rose to address the court. Then he began the task of accusing the prosecutors with the deliberate release of propaganda to the news media. He opened the morning's newspapers, held them up, and pointed to the full page spreads that featured Angel Herrera, drug kingpin. "We want a mistrial declared," he

argued. "Someone in the U. S. Attorney's office is deliberately sabotag-
ing the defendant's right to a fair trial."

The judge blinked, not expecting such forcefulness.

"There's not one word in any of the media stories which is based on
fact," Gavin continued, in the same tone. "It's all based on rumor and sup-
position. A jury should not be subjected to any information during a trial
unless it comes from the witness stand in the form of sworn testimony."

"What do you expect me to do, counselor?" Dart asked.

"Answer two questions. Where did the newspaper reporters get the
information for the stories, and why is the press breaking from tradition and printing stories they know will prejudice the defendant's right
to a fair trial? This isn't coincidence; someone in the prosecutor's office
had to plant the stories."

Gavin overheard Mack as he turned to Doff and said, "This is your
mess. You handle it."

Prosecutor Doff sprang to his feet, walked in an attack-like posture to
the podium and said in a squeaky but commanding tone, "This is an
insult. The U. S. Attorney's office doesn't have to resort to propaganda
to win cases. Besides, there is no evidence the publicity did any harm."

"That's my point," Gavin interjected. "If the court doesn't voir dire
each juror, we'll never know."

"You know my position on that, Mr. Gavin. I asked them yesterday if
anything they had seen or heard caused bias or prejudice, and they
answered in the negative."

"You mean, Judge, they were reluctant to answer candidly."

The judge stared at Gavin with fierce, antagonistic eyes, thinking an
overbearing demeanor would cause him to buckle under.

The show of arrogance caused Gavin to become more aggressive.
"Why don't you," he said in a daring tone, "put Mr. Doff under oath and
ask him if he orchestrated the news stories?"

Dart held up his hand, as if to ward off a thrown object, and said,
"That's quite enough. Your motion is denied." Before Gavin could wage

further argument, he added, "You gentlemen may begin your opening statements when the jury has been brought into the courtroom."

"Nice try," Reilley said as Gavin sat down next to him.

"Shit," Gavin hissed. "With Dart presiding, all we're going to get is politically correct rulings. Justice and fairness will mean nothing."

A few minutes later, Gavin scrutinized the jurors as they filed into the jury box. Their eyes, darting to and then away from Angel Herrera, reflected the impact of the prosecution's orchestrated publicity.

Terry Mack also saw the jurors' predisposition and, wanting to hook them right from the start, scattered twelve packages of heroin across the prosecutor's table. Positioning himself directly behind the heroin so the jury would have to look directly at and over it, he addressed them, "Ladies and gentlemen, the government will prove beyond a reasonable doubt that the defendants Angel Herrera and Ernie Kummer are guilty of the crimes charged in the indictment." He turned and pointed society's symbolic finger of guilt at the defendants. Then, in an unrelenting tone, he outlined the series of events which led to Angel and Ernie's arrest, with special emphasis on Angel's actions when he arrived at the All American Motel in Cicero with a curvaceous young woman on his arm. Turning toward Celia Herrera, the betrayed wife, he cast a compassionate look.

"Judging from Mack's opening statement," Reilley whispered, "Angel is on trial for shacking up with Jenni. He's liable to be the only drug dealer convicted for adultery."

Gavin stifled a laugh. "Mack's a master. With motions of his finger and facial expressions, he's able to tacitly convey important factors to the jurors. But he's also a detail man who will spoon-feed the evidence to them."

As if Gavin's comment was a cue, Mack switched to the events which occurred at the Safe Harbor Motel. "Surveillance agents," he said, "will testify that Sal Veta and Claudio Cillas arrived at the motel, carried a package of heroin into their motel room and then awaited Angel Herrera's arrival." He quickly jabbed at one of the kilos of heroin, and continued, "Then, according to plan, defendants Herrera and Kummer arrived and took actual possession of the package of heroin in the room and constructive possession of the heroin in the spare tire in the trunk of Veta's car."

Professionally done, Gavin thought, as he watched Mack walk to his chair and sit down, a slight smile breaking to the sides of his mouth and eyes betraying a sense of self-satisfaction.

"After that opening," Reilley said in an urgent tone, "maybe we ought to change our minds and address the jury now."

"We can't, Jim, for several reasons. An opening statement is intended to apprise the jury of the theory of the defense, the evidence to be presented and the witnesses to be called. A good defense attorney never gives the opposition a bird's eye view of his case. He protectively holds back his evidence until the last minute so that a prosecutor will not have time to prepare cross-exam."

An owlish look crossed Reilley's face. "Are we holding back anything, counselor?"

Gavin whispered, "I want to keep Fruin and the prosecutors worried—keep them guessing as to whether or not I have a mystery witness who will testify there was no heroin in the motel room."

Mack opened the prosecution's case with its star witness, Joe Fruin, who, with arm raised, swore to God once again to tell the whole truth and nothing but the truth. Knowing that Gavin would be poised at the edge of his seat, ready to object the instant Fruin's testimony became improper, Mack tried to limit his testimony to what he had seen and heard while engaged in the arrest of the defendants. The rehearsed testimony went smoothly until Fruin volunteered information. "Agent Cass told me the heroin—"

"Objection!" Gavin said forcefully, bolting from his chair, determined to muzzle Fruin before he slipped hearsay into the record.

"Your Honor," Mack said in a confident tone, "hearsay is admissible to lay a foundation."

"Hearsay," Gavin shot back, "isn't admissible at a trial. The Sixth Amendment to the Constitution provides that an accused has the right to face his accuser. It's unfair to allow Fruin to repeat what he heard agent Cass say because the person the jury is expected to believe, agent Cass, isn't on the stand and subject to cross-exam or the jury's scrutiny."

"Objection sustained," Dart ruled without comment. "Move on, Mr. Mack."

Fruin's testimony relative to discovery and seizure of heroin in Sal Veta's motel room echoed that given at the suppression hearing, only now he was more fluid, better rehearsed and totally credible. He had psyched himself up for the ordeal of cross-exam and met Gavin's stern, piercing eyes with the self-assurance and confidence of a man who was telling the truth. For over an hour Gavin hammered at him, using every trick he knew to impeach the government's key witness.

Nothing seemed to unnerve Fruin. He stuck firmly to his story, "I recovered that one package of heroin, the one that's over there in the center of the table, right next to where Angel Herrera was standing when I entered the motel room."

The only thing left for Gavin to do was employ a last resort tactic. "Mr. Fruin," he said in a sarcastic tone, "you remember rehearsing your testimony with prosecuting attorneys before taking the stand, don't you?"

"Objection!" Doff screeched. Mack's efforts to control him were futile. Doff's talent for opening his mouth first, then thinking, waved a big red flag in front of the jury and unnecessarily alarmed his own witness. The jurors' eyes and expressions reflected their thoughts. Fruin and Doff must have done something wrong, and Doff was trying to stop Gavin from finding out what it was.

"Rephrase your question, Mr. Gavin," the judge said.

The jurors were now looking at Fruin with suspicious eyes. It was just the break Gavin had hoped for. "Well, Mr. Fruin," he said, "you went over your testimony—what you were going to say and how you were going to say it—with Mr. Doff, didn't you?" Gavin pointed an accusatory finger at Doff.

Fruin's expression changed dramatically from confidence to abject uncertainty, and he answered, "Ah, no."

"Are you trying to tell this jury you didn't meet with Mr. Doff yesterday and last night and talk about this case?"

"Well, yes, Mr. Doff and Mr. Mack."

"So you lied just a minute ago when you answered no."

Doff sprang to his feet again. "Objection!"

Judge Dart glared menacingly at Gavin and said, "I'd like to see counsel at side-bar." He stepped down from the bench and stood waiting for the procession of attorneys to reach him.

Doff arrived first. He argued, "This type of examination is improper. There is nothing wrong with preparing my witness for trial."

Judge Dart summoned his most stern look. "Mr. Gavin, I think your method of examination is egregiously improper." Gavin couldn't help himself. He laughed. It was either that or scream with frustration. He turned away from the huddle for moments, then turned back and said, "Of course there is nothing wrong with the prosecuting attorney talking with Fruin and preparing him for examination. But every first year law student knows I have a right to inquire to determine if the conference in any way wrongfully influenced Fruin's testimony."

Judge Dart said angrily, "That's quite enough. I'm sustaining the objection. No more questions along that line."

Gavin couldn't have designed a better way to end Fruin's cross. Prior to the objection and side-bar conference, Fruin was totally credible, his testimony accepted by the jury as gospel truth. Now his testimony was tainted. The jury thought he and Doff had done something wrong, that they were concealing important facts from them.

Walking away from the side-bar conference, Reilley whispered, "All of a sudden we have a chance to win this thing."

"If we keep punching away, anything can happen," Gavin replied.

Mrs. Batson, the night clerk at the Safe Harbor Motel was the next witness called. She testified that Sal Veta, using the name Perez, arrived at the motel and registered on the night in question and used the lobby phone. "A short time later the man seated at that table, "she pointed at Angel, "approached my desk and asked what room Mr. Perez was in."

"Had you ever seen Angel Herrera before that night?" Mack asked.

"Oh, yes, I saw him at least three other times before that night at the motel."

After Mrs. Batson had stepped down from the stand, Mack introduced into evidence the mud sheets for the Safe Harbor Motel. The telephone company records listed the call from the motel office phone to Angel's home phone on the night of the arrest.

The following day a determined Jim Reilley, thumbs in suit coat lapels and head tilted back, tore into agents Hill and Miller, trying desperately to crack their well-prepared testimony. In a convincing manner, each testified to the search of Sal Veta's car trunk and the recovery of eleven kilos of heroin from the spare tire. And in varying self-righteous tones, each said, "The one kilo of heroin was on the chair next to Angel when the task force entered the motel room."

"They were ready for me," Reilley moaned as he returned to his chair. "Be careful, Matt, agent Cass won't be as easy to discredit on cross-exam as he was during the suppression hearing. Mack and Doff probably spent several hours rehearsing him."

Gavin viewed Cass as the weak link in the government's case. He began cross examination, "Agent Cass, I'd like you to step down from the stand and come over to this blackboard." He paused as Reilley pushed a portable blackboard to the front of the jury box and then attached three large photographs to it. "Can you all see the photo?" he asked the jurors.

The jurors smiled warmly and nodded.

"Mr. Cass," Gavin continued, "you testified on direct that you saw Sal Veta and Claudio Cillas get out of their car, walk to the trunk and remove a taped package, then walk to their motel room. Please show the ladies and gentlemen of the jury just where you were in the parking lot when you observed those things."

Cass pointed to a photograph that portrayed an aerial view of the parking lot. "Right here," he replied.

"From that position, Mr. Cass, you couldn't see what Sal Veta was doing in his trunk, could you?"

"Not clearly."

"So you couldn't see Sal Veta take a package of heroin out from the trunk?"

"No, but I saw him clearly when he got out of the car, and he didn't have anything in his hands. Then I saw him walk to the motel with the heroin in his hand. The only place he could of—"

"Objection!" Gavin said. "It's pure speculation."

"Yes, sustained," the judge ruled.

"Mr. Cass," Gavin continued, "you didn't see Sal Veta or Claudio Cillas do anything with the spare tire, did you?"

Cass jabbed his stubby finger at the photograph. "No. They stood right here, next to the trunk."

"Then they couldn't have gotten a package of heroin from inside the spare tire, where the other packages were stored, could they?"

"No," Cass shot back. "But Sal Veta did get it from the trunk. It was separated from the other packages of heroin."

Gavin glared at the witness, wanting to call him a son-of-a-bitch. Suppressing anger, he addressed the court in a professional tone, "Objection, Judge. Once again Mr. Cass' statement is speculation."

"Overruled," Judge Dart said sharply. "He's testifying as to what he observed." He turned to Cass. "Please resume your seat on the stand."

When Cass was seated, Gavin held up a toilet kit. "This brown kit, " he said, "was recovered from Sal Veta's motel room after the arrests of the defendants, wasn't it?"

"Yes."

"Any other personal items recovered?" Gavin pressed.

"Just a shirt," Cass replied weakly.

Gavin threw the toilet kit onto prosecutor's table, and it came to rest in the middle of the packages of heroin. "Now," he said, "tell the ladies and gentlemen of the jury the truth. You saw Sal Veta take that toilet kit from the trunk and walk to his room with it—not a package of heroin."

"No. I saw him carry a package of heroin."

"Come on, Mr. Cass! Do you really expect the jurors to believe Sal Veta carried a package of heroin around like Walter Payton carries a football for the Chicago Bears?"

Mack growled an objection.

"Yes, sustained," Dart ruled.

"I have no more questions of this witness," Gavin said in a contemptuous tone. He walked to his chair and sat down, eyes riveted on Cass as he walked past him and out of the courtroom. And he thought, that makes two witnesses the jurors suspect of perjury.

Seeing the impact of Gavin's cross-exam on the jurors, Mack decided it was diversion time again. He began fussing with several of the packages of heroin as he removed the toilet kit from prosecutor's table.

Gavin couldn't fault Mack for highlighting the heroin whenever an appropriate occasion arose. It was good trial technique to turn the jurors' attention away from individuals who might influence them and focus it on the substance that reeked of evil. As he eyed the prosecutors, he hoped they wouldn't accidentally on purpose drop a few packages of heroin into the jury box.

Mack closed the prosecution's case when he said, "Your Honor, the defendants, through their attorneys, have entered into a stipulation concerning the heroin. Therefore, I'll not call a chemist to testify." Mack spun on his heels and facing the jurors said, "If chemist John Vogel were called to testify, he'd testify the substances contained in government's exhibits one through twelve do in fact contain heroin, with a purity ranging from twenty-one to twenty-three percent." He turned sharply toward the bench and said, "With that stipulation received into evidence, the prosecution rests."

Several of the jurors were becoming noticeably tired, and when Judge Dart saw the drifting eyes, loss of attentiveness, and restlessness, he said, "It's been a long day and I think the jurors should head home before the rush hour sets in. This court will stand in recess until ten o'clock tomorrow. And Mr. Gavin and Mr. Reilley, be ready to call your witnesses then."

Critical decisions had to be made before trial resumed the next day. Searching for a new environment in which to mull over their problems, Gavin and Reilley found themselves walking through the bustling loop crowds toward the shore of Lake Michigan. Discovering a bench, thoughtfully placed under a large oak tree near the water's edge, they flopped down with legs outstretched and delighted in the fresh lake breeze. The invigorating setting worked magic, soothing over-strained nervous systems. "At times like these," Gavin said, "most lawyers feel like they've bitten off more than they can chew, that they're fighting a battle they can't win. Why? Why do we take this type of case?"

Knowing the self-doubts were only temporary and that Gavin had been in the winner's circle after the vast majority of trials he litigated, Reilley said, "Every criminal defense lawyer hates drug cases. A friend of mine says a lawyer has to be a sadist to defend one."

"Maybe so. A drug case is the easiest case in the prosecutor's repertoire to try. All a prosecutor has to do is put seasoned and well-prepared agents on the stand, open them up with a few leading questions, and then stand back and let the agents tell the story. Impeachment by cross-exam is virtually impossible. And defense witnesses are generally so intimidated by the courtroom, judge or prosecutor that they lack credibility."

"Okay, Matt, drug cases are a bitch. So now what are we going to do for our clients?"

Gavin cleared his throat. "We're going to confront several critical issues for starters. Number one, should I call Angel to testify?"

"Absolutely not," Reilley replied. "He'll make a terrible witness, and Mack will tear his story apart on cross."

"Issue number two. Should you call Ernie and his wife?"

Reilley was certain it was his professional duty to do so, even though the move was fraught with danger. "I think it's Ernie's only chance," he said. "If he comes across as the big-hearted hillbilly he is, the jury may give him the benefit of the doubt. He's not a Mexican, and the prosecutors won't be able to show any past association with drugs or drug dealers, excepting his brother-in-law."

"Have you gone over Ernie's testimony with him?" Gavin asked.

"I've rehearsed direct exam with both Ernie and Sylvia, and I think each will come across well on the stand."

"Okay," Gavin said. "Are you ready for the bombshell now?"

Reilley put his hand on his forehead. "Shoot it, Matt."

"Major decision to make," Gavin said, taking a deep breath. "Should we subpoena Andre Campbell to testify there was no heroin in the motel room Angel and Ernie were in when the agents entered?"

Reilley sat up straight, eyes widened. "Damn! Would he do it?"

"Andre is an old friend of mine," Gavin replied. "We're handball buddies, and as you know there is great camaraderie among handball players. He told me right after the arrest—under a promise of confidence—that the heroin was planted. I haven't told anyone the source of my information until now. I presume you'll say nothing to no one."

Reilley slowly shook his head, knowing he didn't have to profess his integrity.

"I've got a lot of respect for Campbell," Gavin continued. Being a black person with brains and ability, he had to fight for everything he got in a white man's world. And he served his country nobly since he was nineteen years old, as an Air Force pilot during the Korean War, for ten years as a field agent with the Bureau of Alcohol, Firearms, and Tobacco, and for the last five with the DEA. If I called him to testify, and he told the truth, I'd be destroying a good friend because Mack and Fruin would have to turn on him. They'll claim I bribed him."

"You've got a real shitty problem, Matt. You've got to make the call yourself."

"Okay," Gavin said in a somber tone, "I think I'll try to solve it by issuing a subpoena for Andre Campbell. I'll have done my duty, and Campbell will have a chance to do whatever he feels is right."

Reilley grunted, then said, "The shit will really hit the fan at the courthouse. I'll go to the office now and prepare a subpoena. And I'll serve Campbell tonight." He rose and began to walk in the direction of the office, then hesitated, as if expecting second thoughts.

Gavin sat with his legs outstretched, crossed at the ankles, arms folded, and head down. "Go," he said.

*   *   *   *

The night was spent on a bed of thorns, each twist and turn painfully bringing Gavin back to the conscious world to agonize over the Campbell question. From that night Campbell had too many beers and let his anger with Joe Fruin's actions flow out, he had kept Campbell's statements secret from everyone involved in the trial. But as the trial moved toward conclusion, pangs of ethical uncertainty began to annoy him. Knowing he had to make the final decision and bring the Campbell question to closure, he showered and dressed quickly and headed for the courthouse.

Gavin had gotten off the elevator on the 23rd floor and was walking toward Judge Dart's courtroom when he heard a whispered voice coming from a small alcove where telephones were located. "Matt, Matt, just a minute. I'd like to talk to you."

Quickly ending his conversation, Andre Campbell hung up the phone. Turning to Gavin, he reached into the wallet pocket of his suit coat and slowly pulled out a folded piece of paper. His normally bright, smiling face wore an unusual mask: shame, fear, frustration. "I can't believe you'd do this," he said.

Gavin took two steps toward him and said, "Hello, Andre, how are—." He couldn't say more. The position he had put his friend in impacted greatly, and he couldn't bring himself to utter false platitudes. He stared at Campbell, waiting for verbal abuse, expecting him to throw a punch.

"What do you want me to do, Matt, put Fruin, Cass and Hill in jail for five years for perjury and obstruction of justice? Do you really expect me to take the stand and testify that no heroin was in the motel room when they entered?"

"I expect you to tell the truth," Gavin said limply.

"Well, let me tell you what I expect of you, something as important as truth," he replied, voice shaking uncontrollably. "I expect you to honor your promise to me to keep our conversation confidential. You swore you would."

Gavin nodded his head. "Yeah, I know I did, but Angel is being framed. He'll go to jail for a long time if you don't take him off the hook."

"Do we have to sacrifice four good men to do it?" Campbell snarled. "And me, I'd be ruined for life. Jesus. You should've seen the office this morning when your process server dropped this on me."

"Then Joe Fruin knows about the subpoena?"

"The whole mother-fucking building knows by now," Campbell said. "Who you trying to play God with anyway? Everyone knows that was Angel's shit. He owned and controlled it all. It's not like he's an innocent man who was wrongfully framed. I'll bet you a million dollars that if the jury knew the true facts they would find him guilty anyway."

Gavin couldn't respond. The anguish that Campbell suffered hurt him deeply. He turned and began to walk away.

Campbell said in an urgent tone, "Matt, what are you going to do?"

Gavin's voice was barely audible, "The best thing for my client, for you, and for the System."

Chapter 25

▼

WITNESS FOR THE DEFENSE

"Give us your name, please, and tell the ladies and gentlemen of the jury who you are," Jim Reilley instructed his first witness.

Pointing to Ernie, the nervous, but quickly likeable woman said, "My name is Sylvia Kummer, and I'm the wife of that man sitting over there."

"Tell us about your husband."

Sylvia testified Ernie was a good husband and father, and that prior to his arrest he had been employed for six years as a truck driver. Several of the jurors' eyes darted to Ernie when she stated that he spent most of his time with his family. "He couldn't be doing anything wrong," she said, "cuz he sits in front of the TV every night."

"Now, Mrs. Kummer," Reilley directed, "describe your lifestyle."

"We have no money, no property that could have come from selling drugs. We live in a rented two bedroom apartment and drive a four-year-old Chevy."

"Did you ever see Ernie possess or sell any type of illegal drugs?"

"No!" she snapped. "He never used drugs or dealt in them in any way."

A self-satisfied grin spread across Reilley's face as he wrapped up direct exam. His witness' gentle nature and likable persona had affected all within the courtroom.

Mack didn't waste a minute on irrelevant matters. He zeroed in on Sylvia Kummer's most vulnerable position. "Now, Mrs. Kummer," he said, "how are you related to Angel Herrera?"

"I'm his sister."

"And how long have you been married to Ernie?"

Paled, obviously worried she was saying something damaging to her husband, she weakly responded, "I don't remember."

"Oh, shit," Reilley grumbled. "She just blew her credibility."

"A trial is a punch and take deal," Gavin replied. "You didn't expect the prosecutor to go after your witness with kid gloves, did you?"

"Not Mack. I guess the only thing I can do while he tears my client's testimony to shreds is put my hand in my pocket and grab hold of my short hairs."

Gavin raised his eyebrows and nodded. "Grab hold real tight because Mack's going for the jugular."

Mack stared menacingly at the witness. "Now really, Mrs. Kummer," he said, "you can't remember how long you've been married?"

The witness sighed loudly. Her shoulders sagged and she slumped in her chair. "Yes, I mean, I do, a little over ten years."

"And in all that time you and Ernie associated with Angel often, didn't you?"

"Yes."

Realizing Mack had her so overpowered that she lost the ability to think independently, that she would answer yes to virtually any question, Gavin sprang to his feet and screamed out, "Objection! Counsel is badgering the witness." Feigning anger and disgust at the tactics of the prosecutor, he said with great indignation, "I request the court to instruct Mr. Mack to conduct proper cross-examination."

Mack was caught off-guard. He stood red-faced, apparently embarrassed, unable to fathom what he had done wrong.

Judge Dart glared at Gavin, a crooked smile crossing his face. "Gentlemen," he said, "come up to the side of the bench for a conference."

Once again the lawyers trailed to the side of the bench away from the jury and stood clustered around the judge. Mack stood closest to the judge, thinking he would have to explain his manner of cross-examination. But Gavin knew better. He stood the farthest back, arms folded.

"Mr. Gavin, I think you should be cautioned that you didn't put one over on me," Judge Dart said, head tilted back, right eyebrow raised. "You know as well as I that you objected merely to break up and distract Mr. Mack and to give Mrs. Kummer time to recover her composure."

Gavin glanced over at Sylvia Kummer and saw that she was sitting upright and smiling at the foreman of the jury who was seated in the first chair in the first row. And, he was smiling approvingly at her.

Confident his goal had been accomplished, he cleared his throat and began, "Judge-"

He was abruptly interrupted by a peeved judge. "Your objection is overruled, and no more of those tricks!"

Mack lost his edge once Sylvia Kummer regained her composure and the rest of the cross-examination went well for her. Several of the jurors were sympathetic to her plight, and when she was excused, their eyes followed her out of the courtroom.

Ernie lumbered to the witness stand, was sworn, and slumped into the chair. His future depended upon his ability to convince the jury that he had nothing to do with the heroin allegedly recovered from the motel room or with the overall conspiracy, and at first he didn't do a very good job. His ingrained sullenness and thick hillbilly accent contributed to the aura of guilt as he provided background information about himself and his reason for his trip to the Safe Harbor Motel.

Near the close of his direct examination, Reilley asked, "Did you ever use illegal drugs?"

"No," he replied.

"Did you ever possess, sell, or deal in illegal drugs?"

"No, sir, never."

"And, Ernie, did you own or possess, or conspire to possess any of the heroin which was alleged to be recovered at the Safe Harbor Motel?"

"Honest to God, no," Ernie replied sincerely. "I didn't ever see any heroin in the room. I never knew nothing about any heroin."

"I have no further questions," Reilley announced.

Mack sprang at Ernie, tearing into him with a barrage of questions. Surprisingly, he fended them off well and began to come across as a good ol' southern boy. Positioning himself for what he hoped would be a knockout punch, Mack said, "Are you telling the jury, Mr. Kummer, that you got out of bed at four o'clock in the morning and drove Angel Herrera to Joliet as a favor?"

"Yes, sir, Angel had always been good and decent to me, so when he needed a ride I was glad to do it."

Mack wilted. Ernie had come through cross-examination unscathed. Excusing the witness, he returned to join Fruin and Doff at counsel's table, to await the next witness.

"Do you have any more witnesses, Mr. Reilley?" the judge asked.

"No," he replied. "That completes Mr. Kummer's defense."

"How about you, Mr. Gavin?"

"Your Honor, I have one witness, but I need a five-minute recess before putting him on the stand." Gavin glanced at Mack and Fruin as he made the announcement. They sat with their heads bent forward, elbows on the table, hands clamped to their foreheads, tortured by the belief that the next witness would be Andre Campbell.

"Very well, this court will stand in recess for ten minutes."

Gavin walked out of the courtroom and across the hall to the witness room, and approaching the open doorway, he saw a solitary figure sitting in an upholstered chair reading the morning's newspaper. Upon seeing Gavin approaching, Andre Campbell quickly raised the paper to cover his face. It was a tacit signal Jay Doff had ordered him to talk to no one.

No longer troubled by the Campbell issue, Gavin smiled, turned and began walking toward the telephone. He hadn't gone far when the sound of hurried footsteps caused him to hesitate, and he turned in time to glimpse Mack, Doff and Fruin enter the witness room. Returning quietly along the wall and standing next to the door so that he could overhear the conversation, he heard the question he expected.

"Do you think he'll call Campbell to testify?" Fruin asked.

"Hell, he can't call Angel Herrera, and the only witness left is Campbell," Mack replied.

Jay Doff began babbling in a shrilly voice, "I've already warned you, Campbell, what'll happen if you testify any differently than Fruin and the other agents. I'll not only have you fired; I'll have you indicted for perjury, convicted and sent to jail. And I'd like you to know we suspect you've been on Gavin's payroll for years."

Campbell tried to control his animosity, but the pressure generated over the past days overpowered self-restraint. "You fucking wimp," he said as he sprang at Doff. Before Mack could intervene, he had grabbed Doff by the tie and shoved him backwards over a table, his tightly clenched fist hovering six inches from Doff's nose. "You fucking wimp."

Seeing the potential for serious injury, Terry Mack wrapped his huge frame around Campbell, ushered him to a chair, then stood guard directly in front of him, allowing Doff time to slither off the table.

"I've got you now for assaulting a federal officer," Doff sputtered. "And I've got witnesses." He looked to Fruin for support.

"I didn't see nothing," Fruin said leaving the room.

Astonished, Doff said, "Mack, you saw it."

"What?" he replied nonchalantly, "You mean your little trip and fall?"

Doff pointed his finger at Mack and was about to utter a threat when he saw Mack's steely stare.

"Blathering idiot!" Mack said as Doff stormed out of the room.

The tension was extreme at prosecutor's table when Gavin rose to call his surprise witness. He examined the jurors. They seemed to sense something sensational was going down. Walking to a point near the prosecutor's table where he could look into Fruin's eyes, he said, "For the defense's next witness, I'll call Pedro Martinez."

Mack's mouth gaped, and he stared at Gavin. Realizing it was not a mistake that Gavin intended to call the man whose tip made the prosecution of Angel Herrera possible, he rose and addressed the court, "This matter should be discussed outside the presence of the jury."

"What's it all about this time?" Dart asked when he had positioned himself in the circle of lawyers standing at side-bar.

"Quite simply," Gavin replied, "Juan Martinez is the alleged snitch in this case, the one who allegedly was to act as middle man in the sale of heroin by Mr. Herrera to a man from Puerto Rico. Judge Matyan entered an order requiring the government to produce him for trial. Now, I've called him to testify, and I expect the prosecutors to produce a person who has been working for them and is under their control."

The judge was about to respond when prosecutor Doff said in a loud voice, one intended to be heard by the jurors, "Judge, this is one of Gavin's finest charades. He knows Juan Martinez is dead and that his client killed him for revenge."

It was one of the few times in Gavin's career he was embarrassingly dumbfounded. His mind seemed to turn to mud as he tried to grasp the significance of Doff's charge. He glanced at the jurors to see if they had overheard the accusation, and when he saw the shocked look in their eyes, he knew he had only one thing to do. "Motion mistrial," he said. "The prosecutor's slanderous charge was overheard by the jury."

The judge blinked his eyes as concern spread across his face. Not wanting to declare a mistrial, he said, "Gentlemen, let me excuse the jury before we discuss this matter."

Gavin waited until marshal Kerski started the procession of jurors moving toward the courtroom door before he stepped back to the defendant's table and slid into a chair next to Angel. "Don't give me any bullshit," he warned. "What happened to the guy?"

"Don't know, "Angel replied in an unnerved tone. "I heard a rumor Martinez dropped off the face of the earth about a month ago. I figured Fruin grabbed him and was hiding him out."

Gavin's eyes burned into Angel. "You know if he has disappeared, you're in deep trouble. The judge, the prosecutors, and everybody else will think you killed him."

"I swear I don't know what happened to him."

Finding Angel's denial unpersuasive, Gavin walked back to the podium. "I have two motions," he said. "One, I demand that the prosecutors produce Martinez in accordance with Judge Matyan's order, and two, I motion for a mistrial because of Mr. Doff's prejudicial remark."

"Please, Mr. Gavin," Doff replied in a disdainful tone, "spare us the song and dance routine. You know we can't produce Martinez because he's dead."

Gavin stayed on the offensive. "This information the prosecutor has just given has serious implications. If it was known Martinez wasn't available for trial, then the prosecutor should have notified the defendants as required by federal rules. Doff has deliberately withheld information vital for a defense."

"Judge," Doff said, "it came to our attention that Martinez disappeared about one month ago. He hasn't been in contact with his wife or friends. He just vanished."

Again Gavin demanded, "Motion mistrial."

A strange twitch rippled across the judge's cheek, one which was appearing more frequently as the trial progressed. There was no evidence Angel had gotten his revenge on the informer, but it was obvious he believed Angel was somehow responsible for the disappearance, and he was going to make sure Angel paid for the unpardonable obstruction of justice. "It is your duty," he ruled, "to get Martinez to court if you want to call him as your witness. Your motions are denied, Mr. Gavin."

His strategy had backfired, and Gavin didn't like it. He felt like punching his client in the nose as he walked past him and sat down.

Instead, he scribbled a warning on a piece of paper and then slid the paper in front of Angel. 'YOU BETTER COME UP WITH THE TRUTH ABOUT MARTINEZ OR—' the message read.

Angel's face blanked. He shrugged his shoulders.

Dart had watched Gavin, then Angel as he read the note. Disgusted with the turn of events, he said crisply, "Call your next witness, Mr. Gavin."

Continuing to play the game to the hilt, Gavin stood ramrod straight and said dramatically, "For my next witness...I call Dr. N. T. Farley."

Dr. Farley's credentials were impressive: college graduate, Ph. D., thirty years in the field of fingerprints, twenty years with the FBI, author of several books. He was an extremely interesting little man with gray hair and a round cherubic face, and the judge and jury alike hung on his every word. "I was hired," he testified, "by you, Mr. Gavin, to recover and analyze any fingerprints that might be on the twelve taped packages lying on that table. The government provided the packages for examination. I lifted two separate and distinct sets of latent fingerprints from the gray tape which covered the packages."

"What did you do then?" Gavin asked.

"I then took fingerprint samples from Angel Herrera and Ernie Kummer and compared them to the prints recovered from those packages."

"And what did you determine, Dr. Farley?"

"That the recovered prints did not match in any way the fingerprints of Angel Herrera and Ernie Kummer."

"Your witness, Mr. Mack," Gavin said.

Because of Dr. Farley's well deserved reputation for expertise and integrity, and because the gray tape was a prime surface for capturing fingerprints, Mack chose not to cross-examine him. He turned to watch Gavin, to see what his next move would be, racking his brain for the right thing to do if his adversary did call DEA agent Campbell to testify.

Gavin walked to the podium and announced. "The defense rests."

Fruin appeared to deflate as his head drooped. A twisted grin spread across Mack's face. Doff managed to keep his bearing in spite of the palpable shutter which raced through his body.

Reilley waited until the jury had been escorted from the courtroom before he leaned toward Angel and Ernie and said, "That's what I call psychological torture. It'll make 'em better cops and prosecutors."

In on the game plan from the beginning, Angel had watched unemotionally while Fruin had squirmed under the building pressure. Now it was time to enjoy the revenge his lawyer had so cunningly imposed on the real criminal. He caught Fruin's attention with a wave of his hand, and when their eyes met, he said, "Who committed the worse crime—you or me?"

The gleam of competitive spirit returned to Fruin's eyes. "We'll see," he said.

Knowing Angel's and Fruin's propensity to explode and throw punches, Gavin moved quickly to his client's side. "Cool it. Don't say another word."

"Fucking liar," Angel muttered.

Gavin waited until Mack had taken Fruin by the arm and led him out the courtroom door before he leaned back against the table and said, "Damn! Emotions were starting to run high. I thought we were going to have a brawl."

Angel said in a forbidding tone, "That's how this case should be settled. Man against man. Me and Fruin alone somewhere."

"Maybe so," Gavin replied. "Maybe that's how the Creator intended mankind to settle disputes. But for now, we're stuck with the system's rules and we're going to have to play the game in accord with those rules. That means, Angel, stay the hell away from Fruin."

"For now, Abogado. For now."

Ernie didn't feel the same hatred for Fruin that Angel did, and revenge wasn't in his vocabulary. Harboring a childlike belief in the integrity and fairness of the judge and jury, he had remained quiet, considerate and inconspicuous throughout the trial. But feeling the moment of truth drawing close, he turned to Gavin for reassurance. "What you think, Matt?" he asked. "Did I do okay on the stand?"

"You were great," Gavin said, putting his hand on Ernie's shoulder. "And Sylvia was too."

"Yeah," Ernie said, "This ol' hillbilly is going to start treating her real good."

Gavin met Angel's intense gaze and said, "I'm positively convinced that we did the right thing by not calling you to testify."

"Ain't no doubt," Angel replied. "Mack would have made me look guilty as hell. But what do you think? Do we have a chance?"

"Ernie has a good chance; you have a slim one."

Angel chuckled. "That's what I always liked the most about you, Abogado. You never bullshit."

Gavin watched his client leave the courtroom with an alarming resolve in his walk. "I hope," he told Reilley, "Angel's innate toughness doesn't create more problems."

Reilley leaned close to Gavin and lowered his voice as he said, "You worried he'll go after Fruin and avenge a real screwing? Like he did with Martinez?"

Gavin waved his hand. "Don't want to talk about it. I want to believe Angel didn't kill Martinez."

Reilley nodded and quickly changed the subject. "There it goes again," he said, calling Gavin's attention to a young clerk from the prosecutor's office who had wheeled a shopping cart up to a stack of heroin. "The shit is going to be put to bed in a safe for tonight."

Gavin stared at the heroin. "I'm happy to say," he said, "that sometime after closing arguments tomorrow that load of heroin which began its life's journey as an exquisite flower in Durango will be sent to an incinerator on the South Side of Chicago to meet its fate—destruction by fire."

Reilley agreed. "An appropriate end for that load of shit. Angel hit it on the nose when he said the twelve kilos were jinxed from the start."

"Maybe they are," Gavin said. "All who came under the fruit of the poppies' spell suffered some grave consequences. Antonio and

Francisco Alvarado were killed and scores of other campesinos were injured near the poppy fields. Commandante Gonzales and several of his federales were killed waging war against the Herrera cartel. Informant Martinez is apparently sleeping with the fish in the Chicago River. Sal and Claudio will be on the run from DEA agents the rest of their lives, and Angel and Ernie suffered through the rigors of arrest and trial and now face prison for a long time."

"Add to all that," Reilley said, "the fact the seizure of twelve kilos didn't scratch the surface of the heroin industry. Users filled the void created by the seizure by obtaining a fix from another shipment. The arrest and trial of Angel didn't deter him or anyone else from trafficking in drugs. From this lawyer's point of view, our government's War on Drugs is going to injure far more people than it ever helps."

"Let's hope," Gavin said, "you and I survive that war."

Chapter 26

▼

CLOSING ARGUMENTS

Eight o'clock the following morning, Gavin and Reilley arrived at Judge Dart's courtroom door and knocked. They waited only a few seconds before Marshal Kerski unlocked the door and greeted them, "Good morning, advocates. The good judge has decided to hold the conference on jury instructions in his chambers."

"Lead on, Mr. Marshal," Gavin said.

A tinge of nostalgia hit Gavin as he followed the marshal through the small door at the rear of the courtroom, past the judge's secretarial desk and into the chambers Judge Matyan once occupied. He recalled how before each conference, Sam Matyan and he would gaze out the wall-length windows and marvel at the sprawling city and glistening lake 20 stories below. The amenities completed, they would delve into the law applicable to the case on trial, each aware of and respectful of the other's competence. The erudite judge had made the practice of law a pleasure, never hesitating to admit a mistake or to criticize an overly zealous prosecuting attorney.

The atmosphere had changed dramatically. Judge Dart ignored him. Only Terry Mack acknowledged his presence by nodding as he slid into a chair at the conference table. In what appeared to be a two-sided conversation, Jay Doff was telling Dart, "Before coming to Chicago, I was with the Justice Department in Washington for six months. I helped the Justice Department's number three man, Steven Trodd, get the President's Commission on Organized Crime going. Then I was sent here to target major drug traffickers for prosecution."

A rapport had developed between the judge and the prosecutor as the trial had progressed from stage to stage, both seeming so Justice Department oriented, so preoccupied with protecting its image, goals and objectives. Gavin wondered if anyone who opposed the Justice Department could get a fair deal from prosecutor Doff or from the prosecutor in the black robe.

Dart glanced around the table before commenting for the record, "Mr. Gavin and Mr. Reilley are present." He paged through the pile of instructions that lay before him and announced. "I'll give all of the government's tendered instructions, if there are no objections."

There were no objections to the cautionary instructions, for Gavin was confident Mack had carefully prepared the statements of law concerning the jurors obligations and functions. "We do object," he said, "to the government's instruction defining actual and constructive possession. We suggest defendant's instructions one through five be given instead."

"Why so, Mr. Gavin?" the judge asked. "Don't you believe the government proved an actual possession case against the defendants?"

"Absolutely not. As we argued in our written Motion for Judgment of Acquittal at the close of all evidence, for a conviction to stand the government had to prove actual or constructive possession. Neither Angel nor Ernie had actual possession of the heroin. It wasn't their motel room; they didn't do anything which would indicate they took possession of the one kilo, and they were never in possession of the eleven kilos found in the car. As a matter of law, the government failed to prove its case."

"The defendants had the ability to direct and control its possession, and that makes constructive possession," Doff said.

"Wait a minute," Reilley objected, "there was no evidence which showed a relationship between Ernie Kummer and the two men in the motel room, and therefore, nothing to base the government's theory on."

"I disagree," the judge ruled, "the jury has a right to infer actual or constructive possession from the evidence." Your instructions are refused."

"I assume you have denied my Motions for Judgment of Acquittal also," Reilley said.

"That's correct," Dart ruled. "And now that those matters are taken care of, how much time do you gentlemen need for closing arguments?"

"I need two hours," Gavin replied. "Mr. Reilley, one hour," Gavin replied.

Dart tilted his head back and in a condescending tone said, "Mr. Gavin, I can't imagine why you would bother making one at all."

Gavin didn't respond. He raised his eyebrows, then smiled. He'd save his argument for the jurors, the ones who counted most now.

"Quite a spectacle, huh?" Reilley quipped as he and Gavin returned to the courtroom.

Gavin allowed his eyes to drift around the room. In the rows of seats behind government's table sat the reporters from the newspapers and television stations. Sketch artists sat on specially provided chairs next to the jury box so that they could capture, from the juror's viewpoint, the lawyers and defendants during closing arguments. Behind the news media people were several assistant U. S. Attorneys who were eager to watch Mack, the office's premiere trial attorney, give his closing argument. And intermingled with the attorneys, every agent who had worked on the Angel Herrera case sat nervously awaiting the argument they hoped would convince the jury to vote guilty on all charges.

Behind defense counsel's table sat Celia Herrera, eyes directed straight ahead. Angel looked at her and their three neatly dressed children huddled next to her. He smiled, but Celia's face was a frozen mask, unable to respond. Sylvia Kummer with her children pressed tightly against her, sat in the next row, equally horrified.

Putting a hand on Reilley's arm and tilting his head in the direction of the media corps, Gavin said, "They seem particularly frisky this morning."

"And why not," Reilley replied. "This case went from a sensational drug case to a sensational drug and murder case."

Gavin made a fist and punched the air. "I'd like to whack the courthouse reporters for the way they published information to create public opinion. They've made Angel's name synonymous with narco-terrorism."

"Wait till tomorrow," Reilley said. His name will be synonymous with bumping off snitches, specifically one Juan Martinez."

"Yes," Gavin said, "this case went from bad to worse. I wonder—"

Marshall Kerski banged his gavel down sharply, calling the courtroom to order just as Judge Dart pushed through the courtroom door. Dart surveyed the courtroom before indicating with his finger it was time for the marshal to usher in the jurors for the final round of battle.

When the seven men and five women had taken their seats, wide-eyed with anticipation, prosecutor Mack addressed them. He began with the customary "thank you's" and "what's good for God and country is good for you." Turning forceful, he argued that the evidence showed beyond a reasonable doubt the defendants were guilty as charged. Drawing a legally permissible inference, he argued Angel's trip to Durango was for the sole purpose of arranging for the shipment of twelve kilograms of heroin, and that the large sum of money he carried onto the plane was payment for the heroin he received at the Safe Harbor Motel. In a voice rising in indignation, he traced Angel's actions from the time he deplaned at O'Hare Field and was met by Ernie, to his tryst with a young woman, to his trip to the Safe Harbor Motel to meet Sal Veta and Claudio Cillas and take delivery of the heroin. Not wanting to chance a mistrial, he steered clear of any comment concerning the missing informant, Juan Martinez.

Mack turned away from the jury and deliberately raised his closed hand to his mouth and cleared his throat. It was Ernie's turn now, and Mack pointed a rigid finger at him and said, "That man, that man sitting next to his partner in crime, has been proved guilty beyond a reasonable doubt of the crimes of conspiracy to possess heroin and of possession of twelve kilograms of heroin." He kept his finger pointed until Ernie lowered his eyes and began fidgeting with a button on his sport coat. Then he whirled around to face the jury and continued, "Ladies and gentlemen, you have a legal right to infer from the evidence the following facts. One, Ernie Kummer's sole motive for meeting his co-defendant at the motel in Cicero and driving him to the Safe Harbor Motel was to aid and abet him in the commission of a crime. Two, Ernie Kummer was arrested standing several feet away from one kilo of heroin. Don't be fooled. Kummer knew it was heroin. And, three, Kummer knew the eleven kilos in Sal Veta's car were going to be transferred to his car so that he could drive them to Chicago. Ernie Kummer is an aider and abettor and as such is guilty as charged. It is your duty to find him guilty."

Reilley was noticeably nervous when he began argument, voice breaking and hands trembling. However, he settled down once he moved next to his client, put his hand on his shoulder and said, "This man is innocent. He's a victim of cruel circumstances. The only evidence against my client is that he drove his brother-in-law to the Safe Harbor Motel, entered a room to use a toilet and was returning to his car when the drug agents burst into the room and arrested him. There wasn't one shred of evidence presented during this trial which showed Ernie Kummer had anything to do with a conspiracy to possess any of the heroin the drug agents falsely claimed they recovered in the motel room or in Sal Veta's car."

Believing argument concerning the law relevant to the charges would only highlight the prosecutor's thin circumstantial evidence case, Reilley stuck to the facts. Because he believed in his client's innocence, the jurors were swayed by his argument, their eyes becoming fraught with emotion when Reilley said, "Please don't find Ernie Kummer guilty on mere suspicion."

The judge saw the look of independence settle over the jurors. Clamping his thumb and forefinger over his chin, he looked at the foreman for several moments before he declared, "You've obviously heard enough for this morning. We're going to take a lunch break."

"Chrissake!" Reilley said, not caring who overheard him. "It's only eleven o'clock. We could have finished arguments."

The judge was walking to his chambers when he jerked to a stop. Turning to face Reilley, he said, "I don't stand for criticism of how I run my courtroom!"

Reilley didn't back down. "And I don't stand for a prosecutor in a black robe."

"You're close, Mr. Reilley, real close to being held in contempt of court. If I hear one more disrespectful word from you, you'll be your client's cellmate."

Gavin waited until the judge had stormed out of the courtroom before he said, "Big Jim, you're going to have to learn to suppress your outrage."

"Why?" Reilley shot back.

"Because there's no such thing as holding a judge accountable for rulings which are based on vanity and ego."

"Okay, Matt," Reilley said, "then you'd better polish up your closing argument. It's going to have to be the best ever given."

For luck, Gavin wore his three-piece, blue, pinstripe, the same suit he had worn during every closing argument he'd given in the last seven years. And in a serious and earnest manner, with the fate of his client resting on his shoulders, he began argument by praising the administration of justice in the federal system and the American jury system. Although all the jurors appeared eager to hear his argument, he thought he saw in their expressions the admonition: Come on with it, Mr. Attorney. It's up to you to give us a reason to find your client not guilty.

He began with the weakest charge against his client, arguing that the record was void of one droplet of evidence which showed Angel ever possessed the heroin discovered in the trunk of Sal Veta's car. "Think about it. No one told you anything, not one word, that connected Mr. Herrera to Sal Veta's car. How could he have known heroin was in the trunk? Contrary to what Mr. Mack has asked you to do, you don't have the right to infer possession unless there are facts to support that inference. This is not a guessing game. You must be satisfied beyond a reasonable doubt."

Gavin walked to prosecutor's table and picked up Government's Exhibit 1 and began his most difficult task, marshalling the facts which showed Angel didn't possess the heroin allegedly discovered in the motel room. "No one saw him possess this package of heroin, or in any way exercise control over it. Think about it. If he had, his fingerprints would be all over this gray tape. The fact is Mr. Herrera never saw or touched this heroin." He moved directly behind Fruin and continued in a facetious tone. "That brings us to this agent's story about finding this package of heroin next to my client. I'm going to ask you to not believe that story. There was no heroin in the motel room when the drug agents entered. All twelve kilos were found in Sal Veta's car. Then an agent took one kilo out of the trunk of the car and planted it in the motel room. That was a rotten thing to do."

The jurors focused their attention on Joe Fruin. Since his cross-examination, the jurors had harbored the belief the drug agent was capable of perverting the law. They were obviously questioning themselves—could the agent deliberately frame a man?

"Now, ladies and gentlemen, there is one very important thing I would like to discuss with you, and that is the distorted and maliciously orchestrated media coverage this case has received. Let's not kid one another. I know you read about this case in the newspapers and saw it on television. It's only normal that you did, but to let it influence you is wrong." He watched the reaction of the jury as he spoke. My God, he thought, they look like they believe me.

"Think about it," he continued with renewed confidence and rising voice, "what information has been responsible for your beliefs and convictions right now? Be honest with yourselves; isn't it what you have seen and read outside this courtroom?" Several of the jurors nodded their heads.

"Think about it. The media has destroyed your ability to think fairly and impartially. Think about it. What do you know about this case that you have learned solely from the witnesses who have testified before you?" The intensity of his argument gripped the jurors, causing them to become restless, fidgety. "Now who is responsible for this arrogant perversion of justice?" he asked, turning and glaring at Jay Doff. "We all know who's responsible for it, and why he did it."

Jay Doff couldn't resist the bait. Jumping to his feet and moving toward the bench in jerky movements, he screamed, "Objection! There's no evidence I had anything to do with the media coverage."

Judge Dart discerned the damage Doff had done to himself as quickly as Gavin. By making the denial, he had unwittingly driven Gavin's veiled accusation into the juror's consciousness, becoming his own worst enemy. There was nothing the judge could do to salvage Doff's reputation, and he wasn't about to make matters worse. "The jury," he said, "heard the evidence and they'll have to separate fact from fiction."

Confident the jury was now with him, Gavin decided to close arguments with an emotional plea. "Remember, the government, you the people, never loses when justice is done. And justice would be best served in this case with a finding of not guilty on all charges."

Mack bounced up immediately, more to distract the jurors' attention away from Gavin's closing than to rebut his argument. The savvy prosecutor realized Gavin had rung a bell and had dramatically changed the jurors' view of the parties involved in the case. It was his job to get them back, to send them into deliberation convinced both defendants were guilty. Instead of moving to the podium to begin his rebuttal, he positioned himself against prosecutor's table and leaned forward so that his chest was two feet away from the pile of gray-taped packages lying on the table. He said nothing for several seconds, but by sheer bearing and conviction in his case he commanded the jury to focus their attention on the heroin. Poking his finger at the packages, he said, "Tell me, if the defendants didn't go to the Safe Harbor Motel to take delivery of this heroin, then why, just why did they get out of bed at four in the morning and travel fifty miles to Joliet? What other reasonable explanation is there? Don't let Mr. Gavin sway you. Use your common sense."

Mack dramatically picked up a package of heroin and let it drop to the table. Then with an air of dignity, he sat down. Gavin's eyes darted from one juror to another as he weighed the impact of Mack's theatrics. The entire courtroom was affected; no one moved; not even a nervous cough was heard for what seemed like minutes.

There it was, Gavin thought. The question he knew Mack would raise. The question he, as a defense attorney, had no reasonable answer for. The question that would surely cause every juror to rule out the presumption of innocence. Why did the defendants travel to Joliet if not to pick up heroin?

Judge Dart, eager to dispense with the role he considered a chore, broke the stony silence when he began reading the instructions—the law the jury must follow when deciding guilt or innocence. "You, the jurors, are the sole triers of the facts in this case, and I am the sole judge of the law. Before you can find the defendants guilty, you must be convinced beyond a reasonable doubt that the defendants did the things charged in the indictment." For over forty minutes he droned on in a monotone voice, using legal terminology the jurors tried desperately to grasp before giving up on what they perceived to be an incomprehensible liturgy.

"No jury can understand that legal mumbo jumbo," Reilley said.

Gavin laughed. "Nor can most lawyers. In final analysis, the jurors will have to use their common sense to solve problems and determine facts, and that's what makes the jury system work. In their legal naiveté they disregard complex legal concepts and zero in on factual issues they have the ability to deal with. That's primarily the truth or falsity of testimony. Guilt or innocence in a criminal case always depends on a determination of whether the defendant acted in an alleged manner with criminal knowledge and intent, and not whether uncontroverted actions of the defendant violated a criminal law."

Relief registered on the faces of the jurors when Judge Dart held up the verdict forms, one guilty and one not guilty, for each count and demonstrated how the ballots should be marked. "And now," he said, "I'm going to place you in the care and charge of Marshal Kerski until a true and unanimous verdict has been reached."

The trial and attendant pressures had taken its toll, and as the courtroom emptied of jurors and spectators, Gavin allowed a wave of restrained fatigue to sweep his body. Slumping down in his chair, he said, "I'm exhausted."

Angel slid his chair next to him. "Me too, Abogado, even though you were doing all the work, and I was sitting on the sidelines."

Feeling mildly ashamed for not consulting with his client more throughout the trial, Gavin said, "Give me your honest opinion. What do you think?"

Angel shrugged his shoulders. "I don't know. There was too much bullshit in the papers for the jury to give me a break." He rose and began to walk toward Celia and his children. "Thanks for trying, Matt. You did a great job."

Gavin nodded and smiled. "Don't go anywhere," he told Angel. "I don't think the jury will reach a verdict tonight. The judge will call us back in about three hours, and then he'll order the jurors to go home for the night."

CHAPTER 27

▼

UNHEARD VERDICT

The peculiar way Judge Dart looked after he dismissed the jurors for the night left little doubt in Gavin's mind that the judge was confident guilty verdicts would be returned in the morning. Then he'd revoke Angel's bond and incarcerate him on the grounds the Mexican drug trafficker posed a danger to society and risk of flight.

Angel caught all the signals too, and when he and Gavin had exited the courthouse door, he said, "I know I sound like an echo, but the jury is going to find me guilty and that fucking judge will hang me."

"You're probably right, Angel."

Angel extended his hand and gripped Gavin's firmly. "I've watched you wage war against the best legal talent around, and if you can't beat them, no one can. Adios, Abogado del Diablo."

Gavin wanted to say, see you in the morning, but a certain finality in Angel's "adios" caused him to hesitate, thus giving Angel the opportunity to turn his back, round the corner of Dearborn and Jackson Streets and disappear from view. What else can happen in this bizarre case, Gavin wondered, beginning the walk to his condominium. He fervently wished there was some way he could wave a magic wand and resolve all issues for the benefit of all concerned. The trial, a gaudy spectacle, served no beneficial purpose, had no redeeming quality, except to make all the lawyers richer. Maybe Shakespeare was right. Maybe the country would be better off without lawyers.

Angel had no time for philosophizing. It was time to act. Eight miles southwest of the federal building in the heart of the Latino community he glanced at his watch as he slid into a phone booth. His gold Rolex displayed 9:30. He put a coin into the slot, dialed, and then glanced through the glass panes, looking in all directions to see if anyone or anything looked suspicious. "Everything and everybody looks cool," he mumbled.

"Hello," Celia said.

"Hi, Celia, I'm at the phone booth down the street next to the gas station." The phone call was a ritual, performed whenever he worried that either he or his house was under surveillance.

Celia understood the message and immediately went out of the house with her children to check-out the street and alley behind the house. Seeing nothing which would cause alarm, she rushed back into the house, picked up the phone, and gave Angel the all clear signal. It seemed like a matter of seconds before Angel's brooding figure stood framed in the doorway and split seconds longer before she was wrapped in his arms. The time had come; she sensed it. "When are you leaving?" she asked apprehensively.

"Tonight," he whispered as he rubbed his cheek against her moistened eyes. "When that stuff about Martinez' disappearance came up in court, I felt in my bones it was all over."

"Oh, Angel," she gasped, "What about me and the children?"

"Don't worry. As soon as the kids finish school this semester, pack all our things and come home to Durango. We'll have to make our home there from now on." He took a wad of one hundred dollar bills out of his pocket and pressed the money into her hand. "This should get you by for awhile. Now be a good wife and get my travel bag."

"But, Angel, won't the police come after us?"

Angel said, "No. Mexico has a law that forbids extradition of us for a crime committed in the States."

Angel went to his bedroom closet and removed from a hatbox a snub-nosed Smith and Wesson .38 Special and a Browning 9 mm semi-automatic. Unzipping the front of his pants, he placed the .38 under the waistband of his underwear and the Browning at his side under his belt. Totally committed now, if an attempt to arrest him was made, he'd have to shoot it out.

Opening the back door, Angel peered out into the dark, dismal night. "Nothing, no one out there," he said as he turned and took Celia in his arms.

A fresh look of contentment and hope covered her face. "Angel," she said, "I think we will be happy again in Durango. I'm thrilled we're going."

"Me too, Amorcito," he said as he brushed her lips with a kiss. Slipping away from her embrace, he walked through the door and out of sight. Reaching the alley, he peered into the darkness in search of the figure of the man he feared waited in ambush. "No one," he mumbled, reaching for the handle of the Browning. Pulling back the hammer, he started down the alley, traveling only a few yards before he came to a sudden stop, a sense of danger raking his body. Standing directly in his path was his nemesis, society's agent of vengeance, Joe Fruin. Angel's first instinct was to reach for his gun, but he froze for a moment, unsure of Fruin's intentions—and aware Fruin could squeeze off a shot from the gun he obviously held concealed in his pocket quicker than he could draw and shoot.

"Are you going anywhere in particular?" Fruin asked.

Angel's mind reeled, groping for a reason for the drug cop's presence. Was Fruin there to arrest him for Martinez' murder, or did he guess he was on his way to Durango. Angel chuckled and said, "Just a little midnight visit with a señorita."

Watching for the slightest movement by Angel, Fruin said, "I couldn't sleep. I kept visualizing you escaping to the hills of Durango."

Angel walked slowly to within a few feet of Fruin. "No way. I'm seeing my case through to the end. This little travel bag—" Lifting it up, he suddenly threw it at Fruin's face. Recoiling, he reached for the Browning automatic in his belt.

Fruin ducked as he raised his left arm to deflect the bag. He tried to pull his gun from his pocket and shoot, but his body was twisted out of position. He had only one chance and took it, jumping and sticking both feet out, jamming them into Angel's belly just below the rib cage.

Angel grunted as his abdominal muscles absorbed the kick. His gun was jarred from his hand, and he staggered backward to the ground.

Fruin's body seemed to sail outstretched in the air before it came crashing down full weight on his right elbow. He felt the nauseating sound of bone hitting hard concrete and then paralyzing pain shooting up his arm. He tried to roll on his back and reach for the gun in his pocket, but his arm wouldn't respond.

Angel attacked like a jaguar, springing from the ground, digging a well-aimed foot into Fruin's groin, kicking at his prey's head. Stepping back quickly, he unzipped the front of his pants, pulled out his pistol and pointed it at Fruin. "Vengeance is mine," he hissed.

Nausea and frustration rushed through Fruin's body with the realization that he had been beaten, and that he was about to die. He braced himself up on his uninjured arm, a contemptuous look spread across his face. He would accept death without fear or plea for mercy.

Angel cocked the hammer of the gun and took careful aim at the center of Fruin's mouth. "You're a no good prick for framing me," he said. "Did you really think you'd get away with it?"

Expecting a bullet to rip into his face no matter what he said or did, Fruin remained defiant. "Just doing my job as I saw it."

Angel stiffened, his face blanked, and he lowered the gun to his side. "Crawl over against the fence," he commanded.

Fruin dragged himself to a chain-link fence a few yards behind him. "What are you going to do?" he asked, sensing his death sentence had been commuted.

"Take your handcuffs out and put one bracelet around your wrist and the other around the fence post," Angel ordered as he moved in cautiously behind his prisoner. After checking the cuffs, he reached into Fruin's trench coat pocket and removed a .357 Smith & Wesson and the key to the handcuffs. He held them up and said with a chuckle, "I'm going to take these to Durango and keep them as mementos of you."

An involuntary, twisted smile crossed Fruin's face. Angel had taken him on man-to-man and had beaten him, and now he refused to take his revenge in accordance with natural law. "Why?" he asked. "Why you letting me live?"

"Because I'm not a killer. I'm a drug trafficker, a business man who wants to make money and live the good life."

"Give up the drug business," Fruin said. "You'll get caught again for sure, and I don't think I'd like to see that."

"You mean you don't want to see me fried in the electric chair for murder?"

"You talking about Juan Martinez?" Fruin said in a strange tone.

"Who else? You and those punk prosecutors know I didn't have anything to do with his disappearance, but you've got to pin it on someone, and I'm the best candidate."

"I know you didn't do it," Fruin said. "We found out who did and why. I promise I'll give Terry Mack all the info tomorrow. That's part of the reason I came here tonight."

Angel was stunned by the unexpected statement. "How can I believe you?" he said. "You're a crook and liar like all the other cops."

Fruin's knees screamed out in pain, and his tightly cuffed wrists had gone numb. "I've got to sit," he said as he rolled over and sat back against the fence post. "I owe you one for not shooting me."

Angel understood and believed him. It was a matter of macho pride. "Okay, Fruin, tell me who did it."

"After Martinez snitched on you, we persuaded him to turn all the way. He went undercover in a sting operation designed to get evidence and an indictment against nine cops who were giving drug dealers protection in return for monthly payoffs."

"So it looks like the cops here aren't any better than they are in Mexico."

Fruin grunted out a laugh. "Some are, some aren't. The nine cops had been running a protection racket for several years. As long as Martinez and the other street dealers paid off, they were given carte blanch. They could sell drugs without being harassed or arrested by any cops from the district, and they were warned when a raid was going down by cops from another district or by the DEA."

"So how did the fucking snitch buy it?" Angel said.

"A cop by the name of Lafavor was the bag man who picked up the payoffs from Martinez. Since he was in the deepest pile of shit, he was voted the man to put a bullet in his mouth. The cops did the hit right in front of Martinez' house, then dumped his body in the trunk of a squad car."

"Nice story," Angel said in a doubting tone. "Who's your witness?"

"A teenage girl happened to see the whole thing. She watched televangelist Jim Bakker's 'Praise the Lord' show one day and got religion. She then came into our office and told us the story."

"Did she identify the shooter?"

"Yeah. Positive I.D. of the shooter and the accomplice. And Martinez wore a wire when he was doing business with the cops. We have several taped recordings of payoffs."

It sounded too good to be true. To Angel, trafficking in drugs was American capitalism in its truest form. But he wanted no part of murder and the unsavory reputation it carried with it. He believed killing when one's life was being threatened was okay, but never in cold blood. "Are the cops going to be indicted?" he asked.

"Within a month they'll be charged under the RICO statute."

Angel walked to the fence and removed the handcuffs from Fruin's wrist. "Don't move for five minutes," he said as he started down the alley.

Fruin waited until Angel began to disappear into the darkness before he called after him, "That was you who shot down the federales chopper at the poppy field, wasn't it?"

Fruin couldn't see Angel, but he heard his voice drifting through the foggy night air, "The War on Drugs makes all of us act crazy at times."

*   *   *   *

The next morning at 9 o'clock Gavin telephoned Marshal Kerski at the courthouse to find out if the jury had begun deliberation. The affable marshal told him they had, that after serving them coffee and donuts he had locked them up and posted himself in front of the jury room door. Confident that with Kerski's hulking frame guarding the jury room no one would tamper with the jurors, Gavin turned his attention to the stack of client case files which had mushroomed during the week he was on trial. It wasn't long though before concentration became impossible, as it always did when he sweated out a verdict.

Jim Reilley believed so firmly in his client's innocence that awaiting the verdict was one of the most nerve-wrenching things he had ever done. Throughout the afternoon, he phoned Gavin's office several times to venture an opinion as to what the jury was doing at that moment.

The agonizing came to an end at five o'clock when Judge Dart's secretary phoned Gavin and relayed the message, "The jury foreman has knocked on the door and announced to Marshal Kerski that a unanimous verdict has been reached."

Hanging up the phone, Gavin told Tricia, who had posted herself in his office, "We have a verdict. Let's go find out what sort of future our clients have."

Tricia took a deep breath, then mused aloud, "Man has rendered judgment on his fellow man. And thank God the jury was there to render a verdict—not Dalton Dart or Jay Doff."

"You've grown cynical, Tricia. Like this country's Founding Fathers, you've learned the hard way that a judge or law enforcement officer can never be trusted to do the fair and just thing. That's why the framers of the U. S. Constitution guaranteed the right to a trial by a jury of peers. They knew back in 1776 that the only rein on the so-called Good Guys was a jury of twelve impartial people."

Tricia grew confident and optimistic. "Matt, I sense it. The jury saw right through Joe Fruin's bullshit story and through Judge Dart's bias and prejudice. That jury found Ernie Kummer not guilty."

Tricia's attitude was infectious, and Gavin found himself growing optimistic for the first time since Angel's trial began. "Maybe," he said, "the jury saw through the bullshit. Maybe they understood that a normally honest drug cop was driven to do a heinous thing because of his frustration over our system's coddling of drug dealers. Maybe the jury based its verdict on a bottom line total of rights and wrongs. Just maybe they'll find Angel violated the law, but the Good Guys violated it too."

"Let's go find out, Matt."

Heads down, Gavin and Tricia raced down the courthouse hall from one direction while Mack and Doff charged from the other. Though they nearly collided at the door, no one cared to acknowledge an adversary. The conflict had been too intense and the stakes too high for false platitudes.

Everyone is here, Gavin thought, as he entered the jammed courtroom: government witnesses and well-wishers, defendants' families and supporters, the news media people. All except the star of the show, Angel Herrera. Gavin gazed at Angel's chair; it's emptiness made it seem so conspicuous, so out of place. He looked deeply into Ernie's eyes, then Celia's. "Good Lordy, don't tell me," he groaned as he slumped over the table, clasping his forehead in the palms of his hands, all the loosely knit clues whirling through his mind.

Judge Dart was in a hurry to get home, his thoughts being on dinner with neighbors his wife had invited to their house. He burst into the courtroom and took his seat on the bench with a cheerful smile, confident the verdict would be as expected. "All right, Mr. Marshal," he said. "Bring in the jury."

Reilley pushed in close to Gavin and said, "What the hell are you going to do, Matt?"

Still grasping his forehead, Gavin replied, "I'm going to do the only thing I can. I'm going to put my hand in my pocket, grab hold of my short hairs, and stand up and announce to the court my client isn't here."

"What do you mean he isn't here?" Judge Dart screamed in utter disbelief. He held out his hands imperiously. "Marshal, hold up the jurors."

Kerski corralled the three jurors who had reached the jury box and herded them back into the jury room, much to their chagrin.

Dart raised his hand and pointed a flaccid finger to the vacant chair. "Where is he, Mr. Gavin?" he asked.

Gavin rose slowly and looked around the crowded courtroom. Everyone resembled models sculptured in wax. "I didn't notice Mr. Herrera's absence until two minutes before you took the bench. I don't know why he isn't here, but I must assume at this point there is a reasonable explanation."

The judge spied Celia Herrera trying to hide herself by crouching down behind a large woman who was sitting in the row in front of her. "Mrs. Herrera, step up here," he ordered. Without waiting for her to reach the podium, he asked, "Where is your husband?"

"I don't know. I thought he was here."

"When did you last see him?"

"Last night. As he left the house about eleven o'clock, he said he would see me in the courtroom today," Celia replied in a soft voice, repeating the script Angel had prepared for her.

Jay Doff bounded to the podium and in his high-pitched voice said, "I'm going to insist on a grand jury investigation of this contemptuous disregard for the integrity of the judicial system. I can't believe Mr. Gavin and Mrs. Herrera didn't have some involvement in Angel Herrera's disappearance."

Gavin had felt embarrassed until Doff's accusation. Now, contempt for prosecutors the ilk of Doff consumed him. Fighting to retain a professional demeanor, he said, "I suggest we adjourn until ten o'clock tomorrow so we can determine what happened to Mr. Herrera."

"No siree," Dart shot back. "I'm going to accept the verdict in absentia and sentence the defendant in absentia. Bring in the jury, Mr. Marshal."

Tension hung heavy over the courtroom as the jurors filed into the box for the last time. Gavin watched them closely, looking for the usual signals. If the verdict was guilty, jurors heads were usually bowed, eyes fixed on the floor in front of them. Some found something to fumble with, a button, pants leg, a purse—anything to delay the inevitable look at the defendant. This jury is different, he concluded. Their faces reflected the pride felt from reaching a good and true verdict, and they glanced confidently around the courtroom. One woman at the end of the jury box most distant from the judge unabashedly asked a nearby sketch artist from a television station to sketch her and put her on T.V. It was amazing, but the man who was the focus of the jurors attention for several days was gone and none of them noticed his absence.

Gavin swallowed hard, moistened his parted lips, and felt his stomach convulse as the judge asked the jury foreman, "Has the jury reached a verdict?"

"We have," the foreman announced as he stood to face the judge.

"And what are your verdicts?"

"We find," the foreman read from the verdict forms, "Ernie Kummer not guilty on counts one and two. And," he paused to shuffle the forms, "we find Angel Herrera guilty on count one, and not guilty on count two." He sat down, a smile spread across his face, eyes riveted on Ernie Kummer.

The color drained from Ernie's face and his lips turned marble white. He rose slowly from his chair, and with his eyes lowered he shuffled toward the jury, managing to spill out just before beginning to sob,

"Thanks, jury, but honest to God, I'm innocent. I didn't see any heroin in that motel room and didn't know about any heroin deal. I never went near that stuff in my life."

The jurors nodded their heads. They believed him, and in doing so insured that the fair trial provision set forth in the Constitution would remain a deterrent for those in law enforcement who placed their own self-interests above the law and a common concept of fundamental fairness.

Dart was peeved, and he allowed his feelings to show as he dismissed the jurors without the customary thanks for a job well done. His bias and prejudice robbed them of the few precious moments they deserved in the limelight. He directed the same scorn at Ernie when he said, "It has been said one of the worst tragedies in our criminal justice system is to have an innocent man found guilty. I find equally onerous a guilty man being found not guilty."

Reilley sprang to Ernie's defense, "That's a disgraceful and appalling comment. Your mind was so overpowered by prejudice I thank God that Mr. Kummer's fate was in a jury's hands and not yours."

"That does it, Mr. James Reilley. You're in contempt of court."

"Are you of the opinion," Gavin interjected, "that an attorney doesn't have the right to comment on your errors, especially the blatant ones? Do you expect us to be a bunch of emasculated puppets, dancing only to your tunes?"

"I expect you to refrain from making any remark that insults the integrity of this court."

"You provoked fair and necessary comment by Mr. Reilley with your injudicious statement. It was his duty to defend a wrongful accusation made against his client."

"Mr. Gavin," the judge warned, "I think you and Mr. Reilley are going to talk yourselves into jail because that's just where I'll put you if you ever try another case like the one you just did before me."

Jay Doff said, "The U. S. Attorney's office agrees, Judge. Mr. Gavin pulled one unethical trick after another. He misled the jury from the truth."

Gavin watched Doff as he spoke: face flushed, shoulders hunched, and body tilting forward in an attack posture. His face was a mask of hostility, and he spoke in an offensive voice. Thinking any further discussion with the two zealots would result in a contempt finding and jail, Gavin switched the subject. "Judge, what do you plan on doing about Mr. Herrera?"

"I will enter a bond forfeiture and issue a warrant for his arrest." Dart checked his calandar. "December first at two o'clock for sentencing," he ordered.

Reilley silently smoldered for several minutes after Dart left the bench. He was picking up documents and stuffing them into his valise when his emotions erupted. "That arrogant bastard!" he said. "Like most judges he thinks he's above criticism. Why should we be able to disagree with, criticize or lampoon the president of the United States and not a judge?"

Gavin glimpsed a newspaper reporter approaching feverishly scribbling notes. Worried he had overheard Reilley's incendiary remarks and not wanting to add fuel to the fire, he said in a conspiratorial tone, "You tried a great case. Congratulations, Jim." Reilley smiled and nodded just as a portly reporter rudely wedged his way between them and began firing questions in rapid succession. "Where is Angel? Is he dead or in Mexico? Why do you think the jury found Angel not guilty on one count and Ernie not guilty on all counts? Did Angel go on the run to avoid prosecution for the Martinez killing?"

Gavin was about to respond the usual, "no comment", but upon seeing Jay Doff passing, head lowered, sullen expression on his face, he yielded to the temptation to heckle. Thumbs in the lapels of his suit coat, head tilted back, he said in an authoritative tone, "The verdict was definitely a backlash. The jury despised the unscrupulous way the prosecutors orchestrated the news."

Doff's reaction was predictable. He snarled, "You defense lawyers are all full of bullshit. You keep trying to make decent judges and prosecutors the bad guys. Everyone is corrupt and breaks the law except the defense lawyers and their clients. Well, Mr. Hot Shit, I'm not going to let you get away with perverting justice the way you did in this case."

Seeing a sensational story behind the veiled threat, the reporter chased after Doff, attempting to provoke a rash statement. "Do you plan on investigating Matt Gavin because he's a drug lawyer?" he asked.

"That boy is going to be big trouble for us," Reilley said as Doff stalked out of the courtroom.

"Yes, the neo-prosecutors are a different—" Gavin spotted Mack lumbering toward him.

A strong competitive spirit hindered Mack from accepting a loss gracefully, but he did try to conduct himself as a gentleman, as a representative of the United States Government. Offering his hand, he said, "You tried a great case, Matt. And, Jim, your strategy to call Ernie Kummer to testify won the case."

Convinced Mack still didn't know the heroin was planted, Gavin tactfully replied, "Maybe the jury saw something we as lawyers missed and applied an intuitive sense of justice. After all, they did find Angel guilty of conspiracy. He didn't win, you got a conviction and got him out of the country. You did your job."

Gavin stood back and eyed the prosecutor as he commented on Reilley's trial technique. Mack, he thought, was the type of prosecutor who made criminal defense work a priceless endeavor. He was always conscious of his duty to the System, intelligent and talented, and one hard nosed son-of-a-bitch to try a case against. Throughout his career he had lost only a few cases, and when he did, he was always understanding and philosophical, never malicious and vengeful. Gavin found himself sincerely hoping Joe Fruin never told him the heroin was planted on Angel. He'd have trouble handling it.

The truth is, Mack said, "I'm thinking of leaving government service and going into private practice, give civil trial work a go."

"The new method of prosecuting drug cases have anything to do with it?" Gavin asked.

"It's lots of things," Mack replied. "I don't like drug users or dealers, and I'd be the first to prosecute them. But I think it's wrong to suspend their constitutional rights and to bury them in jail for a ghastly number of years for committing victimless crimes. The law enforcement system has over-reacted."

Gavin stalled until Terry Mack and Reilley had gone and the courtroom was empty. Now, it was time for him to perform a ritual. His eyes focused on the empty jury box as his mind conjured up the twelve men and women who had been drawn together from distinctively different cultural backgrounds. He recalled their faces: attentive, sincere, smiling, distraught. Those twelve jurors, good and true, had been the final interpreters of constitutional rights. They cut through the legalese and confusing laws and, by using a proverbial sixth sense, unanimously voted against the objectives of a powerful prosecutor's office and the prosecutor in a black robe, Judge Dart. And they were surely aware that in the minds of many in society they would be considered gullible, or liberals who were soft on crime, or damnable for not exacting lawful retribution. Gavin spoke to his apparition, "Thanks for performing a valuable service to the people of the United States."

Chapter 28

▼

TARGET

Two months had passed since Angel Herrera's startling escape from the grasp of the criminal justice system, and Ernie Kummer's emotional exit from the Courthouse a free man. Matt Gavin was beginning to think that the passage of time had healed all wounds inflicted during the Herrera-Kummer trial. Nothing had been heard from prosecutor Jay Doff, and there had been no evidence of his obsession for revenge. No news is good news, he thought, as he busied himself sipping coffee and reviewing case files.

Things changed suddenly when Tricia burst through his office door. "I swear," she said, "I'll never have anything to do with that man again. I'll quit if you send me over to discuss another case with that creep."

Gavin had been awaiting Tricia's return from what they had thought was going to be a routine conference at the U. S. Attorney's office. Her mood now was surprisingly out of sync with her gentle nature and unflappable attitude. "What happened?" Gavin asked in a concerned tone. "Wouldn't the assistant U. S. Attorney give you the information you were entitled to?"

"Jay Doff didn't want to talk about the Sal Marten case. Instead, he began making derogatory remarks about your professional integrity and ethics. I listened for several minutes before I accused him of being an neo-prosecutor, a zealot who wanted to severely injure defendants and attorneys who oppose the Justice Department's objectives."

"Doff?" Gavin questioned.

Tricia pulled the coffee cup from Gavin's hand and sat down in front of the desk. "Don't look so innocent," she scolded. "You knew Jay Doff had been assigned to the Marten case before you sent me to the pretrial conference."

It figured, Gavin thought, Sal Marten was a major coke distributor in the Chicagoland area, and his bust with fifteen kilos of the white powder was a major news story. "Sorry." he said. "As soon as I filed my appearance for Marten I should have realized Doff would somehow end up the case prosecutor."

Gavin looked sympathetically at Tricia as he said, "Don't feel bad. The word in the legal community is that no one can reach him. He's on a different wave length."

Tricia sighed, relieved for the support. "When I was escorted into Doff's office for the conference, I almost screamed, but then I made up my mind to act coolly professional, to let nothing that creep said or did bother me."

Gavin smiled. "That must've lasted all of one minute."

Tricia lowered her eyes and continued, "It lasted until he got all excited and started raving about the IRS investigation of your tax returns and financial condition."

Gavin examined Tricia's face. He sensed something else was bothering her. It couldn't be just the tax investigation. She knew that was the direct result of Doff's vindictiveness and the Justice Department's new policy to eradicate lawyers who represent major drug dealers. "What's it all about, hon?" he said softly.

Tricia didn't respond for several moments. Finally deciding there was no tactful way to say what was on her mind, she blurted out, "Doff said

I'm not looking at the tax investigation of you realistically because you're my jocker."

Gavin burst into laughter.

A wistful smile crossed Tricia's face. "At least he could have said it was because you're my jocker-fiance."

Gavin got up, walked around his desk, and took Tricia in his arms. "Honey, if being your jocker is the worst thing Doff can accuse me of then I'm a happy man. Besides, I'd go to the gallows for that privilege."

"But, Matt," she said, "he's dangerous. When I told him there wasn't a shred of evidence indicating you violated any tax law, Doff had the audacity to say it didn't matter if the investigation was a fishing trip. He said he'd find something you did wrong, sooner or later."

Gavin walked back behind his desk and sat down. "We've become a big part of the War on Drugs because we represent major drug traffickers. The same rules of war that applied at the poppy fields in Durango and at the Safe Harbor Motel apply to us. Nothing will be fair, nothing will be sacred. The Good Guys will do what they gotta do."

"Doff's a no good louse," Tricia said. He told me he issued grand jury subpoenas for the production of books and records to all the banks and investment houses you did business with in the last six years. And he started a propaganda campaign against you." Gavin rocked back in his swivel chair. "Yes," he said, "that's a sleazy way of doing business."

Tricia was thoughtful for moments before she said, "If I could be objective about you, I'd conclude that the way you litigate drug cases is similar to a guy walking into a cage with a hungry tiger and kicking it in the nose."

"So you think I kicked the tiger prosecutors in the wrong place, huh?"

"Right, Matt. When the jury verdict came back not guilty for Ernie and when Angel skipped town, the prosecutor's office looked bad. They needed a scapegoat. So, they cited you for unethical and unscrupulous trial technique. Add to the foregoing your unpardonable sins of accusing

Joe Fruin of planting heroin on Angel, and then issuing a subpoena to Andre Campbell."

Gavin grinned as he said, "I planned on frightening the hell out of Joe Fruin and his agents by playing the Andre Campbell game all the way to the wire. They thought I was going to call Campbell when I opted for Juan Martinez, then Dr. Farley. The tension was severe."

"Which way do you think Campbell would have gone if you had called him to testify?" Tricia asked.

Gavin put closure on the issue. "There was never any doubt in his or my mind."

Tricia's eyes widened. "I guess we'll never be able to keep agents like Fruin from doing whatever they want."

"Wrong," Gavin replied. "What we did will force men like Fruin to keep a rein on themselves. When he planted the heroin on Angel, it was a spontaneous and compulsive act. Competitive spirit combined with his hatred for everything Angel stood for drove him to violate Angel's rights as well as the law he was sworn to uphold. He rationalized that since Angel was a major drug dealer, he was not entitled to the protection of the law. Fruin learned the hard way that everyone charged with a crime is entitled to several constitutional rights."

"But that was because of our vigorous defense," Tricia said. "What would have happened if a couple of defense attorneys who didn't have the courage to stand up and fight had represented Angel and Ernie?" She assertively answered his own question. "Angel would have gone to the slammer for thirty years and Ernie for fifteen. Our judicial system would have become more arrogant and repressive, and the constitutional ban on depriving a person of life, liberty and property without due process of law would be nothing more than academic rhetoric."

"I'm afraid," Gavin said, "academic rhetoric is about all a drug dealer can look forward to from now on."

"Anyone who deals in dope or goes near dope cases is crazy," Tricia said. She became pensive, then a look of fear flooded her eyes.

Knowing what bothered her, Gavin said, "Go ahead and say it."

She nodded resolutely. "Matt, maybe we ought to think about getting out of the business of representing drug law offenders. It seems we're all alone fighting an omnipotent force of agents, prosecutors and judges. It's a battle we can't win."

"That may be a real good suggestion," he said. If I refused to represent any more major drug dealers, and the prosecutor's office was made aware of it, the tax investigation of me would most likely be dropped."

Tricia's eyes were filled with emotion as she nodded.

Gavin let his mind drift. It would be ecstasy, he thought, to take a one year sabbatical and spend it island hopping in the Caribbean on his yacht. Tricia would be there, and they could fish and dive and comb the deserted beaches with absolutely no worries or time limitations. It would be paradise.

Tricia saw the gleam in his eye and sensed what he was thinking. "Matt," she said sincerely, "I'll go anywhere with you and do anything you want."

Gavin looked deeply into Tricia's eyes and thought what a lucky man he was. Any decision would have to be made with her best interests in mind. He cleared his throat and was about to give his answer when his secretary appeared in the office doorway and announced, "Mrs. Estella Herrera is out in the waiting room. She says her son has just been arrested by Chicago cops for possession of four ounces of heroin. She's sobbing uncontrollably, but I think she said the agents found one gram of heroin in her son's pocket and then mixed it with four ounces of sugar that was in a bowl on the kitchen table." Irene looked stunned. "Can the agent get away with saying the boy had four ounces when he only had one gram?"

Tricia put her hand to her mouth as she studied Gavin's reaction. If he's going to stop representing drug dealers and cruise the Caribbean, she thought, he'd have to start now and turn away the drug case.

Gavin told his secretary, "No, Irene. Not as long as I can walk to the courthouse. Please tell Mrs. Herrera to come in."

Tricia bounced up and adjusted her chair to make room for the new client. "I'll start preparing a motion for bond," she said in an understanding tone.

EPILOGUE

▼

It was Christmas Eve, and Matt Gavin wanted to spend it at home with Tricia, away from the crowded bars and restaurants where a chance meeting with a client or lawyer could result in a loss of the Yuletide spirit. Outside his condominium windows, large glistening flakes of snow drifted by and fell fifty-three stories to the city below. Multi-colored Christmas lights adorned the lakefront and high-rise buildings in the loop, creating a wondrous panorama and adding to the spirit permeating the air. He and Tricia were snuggled close together on the sofa, sipping from glasses of sherry, enraptured with the spectacular view when the phone rang.

The first ring brought about a Scrooge-like effect, and as Tricia reached for the phone, Gavin said, "I'm not here for anyone."

Disregarding his embargo, she said into the phone, "Yes, hold please." She smiled sweetly, "I think you'll want to take this one."

Expecting a family member or close friend to be on the phone, Gavin said, "Merry Christmas."

"Hey, Abogado, how are you?" the caller said in a familiar, rakish voice.

"Ang—" Gavin checked himself, thinking of the likelihood of a wiretap. "Where the hell are you?"

"I'm celebrating Christmas in Durango with my family. We all wanted to say something." Angel, Celia and several children screamed into the phone in unison, "Merry Christmas, Abogado!"

"Thanks, the same to all of you."

"I understand your favorite devil got fifteen years," Angel said.

"Yes, you were sentenced in absentia to fifteen years and fined ten thousand dollars. If you would have been here, you would have gotten the same. It was the maximum the judge could give."

"You mean I would have been eating my Christmas meal in jail if I stuck around?"

Gavin advised his client in a rapid monologue, "It's my duty to tell you to surrender to a United States marshal as soon as possible."

The inimitable chuckle was in Angel's voice as he replied, "I don't think Joe Fruin would like to see me behind bars."

"You're right, Angel. I ran into him in a bar one evening, and after a few beers he told me about the alley episode. I'm very pleased you handled things the way you did."

"Does that mean there's no attempt murder warrant out for me for kicking Fruin's ass around?"

"No warrant, "Gavin replied. "Fruin didn't report the incident."

"Did he say anything else?"

"He wanted the message delivered to you that nine cops were indicted in a nasty police corruption case. Two of the cops were charged with killing Juan Martinez."

Angel chuckled. "Just like Mexico. You can't tell the Good Guys from the Bad Guys without a score card."

"I guess that pretty well sums up the case of United States versus Angel Herrera."

"Watch out, Abogado del Diablo. That load of heroin was jinxed from the start. Everyone who got close to it got burned."

Gavin's eyes drifted around his luxurious condo before focusing on Tricia. "Right, Angel," he said, "we both have to be very careful."